Eden's Shore

Also by Oisín Fagan

Nobber
Hostages

Eden's Shore

Oisín Fagan

JOHN MURRAY

First published in Great Britain in 2025 by John Murray (Publishers)

1

Oisín Fagan acknowledges receipt of financial assistance from the Arts Council of Ireland.

A CIP catalogue record for this title is available from the British Library

Trade Paperback ISBN 9781399815918
ebook ISBN 9781399815932

Typeset in Adobe Garamond by Hewer Text UK Ltd, Edinburgh
Printed and bound in Great Britain by Clays Ltd, Elcograf S.p.A.

John Murray policy is to use papers that are natural, renewable and recyclable products and
made from wood grown in sustainable forests. The logging and manufacturing processes
are expected to conform to the environmental regulations of the country of origin.

Carmelite House
50 Victoria Embankment
London EC4Y 0DZ

www.johnmurraypress.co.uk

John Murray Press, part of Hodder & Stoughton Limited
An Hachette UK company

The authorised representative in the EEA is Hachette Ireland, 8 Castlecourt
Centre, Dublin 15, D15 XTP3, Ireland (email: info@hbgi.ie)

Para el capitán Ronaldo

I

Sea

THE *ATLAS* CAST off from Liverpool in March, moving towards Brazil and winter by way of somewhere else, and within moments of leaving behind the estuary she hit her first swell. Angel Kelly, who had been sitting on a hatch watching the black walls of the harbour diminish, felt his face tighten, his lungs shallow and a heat surge through his throat. He understood, then, all at once, that the sea was alive, that it wanted to kill him, and that there were many things the body hated more than extinction, and that the worst of these was seasickness. Confining himself to his private quarters, he prayed for death.

In darkness, he alternated between hammock and floor; sometimes he leant against the wall, drowsing off, other times he curled up in a corner. Tremoring waves of nausea blossomed in the belly, crawled up through organs until, in serpentine reaching, they kissed his eyes, and everything blurred. He would vomit until he passed out, and then would awaken almost immediately to feel the awful ritual already begun again inside him. By the third day, he was vomiting streams of clear liquid into a bucket through his nose, his mouth too fatigued to open. Waterfalls of nausea sluiced up his throat, and he was guided through inner landscapes by the vagaries of a ragged breath. There was a motion to the body that was commensurate with the motion of the sea; a falling, an unfolding, a decompressing, a jarring, the sense that he had been hurled into the wrong part

3

of the universe and was being taught something, through pain, by a being far greater than him.

Sometimes, still awake, he could feel himself moving slowly into dreams, carried on some presence's back towards a lighted hamlet through a penumbra of tangled forest, dragged about in false spaces that he was powerless to leave. Once he saw a small girl, skin darker than a gypsy's, laying on her side next to him; her gut had been torn open, exposing a meadow of pink flowers, in which roamed a pigeon that moved like a sea creature. It scuttled and pulsed around the wound, until it came to rest and laid a clutch of eggs along a riverlike bend in her intestine, and from these eggs black saplings hatched and grew. More often she appeared to him intact. She came into his cabin, accompanied by a child he recognised as himself, and then they would hold hands, lower their eyes and pray.

One evening, he woke up and felt within him the sea; it was no longer a thing apart. Lighting some candles, he checked the looking glass. He was much diminished, his skin so pale it was as if he had emerged from the powdered rubble of some ruined city. He tried to unpack some of his papers, and then, immediately fatigued again, he lay down in his hammock to enjoy the gentle thrumming of being alive, the creaturely smell his own skin gave off.

Someone had taken care of him during his lengthy sickness; visiting him frequently enough to replenish his stock of fresh water; emptying his chamber pot of vomit; leaving him biscuits. He couldn't recall eating any of them, though he remembered once staring down at them formlessly reproduced inside the bucket, wondering how they had gotten there.

He was awoken by the last candle hissing out. He had, at some former point, fallen asleep. The hammock's ropes creaked slightly, and he stared at his hands, dully blue with darkness, and finally still after so many days of shaking. Moaning wind snuck through the ship checking every cranny, leaving disorder and chill. When the wind hushed, he realised that there was perpetual moaning emanating from the frame of the boat, and that it had been there a long time.

Rolling out of his hammock, he pressed his ear to the wooden floor to hear better the noise trapped within.

A knock throttled his ears, and he pressed his hands against them in pain. Twice more the floor knocked in the exact spot where he had placed his cheek – and then another moan. Someone was calling out, but communicating nothing he could understand, no language he knew.

Terrified, he left his quarters and the shock of the light outside was so fierce that even though he closed his eyes and held his breath, still this light flourished, making his darkness bright like blood, unbearable to witness. The fresh air left him feeling stripped naked and lashed. Invisible bursts of spray scattered across his face and gooseflesh sprang up all along his spine. It was early dawn and the northern star, the last vestige of night, was low in the sky, very near the horizon. Nothing between the grey of the sky and the grey of the sea, the edge of the world blurred. Down by the cockpit, the ember of a pipe glowed with the regularity of a ticking clock, destroying the illusion of grey endlessness. There were shaded forms by the tiller; two sailors on the dawn watch. One of these men moved an enormous heap of ropes from one place to another and was swallowed by a trapdoor. Lines smacked against the hull and creaked upon the sheaves, and above Angel's head, a man was climbing up the foremast, manoeuvring upwards in the harness he sat in.

It dizzied Angel to see the soles of this man's feet so far above him and he leant, blinking, across the bulwarks and stared again at the seething membrane of the ocean, and he was almost comforted by how close the perimeters of the horizon were, how narrow the world was, naught but a little sphere flitting through the heavens – it held no secrets.

At seventeen years of age Angel had gone up to read law in the University of Dublin, where he was almost immediately spell-bound by Rousseau, Voltaire, and flocks of flirting whores. They crowded beneath streetlamps on autumnal nights, kicked mulchy leaves at him; pressed red noses, gapped smiles, and bosoms against steamy pub windows so as to lure him away from the fireplace, the drink and the discussions of politics. He laughed whenever he saw them, as if discovering anew that life was just a wonderful joke.

Around Parliament Street, he would often be seen; a broad-brimmed hat, a cravat and a small book of Montesquieu under his arm, from which he partook of no more than five sentences a day. He flunked classes, wandering between coffeehouses from the afternoon until the early hours, smoking his brains out with tobacco, drinking small glasses of Turkish coffee and discussing liberty; equality; the perfectibility of man and his systems; the separation of powers; the rights of man; the few articles of Diderot which had come to light; beauty; justice; the impossibility of God; the happy century. Secretly, he believed one day he would prove himself to be a great man; publicly, he bragged often of departing to the Americas, and never returning.

In the January of his freshman year, his aunt died suddenly of pneumonia, leaving him a sizeable inheritance, without stipula-tion of any sort, and he drew it down all at once, becoming liberal with his friends, and soon his lively nights began taking a darker turn. Eternal declarations faded behind wreaths of puffed smoke, songs of brotherhood were bellowed out, freedoms were proclaimed on behalf of absent multitudes, and most nights ended with a clumsy mess of fisticuffs.

Life seemed very long for all the forgotten talk strewn at its wayside, all the money it cost to live it, and Angel's friends began to lean on him too heavily, too expectantly, and, despite their increasingly lunatic vociferations, their commitment to progress seemed to be drowning under alcohol.

His aunt had been his only relative, and with her gone, he felt that if he were ever to fall it could only be a fall into nothing. No one loved him anymore. No one lost sleep over him. No one fretted his absences. No letters arrived bearing his name. No one smiled to see him, nor remarked on his pallor, nor, in concern, touched their wrist against his forehead. Nothing attached him to life, and the inheritance would not last forever.

In a packed lounge on Moore Street, each nearly invisible to the other through walls of smoke, Angel blinkingly read a full-page advertisement taken out in *Hibernia: Chronicle of Liberty* that stated that for every acre of land purchased in the uncivilised regions of northern Brazil, the governor-general would grant the adventurer another ten, and, withal, ninety-nine years free of tax on any of its subsequent produce.

Angel folded up his paper and declared that he would take up the brave governor-general on his offer and spend the remainder of his inheritance on cultivable land, establishing, at last, the harmonious society of which they had so often and so manfully spoken.

'Next Christmas, I will be dining at the governor-general's, in São Paulo, or wherever it is he lives. My esteemed brothers should all come with me, to stake flags of liberty in these giving American soils.'

Patrick Edgeworth burst into laughter, and Angel felt a sensation of disgust gliding through his throat like the spread of an internal bruise.

'Why do you laugh, Patrick?'

'There'll be no Brazil,' he said. 'I smoke it, I do, ay. There'll be no Brazil. Come now, Kelly, you have all your inheritance and all of Mecklenburgh Street to explore it with. Come now, be a good lad and dally not with the slate.'

'Do you think all my talk of liberty has been some theatre I play at?'

'I do.'

The waiter filled his wine. Angel felt a moment of stillness. As if for the first time, he saw around the table all the soft, milk-fed faces, leering and guffawing.

'You do not. Say you do not think this.'

'There'll be no Brazil.'

'Am I alone?'

Patrick cupped his ear and leant across another laughing student towards Angel.

'What?' he shouted. 'What did you say?'

Angel didn't answer; he arose and crossed the street to another public house where he drank until closing time.

The next afternoon, his piqued brain still unruffled by alcohol but his affairs quickly settled, Angel took passage to Liverpool in a ship carrying cattle to market, and by midnight was searching a billet by the harbour and passage to Brazil. The water was black and shimmering with lapping susurrations. The harbour walls were black, too. It began to snow. He felt a flake melt on his cheek; glanced up and saw unbroken lines swirling down on him from out of the blank slate of the heavens. A sudden gust sent gooseflesh blooming along his neck, and he hunched up his shoulders so beads of snow didn't hiss down his collar. All was silence. Seeking refuge in a doorway, he saw across the street the windows of the house opposite flicker into illumination as an elderly woman draped in a shawl went from window to window lighting candles, appearing suddenly in each one like she lived inside a magic trick. Soon the windows were full of lit-up whores, all jostling for space to flatten their noses against the sooty glass, their mouths contorted Os of astonishment, become children once more at the sight of snow.

Inside, he was accosted by a London-Irish woman called Molly Sheridan. She took him to a room full of lovers where Angel was brought on twisted sheets to his natural end only from the batting of her eyelashes and the controlled exhalation of her breath. She introduced him to poitín by way of a jar she kept hidden under the bed, and they caroused Liverpool for six days, three of which were entirely lost to his memory. He grew fond of her, and proposed marriage, to which she responded, 'I will not see forty again this side of God's love.' He insisted on writing her out bills of exchange, and then, one morning, he was stalking through cobbled streets, shivering and crying, having separated over some argument whose origin he could not recall.

He found himself down by the harbour again in the white hush of snow, shirts half-undone and tears still hot in his eyes, brandishing his bills at a clerk, demanding he be found a berth to Brazil.

'The *Aurelius*, a slaver and a schooner belonging to the Benjamin family,' the clerk said. 'She is heading to San Domingo tomorrow by way of Dakar.'

'Brazil. I'll have Brazil, or hell.'

'Nothing until May,' he said, checking a ledger by another desk, glancing at Angel over half-moon spectacles.

There was a figure walking by the shop front, a dim shadow against the tinted glass.

'Captain Niewouldt?' the clerk called.

A little man with a red beard stuck his head in the door, setting off the hanging bell above it. He took off his tricorne and smiled in an unassuming manner.

'Is the *Atlas* not departed?'

'I have not been feeling well,' the captain offered. 'Been looking to swap out, but no joy. We shall catch the four o'clock tide. With the French spies, you know, I cannot give too much notice.'

'I have a fare here.'

'In luck so. All passenger berths are yet unfilled; the stomach is gone for the trade, I think. Cold winds of change blow across Europe. Your name, young master?'

'Angel Kelly, esquire, sir,' Angel said, words still a-slur, scalp sweating with drink, tucking in his shirts and checking to see if his black ribbon still tied off his ponytail. 'Adventurer and colonist. I'm going to found a Brazilian city.'

'Jolly good; we'll end up in Santana. You know our business, ay?'

Angel blinked a few times so as to focus his drifting vision.

'I asked if you knew our business, young master?'

'Of course,' he hiccupped.

'Well, then. Chat with my man, Lafcadio, down by the pontoon. He's overseeing the loading and shall give you the summa. If you have the stomach for her, you are most welcome. It takes stomach, you know. It is a hard necessity.'

The little bell jingled once more as the door was shut; the shadow disappeared.

'An uncommonly good fellow,' the clerk commented. 'You'll find the mate a harsher sort, but a certain brutality is required.'

'I'm sure.'

Angel was brought down to the pontoons and introduced to the first mate, a beautiful Brazilian named Lafcadio Naital Oliveira Hinchoa – a man nearer seven foot than six, with olive skin and hair that sparkled like sunlight trapped in filamented strands. Eyes drooping with fatigue, Angel lied profusely: 'Captain gave me the run down, very comprehensive. Very fine boat. Said you were to bring me directly to my quarters. No dally-dillying, he said. Five o'clock tide. You were to send a boy to fetch my luggage.'

The mate brought him to his private quarters where Angel, Molly Sheridan's name upon his lips, passed out almost immediately, only coming to many hours later when he heard the crew on deck, running about and waving, crying their final farewells.

———•◦•———

He appeared, pallid and waifish, at the mess. The chef, a Galician named Hieronimo Sánchez de Villanueva, gave two breakfasts a day, two lunches and two dinners – a rolling meal that never ceased.

'We are think you are die,' the chef greeted him. 'A fantasma, you say? A goose?'

'A ghost.'

'Vale, have a breakfast for you.'

Angel was handed a bowl of oatmeal biscuits, and he hunkered down in a corner of the cockpit where the sea spray would not season his food. Before he had set into his meal a squat man with a face shaped like a crescent moon emerged from the main, walked over to him, reached down into his bowl, pulled out all the biscuits therein, stuffed them into his mouth in one motion, and then walked towards the stern. Angel stood up, cheeks flushing, and the compact man turned on him, and said:

'Nighttown.'

His mouth was still full of biscuits; Angel shook his head.

'What?'

The man swallowed, gasped like a dog, and wiped his lips with his tongue, and then his fingers. 'I am going to drown you in Nighttown. I will do it forever.'

'If you were gentleman enough,' Angel said, 'we'd exchange cards, but you're only a rogue needs lashing.'

The man laughed.

'There is a door in every wave. Open it.'

He clapped his hands and stalked away; Angel returned to the chef.

'I must speak with the captain. I am a paying fare. This treatment will never do.'

'What is not do? You know Marianne Lynch,' Hieronimo said. 'He always have the resent. Maybe, for you, take the breakfast in the quarters proper.'

'I don't know him from Adam. Is he mad?'

'Is an Irish and very liberate, an histrio, you say? He always do the play, yes. Make pretend to be, is very comic.'

'I must speak with the captain.'

The chef pursed his lips; on his left cheek the flayed remnants of a deep burn contorted out like the reformation of a continental map. Deeper burns freckled dark holes under his chin where the beard couldn't grow; and blood vessels, like red lightning, ran through the whites of his eyes, even encroaching onto his blue irises; the effect was striking.

'All the world like speak with the captain,' the chef said, 'but have a bad sick. No one see since Nouadhibou.'

A clatter of plates in the galley; the muffled sound of laughter from full mouths; the thwack of a cleaver in the hands of an aproned boy who cut apart strips of fat.

'You had a who? What are you saying?'

A fly was caught, twitching, in the tangles of the chef's beard. He blinked slowly as though trying to remember something.

'What am I say?' he asked. 'I don't record all, because is make very tired speak the English all the days who go.'

'I'd like to speak with the captain.'

'Mira – go, now,' the chef said. 'Speak with Señor Hinchoa, is the first mate. No can with the captain.'

Marianne Lynch was approaching from the aft, balancing a tall stack of wooden bowls on his head, and Angel passed by the starboard deck to avoid him. Then he saw the Irishman turn around and move athwart onto the starboard deck, also. Angel returned via the prow towards his quarters. He waited a moment on deck, and, bizarrely, saw the Irishman, coming towards him yet again. When Angel got inside his quarters, he leant his weight against the door.

A few minutes later, he was still leaning on the door when there came a gentle knock.

'Sir,' a small voice said. 'I can enter?'

A boy in a bloody apron came in. He was gangly and slight, no more than fifteen, head shaven down to stubble, eyes pale as dazzled skies. He bore a bowl in both hands before him.

'Some biscuit for you,' he said.

Angel took the bowl.

'Thank you.'

'You are not remember,' the boy said. 'I have bring to you the luggages in Liverpool.'

'What is your name?'

'My name is Jacques. I am the cabin boy, from Nantes.'

'I am Angel. Was it you who brought me biscuits when I was ill?'

'Sir, yes.' Jacques hesitated, as though about to turn away. 'The man of the crew is good,' he said, 'but can be aggressive and chalorous. For you, if you want, I can bring something for eat two or three time per day, so you can rest here.'

'Very good. And for this service?'

Jacques blinked. 'Sir.'

'Je te devrai combien?'

'Rien,' he shook his head. 'No, sir. No, only do for nothing. Only help.'

'Thank you, Jacques.'

'Others say you will make a city in Brazil.'

'It is true.'

'Pardon. Why?'

'I would set up a colony that is free from the sins of the old world – a place free from tyranny, discrimination, illegality, religion, persecution, taxation. All will be equal.'

'And can also I come?'

'Yes.'

'Thank you.' He bowed. 'Goodbye, sir.'

'Goodbye, Jacques.'

The boy bowed again and shut the door.

<hr />

The *Atlas* was a large British cargo. Three masts and a topmast; a heaving thing, barnacle-strewn underparts heavy like a warrior gone to seed. The wood that wrought her was dark, full of soft pockets of rot. A forecastle possessed a few cabins for passengers and mail; of which the most spacious and the closest to the stern belonged to the captain. Angel would never have recourse to the main, the open quarters where the sailors passed their leisures and their sleeps. Therein was a long, scarred table around which they sat and drank, playing nightlong games of dominoes that snaked twenty feet, weaved amongst long candles, flaming sun-beaten faces into dull luminance. There were sixty-eight sailors, though often it felt as though there were no more than twenty, working as they did in their different watches, attending their different duties in their different crannies. They were something worse than commoners, Angel felt, more brutish, more predacious, more desperate. Ill-kempt, dull, and superstitious, performing little tics before eating and working: they made circular motions with fingers, kissed sleeves, crossed themselves, touched the soles of feet, the sides of foreheads, put thumbs to eyelids, hummed wordless prayers over knots – all this creating over the vessel an air of private ritual and inviolable secrecy. They were always, it seemed, on the bluff of some violence.

In the end, Angel decided it best not to report Marianne Lynch.

He spent the next few days rocking in his hammock, listening to the moaning in the wood. In the mornings and evenings, he emerged from his quarters and wandered near the prow where the crew was most scant. He stared out at the pleated sea, the ribbed white froths that capped the waves like a million waving hands disintegrating. Jacques came to him three times a day with meals, but he was no company. He was kind and softspoken, but something of an idiot.

At nights, Angel drew up a bucket of seawater, just before the dawn, when the world was at its darkest, and took it back into his cabin and plunged his hands into it. The water was alive and when touched it would grow fiercely luminescent, shining so brightly it lit up the whole room in a pale electric glow. It was a celestial blue, and he could draw spiralling patterns by trailing his fingers through it. He would then throw it against the wall where it produced a brief galaxy, a swirling cosmos of aqueous light.

Once as he was pouring water on himself, a bird cooed just outside his door. Thinking they might be in sight of land, Angel put on his leggings, and rushed out to the deck. Thick clouds, the same darkness as the sea, had made close the sky – two black mirrors playing against one another, the imitation broken only by the inconsistency of the intermittent moon's coruscations on the water. The sails billowed above. He saw Captain Niewouldt by the prow's gunwale, hunched over. On each downward thrust of the vessel more of the sea was brought into vision, like a picture swelling and shrinking. The captain held a messenger pigeon in the cradle of his palms, sheltered in his coats. He wrapped a yellow ribbon around its leg, tied it off, and then cast it into the air.

At first it fell, and then it winged towards the sky, a little blot darker than the clouds it was imprinted against, and began to fly north. Some spray overcame the bulwarks, setting Angel blinking. He wiped stinging salt away from his eyes, and then the pigeon came apart. The green of its chest burst into an oval ripple of blood, and, for a brief moment, the blood was a perfect portal in the air. An explosion was loosed around his ears, overwhelming the ocean's rush, and he sneezed at the acrid scent of gunpowder.

The captain let out a brief cry and stumbled back into his quarters. A slanted rhombus of soft light appeared from the open door, and then it was swallowed up. On the starboard deck, in the lagging aperture between boom and sail, Angel saw the first mate, Lafcadio, holding a blunderbuss across his shoulder, smoke pouring downwards from its broad maw. The boat tacked, the swinging boom obscuring them from each other, and Angel ducked out of sight.

He waited, and then heard bootsteps touring the deck, coming towards him; Lafcadio was approaching. In the shade of the bulwarks, Angel crawled until he reached the stern where a tallow candle glowed in the little window of the navigator's house. The glass was smoked black; within, a bearded man was poring over some charts, a brass compass sauntering its naked legs across watery leagues. Lafcadio called some command and the navigator arose, scraping his chair back, and went out to answer. Angel waited, and then snuck back to his quarters by the starboard deck.

———— • ————

'To whom, other than the captain and the first mate, would I refer a matter of some delicacy?'

'Me, sir,' Jacques said.

He was on his knees clearing away Angel's old bowls and pinching crumbs from between the boards.

Angel ran his thumbnail along his teeth, leaning against the wall.

'Who else?'

'I don't know.'

'What is Lafcadio doing to the captain?'

'I don't know.'

It was gloomy in the quarters. Still, Angel could see the back of Jacques's neck colour.

'Why are you lying?'

'Only help. Please rest here. I ask for you.'

He stood up and bowed.

'You will ask, won't you, Jacques?'

16

'Only help, sir.'

He bowed again and left.

Angel waited a little while, and then decided to go out. It was early evening. The sun was setting, making it look like they were trawling through the bloody aftermath of some frenzy of sharks.

The chef, Hieronimo, stood on the bulwarks, urinating over the side, one of his hands wrapped around the Jacob's ladder, a bottle pressed between his elbow, dank hair flowing in the wind.

'If I mayn't speak with the captain,' Angel called up to him, 'and I would prefer not to speak with the first mate, to whom would I direct an enquiry of some import?'

'The second mate is logic, I think. The Señor Camacho. Him name is Indiana Camacho de Vega. An Spanish man, also but very elegant. Is of Valencia.'

The chef swayed, pushed his cock messily into his pants, engineered the bottle of clear liquid to his other hand and drank from it.

'I am a sinner, or no?' he asked.

'How could I know?'

'The solitude of the life is no end, claro. Even when I am fuck into the other life, I am alway alone. The longing I am not stop never. The sin when is offer, yes, every time, is feel so new and is so nice.'

Hieronimo jumped down to the deck and began producing a choking that at first Angel took for impeded coughing, but then he realised the man was crying.

'You want the Señor Camacho, yes?' he sobbed.

'Yes.'

'Make an reunion tomorrow.'

Before Angel could thank him, the chef had grabbed him by the hair and kissed him wetly on the cheek.

'I find me is very good be alive,' he said. 'Is very good, no? Very strange and very much filled, the life. I love. Yes, I love.'

He hurled the bottle overboard, and then pointed out at the monotonous water, waves cresting pinkly above it.

'Also, I forget me that have something there. A boat. There is there, for much times, but we approach and we approach and she alway away from us. Is strange, I think.'

A speck flickered on the clean line of the horizon. It rolled in and out of view, a vague throbbing on the edge of the world.

Angel pointed at it. 'Is that it?'

There was silence. Hieronimo's distant yellowed eyes glanced up, like small stones studded in dough, his forehead a winter forest of blood vessels.

'What that it?'

'The boat that you claim has been following us for days – is that it?'

'I not record this conversation,' Hieronimo said. 'I think I not say you is a boat, mendigo, but maybe is.'

The sun dipped below the horizon, setting sagging crescents of the ocean ablaze with a sudden whiteness more dazzling than the sun whose shine they had borrowed. Light was fast fading and Angel saw his own hands growing dark in front of his eyes.

That night, the water no longer illuminated when touched.

———◆·◆———

The ghosts in the wood were murmuring. Angel put his fingers in his ears, but still the noise persisted within.

Jacques hadn't returned; it had been more than a day since Angel had eaten, and, in the dark of his quarters, his limbs trembled, and the shadows seemed lively.

The moaning persisted.

He swung out of his hammock, and hammered the floor with his fists, but the sounds did not diminish. A knock sounded in response, but this time it did not come from beneath him; it came from the door.

'Come in, Jacques. Come in.'

A swarthy, fine-featured man poked his head inside, his ovoid face flat and shining like a ceramic plate. His drooping eyelids gave him a lugubrious aspect at odds with the two large ears whose thin cusps the sunlight behind pinked, rendering visible the webs of blood vessels within.

'Indiana Camacho de Vega, second mate, at your service. The Gallego rascal said you would like to speak with me.'

His voice was arch, aristocratic after the English fashion, touched only with the vaguest trill of a Spanish accent.

'Of course,' Angel said, getting to his feet. 'Please, come in.'

The second mate stepped into the windowless quarters. He carried a bottle of rum under his arm, a tumbler in each hand.

'Do you partake, Mr Kelly?'

'Thank you.'

Angel lit a few squat candles in pewter saucers. Camacho sat cross-legged on the floor and poured out two generous thumbs of rum into each tumbler, but then he forgot to pass the second one to Angel, sipping absentmindedly at his own glass.

'Well,' the second mate said, eventually, pouring himself another tumbler, 'what is it you can tell neither Mr Hinchoa nor Captain Niewouldt?'

Angel, slightly dazed by suddenly being in company, was unable to think of anything but the truth. He told the second mate about the captain's messenger pigeon, as the latter filled up his tumbler once more in an offhand manner that made his constant sipping seem almost incidental. He had drunk off his third tumbler by the time Angel was finished.

'He knows he can't carry it alone,' Camacho said. 'It's weakness.'

'The captain is weak?'

'The captain is done, Lafcadio is weak. Have you spoken of this with anyone else?'

'No.'

'It would be best not to say anything. I will know if you misspeak.'

'What is your meaning, Mr Camacho?'

'I will know – that is all. The men are fond of me; they will let me know if you have misspoken. I suppose I am lucky to be so trusted, but then again I have been so long at sea . . .'

There was the clank of winches being twisted, halyards rowsed, the dull slump of a loose cable whipping the deck and screeching in the hawseholes, and the *Atlas* tacked, sending the saucers of guttering candles sliding across the floor like tiny sail boats with their masts on fire. They touched the wall nearest Camacho, illuminating his half of the room and leaving Angel shaded; the bottle of rum had started to slide, too, but it fell into the Valencian's outstretched palm.

'You know, Mr Kelly, on this crossing I keep seeing my mother in dreams, always in the old house. She looks out the window, her back to me, and she is so still that it terrifies me. I go into the next room, and she's there as well, looking out another window. And I go into the next room and the very same thing. But in the old house there was only one room, and it had no window. I go up to her and I am about to put my hand on her shoulder, but I know that her eyes are closed and if I try to wake her I will have to admit that she is dead.'

'I never met my mother.'

'Of course you did. You can only arrive one way. Do you have any opium, Mr Kelly?'

Angel shook his head.

'I'd do anything for a woman, now,' Camacho said, 'to put my head in her lap and breathe her in. Do you know the sweat a woman has where her breast falls over her ribcage? I miss that. And the wild smell that gets all tangled up in the meadow of her cunt; I miss that, too. A woman singing about her lover while she rests her empty hands on her knees; that's all there is to it all, really. How could I give it up? How could Lafcadio ever ask me to give it up?'

He poured himself another tumbler.

'I am not like Hieronimo,' he said, 'a Gallego born to the Atlantic Ocean, a turgid slop that floats icebergs and the brunt of those slaves' bones worth the tossing and is without history – whose only history is the history of squids! I am a man of the Mediterranean, Mr Kelly; where Greek women scented with jasmine ferry jugs on their shoulders, and Sicilian girls with snarls in their teeth dry their wedding sheets on olive trees to show the first blood; where Abd al-Raman forgave the Christians and raised the horseshoe aqueducts; where de Cervantes's left hand was blown apart amidst the glittering surf; where – No! No! No! I cannot take anymore, Mr Kelly. No more . . . Is this it? Is this it forever? I was supposed to be rich. I was supposed to have a command. They used to say in Gandía . . . those afternoons with Inés, the light from the balcony slanted upon the lower part of her face . . . How could I give it up? How could he ever ask me to give it up? I know all about the so-called captain's orders.'

He staggered to his feet, kicking a candle out as he rose that rolled and knocked over the second tumbler that had never been emptied. In his hands were the bottle and the remaining tumbler. He twisted the handle of the door with his forearm.

'Mr Camacho,' Angel said.

The second mate paused, back crooked on the threshold, and stared at him.

'What are those noises coming from below deck?'

Camacho's eyes were surprised, as though he had never seen Angel before, and then he burst into laughter. He left the door open behind him, and Angel heard the laughter play momentarily on the wind, and then it was gone.

From its erratic trajectory, Lafcadio suspected the vessel in the distance to be a Hollow One, a ship unmanned by war, plague or tempest. If such was the case, he would send a party to board her, salvage what they might, requisition the log, and scuttle her, wearing scarves over their mouths to protect them from any noxious fevers therein.

He ordered Quentin Cricklow to keep an eye on it, but then spent the rest of the day watching it himself.

Once, in his youth, he had boarded a Dutch frigate that had been drifting along the coast of Senegal, weighted down by an acreage of barnacles, swarmed by a froth of diverse fishes, and dragging after her densely woven reams of seaweed. He had been the first to board, then; had hauled himself up by a knotted rope grappled to a cleat and spilled aboard. His boots echoed out across empty, tomblike decks. He rifled through defunct instruments; incomplete maps; rusted astrolabes; blunted, demagnetised compasses, the points dragging against the markings. The log was unreadable, a dried pool of inky pap; seven strands of blonde hair pressed between its disintegrating pages. The hold carried an algaed lagoon. Wind moaned through enormous holes in the sails. They had fluttered without interruption for more than a decade, by now so coated in salt they glimmered like a cave of crystals broken open to the sunlight.

'Marry, there she is, sir,' Cricklow said. 'If we set the course we should have her steering athwart our hawse afore nightfall.'

'Set it.'

More loitering sailors joined Cricklow, passing a telescope amongst themselves. They followed it with their eyes and their ship until dusk, when a Swedish carpenter named Fuchs wiped down his spectacles on his trousers and put them in front of his face, at a good distance from his nose and said:

'No sloop, and she is too small in the hull to be French.'

'Ain't got no hull at all,' Cricklow said.

'Where is her mast?'

'La, she has two,' Cricklow said.

By now a crowd had formed that blocked most of the larboard deck. Nearly fifty men had clambered onto hatches, bulwarks, up the rigging. A soft patina of invisible and unfelt rain glazed them.

Angel pushed through this gathering, asking:

'Does anyone know where Jacques is, the boy Jacques?'

Then he saw what seemed to be an island floating very slightly above sea level, its surface pocked with mussels and blankets of bulbous seaweed that adorned it like loosening flesh. It was something slick and animal, like the submerged hump of some rotting leviathan. An olive tree grew out of it, its trunk seven twisting branches. Grey leaves shivered relentlessly, their lighter underside flickering in and out of vision with the wind, giving the appearance of something trying to become something else; even the bark seemed to crawl with motion. On a low limb, almost hidden behind the latticed mesh of sprigs and leaves, was a small girl, perhaps nine or ten years old. She had her back pressed against the trunk, her arms around her knees, her shawl funnelling the wind. Out of reach of the tree's shade, a pale, one-eyed man had been crucified on the severed upper part of a mainmast. His body swayed constantly with the pitch and roll of the sea. The arms were wide across the spars; a loose shirt flapped across the emaciated body; whips of wet hair plastered across his cavernous cheeks, and his whole face was obscured in shade by a faded tricorne hat which had remained stuck on his head by way of a nail hammered through the top of his skull.

'El jardín,' Hieronimo said.

''Tis a wandering graveyard, la,' Cricklow said.

A swell submerged the surface, making it seem like the tree and the crucifix had been discharged, fully formed, from the depths. They tilted back and forth, bursts of whitened water splashing them, and then, like a sigh of release, the bubbling water hissed its way out through the wefts in the seaweed, and then there was the foamy rush of the breaching, the displaced water exploding about it.

'It is the hull of a capsized vessel, in putrefaction,' Lafcadio said. 'It is the fruit of mutiny, only. They have been cast away. This man was the captain, and she must have been—'

Angel looked away suddenly, having noticed something terrible.

There was a noise above; eyes strained upwards. Jacques hung off a sheet, a figure-of-eight coil around his shoulder.

'No, Jacques,' Lafcadio shouted. 'Look.'

He gestured at the crucified man whose head was slouched forward now, the tricorne an inverted black triangle where his face had been; Angel noticed for the first time that the dead man's trousers were flapping wildly, like untethered lines. There were no feet hanging down, the trousers unfilled; only the upper half of a man hung there.

'Get down, Jacques,' Angel called. 'Come down, now.'

Jacques cast the rope, and it landed amidst a tumbling clump of black seaweed.

'Prends-la, 'moiselle,' Jacques shouted.

The wind rose in an ache; the girl didn't come down from the tree.

As the *Atlas* pushed on, the rope wound its way through the reams of seaweed, its knotted end bouncing, and then it plopped back into the sea, and dragged through the water where it created a white rushing furrow in the form of a cobra's hood.

Then they were past it. Jacques looked at the disappointed length of rope in his hands, and then found himself on his back, pulled down by Lafcadio. The first mate knelt over him, and commenced slapping him, open-palmed, across the face. Sailors clustered around them like clotting blood, their faces a mass of indistinguishable shadows in the drab evening. Jacques glanced around, blinking dizzily.

24

'Sir,' he said. 'A child.'

'A cannibal,' Lafcadio said.

He slapped him twice more, and then left off.

The tree and the crucifix cast a faint, joined shadow against the water, and then they, too, became shade. Soon all that was visible were two vertical lines rearing thinly out of the sea, a throbbing spot, stalking closely the water, obscured by every slight pitch of the ship.

Jacques writhed on deck, his mouth and nose bleeding.

'Angel,' he said. 'Angel, please.'

As Angel was moving through the crowd, Lafcadio touched the underside of his chin so he was looking up directly into his face.

They stared at each other silently.

Eventually, the first mate folded his hands behind his back, stepped aside, and Angel helped Jacques up and led him back to his own quarters.

———•———

Late that night, three knocks rapped smartly against the door. Angel awoke.

'Who is it?'

'Marianne Lynch,' the voice on the other side said. 'I will come in.'

The door had no lock. Jacques was laid out in the corner on some of Angel's clothes. He raised himself on his knuckles and watched the door. In the greenish dark, he looked like a coddled embryo, his simple face crimped with the olive bruising that closed over one of his eyes.

'Open the door,' Lynch said. 'Are you alone?'

Angel said nothing.

'Faith, you are alone, Angel, in a way the other orphan does not understand. Do you remember what I said I would do to you forever? First I would teach you to breathe, to float, to forget, to walk across oceans, but you must let me in.'

There was a scuffling of boot heels outside, and then a soft thump as if Lynch had leant his whole weight against the door.

'Five men are going down to the hold,' he said. 'You will join them. You will be the sixth man.'

The sea seemed to have fallen mute. Angel, in dread, waited, his breath held, the hammock beneath him gently creaking.

'Chained in the hold,' Lynch said, 'are more than a hundred and fifty souls, and they are all slaves. The five are going down – and what will they do there? You know.'

'No.'

'You know. You will go, too.'

'No. Liar.'

'It is a secret from the captain what these five do before the dawn watch. Why a secret? What, on such a ship as this, could ever be worth the secret? You know.'

'Go away.'

'Will you join them, Angel?'

'No.'

'When they are thrown overboard, do they feel themselves to be floating down? Or did an angel ever carry one down?'

Angel pushed the palms of his hands against his eyes.

'Shut your mouth.'

'Open the door, Angel,' Lynch said, 'or I'll open it for you.'

He threw his shoulder thrice against the doorframe, setting the wood vibrating, and then the handle twisted downwards.

'No,' Angel said. 'No.'

The commotion ceased; the handle returned slowly to its original position. He could feel him still standing outside the door.

'Only messing,' Lynch said.

Slow, flat waves scrolled across the indistinct sea like black curtains. It was another hour until sunrise. In the great shade of the mainsail, five men silently unclasped latches, hove moorings and dragged weights. Angel, from where he crouched behind the forecastle, recognised Hieronimo, Fuchs, Cricklow, Camacho; the other sailor he did not know.

A trapdoor was opened, and one by one they disappeared, leaving behind only Camacho on watch. The Valencian scanned the ambit of the lightening horizon; in the opposite direction, the huge roaring dark; his eyes came to rest on Angel.

Only once he had been detected did Angel realise he didn't care that he had been found out. He stood up, staring back brazenly. Then, he returned to his quarters.

Jacques was awake, sitting up, his back leaning against the wall.

'Sir, you are ill?'

'Why are you here?'

'I help.'

'No. Why are you on a slave ship?'

'I help the slave. Give the water and the food for them.'

'I saw no slaves in Liverpool.'

'They are bring them in Nouadhibou.'

'When were we there?'

'Before Dakar. After Lisbon. You were sick. I help you.'

'Out. Get out.'

'Sir, yes.'

Jacques rose so quickly the bruise across his face darkened a rich purple. Then he knelt and began folding the shirts and leggings he had lain upon.

'Leave them.'

'Yes, sir.'

Angel looked away as he left.

There came a great confusion, much yelling; boots stamped as they crossed the main. One of the five had been killed below deck; Camacho had fled his watch, unseen. The remaining three suffered to escape the hold, but did not manage to recuperate the body. An alarm was raised.

Lafcadio and Lynch and a few others went down with arms. There followed some gunfire. All noises below were quelled. The dead sailor was brought up to deck, and Lafcadio set to meting out punishments.

From his cabin, Angel heard much he did not understand. He had been sleepless so long it felt like the insides of his throat and eyelids had grown thinner, as if an internal layer of his flesh had been shaved away.

Later, he heard Hieronimo shouting out something in Galician – a language the man hadn't spoken since he was eight years old – and then there was the sound of dragging, ropes shrieking across wood. It seemed like someone was climbing the foremast. There was silence again, and then a thick, soft sound, like a large bird flying headlong into a window, pushed against Angel's door. A few minutes later, it happened again, and then a third time.

He got up and opened the door. Hieronimo was there, hanging upside down. The inverted body twisted idly, the swollen, purple face floating at chest height, the half-closed eyelids bulging. He had been strung up from a spar, his body and limbs wrapped in a length of sail that had fattened him like a swaddled child.

The other two were strung up in a similar fashion. Fuchs hung off the boom of the mizzen, and Cricklow dangled precipitously off the bowsprit, nothing between him and the immensity of the ocean. He moaned in torment, constantly revived by the rainbow spray that exploded up at him as the prow cut the waves. Seen altogether, it was as though three enormous cocoons had made their home in the middle of the ocean. By the entrance to the main, Marianne Lynch sat a-straddle the dead sailor, whose name was Thomas Alderman, and sewed him away into a shroud. His neck had been broken by a chain. Beneath the chalky blue of his face, two links had left their impression across his caved Adam's apple.

'There was a fifth man,' Lafcadio said, addressing the crew. 'I saw him from the aft and so he fled. A coward who fled, abandoning Mr Alderman to his death. And as such, this man abandoned all of you. If Mr Alderman had been a keyholder, we would all be perished now. Why protect such a man? I want the fifth. I want him by the evening watch. Mr Lynch, another turn of the glass and you may take these three down.'

Lynch paused his sewing for a moment and pointed up at the sky with the needle.

'Sir, I've spoken to the Moor, and he says before they're unhanged I've to make a little cross on their foreheads to relieve the tension behind the eyes.'

'Whatever is necessary,' Lafcadio said, his gaze ranging along the crew. 'I go presently to make my full report to the captain.'

None of this did Angel witness. He had closed the door the moment he had seen Hieronimo hanging outside and lain back down in his hammock. Later, he could hear bodies slipping overboard. A whispering and a splash. A whispering and a splash – and then once more.

For several days, Jacques knocked and entered, bearing a bowl of broth, or biscuits and cheese, or salted fish. He would lay the covered bowl out, removing the previous one Angel had left barely touched.

Angel could hear him, but did not open his eyes. He was learning to pray.

He prayed without belief in God or belief in prayer. He prayed until his throat and mouth grew sore, and he felt like he was

choking, but still he prayed. He prayed until there was no difference between waking and sleeping, speaking or silence, and he
prayed for the trembling wretches in the sloshing hold; of each
hold there was, its darkness squarely repeated in a hundred thousand ships that bounded the oceans and millennia. He prayed for
a shrieking mother who smothered her baby as she was being
lowered into the pilot off Santana; for the neck-bound chain-gang
of eight who in unspoken tribal accord jumped overboard as they
were hustled into light. He prayed for the confused girl, wrangled
into a separate coffle from her sister. Please God, he prayed, no.
Please God, do not let her understand. Please God, let her forget.
Please God, let her forget and achieve that lightness that allows
her to float upon the surface of this little life. Please God, give
her the electrifying blaze called aliveness, the sudden shared
perception, the freeing love, the unexpected laugh, the joyous
forgetting, a lover's first touch, a sister's hale call, the giggle of a
baby, the whisper of a tingling word that names the name that
allows the couple to commune; to say yes, yes I will stay here with
you, forever, yes, until I am dead, until all that I am is gone. Please
God, give her something whole and final, or if not give her just a
few brief moments snatched from ravenous death's maw, moments
cached in the flashing illumination of memory with which we
have measured the dizzying breadth of our tragedies and all those
places in ourselves we have lost, all these days we have left behind,
all these friends, all these lovers, all these sisters and brothers, all
these mothers and fathers and all these children, all these hours
and years of work and sleep and prayer and breath and love, all the
fullness of our flourishing and fading existence, all gone soon to
utter eradication. And then let her forget and become light again.
Only forgetting. Only light. Please God. Please God, allow us the
grace of forgetting so that the whole earth may be renewed like
fresh-born skin, the Americas yet unfound, the seas yet unfished,
its fruits yet unplucked, the black lumbering hulls never passing

amidst the wandering gams who slope luxuriantly down to Antarctica where no humans greet nor grin nor grimace, and then, maybe in our forgetting, all the dead would be free and live again, laughing at the memory of that death of theirs that did not so wholly conquer, and so could say – I'm home, mother. Mother, it is me. This is my homecoming. Mother, I have returned. At last, we are together. I have waited so long for you, to see you. I have missed you so much. You do not know what I have been without you. You do not know what I have become without you. You do not know my incompleteness without your love. We are here together, and we are made of love. She is here, and she is made of love. And then she is born once more, and these new eyes are awake, seeing with freshness and vigour for the very first time, and we do it all again – but what, then?

Light.

Light.

Only light.

It was the line-crossing, and Lafcadio had ordered full celebrations. The crew had not given up the fifth man, but he was bone tired of the punishments, the lies, his own sham command. Camacho was biting at his heels, sowing division, whispering rumours about Captain Niewouldt. Lafcadio would wake every dawn hunched in his creaking bunk, eyes closed and clagged with sweat, and something was already waiting there for him, something bright and terrible nestling beneath the ribs. It might all come to a rough end, but if the trade winds kept up, they would see land in two days, and in four more, Santana; by then, it might all be done with.

He could hear them singing already. He stripped naked, palmed gold paint along his broad body, attached a white beard, took Captain Niewouldt's wooden trident and crown from the chest, and then he angled out of the porthole. He climbed up a rope ladder he had secured the night before and shimmied over the bulwarks.

The crew was all there. They wore pink ribbons around their wrists; other colourful ribbons had been tied to the masts. The sails had all been reefed, making the ship seem frail and skeletal. Marianne Lynch stood atop the navigator's house, singing a ballad. Scores of sailors surrounded him, some sitting in the gigs so as to get a better view. Quentin Cricklow was the first to see him. The Cockney wore a wedding dress, and yet it was the rood etched into his forehead, its scab clotted blackly like burnt sugar, that the first mate's eye was drawn to.

'Marry, if ain't Neptune hisself.'

Lafcadio raised high the trident.

'I am Neptune,' he said, 'thy sole master, and you will drink my waters and offer me thy virgins.'

Lynch dipped a pail into the sea, and triced it up. Then he accompanied Lafcadio around the stern. Each sailor the first mate passed fell to his knees and touched his feet.

'Drink,' he said to each one.

Lynch ladled water from the pail, and they all drank. After the first sup, the remnants were poured over the sailors' heads.

When everyone had drunk, the first mate rapped his trident against the deck and called out:

'More virgins.'

Three novice sailors stepped forth and climbed the bulwarks.

'Wait,' Lafcadio said. 'Not yet. Mr Cricklow.'

Cricklow fell to his knees, the tarnished dress slapping the deck heavy as leather beneath him, his eyes brought low but the raw cross still facing up at Lafcadio. It had been so many years since he had been a part of these men's mute complicities and unspeakable solidarities. For many crossings, his position and his dignity had left him without companion. At that moment, he decided to dismiss Camacho as second mate and to separate Cricklow from his fellows by favouring him with promotion. The fifth, when he had been given up – and given up he must be – him, he would have keelhauled into port.

'There is another, Mr Cricklow. I want Mr Angel Kelly, the fare.'

And so Angel found himself roisted awake by a bearded and scarred man in a wedding dress who said:

'La, squire, come hither.'

His hammock was overturned, and he tumbled to the floor. Cricklow grabbed him by the shirt collars and leg and dragged him out into the bracing air where a sudden rush of blood to the head rendered him briefly unconscious.

When he came to, hands were pressed against his back and legs. He was being carried, his light body writhing uselessly against the bearers.

'What is this? No. Stop. No. No.'

'You are in the southern half,' Lafcadio said to him. 'You must give your body to the sea, and only then will it be given back to you.'

Without hesitation, the three novice sailors jumped into the water, the fattest one whooping with joy.

'I can't swim,' Angel said.

'You must learn.'

Angel went to grab at something, and then he spun. The sea was the sky was the sea. A roaring greeted him, and he was enveloped. A thousand hisses; eyes burnt in wet and groaning dark, ears taut and explosive. He pounded his arms against the rushing. The sea moaned and surged. It drew huge sighs around him, tragic and slow, and then his hands breached, and he surfaced, giant commotions in his chest drawing air.

A swell smothered him once more. Two of the novice sailors were climbing up a knotted rope hung over the side, one after the other. Along the bulwarks, a line of faces watched him like a row of heads lining a barbarian citadel, and then there was an eruption of water mushrooming up nearby. Something grabbed his leg, and he started screaming.

'Stop to move, please.'

Jacques gripped his chest with one arm. Messily, he propelled them towards the looming hull with doglike kicks. Angel choked on inrushes of water, floundered, but by then Jacques had reached the rope. Angel reached out and grabbed it, too. The vessel pitched, and on the first dip they were plunged underwater, and then on the contrary roll they were yanked up into the air, light as puppets. After the second roll, Jacques disappeared, and only Angel's hands were left upon the rope.

Gasping, he scanned the water.

The hull above curved outwards, casting a rounded darkness on the water in whose shade Angel was concealed. It seemed like he was under the potbelly of a huge monster, its underparts thickly scaled with warty mussels and hollow-eyed barnacles, all draped with ragged fringes of jaundiced seaweed.

'Yonder,' a voice above called.

At certain tilts of the ship, Angel could see the crew's protruding chins like unfinished necks. He scanned the sea again. Jacques was there, greenly discoloured by the water that covered him. Face down, he floated towards Angel. A rope was dropped which had a loop tied in its end.

Angel grabbed Jacques by the hair and manoeuvred the loop around his waist, then drew it through until he was secured. The cabin boy began to rise up along the hull and then he was out of sight and Angel was alone for some time, hanging on to the other rope.

The shock had gone and now he felt cold tightening beneath his flesh. His left side had gone numb. When the looped rope was dropped again, he pulled his legs through it, secured himself under the armpits and was drawn upwards, the skin around his chest screaming from the flay. As he rose, his swinging body smacked thrice against the boards, razor-lipped mussels cutting his back and shoulders with a pain intensified by the chill. When he was in reach, Lafcadio pulled him up the rest of the way, and then Angel found himself sprawled on deck again.

Immediately, he began crying with the relief of being alive. Sailors, swaying gently in the yaw, looked down at him, from the boom and mizzen, their ribbons gently fluttering. Hieronimo seemed confused, scratching at the cross on his forehead until a trickle of blood shook down to a wrinkle that spread the blood out horizontally. Jacques was still unconscious; Lafcadio stooped down to listen at the boy's chest, trident yet in hand.

'He's not breathing,' he said. 'Hieronimo, get him to the Moor. You, paying fare, you help.'

The chef picked up the boy's arms and Angel his legs. Together, they carried the cabin boy towards the forecastle, to a door in which he had thought only supplies were stored.

'I don't understand. Where is the surgeon?'

'Surgeon take very much the drinks some days and lose the ship. But Flores, he know the physic. Is for this the captain take him for the fare in Nouadhibou. I celebrate the equator now, yes? I go.'

Hieronimo lay Jacques's legs down and departed and Angel, his breath still flustered, was left there waiting. He knocked on the door.

By the stern, the festivities had started once more, but they were muffled, lost in that little distance that passed between the gentle winds. Dancers could be seen along the taffrails; sailors scaling the counterbraced yards, falling off occasionally like scree from a cliff, the grey background of the sky making the men seem stark, tiny, unreal.

Angel knocked again, more urgently, then pushed open the door.

Nothing could be made out in the gloom except for the flicker of moving hands. There was a padded sound. Angel's eyes adjusted – the man was spinning. One leg, planted on the ground, served as a stay, the other propelled him with a kick after each revolution. Right palm faced upwards, the left downwards; his head leant to the right, his tongue protruding slightly. There was a vacancy to his expressions, his movements a perfection of flow.

'Mr Flores? Sir? Can you not hear?'

Still the man spun. Angel tried to grab him by the arm, but only ended up unbalancing him. He stumbled heavily against the wall, his eyes unfocused, his head rolling forwards onto his chest, and then he slid down to his knees.

'I was leaning,' he said, but the words were slurred.

'What?'

'I was leaning towards God.'

'This boy is not breathing.'

Flores crawled over, put his ear close to Jacques's chest.

'Bring him inside,' he said, 'cover his nostrils with your mouth, blow into them.'

Angel dragged Jacques into the centre of the room. He cleared the boy's nostrils with his fingers, and then sealed them with his lips and breathed. Jacques's chest rose, but something else seemed to squirm and shudder within like a second heartbeat. After a few exhalations, Angel was pushed aside. Flores was holding a bowl of dried leaves he had set alight, and in one of his hands was a wooden implement: a hollow tube in the shape of a Y. He put each smaller end in the boy's nostrils and then inhaled the smoke from the bowl and blew it into the opening of the implement. Jacques's eyes opened wide; his legs beat against the floor. Then, Flores placed his hand deep inside the boy's mouth and when he withdrew it, between his forefinger and his thumb, a pink, luminescent tendril stretched tautly from the throat.

His face furrowed in concentration, he stood up slowly, drawing forth the thing until amidst his fist was a thick clump of glimmering roots, and as they grew longer, more light entered them, and the room, in turn, grew illuminated. Jacques was filled with these slick, translucent tendrils, some almost dense as fingers. Tiny cauliflowers of tumescent blue popped out of his mouth, followed finally by a flattened sphere of transparent flab that slopped out like an afterbirth. The creature's featureless head fattened. Four purple circles inside it flickered, and then a kaleidoscopic array of colours started flashing through it, shining so brightly Angel could make out the Arabic script of an open book that lay on the other side of the quarters.

'A medusa,' Flores said. 'Some have never been known to die.'

The creature dangled almost two foot long. Jacques inhaled hugely, and then fainted again, eyes still open, jaw hanging unnaturally wide. Flores walked out the door, the gelatinous thing sucking weakly in his fist, and threw it into the sea.

He returned.

'His jaw has come undone.'

He placed his fingers under the boy's cheeks, and gently exerted them upwards; Jacques groaned, but did not wake.

Then Flores turned to Angel.

'You have a fever coming on.'

'I am fine.'

'Allow me.'

He placed his hands against Angel's forehead, and Angel felt an unusual warmth deep inside his own skull. Something passed between them, something akin to electricity, but subtler, gentler. There was no shock, only a current that suffused Angel's body with calm.

———◆———

When he woke up, it was much later. The quarters were warm, almost like a hothouse; he had sweated in his sleep. There was a blurry outline damp across the floor where the cabin boy had lain. Flores was reading a book across his lap, spectacles upon his nose, two platters of candles either side of him.

Angel watched him silently – he was a slim man with narrow features, deep-set and hooded eyes. African, though wearing European monastic dress – he was perhaps a decade older than Angel, though it was difficult to be sure.

Occupying nearly every surface were books in Arabic, Latin, and French. Many lay open, giving as much an impression of confusion as of learning.

Flores looked up.

'Jacques has gone,' he said.

Angel noticed his accent then, the slight hushing sound when he spoke the cabin boy's name.

'Who are you?'

'My name is Mohammad Ibn Ammar Ndiaye, but you can call me Flores. It is easier.'

'There are a lot of books here.'

'I was writing my doctorate in Montpellier,' he said. 'I still keep the books, though I cannot see now how I will ever finish my work.'

'My name is Angel. I also was a student, for a little while. What is the work?'

Flores laid his spectacles across the open page of his book. 'Those practices which unite Islam and Christianity. This led me to the records of those desert peoples who preceded us, and they are contradictory, a palimpsest of stories. They do not reveal practices; they only tell stories. Many saviours have come already, so many, and they say who is saved, who is not; what is mercy, what is not; where is light, where is death. And so I have gotten lost in the abattoir of history and have lost six years of my life along with it.'

'Captain Niewouldt said I was the only passenger.'

'You were. I am as surprised as you that the captain let me aboard. He would not, at first. I lied to him and said that I had no scruples over the trade; that it was commoner in the Trarza than in the Americas. He said he did not want the confusion of a Moslem. I could see he was nervous, thoughtful even, and I surrendered myself to his mercy. I told him the truth about my mother, and he had a capacity to listen. He let me aboard. The captain of a slave ship did this. It is a great mystery and I saw it as a very fine auspice, but since that day I have not seen Captain Niewouldt.'

'What is this about your mother?'

Flores grimaced slightly, and the expression made him look much older.

'My mother, Amam, is here, held in chains in the hold. They have made a slave of her. In Santana, I will buy her freedom – it is the only way I can see – and, once she has recovered her health we shall return home together, by way of . . . On our journey home, we will take our time . . . see many cities . . . I left home very young, you see. I came to Europe when I was sixteen . . . I haven't seen my mother since . . . I had thought I could . . . Sometimes, I think if I had—'

He gasped, blinked away a sudden film of tears, and turned away, facing the wall, his shoulders rising and falling rapidly like the amputated stumps of wings.

'Could you please go, now. Please.'

———— • ————

Angel set upon the salted fish and red wine Jacques had laid out for him the night before. He ate on his knees, pushing the food into his mouth while yet chewing the previous mouthful, and drinking all the while. In a few moments, he was finished.

He sat back on his forelegs, ecstatic to the point of dizziness. Energy coursed through him, the crackle of his own gallivanting blood enormous in his ears, like sheets of ice rupturing apart inside his head. The sensation seemed endless, and then he felt pushing down upon him a guilt that closed over his throat.

'What have I done?' he said. 'I have destroyed my life.'

He coughed dry tears, mashed his cheeks against the floorboards and beat his fists against his head. He was so alone. Shards of grief reared wildly from the clutching guilt. Memories of his aunt asleep by the fireplace; her left side burnished with lapping light; the slouching head, chin against the chest; the embroidery, a pink flower, unfinished in her lap; sounds escaping her throat from a nervous dream. He had shaken her awake, and she hadn't recognised him.

He saw Molly Sheridan, the pleats of her face deepening with laughter, squinting against sideways gusts of snow. A flake swirled onto her bonnet, melted darkly through the material, dripped down to her eyelash. He had kissed it away and, shivering, she had kissed him back, hard on the mouth. The snow chilled her teeth; the wine dark on the bed of her tongue, and then he saw Flores, tears blossoming, turning away from him again, and the guilt flowed like bile once more up the chasm of his chest. Briefly, he felt a moment of pure and inexplicable hatred for the man.

'I'm so sorry. I'm so sorry. What have I done with my life? I am ruined. I am nothing.'

He gasped and lay on his side; the vividness of his suffering reached an apex, broke apart, and dispersed into a spacious sense of abandonment. The candles were pools in their saucers, twisted short wick amidst them like worms floating in a puddle. His body felt swollen. The fish he had eaten had reached his gut, but its oils were yet rancid against the roof of his mouth.

A slave was screaming below deck.

<hr />

Angel opened his eyes to darkness, a great urgency come upon him.

Someone in authority must absolve him. There had to be some legal manner of establishing that he had had no knowledge prior to boarding that the *Atlas* carried within her human cargo. He was so ashamed, so stupid, such an idiot, such a fool, such a stupid fool – and then he hit upon the idea of asking Captain Niewouldt for his fare back. Would that not be some sort of condemnation; coin being the only kind this breed understood? To castigate the captain for participating in the institution of slavery once they had already arrived in Brazil would seem cowardly, but to force too strongly the point right now was tantamount to suicide – but hadn't the captain let Flores aboard, knowing his mother was in captivity? So the captain must have had some change of heart somewhere along the crossing, himself.

In his mind's eye, he saw Flores reading quietly by candlelight, and grunted in astonishment at the knot of agony pulsing through his chest once more.

'Please, there has to be some . . .'

He was unable to finish. He had to explain to Flores that he hadn't known – and he would offer to pay for his mother once they reached Santana; it was the gentlemanly gesture. But he knew he couldn't speak with Flores now. It was too much. It was too soon. He would ask him for forgiveness for being onboard. He would tell him he hadn't known, but only later, only once he had spoken to the captain.

He arose and opened the door, and found directly outside his quarters Quentin Cricklow, a telescope pressed against his eye making him look like half a brass machine, gazing out at a huge block of dark clouds along the horizon.

It was early evening, and the ocean was turning black, the last spark of red snuffed out by the sun dropping below the water. The white blur of an indistinct moon throbbed dully behind a panorama of clustering clouds like melting fruits. Orbs of golden light emanated from three half-opened hatches; warm sounds of argument flourished in the main. Someone started to sing.

'I have found the continent,' Cricklow said.

What Angel had thought were low clouds was land gauzed and softened by a vast haze. It was too big, too sudden, too there, all before him. Its mass was too grand; human ambition could not encompass such an immensity.

'But we have just crossed the line.'

'A day and a night and a day since we crossed the line. We are well past the Indies, in a nice stiff breeze. You was in your quarters a right little while, la.'

'Impossible.'

He went to move towards the captain's quarters, but Cricklow struck him in the elbow with the brass of the telescope, and a pincer of pain seized his ulnar nerve.

'You are confined to quarters.'

'On what grounds?'

'I has my orders.'

'Nonsense. I wish to appeal to the captain.'

'Appeal? Marry, you're confined to quarters till we're docked. You might appeal thereafter.'

The white fringe of a wave suddenly crested behind the Englishman, and then the ephemeral froth disappeared, and nothing of the sea was visible in the dark.

'When are we going to arrive in Brazil?'

'I am not the wind.'

Angel stared at the cross, now scabrous and loose like a pouch upon the forehead.

'What were you doing to the slaves below deck that morning?'

Cricklow snorted mirthlessly.

'The slaves, la? Who told you? You have spoke with our kid, Flores, might be? Marry, I have made a fortune off the mite this voyage. He gives out ten French livres for the passing of some dried fruits to his mother, and a whole bloody Louis d'or if I let her stretch her legs for a quarter-hour. If we did a round tour with her, I'd retire and establish a pie shop at Margate.'

Angel didn't respond.

'Mr Camacho and myself has a stake on you; the whole crew is taken up with it. Mr Camacho claims no one on the face of the sea would be so stupid as to not know we was a slaving one. He thought you was needling him, but I said you was but a lad; an idealist; a student, with a squawking goose of an imagination. Marry, I never seen anyone so drunk as you come aboard, lowing like a calf the name of some tart . . . Milly Sherryham, or something.'

'Molly Sheridan.'

'Ay,' he said. 'Come aboard full of palaver, off your bleeding head, and no one sees you for near a fortnight. Marry, we all thinks you're dead, and when you poke out thy little lamb of a face, wee sleeping men in your eyes like yellow tears, we've already cast off from Dakar. Such a bloody fool as yourself is an historic find. Enough. That's enough now. Back to your quarters, child, lest I widen thy arse with me glass.'

He placed a hand on Angel's chest and pushed him back inside.

Before the dawn, on hands and knees, Angel opened softly once more the door, and saw Cricklow still standing there, a hanging sentinel against the weakening nightscape. The *Atlas* lurched forward and Cricklow slouched over with a jerk, and then creaked back into position.

He was asleep at his post, arm noosed around a line which propped him up like a marionette.

Barefoot, flesh icy with horripilation, Angel crawled along the deck until he reached the captain's quarters.

He knocked.

'May I enter, captain?' he whispered against the wood. 'It is Angel Kelly. I spoke to you once in Liverpool? Do you remember me?'

There was a stirring behind him. Someone was leaving quarters. Angel stayed very still, holding his breath, and when the man passed out of sight, he tried the handle a few times and found the door locked. Angel took a grapple that was strapped snug against the foremast, went on his knees and engineered a hook under the jamb. He forced the door, flinching at the loud crack, and then he saw, straight in front of him, a mirror reflecting a portrait of a man and a woman on the far wall, above a red curtain.

There was a ruffling sound inside.

'Captain Niewouldt?' he said, stepping in. 'Captain, is that you?'

The quarters were illuminated by two hanging lanterns and twenty or so red candles that had melted into ugly oceans of stacked drippings. A faded globe creaked back and forth in the corner. Cold air like a solid force hit Angel, dust swirling about at chest height. He breathed in the inexplicable odour of resin, the acrid tang of dispelled smoke. A gilded birdcage was affixed to a wall, its meshed door slightly ajar. Three pigeons inside it sat on perches, eyeing him warily, their beaks hidden in the warm green plumage of their breasts. Below them, white feathers and droppings had formed little mountains like stalagmites. An oval portrait hung above a four-poster bed; it had been varnished, darkening the figures. It showed an austere man in the regalia of a bourgeois, a tricorne upon his head. He had a red beard, pursed lips, and dark blue eyes; beside him was his wife. She had soft, slender features, a mousy aspect. In the portrait, they stood facing each other, but their heads were turned towards the watcher, expressions sombre, quietly proud. At the foot of the bed, a clothes chest sat open, revealing a fiddle and bow lying on top of some folded dresses. There was a desk, also, on which lay a compass, some charts, and a leather cup. The curtains of the four-poster bed were drawn, and in the middle of the floor, gargantuan and sprawled out, was the first mate, Lafcadio, shot in the gut. He lay in a pool of blood that had soaked into one of his open eyes, turning it red like a half-filled glass of wine.

Angel tiptoed forward, and the pigeons, spooked, flew out of their cage, and began circling the room. Momentarily, the room was filled with flutters, like some paltry whirlwind. The displaced air from their revolutions extinguished several candles, and then they came to rest on the bed's canopy. Angel stepped over the first mate and, with great apprehension, drew back the curtains.

No one was there – before him a perfectly made bed, white sheets, plump blankets, and feather pillows. He sat on its edge, puzzled, looking down into Lafcadio's stilled eyes, understanding nothing.

He felt exhausted. The urge to lie down on the captain's bed was strong after so many weeks spent tilting in a hammock. Underneath his fingers, the delicious softness of the blankets, and before he realised it, he was climbing in and stretching out, feeling the indistinct merging of his body with the bed. Then, cocooned safely, he found that he was not sleepy at all. His head on the pillow, he turned on his side and stared down at Lafcadio, his gaze drawn towards the blood in the cracks of the floorboards; the boat's rolling making it slide back and forth. Soon, even the leaking blood seemed to become a part of the gentle safety of the captain's quarters. He twisted around, unable to find a position in which he could fall asleep.

Some time later Camacho peeked his head around the door.

'Why are you here, Mr Kelly?'

'Patrick Edgeworth goaded me.'

'Who? More secrets? No sailor on this vessel – that I can tell you. Never mind. It's over now,' Camacho said. 'You look like a little baby; full of snugness.'

45

A breeze from the opened door douted several more candles. The light of dawn was stronger now. A pigeon alighted from the bedpost above and flew out the open door. Angel imagined it disappearing over the Atlantic, solitary, lost, insignificant against the sky.

'Where is the captain?'

'He hanged himself from there.' Camacho pointed at a thin nail that protruded from the wall, only visible from its shadow. 'I don't know how it held up, such a slight thing. It was only ever meant for the hanging of hats, not captains. Lafcadio, of course, tried to keep it a secret, for it is very bad luck altogether.'

Camacho went over to the leather cup, drank heavily from it, and then smacked his lips.

'What a fantastic sup,' he said, running his fingernails along his teeth, now covered in green specks. 'Have you ever tried yerba? A delicious and fortifying refreshment – a truly American drink.'

Taking a flask of rum out of the desk, he poured it into the leather cup and stirred it with his fingers. Angel dug himself in a little deeper under the blanket, his nose poking out over its edge.

'Lafcadio tortured those men; you saw it,' Camacho said. 'Me, he would have done worse to; keelhauled, drowned even. And for what? I ask you – what else are the slaves for, Mr Kelly, if not for the fucking? It only doubles their value if they are begetting – and that with a little, pale child who might work inside the house? Imagine. And if they are not moved nor exercised they are verily like botflies in flesh, waiting to hatch out of their wombs of pus. Their sweats and agues, after one crossing, rot through the boards, diminishing the value of the ship, and if too much value is deemed lost by the insurance it comes out of our shares! He thought he could find me out, repress me. I would not have it. There are many men who seem like leaders because of their tall stature and booming voices, but when it comes to the reckoning, they are found wanting.'

He placed the leather cup on the desk, took out a pistol that had been tucked in the back of his trousers and laid it across the desk.

'I had Mr Cricklow give it out to him that I was the one he sought – the fifth man – knowing he would organise a little meeting with the faithful Marianne Lynch so as to take me by surprise, but it was I turned up instead.'

Angel looked up, away from the fervid Spaniard, blinked a few times, and saw that one of the pigeons atop the bedpost had a little roll of paper wrapped around its leg.

'And do you know why I was able to do it?' Camacho went on. 'Why I could unmake a man who pretended to the captaincy? Because he did not possess any friends. Like you, Mr Kelly – you are a blur; a man outside us. What? You think yourself in some adventure, some fairy tale? You misread every sign; you think yourself haunted, but it is only the living who haunt. You are a minor player in someone else's story.'

Camacho knelt down next the bed so he was leaning directly over Angel's face.

'Be my friend, Mr Kelly,' he said. 'I am the captain now. It is the way of these things, no? Captain Camacho de Vega. Be my friend now and let us carry this man's body to sea together.'

A shadow fell across the floor; Marianne Lynch was standing in the doorway.

'Lo quiero ahora,' Lynch said.

'Sí,' Camacho said. 'Está allí.'

Lynch strode across the room, picked the fiddle and bow from atop the open chest, dashed off a few sonorous notes before he began tuning the instrument.

'Hay motín,' he said.

'Yes, I know there is a mutiny,' Camacho said. 'I have done it. I am your captain, now.'

Lynch shook his head. 'From below. They have hostages; four, I think.'

'You went down this morning?' Camacho asked, perplexed. 'But I told you not to.'

'I never go down. Others go down.'

'How bad is it?'

'Well . . .' Lynch shrugged, the fiddle cradled between his shoulder and ear. 'We are dead men.'

Camacho stepped across Lafcadio's body, pushed the clothes chest away, revealing a trapdoor, which he unlocked with a long, blood-flecked key he had taken from around Lafcadio's neck. Inside were rows of rifles, pistols, swords, cases of bullets, small barrels of powder. For the next while, as Lynch improvised snatches of melodies, Camacho loaded guns with chargers and cloth.

'Can you manage one?' Camacho asked Angel.

'No.'

Lynch took a blunderbuss but carried it over his shoulder so he could also bring the fiddle and bow in his other arm. Camacho stuffed two loaded pistols down each one of his trouser legs, then pulled the blankets off Angel with a flourish, and placed a blunderbuss in his hands.

'I have cocked it for you,' he said. 'You pull that second trigger – and there she blows.'

He armed himself also with two pistols in his hands while Angel lay there, holding the gun at arm's length.

'Witness,' Lynch said. 'You aim like this.'

One-handed, he trained the gun at Angel's chest, and then he winked at him, and swung it over his shoulder again.

'Only messing.'

The two sailors left out the door. Angel rose, his cheeks flushed from the warmth of the pillows. A pigeon had landed on Lafcadio's head, and Angel saw that the first mate's eyes were now closed.

Stepping out through the pool of blood, he left faint red foot-prints in his wake.

———◆———

A silent crowd had formed. Something was coming to an end. There were no shadows, no light; the sun remained beneath the ocean, the silhouette of the day yet a thin line across the horizon. A purgatorial dullness discoloured all. Spray crashed over the bulwarks and sprinkled Angel's hands; there was a snap and a freshness to the breeze. Beside an open trapdoor, Hieronimo lay on his back, nursing a dislocated elbow, his face passive, his eyes watching nothing. Two sailors were leant over him. Sitting along the cockpit, also, were six Africans with their legs drawn up to their chests, four men and two women. Flores argued with one of them in Arabic. She was an older woman, her eyes expressive, a shock of white hair standing electrically against the blue of the morning. The woman beside her was young, her face cherubic. A bruise closed over her right eye, and her nose had been broken, making her breaths raspy flutterings, as though they were being torn out of her. There were welts riveted around the inside of her thighs, and her wrists and ankles were discoloured, encircled with deep impressions from the bands she had worn.

Camacho passed out pistols to men he trusted.

'Explain yourselves' he said.

'We cannot settle them,' Cricklow answered, taking a pistol in both hands. 'They took Jones, Erskine, and Didot.'

He nodded at one of the Africans, a man so wasted away his teeth protruded, as though he hadn't enough skin remaining to cover his face. There was a tiredness to his features akin to the vacancy of death.

'Hisself slipped through the manacles, his wrists had thinned so. Throttled Elmet all the way to his end. The others escaped. These have followed after us, and we have overcome them.'

The man referred to went to stand up, and Cricklow ran over to him and struck him on the forehead with the butt of his pistol. The man sat down again, calmly enough, but then his eyes rolled into the back of his head, and he started convulsing, the left side of his mouth leaping with froth. The older woman Flores had been talking to – his mother; Angel saw now a clear resemblance, in features and gestures both – turned and started shouting at Cricklow.

'La, the very heart of the mischief there, Mr Camacho,' he said. 'Trouble since the first. Were a right Babel down there until that putrid bitch got her way into their ears.'

She had fallen to her knees and was now nursing the man having a fit, pulling his tongue out of his mouth, using both hands to keep his jaws apart. The four others remained mute, sullen. From downturned faces, their gazes scanned the crew.

The trembling rim of the sun emerged palely from the sea, seeming very close. A black line like a serpent wriggled rapidly around its circumference. Angel could look directly into it without hurting his eyes, and then he saw a gentle smudge against the sun's face – a spot of darkness.

He spread a hand over his brow and tried to make it out.

'You are saying there are slaves yet free in the hold,' Camacho said.

'Ay,' Cricklow said.

'Which means they are freeing others. Idiots. Wosniaki, Taussig, Amado, Armance: lay forward and get more arms from the captain's quarters,' Camacho said. 'We must put this down, immediately.'

The boat tacked slowly and one of the booms swung with a clank, the screech of sheets tautening. Angel was still looking out at the gentle sun blasting upwards, trying to understand the black shimmering coming out of it, but it was swinging away from him now. He wondered, then, if the vision were only a mote in his eyes, and not come out of the sun at all. He felt a pull at his sleeve. He turned and saw Flores, and over Flores's shoulder was the continent – so close now, a vast mass of trees and rolling greens, all covered in heavens of swirling mists. It looked unreal to Angel, fake but wondrous, like some stitched quilt draped loosely over the sea.

'Angel, tell them to let me speak to the captain,' Flores was saying. 'I must make my appeal directly to him. He will heed me. Do this for me, Angel. Please. They will listen to you because you are like them. I must explain that it's not her fault. She would not do this; she isn't what they say. I have money, plenty of money. Double, triple, what they would ask for in Brazil. I'm telling you, they won't listen to me. Please, Angel. Please.'

'Look,' Angel said, pointing behind him. 'We are saved. It is land. At last, it is land. We have done it. We are there. We will be in Brazil soon.'

Terror widened Flores's eyes, swept his mouth into a grimace, and then an explosion rang out across the decks. Camacho was on his back, screaming and thrashing; his right hand full of glimmering bone, vined by exposed veins pumping spurts of blood into his own dazzled face. Two of his fingers had been blown off, and his index finger hung, hinge-like, from a flap of skin.

Leaning off the mainmast was Lafcadio, holding a blunderbuss that he could not manage to raise fully to his shoulder. His front was covered with a circle of blood, darker around the holes that tore his belly, and they leaked as he stumbled down towards them, leaving a trail of drops. With great effort, he raised his blunderbuss again, and gestured at Flores's mother.

'There's your problem,' he said, his jaws making frenzied motions. 'There's the captain of the slaves.'

'I appeal to you,' Flores shouted. 'My captain. You are my captain.' He ran over to Lafcadio, dropped to his knees. 'Don't hurt her, please,' he said. 'Leave her be.'

Flores's mother started shouting, gesturing at her son.

'I'll buy her,' Flores said. 'That's why I'm here. It's a mistake; she didn't mean it. I'll buy her now, or put her below and I'll buy her in Brazil. I'll buy her two times; three times; ten times, I'll buy her. Whatever price you'll take, captain. Anything . . . I'll do anything. I swear to God, I will be your slave if you let her go. I swear to God.'

His mother was now forcing out words between sobs, her eyes brimming with tears as Flores lowered his face to the deck, and then he pressed his forehead against the first mate's feet, the blood from the man's wounds dripping down onto the back of his head.

Lafcadio looked down at him once, swayed, and then looked up again.

'All overboard,' he said.

While she was still yelling at Flores, Cricklow and Fuchs grabbed her by the arms and pushed her over the bulwarks, and then they both grabbed the man who was having a fit and tossed him over, as well. Flores rose from his knees, and in three motions had hurled himself over the side. This was done so quickly no one, at first, reacted. She had been led quickly, and had gone over easily, not understanding or expecting what was about to happen, and the man having the fit had already lost his sense, but once Flores disappeared the other four Africans began kicking against their captors, loosing desperate screams.

Angel went over to the bulwarks and looked down as the young woman, and then another man, were hurled over. They splashed, and then their heads popped up again in the middle of the chrysalis of foam their falls had formed. Flores, also, was treading water below, inside the shade of the hull, his head darting from side to side as he called out for his mother, but he was silenced when another African was thrown down on top of him, who in turn had dragged down a sailor after him. They surfaced and tussled together in the water.

Angel put down his gun, went to a coil of rope by the bulwarks and threw it to Flores, but then realised he had neither unwound it nor attached it to anything, so it just sank out of sight. He bent over, intending to throw another rope, but then a swell tilted the vessel causing a severed middle finger to roll its way towards him.

'Mr Camacho,' he called, picking it up. 'Mr Camacho, is this yours?'

He followed a trace of blood and found the Valencian had hidden himself behind a huge cleat, curled up in a dark, hidden place, like a dying cat. Angel held the finger up to Camacho, offering it back to him, when another gunshot sounded.

When the smoke cleared, a corpse was drooped over the edge of the trapdoor, half his face missing, part of the fractured cheekbone shining forth like a gem – but then another man emerged from the trapdoor, and then another. Soon there were more than twenty Africans on deck, and more following. Three children overpowered Cricklow, beating him down with their fists, wresting his gun from him. He managed to escape this heap, hobbling a few yards, only to be taken down again by another man who jumped on top of him.

Fuchs ran up to Lafcadio, and yelled:

'What are our orders, sir?'

Lafcadio, in response, touched one of the holes in his belly and then brought his fingers before his face, watching the blood lighten in the fresh air.

'What a beautiful day,' he said, and then he toppled forward, as Fuchs himself was tackled from behind by a woman who had emerged from the hold in a screaming frenzy.

Dazed by all the noise and activity, Angel watched as a young woman picked up the gun which he could not remember having put down. Suddenly a shadow fell across his face, and then it was gone. The sky was dark with seagulls attracted by the scent of blood. One swooped down and pecked Camacho's finger out of his hand, and then flew towards the east where the sun was now turning the sky a soft and liquid bronze.

The enslaved, in seemingly inexhaustible supply, were still flowing out of the trapdoor, flooding the decks, overpowering the sailors with their sheer number. All around were brutal, brief squabbles; the dark lochia tang of fear, smoke, and screaming, a confusion of languages. So these were the ghosts of pain, Angel thought – all these hidden people. A woman was pointing a gun at him, and seeing her, he wondered at how he could have missed all the life beneath him, sprawling and indestructible, that had never stopped trying to communicate itself.

The woman fired on him, but the shot went over his head, piercing a sail, and a shaft of milky sunlight peaked up through the torn material and hit another sail. Two Africans, having finished hurling a bawling sailor overboard, turned their attention towards him. Another gunshot went off nearby, splintering wood by his feet, and without hesitation, he flung himself backwards, into the sea, and nevermore set foot on the *Atlas*.

———•———

Angel, with the shuddering inhalation of the newborn, emerged inside a shadow. The bulkhead, like some sleeping giant, towered hugely overhead, and instinctually he decided to get himself caught up in sunshine one more time before he died. All around him little tornados of water stirred where sailors and slaves struggled against drowning. One of the smaller anchors was tossed down, cutting a flat sheet of water out of the sea through which transparent rainbows briefly flashed; it landed near enough to a flailing sailor that the man was immediately whisked underwater, caught up in the downward rush of the unravelling chain. Angel flapped his arms in panic, creating a furore of water near his head, and then, soon exhausted, lay flat on his back and drifted.

Soon there was much less flurry in the water; most of the people tossed overboard had sunk beneath, either unable to swim or defeated by the force of their own exertions. From the top of a mast, a huge scream descended like a shooting star. On the unseen decks a gunshot ricocheted off iron and tore through wood, and from where Angel floated he felt as if he were witnessing a holy battle take place, up above in some heaven obscured.

Drifting further away, the scattered noises of fear and ravenous birds eventually became indistinct, soft almost, and Angel would have been at peace if he hadn't felt trapped inside the echo of his own skull by the constant waterlogging of his ears, and a faint, persistent calling. The sound seemed to rise vaguely above the thrashing of the swells, breaking around his head, getting closer. Tilting forwards, he made out Flores paddling towards him, barking out the same syllable again and again. Signs of strain hardened his face, making him look like his skull were attempting to break out through its sheath of skin.

He was almost on top of Angel before he saw him, wide-eyed, throwing his head backwards and forwards, scanning all around him.

'Am,' he said. 'Am. Am.'

He spluttered, coughed water, and went under momentarily, and then scrambled back to the surface.

'Come here,' Angel called.

Flores's eyes passed over him a few times, but they didn't recognise him. The boat was small in the distance. The sky now an unbroken blaze of azure, solid as a painted wall. He twisted around and paddled back towards the boat.

'You won't find her,' Angel shouted after him, but Flores, insane with grief, never turned around.

Flores's head got smaller as he moved away, then, halfway back to the vessel, puny and dark, he waved his arms a few times before he disappeared – and then all was quiet except for the inhuman rushing of the swells.

A seagull landed near Angel, framed between his pointed-up feet. Everything changed slightly. Sea and sky both became a darker shade, almost identical in colour to one another. His own skin became softer, thinner and more mottled; it seemed to have the same consistency as apple skin. He touched his arm with his fingers, quickly pulling away when he felt no resistance in his flesh, as if he were turning into liquid. Warmth leaked up his spine, and stopped him shivering, and then a gentle swell swept over his head, enveloping him. Inside him, everything trembled, and he felt a brief wonder of pride that he had lasted longer than any of the others who had gone overboard. He was coming apart. In final inspiration, he looked up, directly into the morning sun, so that the burning imprint it left on his retina would be bright enough to guide him into his death.

He sank down.

———◆———

Ears thumping with pressure, he landed on his back, fallen gently to a sitting position onto a cushion of streaming sand that passed him by, the granules moving in antlike paths around his body. The surface was close. It sloshed above him with the unity of a perfect, unbroken membrane. Stretching out his hand, he heaved through heavy water, and sank down again without breaking the surface. A trick of the light had fooled him, and the resulting disappointment he felt revealed to him that he wanted to live.

The possibility soon occurred to him that he was on a single jutting thing, some rock, that had erupted freakishly from the sea floor, and that all around him was only cavernous depths. He envisioned waiting on a little submerged island of sand until thirst made him leap to his death again – from one underwater to a deeper one. Jumping up and down a few times to get some air, he decided to at least try to move towards the mountains, feeling that at each step, nothing might be beneath him. He waded

56

beneath the ocean, every second pace leaping up clumsily to take a breath and reorient himself in the direction of land. The noises underwater were huge, the sand under his feet always shifting. He kept his eyes closed most of the time as they had grown raw with salt, and then he saw a huge shadow swish by, so close he could have reached out and touched it. It was as thin as his wrist, but enormously long, longer even than a ship – and then it had propelled itself back into darkness.

Fear of the creature made Angel lose his concentration; the sand beneath his feet gave way. He had stepped into nothing and was sinking down. His arms flailed and he grabbed a handful of sand that leaked out of his grasp, and then he scuttled sideways, enraged bubbles bursting from him, and kicked until he breached the surface. Breathing shuddering, he extended downwards a toe, and found he was now standing with his neck above water.

He was, he realised, on a pier of sand, not wider than two men; he wondered if it could stretch all the way to the mountains.

'Am.'

He looked behind him and saw the boat a carbuncle on the horizon. Flores was swimming by, still grunting his monosyllable, though now it had lost all consistency and shape, barely a moan.

'I thought you dead.'

'Amam.'

'Amam, yes.'

Flores looked up, saw Angel, and then turned away again, his fatigued arms flapping weakly against the water.

'No, you'll die,' Angel said.

He managed to grab one of his legs, and Flores began thrashing against him, but Angel had already wrapped his arms around his neck and was dragging him under. Flores, not knowing he could put his feet down, wore himself out by trying to swim away, while Angel just stood, and waited. Eventually, Flores weakened and collapsed into Angel's embrace.

'Am,' he gasped. 'Amam.'

'Stop,' Angel said. 'She's gone.'

Flores's face was momentarily transfixed in a rictal mask of hatred, and then it relaxed, suddenly, becoming deathly still, his body limp.

Angel waded towards the land, dragging the catatonic Flores gently after him.

The water was at his navel now. The low mountains were becoming more distinct: white ridges and sheer jagged faces against which swooping birds appeared only as the momentary cut of a falling shadow; a still haze enshrouded the peaks. The land beneath the mountains quickly abbreviated into the sea, and around Angel's waist, the waves were growing brisk as the current changed, churning black so he couldn't make out his path clearly anymore.

The land, which had seemed so close, would come no closer. He felt deceived and wanted fresh water; wanted the sun to go down; desperately, he wanted an orange – this want affixing him as uncontrollably as a sexual urge alighting suddenly in a dream. He would have given anything for the flesh of the bursting fruit overflowing his mouth; would have eaten the skin, the pips, sucked the juices dry, licked the claggy stains from the lines on his palms.

In early evening, he fell to his knees, leaning heavily off the bobbing, supine Flores, blinked a few times, and then collapsed in a stupor, his head upon his companion's chest, where he heard, against the murmur of the water, the other's shallow breathing. A swell, larger than the others, momentarily put them both under, flushing into Angel's nose and reviving him, and when he looked up again he understood, finally, how close he was.

He could see it now, all coming together, like the final touches on a painting – details, previously blurred, suddenly rendered clear. The forest, in the direction of the sea, ended in sheer cliffs, their base an orchestral cacophony of explosive waves. Between two broad cliffs, a strip of sand gleamed like filed-down teeth, its starkness fading back into the teeming growth of the forest, where huge, hairy trees in one joined body curved gently up humped mountains, the fringe of foliage thinning out towards the summit. The higher leaves in the forest had been tinted gold in a faint, almost dreamish light that made them seem unreal. Conical, white flowers like inverted hives popped out amidst branches, sprightly and unexpected; huge leaves, broad-faced and dark, slumped heavily under their own weight. Poignarded by the mountains, the undersides of the night-gathering clouds were faintly empurpled, and below this a black vein of a river weaved down a mountain face, where it was lost in the knotty tapestry of trees.

Soon, the sunset was a streaky mess, blurring the vista once more. There was an effervescent softness to everything, the universal relaxation of unhuman silence hinting at something beyond itself. The wind, as though tracing the earth with an invisible finger, pushed a path through the top of the forest, swaying a narrow line of trees gently in a long, arching serpentine motion that went all the way down from the mountain to the sea until, where he knelt, Angel felt it run through his hair. A set of tall waves broke their force against him, setting him stumbling. He made out the faint echo of screeching monkeys travelling across the water, carried on the wind. A shimmering flooded his body, a holy exhilaration. He had leapt through half a sea. It was amazing to have survived, and it was not so far now. Sparkling fish had gathered in circles around Flores's body and were nibbling at his chest, eating away the sun-rawed flesh. When Angel rose, their circles disintegrated like bursting halos.

As the evening faded into night, the aromatic, woody odours of the forest's flowers released themselves. Contrary winds rippled the water. The buttery face of the moon appeared from behind one of the sulking mountains. From the moment it appeared, Angel's wading broke apart a shimmering reflection of the moon with every step, scattering beneath the darting fish that still shadowed him. The water was knee-deep now. They would not make the beach, Angel saw, his elation dimming slightly. He had envisioned lying on sand, but his path had taken him towards the pockmarked base below the forest. Dragging Flores's inert mass after him, he trawled his way across a dripping, lunar landscape that would disappear with the tide.

The forest appeared above him quite suddenly. Intertwined limbs barred entry into a smothering thickness from which frogs rumbled and cicadas whirred, loud as any capital's thoroughfare. Its interior darkness was vaguely marred by hovering constellations of luminescent insects. Angel leant against a tree and his hand came into contact with something sticky. It was sap, bitter and sickening, but he licked it until his tongue cramped. Then he fell to his knees and ate a handful of soil. When he was finished, he sat down, his back against the trunk, and gazed down at the moon's reflection, a white pyramid-shaped blanket draped over the broken mirror of the sea, stretching out over the edge of the world. The flashing stars were so plentiful it was as though the heavens were just about to begin dripping down on his head. And then a low star trembled and fell, streaking fast into the watery horizon. Angel's body, given the chance, stiffened up immediately, forbidding any more movement. He keeled to the side, his face against the earth, and lay there, frozen in wondrous fear, until he passed out.

—•—

'They're coming,' Flores said. 'We have to go.'

Angel opened his eyes, and everything was swirling and close. The light was too bright, the air too thick in his nostrils. Birds were screeching overhead; the treetops were raucous. A whirlwind of flies blustered near his ears, and his breath was hot in his mouth. His neck and cheeks itched with sunburn and he felt as though he were wearing someone else's face and hands over his own. Mosquitos had decimated his flesh, raising scores of poisonous little islands across his arms. His hands trembled so much they had no outline.

'What's happening to my body?'

'You've taken a fever.'

Over Flores's shoulder stood his mother. She looked silently at her son. There was a young girl there, too, carrying an earthenware jug full of water. She brought it to Angel's lips, and he drank a few gulps, and then started spluttering. When she took the jug away from his mouth, he saw inside the water were three twisting worms, swishing their blind heads out at him.

'This water isn't safe,' Angel said. 'There are creatures inside it.'

'No, there aren't,' Flores said. 'We have to leave here. Your temperature is far too high, and they are about to debark.'

'If it's your mother, is the girl also not real? I saw her in a tree once when I was waiting to be saved.'

'Her name is Esa,' Flores said. 'We are near a town, and she will bring us there. Can you walk?'

'I didn't know, Flores. I didn't.'

Underneath Angel's hands a tuft of thick reeds grew out of white soil. He pawed at the earth, then started shovelling it into his mouth with both hands, swallowing so fast he began to choke.

'Stop, stop.' Flores slapped his hands away from his mouth, grabbed him by the wrists. 'You must stop.'

Amam was still staring at her son, her breath visible in the slight rise and fall of her shoulders.

'You must do what I say now no matter what you see,' Flores said.

'I don't give a tinker's eye if Molly is the captain's wife, nor what her pigeons say,' Angel said. 'I am what Brazil is, and the messages

I received. No. O, no. Please, my secret is everywhere. O, no, look. Look. It's all coming apart . . .'

There was a pillar nearby, shaped like a jutting fang, emerging from the sea. It was starkly white, only temporarily separated from the mainland by the high tide, and then, all at once, it heaved and bristled. The rock had become monstrously alive, darkening and scattering itself in flying shadows. Angel thrashed uselessly against Flores's grip and began praying deliriously.

The surviving crew of the *Atlas* had been expelled from their vessel by the mutiny of the slaves and were coming ashore in six rowboats. The flock of seagulls that had nested upon the pillar had been stirred to flight as these sailors passed beneath them, but Angel, mad with fear, didn't know this. He thought all creation was coming undone.

Dear pápa,

¡how are you? I am fin. Thank you for asking. I love you two. The Sister Carmen make us to writing the many leters in this times, all is goode salve the inglish, but is all we must to make, I think ¡is too much! I am talk about my thinks. I not like the eschool, the leters is tired. I like Berenice, is the best friend. Have the jung brother, who nambe Roberto, I acquant him one time. Fatima sleep in the bed with me, but opposed side. «¿is coming the boy you is love?» she is ask I for have a joke «¿is sending you the mensages?» «¡I no know!» am repond. ¡am very annoy! Fatima and my self not like very much, but hairs is very pleasing and longs and blacks &c. valley, is suficient thinks in this hour. One think more, pápa, this nadividi who come, please buy to me the bird is green can to sing so can to sing the rosari with me and am not then I so tired and boring in the nigts who is solitaries. Am miss you.

May the GREAT LORD preserve You in Safety, Evermore, Srta. B.T, &c.

Land

FLORES AWOKE GASPING in the night, turned and saw, on the threshold of the granary, illumined by moonlight, a white bull terrier holding in its jaws a dead pigeon. The following day, he questioned Esa about it, but no matter how he tried, he could not make himself understood to her. He was already forgetting details of the creature's appearance, and when next he thought of it, he decided it had been only a dream.

Almost a month, he had been trying to learn the language. Each morning, for a few hours, he sat in a circle with several children and they took turns drawing shapes in the earth with a stick, pointing at them and naming them, the necessity of a single drawing stick having become apparent after the children had the first day drowned him in a competitive confusion of symbols and yelling. This learning was his only interaction with the townspeople; the adults kept their distance, often entirely ignoring him, except for the mothers of the children who sat with him; these brazenly stared at him, with either suspicion or contempt, Flores couldn't tell which. Still, the children would come to him each morning, and stay for an hour or two until they were bundled inside. They would emerge later, playing together, and he would watch idly from a distance, having no other activity with which to occupy himself. In the evenings, the children ran around while the townspeople chewed tobacco from a communal pot and drank a bitter alcohol out of small, wooden cups. The adults stood outside in several large crowds that were broken up by age and sex, laughing and talking. The men and women, while of a certain age, were usually separate, but the oldest and the youngest mingled freely.

The centrepiece of the town was a huge wooden building, its only distinguishing feature being, apart from its size, its strange roof: a type of dome, made of a much paler wood than the rest of the structure, whose topmost arc was flattened by an unexpected decapitation. This left the feature looking incomplete, although at later hours of the day the light would often hit it at such a slant that it sent a type of silhouette riding across the absence, an invisible curved line that completed an implied arc, suggesting a black pupil emerging from a white eye. It was a trick of perception, immediately striking. The building itself was communal, multi-storeyed, and the majority of the townspeople lived there. Around it, like seeds dispersed from a flower, sat twenty or so smaller, more irregularly fashioned houses, laid out in an arch which created inside its embrace a kind of plaza where a huge tree grew, and where the townspeople spent most of their days conversing and preparing food. As far as Flores could make out, these smaller buildings seemed to be without fixed occupants, purely functional in nature, used for giving birth; dying; lovemaking; healing; cooking; rituals and chanting – anything that demanded privacy, separation or enclosure.

Flores and Angel never got to go inside any of these structures; they slept a little way outside of the small town, in a stone granary with a raised floor covered with sacks of maize and pressed flowers. At this slight distance from the main body of the town, the wild animals were much less timid. Small creatures shuffled past them at night; the ceiling held a score of silent, unfurred bats, whose angular limbs and shrivelled skin looked like burnt corpses, and a slack nest of white muck and rotten flowers rounded out an upper corner, below which lay a gummy pyramid of hardened guano – the nest itself empty, its builders emigrated to another continent.

'Why do we have to stay?' Angel had said, a few days after he had emerged from his fever. 'They don't want us here.'

'They took us in; have fed us, do us no harm.'

'It's not how I imagined it would be,' Angel said. 'They don't smile at us; they don't greet us – nothing.'

'This is a type of quarantine, I think. We carry diseases. They only let the children speak with us, because they don't get sick in the same way.'

'If it's a quarantine then why is the girl being kept with us? Is she not one of them?' Angel asked, referring to Esa, who was nearly always with them during the days and the nights.

'I don't know,' Flores said. 'She's a little older than the other children. Maybe she spent too much time with us the first day and is considered infectious.'

Angel shook his head. 'Quarantine doesn't explain the animus I feel directed towards her. She is also apart.'

It was true that the townspeople rarely acknowledged her, never raising their eyes to greet her, as seemed to be the custom with the rest of them. She appeared to be an orphan of sorts; never playing or working with her peers; spending all her time with Flores and Angel, though some evenings she spent with a group of older women, sitting quietly as they cooked.

'What do you think, then, is happening?'

'I feel we – you, I and the girl – are under some moral opprobrium, some type of banishment before we are used for a ceremony.'

Flores felt a flush of anger course briefly through him. 'Ridiculous,' he said. 'That's ridiculous.'

'It's not ridiculous.'

Angel's voice cracked over the words. Flores looked at him, and then looked away quickly, his eyes watering at the mere sight of him. He was almost vibrating with nerves and had become terribly thin. Flores tried to put down his anger against the youth, but he could not, and so he left.

He went to Esa and, carefully as he could manage, asked her about their status in the town, but in the flurry of her response he understood almost nothing. More slowly, he asked her to speak again, and then spent the best part of an hour trying to untangle some meaning from what she said.

'She knows we are from the sea, but many from the town think we come from beyond the mountains,' Flores reported back to Angel later that evening while they were eating together. 'There is a town there called Santa María, and they don't like the town so much. Esa said she was supposed to protect us so she could grow up, but I have no idea what that means. Maybe, I misunderstood.'

'What if her name isn't Esa?'

Flores didn't know how to react to this. He thought for a while, and then started eating again.

'Answer me.'

'Her name is Esa.'

'What if Esa means "no more", or even just "no"?' Angel said. 'What if they are tired of all your questions and they are telling you to leave them alone?' Angel put his bowl down and gesticulated. 'What if there is no referent; nothing to say this is this, that is that? What if, way back, you made a mistake at the beginning of your learning and it has brought you to some place where now you and they communicate, thinking you are saying the same thing, but talking at cross-purposes, never knowing it?'

'The fundamentals of language are common. Question and answer. Action and reaction. Being and doing. Present and past.'

'Well, then,' Angel said, 'what if they are lying?'

'Why would they lie?'

'Why would anyone?'

Angel's eyes were bloodshot, and he had started shivering again. 'You are still sick,' Flores said. 'They put bark in the food to repel the insects and your stomach hasn't adjusted to this yet. Sometimes new climates hurt us. I remember when I first arrived in Montpellier: it was winter and everything was dead; all the trees were skeletons; everything was so without light that it seemed no one was ever truly awake. I couldn't believe people could survive in such a place. All the faces I saw seemed hateful and suspicious, but it was my own sin I was seeing in unfamiliar faces. It is a reflection, a repetition of yourself. Do you understand? It goes, the feeling, and you change. You should cool yourself down in the river more often; rest during the days, and sleep more.'

Angel shook his head. 'It is you, Flores,' he said. 'I cannot sleep because of you. I have gone out of my mind with sleeplessness.'

Instantly, Angel frowned, seeming to regret what he had said. He turned his head a few times, then waved his hand in a motion somewhere between a farewell and a dismissal and left towards the granary.

Since they had arrived in the town, Flores had woken Angel up each night with his sobbing, and the younger man could not return to sleep easily. And so the Irishman grew more impatient and resentful; suffered from restlessness and dark moods. His responses to Flores were clipped, sparse, often erratic, and his few dealings with the townspeople were carried out in an arrogant fashion. Most of his time was spent sitting in the shade of the granary, his guts clenched in pain, scowling like a petulant child amidst a haze of insects, hating everything and losing weight.

Flores felt responsible for him, but there was nothing he could do to stop his nocturnal grieving – the tears were autonomic responses to his dreams, dreams he couldn't even recall, their only trace the heavy eyelids, the unease inside his chest like he had been filled with shards of glass and shaken. He felt he should express to Angel how completely grief had defeated him. There was nothing of his old self left; no intelligence, no personality, no past. Nothing made sense anymore. What remained was the congruent nature of reality: its constant surfaces, its tactile and encompassing nature, and all this had stunned him into an unfeeling submission.

One night, as a peace offering but also by way of explanation, Flores had recited a poem.

> *The moon, who is not a fish,*
> *Is moved when she is spoken to*
> *By the land, who has seen her naked.*
>
> *And the sea is always whispering*
> *That she will not be loved until*
> *All her flowers are given back to her.*
>
> *We are born in between,*
> *And are sad in the evenings,*
> *Hearing them hiding, as they do,*
> *Underneath our balconies*
> *And beyond our senses.*
>
> *O stop! What is this?*
> *Sometimes*
> *A river approaches.*
> *Sometimes, without fear,*
> *Dawn's flowers are open.*

They were in the granary. Angel and Esa lay on sacks of maize. Esa faced into the wall, her spine curved outward, the ridges visible; a moonbeam fell through a rupture in the roof, bathing her feet in light and making the tears on Flores's cheeks glisten.

Angel turned towards him, his emaciated face ghastly in the night, his hair draped over his eyes like frayed tassels.

'Did you write that?'

'My mother did,' Flores said. 'It is much more beautiful in Arabic. It sounds too plain and arbitrary in English, I think. Her style is pliable, but not so plain. I wish I could do the words justice.'

'What was she doing on the ship?'

Flores looked out the small hole in the roof. A few stars perforated the darkness. Errant monkey shrieks were carried in shadowy echoes across a high breeze. Swathes of insects clicked in a rising crescendo and then fell silent all at once. Sometimes, in the hour before dawn, he could hear the sea coming in.

'Amam was an amanuensis in one of the courts of what Europeans call the Trarza emirates. There was a crisis of succession, and the successor was brutal, and my mother . . . She was outspoken, and she advised against . . . I don't know. I don't know, for sure. The successor, he punished everyone who had had terms with his predecessor. The clerks requested death. Instead, when a caravan came up from the interior, they were sold into bondage, and transported to the coast. Maybe one or two of those you would have seen aboard would have been in the courts with my mother – maybe. I wouldn't recognise them, anyway; I had been gone so long. The others, I don't even know where they're from. My brothers-in-law had the caravan followed and sent out watchers to all the ports to see what ships she might be on. You see, before you are transported, you are split up, but when you arrive at the coast, after a long journey, all on foot . . . There are these buildings, like pits with no roofs where you are kept for weeks. There are no partitions, and they are so vast and crowded, and the . . . you can't breathe. You lose your family, your tribe, your companions . . . in the push. They are always pushing, and you can go under. You are lucky if you survive . . .

71

Older women are considered useless, and they . . . I only knew from . . . I – Sorry, I . . .'

Already shuddering with sobs, he began choking. Everything inside him was coming apart, collapsing in on itself, and the stars above him were lurid in their meaninglessness.

Angel stared at him while he cried, his mouth hanging open, his gaunt face blank.

'I must say,' he said, 'the Americas have been a huge disappointment.'

———◆———

Angel lay on his back in the granary, his eyes clenched against the light, willing himself to sleep. A bead of sweat trickled across his navel, but then it stopped trickling. It pressed slightly too heavily against his flesh. He opened one eye: a tick, full, round and black, had bloomed from inside his navel, and now lay sated atop his belly like a tiny dolmen on a white plain.

He brushed the creature away, and started to paw and pinch at himself, searching his flesh for other holes, groaning in disgust; and then he saw the tick still laying there, near his feet. He stamped on it with his heel and ran out of the granary.

He appeared over Flores while the latter was sitting, learning with the children.

'What is this nonsense?' Angel said, pointing down at a rough picture one of the children had drawn – it portrayed the figure of a man rolling a circle downwards.

'Verbs of motion.'

'Why don't you teach them English so I can talk to them? I need a guide.'

Flores looked up at his companion. Oily sweat glistered unhealthily across his pale skin; a fragment of milky crust flaked his lower lip, and a greasy rattle in the back of his mouth under-scored his every other word.

'We are guests here.'

'If there is another town upriver, let us go.'

'I have no wish to go anywhere,' Flores answered.

'I'll go alone, then.'

'Where?'

'Home. I am well enough now to travel, and I want to go home. It was a terrible mistake to come here. We'll find the civilised town beyond the mountains, Santa María, and from there I'll write to my aunt's solicitor. He should send me a promissory note, and we'll be able to return home. Tell these children to fetch me a guide – and come with me, Flores. An air of devious malcontent lingers over these savages. Where do they go every day? Last night, I saw a lean man slink out of the forest with a sword whose handle was a bird. He had the unsettled look of a conquistador's ghost. They must have done something terrible to him, and now he haunts them. He will be back. I know it. Let us leave now, immediately, before something happens that cannot be repaired.'

Flores shook his head and turned his attention back to the children.

'You have lost your nerve. You are talking nonsense.'

Angel, infuriated, dragged his heel across the drawing in the earth, destroying its form. 'I saved your life.'

'If I have not yet expressed gratitude,' Flores answered, 'it is because I have felt none.'

The children were silent, looking at the two men. One of the younger girls, misunderstanding the nature of their argument, took the drawing stick from Flores and presented it to Angel. He looked at it dumbly for a moment.

'Thank you,' he said, and the child answered at some length.

Angel looked so foolish and lost, holding the stick and nodding at the chattering child, that Flores felt his heart soften.

'Draw something,' he said. 'We are all trying to communicate.'

Angel hesitated momentarily, and then got down on his hunkers and began sketching in the muck.

'The townspeople here tend a type of pink flower,' Flores explained, as the other drew. 'You have seen it. As is the custom, Esa gave you one when she brought you to town. It is rare and only grows in the pale soils of this part of the forest. They harvest it for trade. Once a year, they deliver them to Santa María. This whole town is only placed here so as to be near to this flower. It is a precious ingredient in many types of medicines and perfumes, and, of course, it is beautiful on its own.'

Flores looked at what Angel had outlined in the earth. It was almost a scrawl, crude and uneven, trailing lines out of one circle that held inside it another circle.

'What is that? A jellyfish?'

The children started laughing at the drawing, pointing at it and stamping their feet. Then Abo, one of the more mischievous boys, in a perfect mimic of Angel's former anger, dragged his heel across the sketch, and wagged his finger. Angel, in response, dropped the stick, and left.

Flores watched him stalk back to the granary. After a while, the children used the opportunity of Flores's inattention and began crowding around one another, all drawing different things in the earth with their fingers, appealing to him to look at what they were making.

A woman who was shucking corn in the shade of one of the houses began singing. Two men wandered past her, carrying sacks across their backs. They stopped and listened for a moment. A rooster crossed the plaza in an interminable zigzag. Flores had lost his concentration; it would not come back again that day. Nearly a month he had been here, and what he had learned was incohesive, and even if he ever learned how to converse comfortably with the townspeople, what did he have to say to them? His memory was broken. He couldn't remember the words. He was becoming absentminded, vacant. He hadn't written in so long. His doctorate had been on the ship – all those years of work lost in a moment. An earlier copy of it existed, still – some juvenilia – back in Montpellier, but it didn't matter; he would never return to Europe. He didn't care about his doctorate, the town, its language. All these doubts, all these thoughts, all these fears – all this was nothing but subterfuge and pretence. Everything he did was to allow him to forget for a few moments . . . Flores was already walking away.

In the granary, he lay down on his side, his right ear pressed against an empty sack, and watched the day spin away. The cadaverous Angel lay on another sack of maize, his back against the wall.

'It was an eye,' Angel said.

'What?'

'It was an eye, to see with. I drew an eye. And I'm leaving tomorrow. Come with me.'

They were not together, Flores felt, they were merely proximate, both watching the same nothing. The forest was a huge lumbering thing that trembled over them, groaning and enclosed. Beyond it, the indistinct blue of the mountains. Some white chickens pecked their way towards Flores, their eyes vacant and stupid. The rooster crowed behind them, sovereign and sentry over his idiot harem. A woman near the granary was spreading a shawl across some shrubs so as to dry it; another was carrying a basin of water on her head into one of the smaller buildings. The way she moved reminded him of his mother, and he felt the need to be alone. He made some brief excuse and left towards the forest.

———•———

Angel sat up slowly and, with the slight compression of his core, a string of shit curled out of him. He was aghast.

'Flores?' he whispered.

75

Greasy warmth trickled down his thighs, mashing into the hairs on the back of his legs.

'Esa?'

There was no answer, thankfully; he was alone.

He crawled to the entrance of the granary. It was late afternoon. Along the plaza, a few men were constructing a type of awning beneath the tree. Beyond them, diminutive against the tall sun-scorched walls of the communal building, women ground flowers and paste together in large bowls to make paint; others beside them sewed together feather necklaces, and a woman named Kiri was demonstrating to Esa and three other girls how to perform a sweeping dance step. They were all in the midst of some preparation; no one was looking in his direction.

He stole bandy-legged away from the town, and trotted into the forest, the screeching of monkeys and trilling of birds spongy in his ears. Stunted trees, starved of light, grew jaggedly through an outcrop of bushes that crawled with a floating city of flies. A tree glimmered from a scab where its bark had been nibbled away; jaundiced fuzz hung down from limbs like long beards, brushing softly across his shoulders. A spangle of light showed a gossamer-thin filament running into a tree limb where it blossomed into a silver mesh of web. Doughy pods hung there, the dangling wombs writhing from within. He pushed his way past squeaking rushes; the tattered hands of leaves fluttered by; crowns of buds like closed lips jointed silently along the knobs of branches; mosses furred limbs tightly like velveteen sleeves, and the interplay of all this layered confusion of jagged angles and soft circular fronds was a shadow play of dark thunderbolts against the blazing sky – and then he saw the black gliding of the river and he tore down his leggings, pressed his forearm against a tree trunk for balance and unclenched his bowels.

His mouth dripped with the diluvial moisture of rotting undergrowth; he could taste the forest's damp. Insects pullulated

cacophonous in his eardrums, and his sweat was a cold embalm-
ment; he could feel his coccyx jutting out of him like a peg.

He shed his clothes, and waded into the river, making fists in
front of his face – the skin along his wrists seemed to him brittle,
and old. His ribs stood out like rows of prison bars; a green river
of veins ran under his armpits as though he were illuminated from
the inside.

The light was too bright, his body too repulsive; he was stunned
by his own corporeal degradations. He looked away from himself,
into a glint of rainbow light shuddering against a concentric
ripple. He felt an itchiness within his chest, and put his head
between his hands, shivering with nausea.

'Angel.'

He spun around so quickly the root of his tongue flashed
numb, the dull shock repeating in the back of his mouth.

'Here I am.'

He looked up; Marianne Lynch was sitting on a limb of a tree,
the same that Angel had earlier balanced against. The man was
mostly shaded by foliage, but his face was still vaguely luminescent, greenishly reflective of the gloom.

Angel scanned the banks, the trees.

'It's only me,' Lynch said. 'Cricklow was sent to fetch Flores; I
accompanied him part of the way, but said I'd take a gander down
by the river.'

'What does he want with Flores?'

Lynch was swinging his right leg back and forth; his left was
tucked beneath him.

'Captain Lafcadio wants to challenge him to a duel,' he said,
'but I'd say that sad-eyed Moor never handled a pistol in his life.
It'd be nibs and quills he'd be more used to. So that's the last of
our kid, Flores, the one you thought you saved.'

Angel took a step back, felt the muck rising up through his
toes; he took another step, and then the water was up to his chest.

'You go that way,' Lynch said, 'you'll get scooped out to sea – or you make it across and a panther is tucking into your guts by night-fall. Come with me; you'd be better back with your own kind.'

'You're not my kind. You're killers.'

Lynch held out his palms, his expressive face suddenly forlorn. 'These hands,' he said, 'these hands have never killed anybody.'

'You're a liar.'

'You've suffered a great loss, haven't you? You're a sail loosed in a storm, small against the sky. And now Flores is gone, too. Of course, back at camp, Jacques is waiting for you, and he'll take care of you. He misses you, Angel, it's true – but that's not enough, is it? You've an aloneness in you that is something worse than the aloneness of flesh and mind – you've lost heaven; you're looking into an abandoned universe.'

A line of insects skated between the banks, slightly above the water; their wings popping loudly like candles sputtering out as they moved towards Angel. He had been standing still for so long that the cold was knitting into him.

'What are you saying?'

'You've lost heaven, and what is heaven but elsewhere? For orphans like you and me, that elsewhere was always the Americas. We used to have other heavens, but they're gone now. Maybe this place should have remained a dream – though I cannot imagine the Americas discovered and not moving towards them. I cannot imagine the continent untaken; the seas unsailed, the plains unblighted by riders, the mighty storms unwitnessed by those of us who dared venture out. Once it is there, you must go. So, I went and I was standing right in it, but, at that same moment, I had lost it. I couldn't see the Americas anymore, and so I made them. I made them until I could see them and now I am them. You say I am a killer, Angel? No, never. I am an artist, and I am creating the Americas, and it is heaven. And if you let me, I will show you how.'

78

He dropped down from the limb, landing sleek as a cat beside the sodden heap of clothes. Angel stretched his right hand out in front of him as if to ward him off, but he could not maintain it. The arm dropped back down, submerged.

'I can't,' he said. 'I can't do this. I have nothing. It's too much. I can't keep . . . I can't.'

'I know,' Lynch said. 'These things go hard, but are soon ended.'

A ripple traversed the river slowly, a series of concentric circles blooming after it. Angel, his knees sinking, his spine coiled, and his eyes upturned, watched it culminate in a discreet hooded slip of white that splashed once, and then disappeared.

Lynch was in the water now, wading towards him.

'But let's begin how it has always begun,' he said, 'with a breath and a baptism.'

<hr />

Flores gazed at the women washing tubers in the shallows of the river, imagining himself floating along on his back, dragged out the mouth until he was in the sea.

The forest was plentiful behind him; it tapered off into darkness. In the distance, beyond the river, evening sprang up oblong shadows beneath the buildings. Edges blurred in the shade; the reeds on the banks cast thin shadows of a machine-like straightness, suddenly undone by a breeze that rattled their stalks and made them appear, in their totality, as the gooseflesh of a terrified child. Further upriver, one woman was washing her hair, her naked back turned to him.

Very briefly, the pain in his heart flared up again, acute, enormous. There she was humming to herself as she moved through the marketplace; cautioning his little sisters. He couldn't breathe; he couldn't – and then, as though broken by the weight of itself, the pain softened and he noticed himself gasping in air.

79

Pessimism, along with the shadows, had slunk in on the folding wings of this twilight, and it clung darkly to his fear. He had made so many mistakes; he had abandoned his family the moment he reached his majority so as to better study God; had spent nearly twelve years praying, debating and pondering his nature, and it had all been a waste; it had all been a lie.

The day's last light fell upon the water, glinting harshly. The woman was making her way out of the river. Unified by the water, her hair like a heavy rope slung down over her shoulder. Tiny silver fish swam in one harmonious body around her feet. Amam was still sinking somewhere; the sea was so deep – and then he heard the crackle of sticks coming apart underfoot and he looked behind into the forest and saw Quentin Cricklow's head behind a tree, some way off in the shade of that cacophonous forest – and then the sailor was gone, the pale, floating face marked with a cross swallowed up in the inner darkness.

It was almost an apparition; and, even through his grief, Flores felt a flinching nausea at the sight of the man, who then stepped out from behind a nearer tree.

'How goes it, Flores?' he said. 'Having a gander at that fine naked creature, I see. Marry, 'tis an average breed here, though perhaps I am too used to the painted whores of the Caribbean: Antillean mulattresses with jewel rings in their navels as can fold their tongues sideways. La, I misses them. Here it is all thick thighs, lacking breasts and squatness; the thickness of the cheekbone is not to my fancy at all, o, and they dress far too similar to the gentleman, I find . . . Jesus Christ, boy – what has happened to your face? O, I see. Just having a little cry to yourself.'

The Cockney had leant forward and Flores could see that underneath his shirt a pistol was slung across his chest by a thin piece of rope.

'What are you doing here?'

'Captain wants to speak with you.'

'Where was he during the crossing?'

'Being dead. Lafcadio's the captain now.'

Flores glanced up, blinking, eyes adjusting to the forest. The purlieu within was dull gloom, the only shine coming from the trails slugs left, slick and glimmering. A small monkey was sitting on a branch, partially hidden behind a mottled pattern of swaying leaves.

'I don't want to speak with him.'

'Nary a one of us does neither' Cricklow said. 'He is gone lunatic from pain, and will pass straight out, eyes wide as the gates of heaven. Then, night come, he does raise his head like so, marry, and pick up the sentence he left off as though there were no time in between. It is very queer and bothersome. Yet he is the captain, and you, you are summoned.'

'How long have you known I was here?'

'What matter?'

The monkey stared down at Flores with sad, amber eyes. It had silver fur, a perfectly circular face, and fine, black hands wrapped around a drooping limb which rocked gently with its weight. The fingers were delicate, thin, aristocratic almost; even the fingernails seemed to have been rounded off in perfection.

'Why haven't you moved on?' Flores said. 'Surely, you are never more than a day's march from a European city.'

'La, I wants to, and it wouldn't be no problem if we knew the *Atlas* had scuppered; then the corporation could draw down the insurance and we could find ourselves another berth. But, says captain, we must wait until we are sure she hasn't been tugged in by some busybody man-o'-war. If enough time goes by without word, we will know she has shipwrecked. Then we march into whatever town, and put in a claim, saying we were destroyed by a tempest. You see, it must be an act of God.'

'The rebellions of the enslaved are not considered acts of God.'

'Not in the city of London. Come along. The hour grows late.'

'I will not come.'

'You will.'

'Shoot me if you would, but I will not come.'

Cricklow snorted. 'I ain't the one is gonna shoot you. Look, Flores, we're out of every convenience, and the rum is running low. Captain has been mighty strict on the rationing, but he does pass out so much these days that we have become a mite free of late. We've no choice but to take a town – that little one as you're in – but captain wants to see you beforehand.'

'What for?'

'That's his affair.'

Cricklow turned around and walked deeper into the forest. The little silver monkey trailed along a high branch after him, as though shadowing him in a higher dimension. Flores followed into the forest for a few moments, not realising what he was doing.

'A colony of seals arrived from the sea this afternoon,' Cricklow called over his shoulder, 'and it is thusly that the crew are sweating out their tantrum, marling over our divisions. Marry, the sound of it does go very hard on the ears. By the by, is there much rum in that little savage town of your'n?'

Flores, suddenly tired, went to lean against a tree. He withdrew his hand: pink beetles were emerging from invisible pores in the moss that blanketed the bark; jagged plates of fungus grew along the trunk like diseased balconies, and a liquid, thick as treacle, trailed along the lower branches, dripping down with an impossible slowness.

When Cricklow heard he wasn't being followed, he turned back, and then, a moment later, the monkey did, too, holding its humanly hands together as though in prayer.

'You have no rights over this place,' Flores said. 'You should leave the people here alone. They are nothing to you.'

'I'n't that the nub, and i'n't that why you'll presently come thither. If we are sans convenience wouldn't we not better go to some convenient place as has convenience? And ain't you precisely the one to take it up with captain. Come along, now, my boy; tarry not.'

He traipsed off into green-hued darkness, and Flores and the little monkey followed after.

———•———

From over the sandbank that bordered the mouth of the river came some scattered barking nestled amidst the broader threshing of the sea that spilled against the shore. Cricklow – and the monkey after him – waded across the shallows, climbed up the brief summit, Flores lagging behind.

Evening was coming down all around, gentle and smothering. Two stars hung low, almost touching the sea, and Flores wondered briefly why he never saw new stars appear; why they were always already there. He caught up with Cricklow and watched the scene below, sinking slightly as the sandbank came apart under his weight.

The tide was high. The whole beach was littered with the scattered blobs of dead seals, like inky fingerprints smudged against the earth. Three bonfires blazed in a triangle, and in their midst, glowing orange, the surviving crew of the *Atlas* was building a tower of slaughtered seals. The tower stretched high as four men; a few sailors at the base packed tight the corpses so it wouldn't topple over. By the light of the bonfires, obsidian eyes glimmered brilliantly out of the heap of flesh. A smattering of seagulls rested thereon like feathery rosettes pinned against the mass. Occasionally, the tower would sway, as though on the verge of coming to life, and these birds would alight, circle and land once more.

Two stray pups, seeing Flores appear over the rise, shuffled towards him, whiskers and noses pointed to the sky. They were sleek creatures with naked, doglike faces, and eyes so black there was little there that might distinguish them from the dead.

Hieronimo stumbled after them, a bottle in one hand and a rock in the other. He managed to get on top of one and stove in its head, but while chasing the second, he collapsed.

The escaped baby seal trundled by Flores, yelping in a terrified squeak.

'You should have taken thyself to the sea, my lad,' Cricklow said.

With a cry, the chef rose up from the sand, spitting and blinking. He started crawling around, the rock and bottle gripped with one arm to his chest, and then he stopped, spying the silhouettes atop the sandbank.

'Is you, Flores?' he called. 'Is you, in my nights? There are you?' He petered out, squinted up at them again, and then let his head fall down to his chest. 'So much die . . . so much. I am forget . . . Is you, Flores, is?'

The monkey hid behind Cricklow's legs. Hieronimo began to groan, dipping his head once more, a despondent shade against the sand, like a statue brought in on the breakers, now half-buried, beached and slanted and forgotten.

'Am . . . am . . . have the sick . . . Where is? . . . Am sole . . . so lone in the sea . . . Yo falta mucho . . . Go Nighttown . . . Where is? Yes, I see. Please. Ayúdame, Flores. Forgive, Flores. You are so special; is the light from make a shine. You are a shine. I am so sad. I don't want hurt . . . Please, forgive. Please. Forgive, or no? Please. Forgive.'

Flores felt himself on the precipice of some obscene and unwanted revelation but was spared by the sound of Hieronimo snoring – and Cricklow burst into laughter.

'Follow me,' he said.

Positioned where the forest gave way to the sand stood two huts made out of hairy driftwood, huge leaves and boards salvaged from the hacked-up skiffs they had come ashore on. Under the canopy of one of these, Lafcadio and Camacho were in heated consultation, poring over a document in a pool of candlelight. Camacho kept his mutilated hand hidden in the pocket of his jacket and gesticulated with the other; Lafcadio, with his deathly face, leant off two cumbersome crutches fashioned out of saplings. He wore only breeches discoloured by seawater and time, and a patchwork leather coat draped over his shoulders. Reams of cloth were bandaged around his bare stomach like a cummerbund, the fabric darkened from where his wounds still leaked. Jacques, the cabin boy, was there too, ensconced on some kind of ramshackle chair made of netting, bark, ropes, and a cutting of sail, and every now and again his face contorted horrifically into a sneeze. In the second hut, further down the beach, men slept on the sand, hunched like slugs coming out of the earth after a flood.

As Flores approached these huts, the rustling of the forest grew indistinguishable from the breathing of the sea, the clicking and whirring of its insectivorous hunger doused in an oceanic splendour.

'Flores,' Lafcadio said, as he entered the flickering sphere of candlelight.

On the table, by the platter of candles, was a mound of scrunched-up slips of paper, fluttering gently; there were also some knives; a huge key turned green with age; a chicken bone; a buckle; a needle; a hollow tortoise shell; a soiled pair of women's stockings; three empty bottles; a little pile of cracked seashells; and a cured seal skin on which was written a long tract, the writing so faint Flores couldn't make it out.

'Jacques,' Lafcadio said. 'Fetch the gift, and also the two pistols off Fuchs. I want my hat, too. – Mr Camacho, you can go now.'

The cabin boy stood up and hastily left, leaping over an injured seal pup that was wriggling by, and had dipped accidentally into the candles' penumbra. Camacho furrowed his brow, about to say something, and then left, too, though on the way out he picked up the wandering pup by the flipper and threw it over his shoulder.

'This crew,' Lafcadio said. He staggered over to the vacated chair and collapsed into it. 'Even with Camacho I have had to make a marriage of convenience, but they are fraying again, desperate to go north. It goes so heavily.'

Jacques returned with a long strip of cloth draped over his shoulder, a rosewood box, and two bottles in his hands – one of red wine, and the other of a clear alcohol. He placed the rosewood box and clear alcohol on the table, uncorked the bottle of red wine and handed it to Flores, all the while sneezing in quick little bursts like a spitting fire.

'Where is my hat?'

Jacques nodded and went out again; then Lafcadio gestured at the bottle in Flores's hand.

'That's for you. It's a gift.'

'I don't drink alcohol,' Flores said. 'I came here to discuss the town you have had your man, Cricklow, surveilling.'

'Maybe we'll get to your town. Perhaps – but first I want to ask you whether or not there is a natural order on a ship?'

Flores glanced out at the beach. The tower of seals was so high it didn't even begin to taper off in the vista afforded him from the hut. Some of the sailors were carousing in the surf, their silhouettes visible against the waves' evanescent whiteness.

'I don't wish to discuss anything but the town.'

'I do. Is there a natural order on a ship?'

'Whose ship?'

'Any ship; it doesn't matter which.'

'It does.'

'They are all the same – wood nailed together with a piece of cloth that moves them around the froth of the globe. And I am the captain of the crew which lives upon this wood, and I must ensure their safety, come what may – against ocean, gale, leviathan, the many warring nations, but mostly, against themselves. So much that is inevitable is wrong, yet I remain the captain. I am right by my lights. Do you understand that I must be what I am?'

'A murderer.'

'I am the captain, and she was the mutineer – a good one. She drew us to an historic truce. We lost the ship but kept our lives and just enough materials to get by on for a little while. It was a good coup she did, and it will always be my disgrace, though I was beset by circumstance, and could only acquit myself as best—'

He seemed to drift out of consciousness for a moment, his eyes closed, wincing in pain.

'Well?' he asked, suddenly.

'What?'

'Will you forgive me?'

Flores was struck dumb again. The captain pulled a crutch across his lap, and they held each other's gaze for a few moments. Eventually, Lafcadio waved his hands.

'Honestly, your big sad face and your big dog eyes can go fuck themselves,' he said. 'If your mother had kept her peace, many more would be alive – her also. And I'd have my ship. Look at you. You would think your mother was a slave for some other reason than because there was work to be done and a whole world to do it in. You'd think it some personal affront to you. Haven't you your own slaves over yonder? Who sold them to us, Flores? Who?'

With these last words, the captain groaned hugely, pushing both his hands across his bandaged belly.

'You are tortured by what you have done,' Flores said.

'Tortured by four pieces of broken metal in my gut, not you,' Lafcadio said. 'Damn you. I know what I am, and your mother knew what she was – but what in the hell is it that you are, Flores?'

Jacques returned, carrying a tricorne.

87

'Open the box,' Lafcadio said.

He leant forward and Jacques started to unwind the soiled bandages, moving round him like he was a maypole, until his cavernous front was finally exposed.

'Open the box, Flores, I said.'

But Flores could not move anymore. As the final layer of cloth came away from Lafcadio, a raw stench sent a tidal wave of goose-flesh rising across Flores's back, his arms, neck, and scalp.

The captain's gut was pocked by four pustulent holes gathered closely together. The most central one, a little above his navel, was tumescent and blue, almost the size of a baby's fist; surrounding it were irregular canyons of tallowy fat, purple muscle and a weblike mesh of tissue. When he inhaled, the four holes expanded like softly opening mouths, veins widening and red flaps detaching; and then, in exhalation, the wounds wilted, becoming puny again, coils of pus eking out of them. Deep down, occasionally, like buried treasure, the flashing glint of lodged bullet.

'Open the box, I tell you!'

Flores unlatched the rosewood box. There he saw, lying cross-ways and inlaid in red cushioned felt, two bright pistols, both embossed with ivy designs twined around mother-of-pearl handles.

'Jacques, a pistol and the rum.'

The gun was passed to Lafcadio and the bottle of clear alcohol from which he drank angrily, glaring at Flores out of the corner of his eye all the while, and then Lafcadio began to pour splashes of rum onto his naked belly, a sheen of sickly sweat flourishing across his features, biting the hand that held the gun to stifle his own groans.

Flores – staring now at the gun in Lafcadio's hand and feeling at last at the end of all things – took a swig from the bottle of wine.

It was bitter and set him coughing. Even once it was swallowed away, the substance clung darkly to the back of his throat and the underside of his tongue. He drank again, and then paused to take a breath, shivering and gasping at the taste now grown so wondrous.

The captain, the pistol across his lap, watched him drinking. Strip by strip, the horror of his corrupted flesh was concealed by the fresh wrap, which already was stained in a descending fringe of bright scarlet.

'Jacques, my crutch.'

It was becoming difficult to swallow, but Flores continued, his eyes clenched shut against his own gagging – and then the bottle was finished.

He opened his eyes and was dazzled by his surroundings. It was all new. There was beauty in the glowing dead eyes of the seals outside; in the blurring above the candles, whole visions flickered by; even the pistol Lafcadio gripped glistened with magical invention.

'We will do twelve paces in this room as the light is best here,' Lafcadio said. 'The sand is a natural disadvantage to me with my crutch, but so it goes. We will need no seconds.'

'What are you talking about?'

'For our duel – we will remain here.'

Flores burst into laughter.

'Why are you laughing?'

'You are so stupid,' Flores said. 'You're such an idiot.'

'Pick up that pistol, boy.'

'No, I won't. It's too silly. You're so silly.'

Lafcadio retracted into his seat like a snail shocked by the glancing touch of a finger.

'I had your mother killed. You do not understand. What I am offering you is something rare, something precious.'

'But I'm not a . . .' He had to break off from speaking; it was too funny; he could barely breathe. 'I'm not like you. I didn't come here for that. The reason I came here was to . . . I wanted to say . . . No, there was something. The only problem is I don't remember what it was.'

His laughter redoubled, and he was almost falling to his knees with weakness at the power of his giggles – but Lafcadio was no longer paying attention; he was looking somewhere beyond Flores.

'Is that . . . Are they . . .?'

He gripped his crutches, hobbling out of the hut.

'Get down, you fools!' he yelled.

The tower of seals was silvery outlined at the top, and at its base, bathed in orange light from the bonfires, many sailors hollered. High up, silhouetted against the stars, two men raced towards the summit with the agility of sailors who had lived a lifetime amongst Jacob's ladders. Then, with the touch of a bare foot, a seal was dislodged, and with this the whole structure collapsed in a flabby susurration of flesh – exposing behind it the full and glistening moon. Four sailors and two bonfires were immediately interred beneath the tumult. Other sailors sprinted away from the brief avalanche, dashing into the sea – and in the captain's hut, a fat seal spun by the laughing Flores, douting the candles with the whistling swoosh of its gyrating momentum, before cannonballing into a supporting pillar and sending a portion of the leafy roof fluttering down over his head.

'Lo siento,' Hieronimo cried out, amidst the yelling and moaning of the men and the whispering of the surf, taking full responsibility for the turmoil in which he had played no part. 'Forgive.'

Flores, his laughter dampened by an unknown substance in his mouth, brushed leaves and vines off himself and staggered away down the beach. Everything was nacreously bleached by moonlight, and he was confused by it all. Hiccuping, he weaved awkwardly through murdered seals and floundering men until he could see the black band that demarcated the river from the bone-white sand.

'Forgive.'

There was someone pulling on his arm – it was Hieronimo; the man had followed him, and when Flores turned to him, the Galician fell down to his knees in supplication.

'I need,' he said. 'I lose all. Forgive.'

Flores raised the palm of his hand to him; he could not remember the man's name.

'Just a moment, please,' he said. 'I have something to attend to.'

He wheeled across the sand until he reached the mouth of the river, and there he collapsed on his hands and knees and vomited a flood of pure wine into its dark waters, watching out of the corner of his tearful eyes the red liquid drowning the full moon therein reflected.

———•———

Forgetting immediately his dream, Flores tried to open his eyes, but they were stuck together; he popped them apart with his fingers. In glinted the merciless light. Cicadas and crickets were everywhere engaged in a clicking crescendo, making his surroundings seem too close to his senses. Beneath him, the earth shifted. He flinched, fearing once more that he was at sea. Still, on occasion, the shadow of the sea would contort his movements and tense his muscles, and, sometimes at night, when he was rocking back and forth in his hammock, listening to the sails fill and the lines rattle, he would suddenly feel himself to be far too still, and would jolt awake, terrified, only to find himself in the granary, under the forest, on the outskirts of the town, and would realise afresh that he was not on the *Atlas* anymore, and would remember all that he had lost.

He was not in the granary now, though; he had passed out behind it.

Esa was still talking, as she had been in his dream, her hands gentle upon him. The left side of her face was painted red, and she

91

was wearing bright clothes. It must have been nearly midday; the sun was at its summit, and the heat thick. Rising, he spat a few times; the back of his throat pocked by crustaceans of phlegm, the canals of his nostrils narrowed as though fringed by ice, and his skin was too tight across his face.

Stumbling over the words, he told her she must bring him to the king of the town, the one whose name was Iaen – but he had forgotten the word for 'king', so he just said 'Iaen' again and again. He was trying to figure out how to explain that fifty or so armed men would arrive soon, but there was no flow this morning; he made some gestures signifying a very tall man, and then he stopped, giving up.

Esa took him by the hand, and led him around the granary to the plaza, and the first thing he saw were the makeshift canopies, the broadest of which had been propped up off the central tree, and the painted faces of the townspeople.

A young townsman stood out in the open, his arms feathered, the right side of his face painted a resplendent red. He looked at Esa, his shadow shrunk to a concentrated pool of darkness under the vertical light, but Esa didn't look back at him. She remained speaking to Flores, and leading him by the hand, and then he saw, standing at the edge of town, the surviving crew of the *Atlas*.

They were like some primordial rising, emerged from the overhanging forest and dripping wet from the river. Out of this feverous apparition of writhing paleness and searching glances came an impression of salt-glimmering clothes, blades flashing; leather shoes blistered from seawater; arms flaked with seal blood, viscera up to the elbows; sleepless eyes in lean, ravenous faces blushed with sunburn. The captain's eyes were pincered with pain or light, but it was Marianne Lynch who separated himself from this carnivorous herd.

Taking a few steps forward, he called:

'Flores, come parley.'

'What is this?' Flores shouted out, across the plaza.

'Flores, my boy,' Lafcadio called also, 'come parley.'

The captain leant on Marianne Lynch's shoulder, the other arm occupied with his crutch, and hobbled forward. Flores moved to meet the two of them. Many of the townspeople were drifting discreetly away, children in tow, back into the communal building.

'Well, then, my boy,' Lafcadio said, 'I have forty-six men who have come through hell and they are looking for respite. Mr Lynch came to me this morning with the bright idea that you might translate our needs for us. So have these Indians produce something to mollify my men and cater to their comforts for a few days before we pass on to a more tamed place.'

Even hunched over his crutch, the captain stood a head taller than Flores. Traces of his majestic handsomeness remained yet visible beneath the warp of his protracted dying.

The light was fierce, unhealthy; Flores blinked slowly before its brilliance, his right eye blurring slightly, trailing sagging lines of yellow light.

'How did you know I was learning their language?'

'It is in your nature,' Lynch said.

'I will not help you.'

'You will translate, Flores,' Lynch said. 'For we will communicate ourselves come what will, but it is only you who might deliver the message with words. Go to it. The alternative is unthinkable to you.'

'You misunderstand,' Lafcadio said, his forehead cleaving hugely in wrinkles. 'I am being moderate. There is a man coming up behind me who would promise more than I would; a man who would not parley. You must respect us, Flores. My crew get restless unless they feel they are being respected. You know this.'

'They will think I am like you.'

'That only makes your sacrifice all the greater,' Lynch said.

Lafcadio patted Flores on the shoulder. 'Have them give us a gift, boy. It need not be much. Some few baubles is all, a little gold or silver – just an offering.'

'This is not some fairy tale,' Flores said. 'This is not El Dorado. You have mistaken the nature of these people.'

'Test our mettle, Flores,' Lynch said, 'see what it comes to.'

Flores walked alone along the plaza, skin prickling with the many eyes that watched him. He approached the canopy where Iaen stood, grey-haired and still. He carried a staff off which had been tied several metal bands, and listened as Flores struggled with his words. Then he shook his staff, and a clanging sounded out. He addressed some words to the crowd, and then departed into the communal building, several women following after him.

More townspeople shuffled away from the canopies into the communal building, the ceremony abandoned. Guilt constricted Flores's chest; like a ghost it ran through his blood.

Finally, some women emerged from the communal building, holding sacks in their arms. They pushed pink flowers into the sailors' hands. A pregnant woman named Suya came up to Camacho and slipped the stem of a flower between his remaining fingers, and gestured for him to smell it, to rub it against the skin of his eyelids and his throat. He looked at the flower for a moment, and then opened his fingers so it fell, petals first, down onto the pale earth.

———◆———

The crew evicted everyone from the communal building and decamped inside. The reaction of the townspeople was at first confused, then rowdy. There was shoving, protesting, harried and fitful motions of dissent. A child started crying, and one of the sailors slapped its face, starting a scuffle with two outraged townsmen. More joined and swarmed over the offending sailor, and

Iaen tried to break up the squabble by shaking his staff, ringing for attention, calling out various names to help him.

Lafcadio, who was scanning the crowd, extended an index finger towards Iaen.

'Now, Mr Lynch.'

Lynch nodded, and pushed his way through the crowd, and then found himself face to face with the woman named Kiri, two of whose children – Abo and Sami – Flores had spent much time learning with. She was wearing two ceremonial knives skewered through the front of her clothes and was shouting at Lynch. Lynch, barely slowing his pace, grabbed her by the hair, and kneed her in the abdomen, and was soon pushing once more through the bobbing heads. It had been a flickering motion, so quick Flores only pieced it together once it had already happened.

'You can't,' Flores said. 'That's not—'

'Hush,' Lafcadio said. 'You do it to one, so you don't do it to many.'

Flores ran into the melee and found Kiri winded on the floor; he went to help her up, and she lunged at him, striking him across the face. A little deeper into the crowd, Lynch reached Iaen and punched him once quickly on the temple. The old man blinked a few times in shock, stumbling backwards. Lynch closed the gap and punched him smartly again, this time in the forehead, and he fell. Wresting the staff off him, Lynch took hold of his ankle and dragged him out of the building. The tussling crowd quietened.

Once Lynch was certain he was far enough into the plaza to be visible to all, he sat down in the dirt, spread out his legs and pulled Iaen up to him, so that the man's back was flat against his own chest. Then he put the staff lengthways across his throat and ran his two elbows underneath it so that if he flexed his arms back, it would kill him; there was a certain lovers' intimacy within the brutality of the pose.

Lafcadio made an anticlockwise motion with his finger.

'Clear it,' he said.

The communal building was emptied without further resistance, and then it was the sailors who were fighting one another, claiming the cells in which they wanted to sleep. Flores, still dazed by the blows he had received, kept close to the walls. It was his first time inside the building. It contained five levels, each one opening onto a single stair that ran in a diagonal line, uninterrupted, all the way up to the skylight. Individual rooms were stacked on top of one another in the form of cells in a beehive, and each of these living spaces opened onto a narrow hallway that ended in a sheer drop, except for the point where the stair intersected each level.

Flores had never seen anything like it. He wanted to climb the stairs, to examine it more closely, but the irritations of his body had grown too myriad – his throat and eyes seemed covered in a scabrous film; his fingers itched, even his heart seemed to itch. There was a shimmering in the bottom of his field of vision, and his every inhalation seemed to blow open his guilt, renewing it with an almost supernatural tenderness that perforated his lungs. He sat down, clutched a step, and waited.

Hieronimo emerged from a cell on the third floor and called down that he had found alcohol, and soon sailors were tumbling down the stairs, hauling pitchers against their bellies, stains growing on their fronts from where the dark liquid sloshed onto them. Amidst all the rushing, Flores was guided outside.

The sailors formed little circles along the plaza, each group crowding around a different pitcher. Flores pushed through one such circle and took a cupped handful of the alcohol and drank it down. The wine of the previous night had been bitter, yet soft in nature, but this liquid was harsh and choking.

His hair was tousled; someone said something he couldn't hear. He took another drink, and then tried to break out of the circle, but too many hands, rough and loving, were restraining him.

He drank again.

<hr />

The crew sated themselves with alcohol and tobacco until they had grown merry, exhausted, or lost in their own games. Eventually, the townspeople started drifting back into the communal building, returning quietly to some of their affairs and chores, leaving distance between themselves and the sailors who lay about in the plaza.

Flores reeled into the granary, and all at once the sacks on the floor seemed to jerk further away, their shadows diffusing towards him, the angles doubling and stretching as if to reach out and envelop him. He went to lean against the wall to balance himself but missed and fell to his knees.

Nearby, someone was breathing.

'Angel, are you there?'

There came no answer – only the breathing, deep and peaceful.

'My eyes, they . . . I feel so tired.'

He tried to focus his line of sight towards the breathing, but the jagged shadows continued to twitch and repeat themselves, and, when he closed his eyes, everything pitched and tilted within.

'Goodnight, Angel,' he said.

Outside, the sailors later got their second wind after Cricklow shot a chicken. Its head exploded in a bloody mist; the gunshot lingered, and the sailors cheered and soon many of them were chasing after the birds, burying them up to their necks to use them for target practice. The resulting squawking agonised Flores, before being abbreviated by the huge thirst that, abrupt as a thunderclap, overspread him in a headache, and he arose, his vision somewhat cleared, and saw the granary was now empty. He went looking for something to drink.

Under the tree in the centre of the plaza two sailors sat around a simmering cauldron – Lafcadio lay on his back, his neck perched off the trunk, silently regarding the fire; and opposite was Marianne Lynch, who smoked a long pipe on his side, hand holding up his head as though he were stretched out upon a divan. The whole town was falling into dimness, and the shadows, thrown off by the fires, ranged monstrous and thin, dancing out far beyond their sources, and the underside of the leaves flickered and shimmered with that honeyed softness particular to those final moments of twilight.

'Here he is now,' Lynch said, 'the sad-eyed Moor.'

Flores ignored him and addressed himself to the captain. 'Will you not put order on your men?'

'The eyes are open,' Lynch said, 'but no one is within.'

Lafcadio was indeed insensible, sprawled out like a stuffed puppet, eyes unseeing, the huge, wilting face like a cracked gargoyle in the rain.

'Come sit,' Lynch said, gesturing with his pipe.

Flores peered into the cauldron and was disappointed to find not alcohol, but only a swirling stew of tobacco. He took a fallen twig from the ground, dusted it off, poked it into the juice, withdrew it and then sucked on the dripping stick. His mouth salivated, giving him some relief, and he almost collapsed into a cross-legged position, attempting to ignore the deathly captain beside him.

'I can't stand to see you swallow your thirst so.'

Lynch offered his open flask; Flores took it and drank hurriedly.

Sailors were stumbling around, shouting at one another. Fuchs was carrying two chickens above his head like trophies, and Hieronimo was stumbling after another, bending over so slowly to catch it that it managed to stroll away easily each time.

'You must hate us very much,' Lynch said.

'Yes.'

He took another long draught; Lynch watched him.

'We appreciate your help today. Faith, you made our little conquest fair handy for us.'

The townswoman, Suya, was walking into the communal building now, her form darker than the blue evening, both hands under her own belly, dripping water from the river where she had gone to take the weight off her strained back. Flores saw her disappear, and tears rose in his throat. He blinked, looked at the ground.

'You have corrupted me.'

'O, no. No,' Lynch said, grimacing. 'You can't believe that. There is no corruption; there is only compulsion. We are compelled to go out, to go further, to become boundless. We are compelled to create and be created. It all happens despite us. If you don't understand this, none of it makes any sense.'

Still looking down, Flores shook his head.

'We were made free. We could have come here with love in our hearts.'

'You're not listening, acushla,' Lynch said, pointing the stem of his pipe at Flores. 'Fooling yourself into believing you have agreed to creation is what is called love. Love is a glimmer on the object seen at a certain slant; a kindness bequeathed after the fact, an addendum to creation. It is a lightening varnish that allows the structure not to feel its own weight cracking it apart. True surplus, pure gift – and hence unnecessary. You saw that woman, the pregnant one there, who passed from the river. You watched her, didn't you? Say I had taken her against her will but eight months past, and though I had hated her and given her seed entirely in hate, she would love the made child. Is God not good, Flores?'

The film of tears was like a membrane itching Flores's pupils; he tried not move his face.

'What is this?' he said. 'What do you want from me?'

'I only want to be your friend,' Lynch said. 'You see, I like you uncommon well.'

99

A few of the crew started letting off bullets. A stray hit the tree above Lafcadio and bark shattered around him, covering him in flakes. Marianne Lynch was still speaking, but Flores couldn't hear him anymore; a high note was ringing in his ears.

The full moon seemed to be coming closer to his face. He curled up on his side, twisted his ribcage in a huge serpentine motion as if to shake his skeleton out of its flesh and clenched his eyes shut so firmly it made his face shake and the bones in his neck rise. He sucked at the flask until he passed out, the rim yet against his lips.

Night fell. A few bulbous clouds hung low like severed heads, still and separate from one another. Sailors, damaged flowers in their hair and inside their frayed buttonholes, played cards around a fire, and even though they sat close together, they were all yelling. Their gesticulations were profound, conversations cutting across one another. Fingers pointed, eyebrows cocked, drunken sighs expelled. Camacho was standing in a squat, continuously in the process of getting up and sitting down again, telling an obscene story about what he had done to a Creole girl with one of his toes, pointing the absent forefinger of his right hand all about him. Fuchs and Cricklow were tossing a dead chicken back and forth between themselves, and each time one of them dropped it their laughter blared higher. It was an enclosed circle of pandemonium: spat wads of glistening tobacco, torn playing cards, bottles and feathers lay scattered, forgotten, half-buried. Two brown snails had slunk onto Lafcadio's cheek, leaving shine like tears, but then the two trails had become one as the smaller snail had clambered onto the other's shell, and was now riding its fellow down the long body of the captain. They sailed past the neck's legions of broken blood vessels, and then across the shoulder and down to the cresting wave of his flaccid bicep, and, amidst all Lafcadio's enormous dying, when the snail touched the creased groove of the crook of his elbow, he was tickled into waking.

'I am alive.'

'Ay,' Lynch said.

'Was that Flores, or a dream?'

'He is here, too.'

'I see him in my . . . Why did he take him on, unless he . . . A paying fare in Nouadhibou . . . only ever in Liverpool . . . The captain knew. He knew. He knew the mother was there . . . The captain knew he would not cross again.'

Lynch shrugged.

'Maybe.'

Lafcadio's eyes glanced down over his own body.

'Would you remove these snails, Marianne?'

Lynch plucked the creatures off, watched their flabby verges retract suddenly, placed them gently on an exposed root. Immediately, they started heading back towards the huge beacon of the captain.

'How long will we remain in this town?'

'I think I might be . . .'

A wave of noxious pain flooded through Lafcadio setting him trembling, and then he was given a brief release. He gasped and spoke hurriedly:

'You cannot let Camacho be captain. He has nothing in him. I never wanted the command. I did it because I . . . He has no honour, no discipline, no forbearance. It has to . . . I did so many things. So many things . . . I hurt women. They were women. It has to mean something . . . You must stop him.'

Lynch's pipe had gone out. He took a crisp leaf from the ground and placed it in the blue flames under the cauldron and then placed the smoking leaf in the bowl of his pipe and sucked at it.

'It was me that arranged the parley at which you were gut-shot,' he said. 'It was myself that betrayed you, and you know why I did it, don't you?'

'I thought, now . . . I know you. I know what you are, and I thought, now, with all . . .'

The captain gasped again and passed out for the final time; his eyes shucking up, the yellow crescents staring out blindly. Lynch removed the flask from under Flores's cheek, and pocketed it, and then squinted up at the contrary motions of the trees that bordered the town. Lynch counted the silhouettes of the sailors by the fires, and then glanced back towards the forest.

Some pale and new man, he saw, loitered there.

<hr />

Chuck Benjamin stepped out of unrelenting wilderness, his gait resembling that of any gentleman enjoying a Sunday stroll. He swung a cane whose handle had been carved into the form of a phoenix, and wore a white, fitted coat with a tail, and a broad-brimmed hat cocked rakishly askew. Alongside him was a glum, little Chinese boy named Xiaoguang Lee, carrying a pack which towered over his shoulders. The boy was perhaps ten or eleven, and he held the leather leash of a white bull terrier named Cicero whose bony slab of head and abbreviated tail rose like surrendering flags above the tall grasses.

They came upon the moonlit town; Benjamin scanned the plaza. Deep sockets of trampled muck scarred the earth where there had been dancing; dead fires left holes in the earth larger than cannonballs' scars; dreaming men turned on their sides; rainbows of chickens lay stretched out on their backs, wings spread in cruciform, their sodden feathers fallen off them like scattered petals at a wedding, globules of blood bubbling across their breasts. The lonesome cockerel, undaunted and unaware, wandered through the aftermath of the massacre, never pausing over the exploded bodies of his clutch. Only one fire remained, around which twenty or so sailors sat, playing poker with three shuffled packs of cards. Hieronimo, far from these, was splayed out on his back in front of one of the smaller buildings, his arms and legs maintaining a sticky membrane of feathers, stripped of nearly all but their twisted, hollow shafts. Each of his hands pushed a bottle of spirits down into the earth as though he were afraid they would come untethered and float away.

Benjamin tapped the sole of the chef's boot with his cane.

'Where is the captain?'

Hieronimo's bloodshot eyes widened at the silvery adumbration of narrow face turned up towards the moon, the unclouded gaze free from expression.

'Who is?'

'Donde esta el capitán?'

Hieronimo blinked so slowly he felt his head falling forward with the weight of his own descending eyelashes. The cross on his forehead demanded scratching, but he was afraid of falling over if he moved, and he noticed then the bull terrier, its head the flat wedge of an executioner's block – and a huge remorse spread over him.

'Am sorry for all, sir, no time,' he explained. 'If I have all way the same too many speaking at me with captain. Forest is mouths. Little mouths all the days who is, all the days, which don't forget are when you want to. And if I am see me, what then?'

Hieronimo went to take a sip from one of the bottles and ended up pouring most of the alcohol into his eyes. He fell on his side, grunting.

'If you don't answer me presently, I will strike you.'

'She is with a tree in the centre of the place. Him name is Lafcadio Hinchoa. Have the big stomach who is full of the blood is blue. You find. Lo siento. Am sorry.'

Boy and dog following after him, Benjamin strode across the plaza, arching his cane out in long and conspicuous strides. When he came to the tree, he saw beneath it a cauldron filled with cooling tobacco, on whose oiled surface floated a solitary, pink flower.

There were two men around the cauldron, one had his face hidden, curled up in a ball like a hedgehog; the other was splayed out and staring up at him – a tall, blonde man with an impossibly engorged belly wrapped in bloody rags.

'Captain,' Benjamin said to the blonde man, 'I would like to buy your town off you.'

He stood and waited.

Eventually Camacho came jogging across the plaza, still holding his hand of cards. He came to a sudden stop in front of Benjamin, as though yanked back by an invisible string, awestruck at this civilised apparition.

'Who are you?'

'If I poked this man's belly he would burst open. This fellow cannot be your captain – he is in his final descent. Look me in my eyes and tell me how drunk you are?'

Camacho stared into the man's pacific blue eyes and said nothing.

'Hold my gaze,' Benjamin said. 'Tell me your name and your condition.'

'I am Indiana Camacho de Vega, the second – the first mate of the *Atlas*.'

'Mr de Vega, get my boy something light to drink. He has travelled much for a little boy and could use some respite. No whiskey.'

'Sir, I must know who you are.'

'Chuck Benjamin, American – but go take care of my boy and I shall give out more palaver.'

Benjamin tapped his cane and spoke a few words in Mandarin, and Lee snatched the cards from Camacho's good hand, and then ran off to the fire and took the first mate's former place in the deal, much to the befuddlement of the other players. Camacho went to the communal building where he washed his face and forced himself to be sick, and when he came out again with some of the townspeople's alcohol in a bowl, he saw the child smoking a long-stemmed clay pipe, his face serious, a small pile of coins laying in his lap.

Back beneath the tree, Chuck Benjamin asked:

'Do you claim this town?'

'Yes, sir.'

'And this is your town of Indians?'

'Yes, sir.'

'And you have moved upon them?'

'More or less.'

'Más o menos. You have no legal entitlement.'

'We were—'

'You have none, I would know. Does anyone else know you're here?'

'No.'

'This is important. Think carefully – does anyone else know you have come ashore here?'

'No, sir.'

'Good. Do I have your attention Mr de Vega?'

'Yes, sir.'

'Are you sure?'

'Yes, sir.'

'The Benjamins are a family business. We are two boys, Osgood and Charles – I am Charles, the eldest, but you can call me Chuck. Then, of course, there is Momma Dearest. We run a coastal town called Santa María three hours to the north of here, but, as of late, we have grown restless. Are you still following me, Mr de Vega?'

'Yes, sir.'

'Good. Now, I have a special interest in any gathering of Indians around these parts, and you might say I have some rights to them too, but I do not think I will have to lean too heavily on my rights in this instance. Like I said, Mr de Vega, we have exhausted Santa María. She is not well-placed for investment, being on the cold front of three squabblesome empires, and the local Spanish landlords have grown annoying – always stupid, but now proud and difficult, too. I am wasting precious hours of my life playing politics with peripheral imbeciles; it is beneath me. We must start again, and I will make this place here the new capital of the colony, but you'll have to give me ten years or so, but in the present tense – the only tense you exist in, Mr de Vega – it is the time for a transitionary venture. I am willing to offer you five dollars for each acre of this town, thereby giving you, by my appraisal, a total sum of seventeen dollars and two bits, and I would be willing to give every last one of your men gainful employ and you personal foremanship over the whole caboodle. How strikes this you, captain?'

'Foreman of what?'

'The mine.'

'What mine?'

'We are standing on it.' Benjamin said. 'We are standing on a gold mine made of shit.'

'A gold mine?'

'No – shit.'

Benjamin struck his cane into the earth, twisted it, and then brought its tip under Camacho's nose. It was covered in a little wedge of white dirt. The Valencian flinched away from the outstretched cane, which looked impossibly long between his eyes.

'It's guano; the town is built on it.'

'Is that valuable?'

'Valuable? Europe is dying – and yet in her lazy dotage of good American eating she has borne fifty million more whelps out of her than she should have, but you take this here guano and you mix a little bit of that in with that exhausted European soil and, revivified, Momma Europe will smile once more upon her children. This guano is so potent that a few thousand barrels of the stuff'll nourish crops as'll feed that whole continent for a decade . . . And, Mr de Vega, this ain't coal, nor diamond – none of your tawdry hassle of mining. No pickaxe, no flint, no iron, no nothing: a shovel and a pulley is all. You could peel this off with your fingernails it's so soft – easy as slicing momma's apple pie on a Sunday afternoon. We'll pick up our fortune with a spoon, Mr de Vega, and Momma Europe, she'll pay us well for it.'

Benjamin at last planted his cane back in the earth, breaking Camacho's rapt attention.

'I'll give you boys half a dollar a week for overseeing the labour, and to you I'll give a dollar and a half a week, and I will put seventeen dollars plus change in your hand this time tomorrow, and four dollars right now.'

Camacho looked beyond the open vista of Benjamin's blue gaze; to the low mountains hunched up in darkness, all wreathed invisibly in gently shivering forest, and then he ran his incomplete hand through his knotted hair.

'You want the Indians to be miners,' he said, 'and you want us to oversee the Indians.'

'O, I wish you were right, Mr de Vega,' Benjamin said, shaking his head, 'but no one on God's green earth can make an Indian work. Lord knows we've tried. If I could help an Indian I swear I would, but I can't help an Indian as can't help himself. You give him a dollar, he'll put it in his mouth. You chain up his family, he'll fetch something for you for a day, and then disappear off into the forest. You put him in your debt and he'll think you've given him a gift. You burn the soles off his feet and he'll run away from you on his hands. The working day is a mystery to these folks. No, the reason I'm following Indians is, well – have you ever seen shit on its own?'

Camacho hesitated and remained silent.

'The answer you're reaching for is no,' Benjamin said. 'Shit has flies on it. It makes noise, buzzes, smells. Insects crawl all over it. Heck, it seethes. It's more alive than most of the men it comes out of. Now, if you're looking for shit, you follow the signs. Sure as day, your local Indian'll have set himself up near some wonderful curve in the river where the water tastes just right; his little house'll be positioned so it catches the sunlight just right; and he'll have set his crops up on a nice little pile of guano, all mixed up, all nice and consistent with the soil, just right – but did you ever pick up shit with flies on it?'

'No, sir.'

'That's exactly right. You can't pick up shit as has flies on it. You've got to shoo them away. Come now, Mr de Vega, be serious. I got three hundred Chinamen half a day from here could be set up cutting slabs of guano and barrelling within two days. I got a contractor as could set up a landing pier down by that there beach in three weeks. I got a man as can hack through that forest for you and set up a mailing line, allowing you and your boys to talk to your mommas. I even got a clockmaker from Philadelphia City as will set up a big clock right over yonder. We'll get a church, a saloon that sells old cigars that taste like oak trees in autumn, and a little post office with a glass window so clear you can see yourself in it when the sun falls good and soft on it. And, Mr de Vega, I think this guano will hold out for some time. I think this town is, in your parlance, what we call la veta madre – the big one. The steam off all this shit, restocked by all these birds every sweet-nice day, is rising up to God, saying – "Here I am, Mr de Vega. Hallelujah. Here I am. Come pick me up. Barrel me, and sell me in London, Paris, Madrid." Can you hear it, Mr de Vega? Can you hear it?'

'Could I have some shares, too, as well as my wages?'

'Standard practice. There is one more thing – what is this?'

He gestured his cane towards Flores, who had at some point unclenched his body, exposing his face to the sky, eyelids twitching with nightmares, muttering unfinished sentences to himself.

'That's Flores.'

'That's your concern is what it is, not mine,' Benjamin said. 'I'll be returning at this time tomorrow, and, by then, all this – all this – must have been already resolved.'

He withdrew a golden watch from his breast pocket, clicked it open, glanced at it once, closed it and concealed it once more in his pocket.

'It is half past seven now, and Momma Dearest will take to fretting if I am not sparkling-fresh at breakfast tomorrow. The deal is done. Cicero will act as surety; he will be useful to you.'

He called out for his boy, and then spun on his heels, his cane swinging back and forth like a pendulum. Xiaoguang Lee gathered most of his winnings into his pack, balanced it on his back and then came trundling up to Camacho, his face flushed from alcohol, pipe smoke trailing after him.

'Give him four dollars, Lee,' Benjamin said, not looking back.

The child slapped a fistful of grubby coins into Camacho's good hand. He squinted down at his palm, flicking through them, and when he looked up again, the man and boy had already disappeared back into the forest, the leaves still swaying in their wake, and then he felt something damp and warm seething against the sensitive scabs that covered the stumps of his right hand.

A white bull terrier was sitting beside him, tongue lolling out of its mouth, panting up at the moon.

———— • ————

Streaks of orange light cut veins across the sky. It was colder than he had ever expected it would be here. The plaza was empty save a score of sleeping sailors huddled around smouldering ashes and the torn-up chickens dotted upon the earth. The full moon was yet there, far away and fading into day, like a pale fingerprint sprinkled with specks of blue powder.

Jacques waded through whorls of knee-deep mist. The fibrous, moist legs of a creature landed on his face, and he brushed it away as gently as he could. He checked several of the surrounding buildings, until he came at last to the granary. A young girl slept there. Quietly, he took an empty sack from near her feet and brought it over to the tree in the middle of the plaza. He draped it over Flores's torso and legs. Flores stirred, his cheeks beaded in a sliding sheen of dew, and then he turned on his side, and Jacques saw that all night he had been wearing on his head, like half a wooden crown, a shard of bark.

Jacques pinched it off, tossed it into the ashes of the fire.

'Is the captain dead yet?'

He looked up. Lynch was standing there, leaning against the tree.

'No. I bring him inside, and change the wraps,' he said. 'It is become cold.'

'Do you have a cold, Jacques? Do you have the grippe?'

'I think yes, but I am fine.'

'Let me help you.'

Together, they lifted Lafcadio and hauled him towards the communal building.

'Do you like it here, Jacques?' Lynch asked.

'Yes.'

'Would you like to live here?'

'I will, yes.'

'Who will you live here with?'

'My friend, Angel, I will live with.'

'A friend, yes. And what about the Indians – will you live with them?'

'Yes, I will live with them also.'

Over the forested mountain rose a sudden meeting of birds; they darkly swirled themselves into the form of a gentle whirl, parts of it spilling away, moving indecisively towards town.

'If you stay here, Jacques,' Lynch said, 'you'll kill them.'

'No, only help.'

'It's not a choice. Once twenty million lived on this slender strip of coast, and this not so long ago. In vast, connected cities, right here; cities far bigger than Liverpool or Nantes – and now, nothing. They were killed with our breaths, Jacques. Nothing more. It was sickness as won the Americas. If you meet an Indian, he will die of your disease, but not you of his. That is what being chosen means, Jacques. You are chosen; they are not. You are death to these people. Your sickness is probably already in them.'

The flock of birds had moved in over the town, throwing flashes of shade like falling leaves. One broke away from the others, and glided towards the ocean, its wings still. Jacques watched it. He wondered if such creatures ever got lost. It disappeared into the clouds, and he remained looking at the dim, closed-off sky with his soft eyes.

'I only help.'

'You want to, but you hurt them.'

There had been a Sunday in Jacques's childhood when a burning fever had left him almost blind. The sisters had taken all the other foundlings to morning mass, and once his sight had recovered he grew scared amidst the many rows of empty beds, the high ceilings, the black crucifixes that scored the walls. In his shift and his night-cap, he had fled, trying to catch up with them, but the other children were too far ahead. It was December. Fields lay fallow, the rises covered in hazes from which a veiny lattice of tree branches emerged. He trotted down an empty country road, dwarfed by every gate and bush, terrified that he would never be able to find the others, and then, from a frost-glazed copse, appeared a doe and her fawn sniffing the air in concert, three ducks, a goat and a cat, and all these creatures followed him until he reached the steps of the church where the next mass was being called with a peal of clamouring bells, and from that day on Jacques knew that he was not alone.

They passed inside the entrance of the communal building, and then Lynch, without warning, let go his grip of Lafcadio's legs, and the falling weight of the captain's body sent Jacques to his knees.

'There's no point changing his wraps,' Lynch said. 'He will be dead by nightfall.'

Jacques set himself to rearranging the captain's legs so they weren't riding up underneath him, and then heaved him up against the wall by himself.

'Of course,' Lynch said, 'do what you think is best, acushla.'

He ruffled Jacques's hair, and then the youth looked up at him, his eyes steady.

'It is true what you say of my breath?'

'It is true.'

'I must hurt them if I live here with my friend?'

'You must.'

Lynch departed; Jacques fetched the captain's crutches and then changed his wraps. When he was finished he sat on his forelegs, hands resting in his lap, and looked up at all the cells. His face contorted briefly, and he sneezed three times in quick succession. He wiped the drip from his nose, and turned his face upwards again, now towards the aperture in the domed ceiling.

<hr />

The crew woke, yawned, began drinking. A line of six sailors urinated against the communal building. Hieronimo, who had woken drunker than he had fallen asleep, wandered around, knitting his big brows together, looking like a skinny bear recently arisen from hibernation. Flores, too, awoke, alone now beneath the tree. He found himself covered in the heft of an empty sack, his bones a numb torment of stiffness. It took him a long while to sit up, and when he did all the drunkenness that had been latent inside him sloshed once more to life.

Townsmen, in small groups, left to the forest, all of them coming out of the communal building, having last night reclaimed their cells. Several children darted across the plaza, full of a bottomless energy; Flores would never go to them again – everything he learned would be used against them in the end; yet without learning in the day a huge emptiness stretched mercilessly out before him. All the hours until he could sleep again were taunting monsters; even the gauzed sun was teasing him with the moribund slowness of its arc.

There was a figure by the granary. It was Quentin Cricklow. He held a bowl of water with a half-opened cut-throat razor dipped into it like a fishing rod, leaning off the entrance with his marked forehead pressed against the inside of his wrist. Next to him was a white dog lapping up a puddle of blood. It wagged its tail with a forlorn slowness; its yellow eyes upturned, watching Flores approach.

'Marry, 'tis the sad Moor,' Cricklow said, staring in at Esa, asleep. 'They say children have the whole future already in the citadel of their minds. Espying her, I'd well believe it.'

Flores looked in.

'Where is Angel?'

'A fine question.'

'Why are you here?'

'Mr Lynch let me filch his razor for a shave, but I were about to set me down when I realised I'd lost my bloody monkey. Would you believe that?'

The dog raised its head, yawned, its tongue shivering electrically, and then it lowered its mouth to the puddle again, where a few ants, separated from some harvesting colony, were twitching and drowning.

'Whose blood is this?'

'La, so many rude enquiries early in the day. Scrinch not thy dirgeful phiz, Flores, 'tis but a chicken's blood.'

He produced something from his pocket and tossed it; Flores caught the jostling object against his chest – it was a flask full of alcohol.

'I don't want anything from you.'

''Tis Lynch's, not mine. He were keen you got it.'

The puddle of blood was diminished now, slick and oily against the earth. The dog drew its head back with directionless defiance, eyes ranging masterfully across the plaza. A fuzzy halo of pinkness around its muzzle marred its white perfection; a single drop hung from its whisker. Flores's brain was fizzing with some kind of decompression.

'I feel terrible,' he said. 'I can't continue in this way.'

'La, sup and feel cheer.'

A sailor was singing a shanty. The voice blended in with the murmurings of the forest, was overpowered, and then trailed off, the subsequent verses forgotten. Flores looked at the constant flux of agitating sky, waiting for a slight glimmering effect in his vision to dissipate.

He drank from the flask, gasped, and then drank again.

'Thy stormy lover approaches,' Cricklow said.

Kiri was coming towards them, accompanied by a middle-aged townsman called Atta.

'War ring,' she said.

Flores shook his head.

'Warring.'

'Wars sing,' Atta said.

Flores grimaced, shook his head again.

'Iaen,' Atta said.

'Iaen,' Kiri repeated. 'Donde? Onde ela está? Flores – donde?'

'Donde está Iaen?' Atta said.

An embarrassed blush spread across Flores's face – they had been trying to speak English, and he hadn't realised it.

'Where's Iaen?' he repeated.

Of course, he thought; the townspeople could speak Latin tongues; three centuries they had been coming here, but when he had arrived, out of stupidity, out of some misguided idea of respect, he had tried to speak to them only in their native tongue, and so – all these weeks – they had been humouring his own ignorance unnecessarily.

'You want to find Iaen,' he said, having forgotten every trace of their language. 'Is he gone? I'll ask Marianne Lynch. He was with him; he'll know. Yesterday, he . . . Eu procuro Iaen . . . Procuro a verdade . . . Voy a encontrarlo.'

Cricklow was laughing. Kiri went into the granary, woke Esa, and led her out by the arm. Cricklow whistled as Kiri passed by him, tapping the razor handle off the bowl, and Kiri let go Esa, and turned back towards Cricklow.

Flores stepped between them.

'I will find Iaen,' he said. 'Eu o encontro.'

Cricklow whistled and tapped the razor against the bowl again, and Kiri cursed him, and took Esa's hand. When they left towards the communal building, Esa glanced sleepily at Flores, and he knew he would always remember this moment – her being led away, looking back over her shoulder at him with the attentive, simple eyes of a watching child, half-asleep, not understanding what was happening.

Guilt was throttling him again, the slaughtering clutches of some final breakdown crowding him out.

'Whither the Moor?' Cricklow said.

Flores was already stumbling away, but he didn't know where he was going. He realised, unconsciously, he had been heading towards the sea.

'I must find Iaen.'

'Find Mr Lynch, you'll find him. He were just speaking to him. I'll take you to him.'

'Is Lynch far? I am so tired. I've never felt so . . . I never felt this way. I don't know what's happening to me.'

'Sleep not, la, or you'll miss him. You must drink through it. Drink, drink. Take a drink and follow me. I shall bring you to Mr Lynch. Take a drink, Flores.'

The dog slumped down politely on its hindlegs. Flores blinked at it, an unwanted sense of wonder, vast and formless, overcoming him. He stared out at the plaza. The nothing of it all, splayed out like a field of corpses, begged acknowledgement or burial.

He took another drink.

—•—

Someone was always drowning. A panic in the chest swelled up a dilating heart; like a bubble it grew until he was trapped inside its dimensions. He was being consumed, but there was some easiness to this abandon. At least, he thought, I am nobody's anymore, but if I could just save one person – and then the idea, incomplete, escaped out on his breath, lost.

A cool wind whipped low over the ground, coming up to his neck like a guillotine. A flying seed with a feathery appendage landed on his face, and when he peeled it off he saw a little ant clung to the stem by all of its legs, hanging on as it was blown about the world. Flores let it go, hoping it would float off again, but he had ruined the sleek distribution of its parts with his clumsy fingers, and it fell heavily down to earth.

'I called myself Flores because I liked looking at the flowers,' he said. 'Call it proselytising if you will, but what is a baptism to changing the name your mother gave you, but I believed it all . . . I believed everything . . . The first . . .' He took another drink. 'I loved the nativity. I loved it, so much; those people and animals, together, all in a moment . . . Before all else – kings, Caesar, state census, exile, commerce – there was the family, there, together. The child is safe, the mother exhausted.' He was laughing. 'A stable. Sighs, voices, blood, goats, donkeys . . . all that mess . . . all that . . . life. There would have been a scent of manure, dust unsettled, leather harnesses slung over posts, mice shuffling in the hay – and then there was the child, of course, the heart of it all . . . and then he opens his eyes.'

Angel was laughing at him.

'What on earth are you talking about?'

'The first nativity.'

'Could be said of any sow with her piglets.'

Angel's face was rent in two by chiaroscuro, his voice a mock-whisper. Flores blinked, nodded emphatically.

'It could. Exactly. Of course it could. That's what I mean.'

Cricklow – or was it Camacho? – had said Marianne Lynch would be back in a moment, but that was so long ago now. The shadows were long, thinned, hysterically shimmering; evening was rising up out of the ground again. The wind played chiming songs along the howling mouths of the empty bottles that lay sideways across the earth; the seeds of some windborne plant drifted by; its pink burrs stuck to his sleeves. He thought he had seen this seed before, but he couldn't remember. The cold in the air hurt the tip of his nose. Someone offered him another drink.

'Why is Marianne Lynch not here?' Flores asked. 'I am tired.'

A belch of impossible duration rumbled through him, and once he had finished he had to gasp for air; Angel patted him on the back.

'He'll be back soon. Drink up.'

'I don't want to drink anymore; I feel sick.'

Angel touched the underside of the bottle in Flores's hand and brought it gently up to his lips; then he pulled at Flores's hair, so that his face was tilted back, and Flores swallowed twice, before pushing him away. He stared once more into the smothering sky, felt his fingers tight and wrinkled with cold, the chilblains of a thousand winter mornings shuddering through his knuckles, and he was there alone again in Montpellier, with his books, his papers, his prayers, the families of mice rooting through the walls, the burning candles, the sooty glass dewlapped with frost, glancing down at the huge sloped trees in the broad avenue, the charwomen passing behind the carriages, the other students all returned to the provinces, feeling once more like he was left care-taker of the whole world.

'Please, no more, Angel.'

Angel gripped his hand and pressed it against his own cheek.

'You'll catch your second wind,' he said. 'You are not such a bad Moor. I am glad th'art here. I mean this, Flores. Truly, I mean this.'

'After I became a Christian, I spent every Christmas alone,' he said. 'Isn't that strange?'

'Passing strange.'

Flores rested his chin down in the pit of his throat and hiccuped again. He hadn't wanted any of this; all these worthless memories; all his youth wasted; these fingers gone crooked with cold. He had never wanted these lips to tear and shiver, had never wished to breathe every moment of every single day. The body was solitude, an indivisible oneness creeping back into the nothing. Flesh didn't unite – it was the means of separation. When you touch someone you do not become them. Press too hard on the skin and you hurt them. If only there was something to say, he thought; something to be communicated; someone to speak with – but how could that ever be enough? If only he could save someone.

'When I was a child our town died,' Fuchs was saying, across the spent ashes of last night's fire, jogging the child, Abo, on his knees, feeding him a bottle of alcohol like he was a sucking lamb. 'There used to be fortifications, but with the new cannons they may as well have been made of skin and feathers. My father put me in the pantry and said, "Don't you move, child," and when the soldiers finally came in with my mother half her face was missing, the flesh hanging off the skull like potato peel. And she was naked, but only the lower parts. It was all bloody in that darkness from whence I came. When she came towards me I turned away, afeared, and then, so did she, and we were there in the shade of the pantry, both of us not looking one at the other.'

His face had blenched in the telling; the child in his lap tracing his finger against the scab on his forehead.

'I suppose that is some kind of excuse,' Flores said.

'Excuse for what?'

'For what you are.'

But Fuchs didn't understand; Flores stared at him brazenly and felt no kinship with him. None of these men could share the same creator as his mother. What arrogance to think the divine finger-print could be upon them; what frailty to have ever believed that their forms were endless, repeated, that, as one, they would be returned to the loving source of all things. All around the fungible faces were sharp and arbitrary, always in the process of discomposing, always splintering into laughter, the skin so harsh and ruined it was as though they had all been carved by the same careless axe. He couldn't look at them anymore; he turned towards Angel.

'You know, I dream of my mother sometimes,' Flores whispered, 'that's why I keep you awake at nights. I would like to see her again, just one more time.'

Angel recoiled slightly. Flores blinked and saw that he had a cross carved into his forehead. He was about to say something, and then he realised that it was Quentin Cricklow. He was without a beard now, seeming smaller and weaker, like a peeled egg; the razor that had shorn his face had revealed cheeks and chin pastier and more unfinished than the creased teak of his forehead.

'You are not Angel.'

Cricklow shook his head. 'I am not Angel.'

'You are the one.'

'What one?'

'You threw my mother.'

'I do not recollect that.'

The whole time he had been with the crew Flores had thought he had been sitting next to Angel, but Angel had never been there.

The profundity of his mistake, its continual nature, the creativity with which he had invented Angel in Cricklow's dissimilar features, astonished him.

He looked around – Fuchs was wrapping clothes around sprigs and then dousing the old fabric in black alcohol, laying the moistened sticks by his feet when he was finished so it looked like he was nesting himself in his own funeral pyre; he laughed wildly at a joke he was pretending to be able to hear; a few townspeople were milling about on the blurred edge of the light like midges out the corner of his eye; smoke came out of one of the smaller buildings, but he couldn't see Angel anywhere.

'Where is Angel?' Camacho said.

Flores looked up, astounded once more. 'I was about to say that.'

The Valencian was propped against the tree by his forehead, urinating upon the trunk, blinking away the mist of his own rising steam.

'Do you know where he is? Have you seen him, Flores?'

'No, I don't think so. Not since this morning . . . no, yesterday morning.'

'The cannibals took him last night,' Camacho said.

'Why would you say they are cannibals?' Flores said. 'I don't understand some of the things they do. When I . . . I thought . . . I could read them, but then I realised I was just inverting . . . what I was seeing was myself, or my opposite, not them. When I knew this . . . but to go from feeling alone to assuming something like that . . . They are not cannibals, Mr Camacho, I am sure of it. I didn't even know they . . . Speak with them yourselves; they have Spanish and Portuguese. Speak with them.'

'Cannibals, I say.'

'Of course, they are cannibals,' Fuchs said. 'How could they not be?'

The child on his lap had vanished, and, for a moment, it startled Flores, because he couldn't remember Sami having left – or was it Abo who had been there? – but he remembered him being gone; it was a closed space in his mind, something sealed away from him. The sky had grown darker, invisible behind the thick clouds, and it was so cold his eyes had started hurting.

'I was supposed to be looking for Iaen.'

'Iaen, la?' Cricklow said. 'I thought we were looking for Angel?'

There was a bottle in Flores's hand; he raised it to his lips and drank.

'Iaen is their elder, their king,' he said. 'He welcomed me into this town, and Angel, too. Esa brought us . . . Where is Esa?'

'Marry, you don't know who you're after, at all.'

Camacho shook his cock and stuffed it back into his trousers. His stream of urine was diverging into three different paths, rolling towards separate, oblivious sailors.

'I'm worried something has happened to Angel.'

'What's wrong?' Fuchs asked.

'He's missing,' Camacho said. 'Stolen by the cannibals. We must find him . . . O, Angel, if one hair on your head has been misarranged, if one whit of your heart has been saddened, I will raze this tribe. What have they done to our poor, innocent boy? O, these liars, burn away the flesh of these liars' faces . . .'

A sheath of taut bones had risen up in his neck like a cage; he held the centre of the circle, standing in the dead fireplace, the soles of his boots blackened with the ash.

'Find him, men!' he called. 'That is an order. Find our Angel. Let me witness his life. You, there, start in the scattered houses, and you, you trek the surrounding forest – and let no opportunity pass to interrogate the savages. This is a small place. Within the hour we shall assemble yonder.'

The sailors arose in one body and scattered apart, calling out Angel's name.

'Angel!'

Flores was left sitting alone, energy leaking out of him in flagging pulses. His head drifted down, his eyes closing over, his body rocking forward into sleep, but each time he reached the tipping point, the sensation of his own falling would jolt him awake.

'Angel!'

He started rooting around in the muddy remains the sailors had left behind them, rifling through the spent bottles on his hands and knees, shaking them and tossing them away. One small bottle lay on its side in the sodden puddle, still sloshing with alcohol behind the verdigris blur of dark glass. He gulped it down, tasted ash and chewed tobacco in it, and then spat and coughed.

'Angel!

A dog was barking somewhere behind the communal building; Fuchs was stacking kindling in the formation of a little temple against a door; Cricklow was in the granary filling up a sack; a woman carried a knapsack of maize into the forest; a man followed after her, holding a child's hand; the moon was invisible, but its disc imaginable from the illumination it gave to the iterations of flowing vapour that passed its obscured face; Hieronimo climbed onto one of the lower buildings, crawled along its roof until he came to the vent from which a little smoke rose and saw, hunched below, a few women on their hunkers, preparing a huge cake in a shallow hole in the ground, and from where he was perched he could also see all the environs – the mass of dark forest bobbing up and down like horripilated fur coming undone by gusts of wind; the squat mountains tumescently emergent from it all, their sloped sides like hardened sky in the distance, and between one of their disappointed curves, in a sliver like an opening eye, came the flash from the shimmering cosmos of sea beyond.

'Angel!'

A monkey's shrieking answered from within the forest.

'Angel!'

The crew, in the assiduity of their searching, became alone and dissonant to one another. Aimlessly, they trawled, yelling out the name. Once hope of finding Angel had diminished, the utterance became a plaintive moan, the single word overlapping itself so often that it was rarely sounded out clearly, ricocheting in unfinished laments across the twilit town, and then a drunken sailor would stagger to a halt, turn around, wide-eyed, to see the nothing that was behind him, and come to realise, with a shock parallel to grief, that there had never been any echo, only the sound of another man's solitary voice unanswered by the same lack.

'Angel!'

The communal building was illuminated from inside. Light poured out in a long rhombus shape that almost stretched as far as Flores, making everything else in the plaza seem much darker. Then the long shadow of a behatted man cast itself across the length of the plaza, its head alone the length of two men, and Flores followed it with his eyes and saw the broad spectre narrow like a funnel until it joined the feet of a form standing in the entrance of the communal building.

'Angel!'

It was Camacho, wearing a tricorne. He leant against the entrance in the pose of a waif, legs crossed one over the other, hands joined over the belly, shockingly diminutive atop the awesomeness of his own projection, and yet he was the master of all the shaded forms that staggered and screamed in fruitless hunt through the fall of night, his doleful oval of a face surveying it all.

'Angel!'

Some pale body passed by, heading in the direction of the communal building, and then a drunken sailor obscured Flores's view momentarily, and when the sailor passed out of his line of vision, Flores saw the person had gone behind the communal building and disappeared into the forest.

'Angel?' Flores said. 'Is that you, Angel?'

He stumbled jerkily across the plaza with the sloppy, imprecise motions available to his limbs, and pushed into the forest, past crowding leaves and brush until everything around him was rustling, cobwebbed darkness.

'Angel?'

A finger reached down and caressed wetly his cheek. Flores threw himself to the ground, but then nothing more touched him, and he flipped onto his back. The leafy ceiling was a lower, closed-off sky whispering at him, the false impression of some leaning bush that ranged out and looked like treetops from where he lay. Within this bush grew a white tree, its bark bearing the consistency of diseased flesh gone livid. Silvery hoods and collapsed pockets of fresh spiderwebs wove the lower branches together; the higher limbs were sleeved with spoiled wedding veils of the stuff. Two black vines, come undone with some breeze, crossed and uncrossed over each other like pendulums; it was one of these that had touched his face, and, between them, but higher up, waited a brief rope, its end terminating in a loop. On tiptoes, Flores managed to touch it, and he found it had no give. It had not been tied with a hangman's knot, but a Boling knot – a sailor's knot. Someone had died here, Flores knew; and someone else had lately removed the body.

Spectral hush engulfed the town. Angel was no longer called after. The only movement was a small fire beside which Quentin Cricklow perched under the tree, his chin resting on his fist, light bouncing against his sodden features. He stared pensively into the flames, his shadow guttering behind him.

Flores went towards him, but came to a stop when the front of the communal building slid into view. There, in immaculate quiet, partitioned amongst themselves by the single strip of light irradiating from the interior, knelt forty-odd sailors assembled in a few arcing rows. They were praying; their hands drawn together, their eyes closed, their silence so forceful that Flores felt he had stumbled across an exposed crypt.

He walked through the rows of praying sailors, until a rope-toughed gnarl of hand took him by the wrist; it was Marianne Lynch. Flores pulled uselessly against the grip, but the Irishman only raised a forefinger to his lips. Rising, he led Flores beyond the sailors, until they were out of earshot.

'You would put yourself between a man and his grief?' Lynch whispered. 'You are mad to do it. Leave now – go south.'

They were closer to Cricklow now. He was still hunched over, a black silhouette against the small fire. Detached from the greater body of the sailors, he seemed like a lonesome raft cut loose, drifting beyond its mothership, unheeded signal shining. He turned his face towards them and Flores saw he was covered in blood; his hair was a thick, dripping mat, his face a black stain against the push of flames.

'Why is that man covered in blood?'

'You are free,' Lynch said. 'No one will remember you. Go now.'

'Someone was hanged over yonder, and now that man is covered in blood.'

'Them who hang themselves are none of your concern. Are you listening to me?'

'Whose is the blood?'

'Attention, Flores. Pay me mind. Our discussion is no trifle.'

By the entrance of the communal building, Camacho crossed himself and got to his feet, his face emerging into the light as he did so.

'Get in there, ye good men of the *Atlas*,' he said, 'and upturn every last cell until we have found our innocent Angel.'

The sailors crossed themselves and arose. Flores felt a slight breath on his fingers; the white dog was sitting next to him, its belly and hindlegs coated with spasms of congealed soil. In a languorous swipe it licked at his wrist, and then Lynch slapped Flores across the face.

'Attention, Flores,' he said.

Without thought, Flores punched Lynch in the mouth, setting the man stumbling backwards. Flores's hands tingled with the aftershock of the blow, his whole body suddenly alive with a magnificent electricity.

Lynch stretched out his jaw a few times.

'You are like a bitch in heat for death,' he said, 'but I won't do it.'

Two sailors had come out of the communal building. One carried a sack, and waited by the entrance, while the other, Fuchs, moved amongst the men, handing out the torches he had spent the evening constructing. The sailors, on receiving these, went over to Cricklow's fire, setting them alight, and then filed into the communal building, taking objects of glistening silver out of the sack as they passed by, the guns and cutlasses lapping reflectively beneath the proliferating flames.

'What nightmare have you concocted up?' Flores said.

'Will you not go?'

'What is this mischief?'

Lynch grabbed Flores by his ears, pulled his head down so he was doubled over and then, with a brief pulse, kneed him full in the face. A crack of bone snapped within Flores's skull, followed by a huge trembling of fluids gurgling above the roof of his mouth. He heard many tiny vessels drip inside him, an enormous scraping of cartilage like the calving of a glacier, but it was a hearing of himself from within, bypassing the ears entirely, and for some time this dark crashing inside his face was all he knew.

Voices jostled above, thrown back and forth as though carried by floating ships. Liquids unclenched inside his skull. Forced to the ground, he opened his eyes and Lynch towered there, the underside of his chin shading him from the sky like a summer tree; the crooked nostrils like two misshapen lungs, dilating in and out, the globular curve of the white sclera. The man seemed very far away, on another plane of existence from the jolting bones that moaned under Flores's own sight.

'Stay down,' Lynch said.

Flores drew in a breath that set off a snagging click behind his nose, and he knew if he didn't turn over he would suffocate. He tried to push himself up, but Lynch planted a boot on his chest.

'Stay down, I said.'

Arching his neck back, Flores saw the world upside down – a slim strip suspended above nothing, a flimsy material floating against a fantastical void, and in the inverted world he saw Marianne Lynch striding away to join the procession of men who held torches and who hurled themselves one by one into the open jaws of a flaming mouth, and then Flores was drowning in himself.

In this pulsing and surrendering darkness, he was rolled onto his side, his nostrils were cleared, his back was struck forcefully and blood poured out of his mouth and nose, some fluttering in tears out of his closed eyes, decompressing slightly the torturous press in his skull. Still, there remained some fragmented blockage in the space above his mouth, and he coughed with his mouth closed a vital, focused breath, expelling the burning element from his flattened nostril. He gasped, and the world unblurred. Drooling, he felt his own face – the smashed nose; the clicking cheekbone, the canyon-like ridges under his eyes. Next to him lay the substance that had almost killed him; an unthreatening sliver the breadth of a fingernail, a shining chip of tiny bone glazed in a light patina of blood.

He looked down at it. Whatever had been taken from him, he had remained whole. However they had disfigured him, he had remained intact. There were no secrets left in the universe, nothing hidden in the coming devastation.

———◆———

The swooping arcs of torches undid and remade shadows, illuminating an orblike tableau vivant on whose tenebrous verge Flores found himself. A yellow halo spun around a swirling procession of sailors who grasped at each other in comfortless torment – all else in the interior's purlieu was unseen – and at the very heart of all this light was the corpse of Jacques, the cabin boy, held up on one side by the bloody Cricklow, and on the other by Fuchs. The sailors hovered around the remains, a writhing jumble of backs.

'We have found Angel,' Cricklow said. 'The only innocent is gone.'

'Alack,' Fuchs said. 'Alack, that there be such villains in the universe, such demons in the forest, such sinners in my father's house. He prayed for us, and now he is gone.'

'The friend,' Hieronimo cried. 'The friend depart.'

He stumbled towards the body, flailing his torch so wildly that his own eyebrows started smoking, and Marianne Lynch pushed him away, and approached the corpse himself.

'O, my Angel,' he said. 'Is it because you loved God too much? They could not stand it! O, if only these sweet lips could tell one last secret! Who has done this to you?'

He planted a kiss on Jacques's lips so firm that it sent his head lolling back, showing a slight, discoloured indentation coiled around the neck.

'Hark!' Lynch said. 'What is this I espy?'

He squeezed Jacques's cheeks, pinched the lips ajar, snuck in his fingers into the mouth and pulled out a pink flower. He held it up for all the sailors to see.

'Why, I were given a pink flower just like that one the other day,' Cricklow said.

128

Lynch threw his head back, his gestures huge and lurid, and his eyes, in the play of torchlight, became pockets of shadow.

'By whom,' he bellowed, 'was such a little pink flower given?'

'By them as what is above us, I'd hazard, Mister Lynch,' Cricklow returned. 'It was them Indians what done our boy, Mr Lynch. They done him as he was a little doggy what needed drowning, la.'

The crew collapsed into a renewed tremor of moaning, hand wringing, terrified crying, cursing and cowering. There was to all this some obscene funerary theatricality, but it was overpowered by the obsessional nature of the mob who flustered raptly within the scene, and Flores understood, then, that though the lie was staggering, the fear, somehow, was real.

'And I know wherefore,' a voice called out from above.

Scores of eyes turned upwards, searching out, to no avail, the source, and Flores looked up too, into the darkness of the ceiling, past the long, dancing shadows the torches cast, past the shaded forms of the townspeople watching him from above. Confused, expectant faces stretched out along stacked corridors: mothers held children in their arms; men spoke to one another in quiet tones. Flores, seeing them, like this, on high, felt fully the vastness of the gulf between himself and them, the impossibility of its interpretation – and then Camacho stepped out of the shadows of a corner cell on the second floor, holding a large urn against his chest.

He descended the stairs, and went around, from sailor to sailor, showing each man the contents of the urn. One by one, they peeked inside, blanched, turned away. Eventually, he came round to Flores who saw therein a slender white foot, cut off above the ankle, the toes lost in pink petals; and within the dark half of the urn, buried deep in flowers, glinted out a little metallic shine.

'Whose foot is that?'

'Look you down, Mr Lynch.'

The Irishman dropped to his knees, examining Jacques's corpse from below. He harrumphed loudly, squeezed a trouser leg together, and then peeked into the empty socket.

'Angel's foot is missing!'

Camacho plunged his arm into the urn and picked out one of the pink flowers; Lynch stood and held up the one he had taken from Jacques's mouth.

'Why, bedad, they are the same flower.'

All the sailors gasped, several yelled; Hieronimo fell into a faint, and was caught by another sailor; sobbing and moaning grew everywhere audible.

Camacho placed the urn on the ground.

'It is decided then,' he said, 'the Indians murdered Angel so as to cannibalise him. Cannibals every last one, murderers all. We must save ourselves. There is no choice.'

In the furore that followed this accusation, ecstasy engulfed Flores, and he could feel the violence opening up, and him at its very heart. They were liars all, convincing each other of their awful necessity, and he was their most vital part, that which they would never be free of – the truth of themselves. They would kill him for it, and he would have, at the last moment, his rhapsody and his righteousness; his suffering; then, would be no more.

'Liars!' Flores called. 'Liars!' shouting it again. 'Liars!'

He called it until they all heeded him.

'Such lies!' he said. 'Every man a liar! The body is not Angel's; it is Jacques's – he was hanged in the forest, and you have trifled with the lad's remains . . . It is not Angel, I tell you, and I tell you that you know this already. No. You, of the *Atlas*, have no cause for vengeance. There has been no murder done here, none beyond your own machinations, your own slave-driving. You are the murderers. You. You. You. Murderers, every last one.'

Amidst the blended commotion of the crew's faces, one single visage was unmoving – it was Lynch, staring at him.

'Whose body, then, Flores?' he said.

'Jacques's body,' Flores said, 'and that man' – he pointed at Cricklow – 'hacked it up. Look – he is besmirched in the blood of the mutilation even now.'

In response, Cricklow shook his head vociferously, the sprayed drops of blood setting Fuchs beside him blinking.

'Marry, I do not know him.'

'Me neither.'

'Nor I.'

'Who is Jacques?' Camacho asked.

'And why would we do it?' Lynch asked.

'I do not know why,' Flores said. 'I only know it is.'

'Who are you to question thusly our grief and our terror?' Lynch said. 'To come between us and our love?'

'I am your witness,' Flores said.

'You are my witness, yes?'

'I am your witness, yes. Your love is a lie. Your passion is a play. You only seek an innocent man to make a guilty one thereafter. You are the guilt you seek. You possess a nightmare in you, and you say it is the reality of another man, but what you may hide from yourselves you will not hide from me . . . I saw murder – I see it still. Will you stop? Will you ever just—'

'Hush,' Camacho said, tapping the urn with his foot, setting a few petals drifting out. 'This is my Angel.'

'I love Angel,' Hieronimo said. 'Am infirm with the love.'

'They are cannibals that took our Angel,' Cricklow said. 'Wild men as would eat us in our sleeps. Savages. Cannibals. Silent watchers.'

'And we will have our loving vengeance,' Lynch said.

There was nothing more to say, nothing more to contend with. He had spoken so much and nothing had been heard.

'Look at the Moor; look at how calm he is,' Camacho said. 'His face is all stove in, and still no tears shine forth. Cold, cruel and uncaring, untouched by love, you are, Flores. Why don't you mourn our Angel?'

All the sailors' eyes were trained on Flores in a glimmering conglomeration of tears. There were so many eyes; they crowded around him, overwhelming him, closing in. He wondered how long they had been coming closer, and he looked away to free himself from the sight of them, and saw, far apart, Lafcadio over by the wall, facing inward, crumpled and strewn like a tossed doll, but Flores did not want to see this in his last moments so he looked up and saw through the circular dome of skylight that some of the endless cloud had come undone. Several stars – five, six, seven – he lost count. They were always there, always waiting.

Camacho knelt down, plunged one hand into the urn, grasping for something hidden, and Lynch seeing this, put himself between the Valencian and Flores.

'You are the witness, yes?'

Through their tears, the crew started jeering. Hieronimo kicked his shin, and another sailor sent a stray punch grazing across his ear. Flores tripped and fell but managed to scramble up to his feet again.

'Will you ever stop—'

Lynch broke through the sailors and went to hold Flores in an embrace, but before he could surround him entirely, Flores rose up his hands against him and pushed him away.

'Will you—' he said, and then his head was whipped back, and above him, like a bolt of lightning, came the flash of the razor. A pinch shuddered through his right eyelid, and then Marianne Lynch was so close and so bright. Flores grabbed his own caved-in face, felt wetness there – a single spurt of warm fluid pulsed against his palm.

'Are you bearing witness yet?'

Lynch brushed Flores's hand away from the leaking socket and kissed his forehead. Flores broke away; staggered a few steps towards the entrance, and then turned back to see that between Lynch's fingers dangled a bloody stem from which his right eye was swinging. The eye was mostly hidden, nearly entirely enclosed within a shield of pink flesh like the sepal covering of a budding flower.

'Will you ever stop murdering my mother?'

Flores wheeled out into the night.

———•———

Smoke interrupted Lafcadio's breathing, and he was revived into some close pandemonium. The pain in his gut was gone, the massacre long begun, and in the fiery surroundings he felt a momentary abeyance.

'Jacques,' he called. 'Minhas pistolas.'

Tumescent clouds, all brilliantly white, floated near his face. A sailor rolled by, locked in battle with a corpse whom he kept stabbing in the chest with a knife.

'Attention,' Lafcadio said.

The sailor's face looked over the shoulder of the corpse he embraced. 'Captain?' he said.

'Where is Jacques?'

'Gone, sir.'

'Are many gone?'

'I couldn't say, sir.'

'Bring me my box of good pistols. On the first floor, in the left-hand cell nearest the stair.'

'Ay, captain.'

The sailor pushed the body off himself, and disappeared, running headlong into a tumbling wave of smoke. Lafcadio hobbled after, but when he passed through the veil, he found himself entirely lost in more smouldering clouds. He followed some brightness until he came to a fire around which three men hunched, warming their hands. Coming closer, he saw that his eyes had deceived him – Fuchs was pinning down a townsman, covering his mouth with his fist, while another sailor sat on the man's chest, holding his legs like tongs so as to roast his feet over the flames.

Lafcadio passed by and came to a wall along which splatters of viscera clung. From each smudge trailed red drops that pointed down to a prostrate body lying with arms outstretched as though in worship of the patterns that had emerged from their own flesh. He walked by the row of corpses, all executed with cutlasses or guns, the stench of gunpowder pinching his eyes, until he came to a corner and saw that no matter how far he went the bodies would stretch across an endless border. In death, the townspeople had become more similar – the clothes plain, and modest; no paints on their features anymore, both men and women wearing the same shoulder-length haircut. The dead were mainly adults, but there was the occasional child.

Gunfire sounded from somewhere. It was becoming even more difficult to breathe, and visibility had diminished to almost nothing. He made his way back towards the dampened glow and saw the tortured townsman was face down now, his face invisible under his black hair, his lower half alive with blue flames. The sailors were gone save one, who lay on his side, legs crossed at an angle of repose, holding something in his arms. It was the one he had sent upstairs, dead from a deep wound across the neck; he was holding yet the box. Lafcadio used his crutch to tap it away from him and saw its latch had split in his fall. Kicking it open, he found the pistols, perfectly laid out and intact, both still loaded from the aborted duel two nights ago. He cast aside his crutches and took up the pistols, but with all this sudden motion his stomach muscles yawned in a rictus of pain. The tearing feeling permeated the flagging matrix of his core, each fragment of bullet within seeming as huge and alive as any organ, and he screamed, and his screaming called forth some hidden person. Footsteps clambered down; he could hear them, and this put him immediately in his whereabouts. The stairs were just behind him; the entrance a little to the left, no more than ten paces away.

'Stop,' he called, 'or I will be forced to shoot.'

The sound of shuffling feet was almost above his head now. A wreath of smoke drifted into his mouth, and everything seemed very close to his face. Then, another blast of smoke billowed down, shrouding entirely whoever was there, and the footsteps were so near he was certain he would be trampled. He raised a pistol upwards, and fired, as, clenching his teeth, he charged towards the entrance – and found himself on his back.

He had almost knocked himself out, and through his dizziness, realised the entrance had been behind him, and he had run head-first into the side of the stairs. He went to stand up, and tripped over, collapsing face down into a burning stair. It was his own wrap, come undone and slick with matter, that had tripped him. The whole building was crashing down, and it was something fundamental to his own bodily structure, too, he felt. Searing annihilation before him, he lurched away in fear, but the illumination remained no matter where he turned. Trapped inside white light, he was spewed forth into the night, his beard on fire; his head become a beacon to the world. Screaming, he tripped face first into muck, extinguishing himself in the earth. Then he plastered his face in pale muck to better cool himself, but when he touched his cheeks sheaths of flesh fell away, so hot they burnt his fingertips, sticking to his hands like viscous liquid; his beard, too, came away in a foul-smelling ash, oily and seeping. The wrap was also on fire, burning down in cinders from its end, so he undid it and cast it away, exposing his distended belly to the air. Even the breeze was hot, and it was only then he realised that he had made it outside.

He sat there, his legs splayed out wide, looking through his blister of tears into a night that possessed the luminance of an overcast morning. The communal building roared behind him, its heat pushing forcefully against his back. The space he had escaped into was yet another pandemonium, only more visible in its hellish constituents, and Lafcadio, his flesh smoking, watched it all in a listless stupor. Three sailors crowded over a fallen woman; all covered in soot and sweat, they flopped against each other like some strange multiheaded beast; another woman limped in the same spot, the continuous motion of her arms and legs getting her nowhere as a sailor held her ankles; at the door of one of the little buildings, a strange, white dog was raised on its hindlegs and clawing with unrelenting motion, as next to it, Hieronimo, one eye closed, was attempting to light some damp kindling – but all this was peripheral to the obscene circumambulation that took up the majority of the plaza where about thirty townspeople had been corralled together and forced to run in a continuous circle while sailors shot into their number with pistols and blunderbusses, never allowing them to slow, forcing them to trample over the fallen.

A ball of burning flames flew across the sky, too low and too close to be a comet. Lafcadio looked behind himself at the communal building and saw another fiery ball fly out of the skylight, straight up into the night. It spiralled down, a thing of shrieking flames, and landed in his lap. It was a pigeon, its eyes open, its head a burning crown.

'A phoenix, sir, but even phoenixes are brief, at the last.'

Lafcadio threw his eyes up. Marianne Lynch was above him, pensively gazing up at the blur of thinly veiled moon while he smoked his pipe.

'Where is Camacho?' Lafcadio croaked, some skin on his lips coming away on his tongue.

'By the tree. I will take you there.'

He hauled Lafcadio to his feet and led him by the hand around the edge of the plaza – around the shuffling circumambulation and by the whistling, shrieking forest in avian uproar at this false morning arrived at night, and then a townsman broke free from the circle, feinted his way past a sailor wildly swinging his cutlass; kicked another in the belly, and disappeared into the forest.

'That is only the fourteenth one as has gotten away by my count,' Lynch said.

'Why don't they resist?'

'Hostages. Their children, of course.'

They moved on in silence until the tree came into view; the captain recognised it as the same one he had spent the previous night passed out beneath, but now it was utterly transformed. Thick white leaves fluttered at him like a thousand, winking eyes, and on the lowest bough an elderly man had been hanged upside down, stripped naked and castrated, his hands trailing in the dirt. Lafcadio recognised him, beyond the transfigured features of death, as the king, Iaen; and directly underneath him a pregnant young woman lay dead on her back, splayed across the ashes of last night's fire, a cut through her belly.

Cricklow stood by the tree, too, red-faced and holding a blood-ied razor in one hand and a pistol in the other, discussing something with Camacho, who was holding some kind of a jug in front of him.

'O, la,' Cricklow said, ''tis the captain, blonde hair burnt black as an Ethiope's – and you was once so handsome.' He tapped the cross on his own forehead with the tip of the razor. 'I confess the bursting of thy phiz has rendered me passing whole again. O, la!'

He approached Lafcadio, searching around in his pocket, and then showed him something in his hand.

'I'n't I done well by our innocent Angel, sir? I shall shave it, and I shall cure it and I shall employ it for the holding of my tobacco, I thinks. 'Tis not thick enough for coins; I'll needs harvest a womb or a face for that, sir.'

Lafcadio looked away from it while pointing the two pistols at Cricklow's middle.

'Get him gone, Mr Lynch.'

There was no response; he tried not to look behind himself.

'Lynch ain't with you no more, sir.'

Lafcadio tried to gather his concentration on Camacho rather than getting lost in the stark horror of the tree, and then a burnt eyelash drifted into his eye, cutting his vision in twain. In his sight, Camacho and the dead woman were to the right of his eyelash and Cricklow and Iaen were to the left.

'Does you like my Christmas tree, sir?'

'Get you gone, Quentin. You are a saucy article, but not the villain for me this night.'

Cricklow looked to Camacho, who nodded, and in response, Cricklow shrugged, and left. Now only Lafcadio remained by the leafy end of the low bough, and Camacho by the trunk.

'You will never be a true captain,' Lafcadio said, rubbing the eyelash away with his thumb so as to unify his vision. 'Listen to me, Camacho, you have no authority; you are not a man; you have not even that authority which is proper to a boy. You are a primped corsair, a cunny-faced trout, a moaning, loathsome bitch-child. Will you answer me, little dog?'

Camacho's nostrils flared slightly, but he said nothing. Lafcadio raised up the pistols as much as he was able, letting them dangle by their trigger guards.

'We are to duel, Camacho, though I know your cowardice rejects it. Twelve paces, no seconds, one shot, placed upon by chance. I have two pistols here, one spent, one loaded. You may choose, without foreknowledge, the one you prefer – the one in my left hand, or the one in my right hand? Come now, bitch. For my part, if I chance upon the empty one I will walk through your bullets once more and stove your face in with my open palms, and then I will load it with these fragments you have left in me, and—'

Camacho put his left hand in the jug, withdrew a small pistol from it and shot Lafcadio in the chest; the captain fell on his back, still seeing the flash of white exploding from the muzzle. The world was spinning, and then he realised that it was only Iaen's body turning gently above him.

'That that would stopper up his long-talking mouth,' Camacho said. 'And would that I had gotten him in the chest the first time.'

'Marry, the gut-shot will end most in a day, sir,' Cricklow said, somewhere nearby. 'Indeed, he were an hardy one.'

There was something up in the tree, only visible from Lafcadio's vantage on the ground. High up, amidst shivering leaves, was a young girl, the blackened soles of her feet dangling over the edge of a huge branch. She held a man's head in her lap. It was Flores, draped out along the bough, his legs folded underneath him, his arms supple and lifeless, and then, suddenly, the leaves and the tree, the body, the night sky, it all disappeared – two men loomed above, throwing dense shadows on him.

'Anyone but you,' Lafcadio whispered.

'What did you say?'

'I believe what he said, sir, is, "Ga ga ga."'

Cricklow hunched down over the captain's body and disappeared below his line of view.

'What on earth are you doing?'

There was a scraping sound of metal off metal, and then a pop. From the sounds Lafcadio realised parts of him were bursting open, but it was not his body anymore; he felt nothing.

'I likes to have keepsakes.'

He was rooting around in his belly, searching with his razor, and Lafcadio tried to raise his head so as to see, but he felt too dizzy.

'Qué olor!' Camacho recoiled, covering his face with his sleeve. 'Stop it, Quentin. It is too disgusting. What is that? Such blue accumulations inside a person . . . How is it possible he lives?'

'Almost finished,' Cricklow said, wedging another fragment out of the captain's belly with the edge of the razor. 'Marry, he were all bunged up, and now he's leaking out and getting all trim again.'

Cricklow's leering head emerged into Lafcadio's view like the moon rising up over the horizon. He wiped one of the bullet fragments on his shirt and then put it before Lafcadio's eyes. 'See, captain, your body polished them,' he said. 'You are an oyster to make such pearls. La, how you made them shine . . . Here, Mr Camacho, will you have one?'

'No. Get off him. Give me that.'

The horror of his own men scavenging over his motionless body was too much for Lafcadio to bear. He wanted to see the little girl and Flores together in the tree one last time, but he was afraid the two sailors might follow his gaze and find them. With his last smattering of will, he jerked his neck away to look at the dead woman, and he saw, in the midpoint between them, a snail on whose brown shell the moonlight was reflected in a glistening swirl.

'We will make sure of him this time.'

A shadow confiscated the glimmer of the shell; Camcho's flat, warped face, instead, loomed there, growing ever larger in the twisted whorl as he kneeled down over him.

Three sawing motions of the razor sufficed to open the captain's windpipe.

———◆———

The fire bloomed so high it licked away the threads of cloud, at last unravelling them until it revealed the full moon. Flores stared at the exposed orb, sweating profusely with the rising waves of heat, and hearing inside his own skull the dripping formation of a tiny lake of blood. He found the lapping sound in his socket curious only; he was without pain now, only called back into his body by the intermittent itchiness of his torn eyelid, and Esa's fingers, warm and damp against his scalp.

When the communal building collapsed embers splashed across the plaza, the destructive orange thrum still persisting inside the wooden fragments that had spiralled across the earth in strange, unreadable patterns. Camacho and Cricklow had long since abandoned the base of the tree, but Flores still sensed motion below, and, even in this newer darkness, he was too wary to descend. Eventually, Esa touched his cheek, and gestured towards the forest. He rose up from her lap and a small pool of blood spilled out of his face, and, immediately, he was back in the entrapping horror of his own body, hearing again the thin edge of Lynch's razor scrape against his cheekbone, the deafening snap that had resounded inside his face. Blood dripped down his cheek and into the hollows behind his clavicles, but he slowed his breath and ignored it, beginning to climb down, helping Esa where he could. Once the foliage had thinned out beneath him, he realised that the motion he had sensed from above was the swaying of hanged bodies, the heated air ruffling their hair and billowing their clothes. Finally, he leapt to the ground, and asked Esa, with a whisper, to jump down into his arms, and he caught her. He led her away from the tree, through Lafcadio and Iaen, beyond the body of Suya, both his hands draped over her face so she wouldn't see.

The silhouettes of men in the plaza were dotted amongst the embers like tall charcoal ghosts. They had begun drinking again, waiting for the heat to fall away, stacking the cooler bodies that had perished along the periphery of the town. Some sailors had fallen asleep on their feet, exhausted; others were dragging what objects they had plundered to hidden places. Voices, slurred and indiscernible, called to one another; a solitary laugh sounded out. Flores moved towards the oceanic breeze breathing from the dark insides of the forest, relishing the touch of it against his skin, shocked at how much cooler it was on the ground than it had been in the tree. For the first time, he wondered how he had found himself up there, and then someone grabbed his throat from behind.

Esa broke away, and Flores wrestled against the unseen hands; they were not strong. He spun around to see Hieronimo, holding a bottle in one hand and a pistol by the barrel in the other.

'Die anymore,' he said. 'The dead is a crowding place. What if am die and have to only me? What, then? Entonces, the person who arrive the last take him, who signify the Brazil is mine at the arrival, but the infierno is also of me . . . Please, for favour me. Flores, kill my head.'

He offered the gun to Flores, who took it, and began to back away. Hieronimo took a drink. His hands were covered in burns; his whole right arm was a raised sheath of pink, shining blister, almost double its original size. Then the chef slouched forward, baffled; he burped once.

'Here is come all who I am.'

Looking directly at Flores, Hieronimo started silently vomiting a black liquid out of his mouth that was neither blood nor bile. He fell to his knees, getting sick in long, uninterrupted heaves; it was a glistening substance of the likes Flores had never seen before, and there was so much of it that it was inconceivable such a small man could contain so much endless flow.

'Jesus, no,' Hieronimo spluttered. 'Dios lo quiera, no.'

A popping sound gurgled within his nostrils, and then the stuff started leaking out of his nose, too, but his tearful gaze on Flores remained lucid. Transfixed, Flores went towards him to lay him on his side and clear his orifices so he wouldn't choke on himself, but then he felt Esa tugging at his arm, dragging at him, and he followed her into the forest.

———— ·•· ————

Shadowy growths rumbled in the treetops where a plethora of terrified birds were hidden, squawking and twittering within; the moon flitted behind leaves as they sped by; a troop of squat, nocturnal apes with lugubrious countenances trailed after them, eventually halting at a weblike tree, as if held there by unspoken treaty. The cold of the night had robbed the forest of its mulchy confluence of scents, cloaking them within the neutralising chill of the ever-falling dew.

They came to a large, perfectly circular clearing whose floor was laid with cut, polished stones so clear Flores could see his own form faintly reflected thereon. The black stones were laid out in some vast, curving pattern. He tried to imagine the design from its parts, but its surface was too broad and he was too close; such an arrangement could only ever be discernible from above, with the eye of some impossible God. Within the forest on the far side of the clearing, a long train of yellow light moved, like the crawling of some giant luminescent centipede.

Two ponytailed men appeared beneath one of the ancient trees at the edge of the clearing. One ran ahead, scanned around, then shouted something in Mandarin to his companion, and, together, they dropped back into the forest again. Soon, the caravan of light changed direction and began bearing down on the clearing. Flores found a narrow hollow beneath one of the black stones where he and Esa concealed themselves.

First, path-clearers came, bent over and swinging machetes in low arcs against the undergrowth. They wore black knee-length robes and sported braided ponytails beneath conical hats; in their waistbands were tied long bamboo sticks off which lanterns hung that bobbed, making it look like they were fishing in the undergrowth with lures of light. Following these, like some sombre masque, came a parade of several hundred men carrying long lengths of timber on their shoulders; barrels full of tools on poles; sacks of rice and maize across their backs; fattened by huge coils of rope wound around their waists, all flanked by lantern-carriers. In the very midst of all this was a plush, curtained litter of a lavender colour, borne on the shoulders of four shirtless men. Around this litter, two European dandies ambled. They were almost physically identical, but of various ages, like two fruits stretched along a bough in assorted stages of ripeness. Both wore broadbrimmed hats, sported waxed moustaches, large signet rings, and each bore a cane. Their coats, though, were of different colours, their collars of different sizes, their signets different designs, and the handles of their canes were each carved into a different species of bird. This litter, the centrepiece of the caravan, was followed again by another hundred labourers, and the occasional foreman who yelled out brusque orders and encouragements. Finally, bringing up the rear, came a pack of long-toothed burros, laden with fresh water, all of whom passively accepted constant prodding and harassment with nothing but the melancholic protest of their tails, save one enraged yearling who clicked disappointed bites out at all who passed.

A child smoking a thin bone pipe emerged from the purple curtain of the litter and spoke to the eldest dandy. The man listened, nodded, and then called a single syllable that was passed up and down the line, and the entire lumbering caravan came rocking to a halt. The litter now sat in the centre of the circular clearing. The man tapped his cane, whose handle was in the form of a phoenix, up to the litter, and waited beneath the curtain.

'An unreasonable proposition, momma,' he said. 'I can brook no more tarrying. If these Chinamen get time to fill up their pipes that's the night's work gone. Tell me what I am to do with two hundred sleepy Chinamen in a forest come midnight? We keep moving.'

A crooked finger emerged through the curtain, pointing at the stone beneath which Flores and Esa were hidden.

'So I am to be responsible for every sparrow that falls?'

There was a pause. The path-clearers, unnecessary in this open space, were speaking in hushed tones, laughing amongst themselves. One of the men behind the litter carrying rope around his waist sat down and began tamping a long pipe; three other men bearing barrels on their backs undid each other's straps and stretched out their limbs, massaging one another's necks and shoulders; a few lantern-carriers trailed back towards the end of the caravan and crowded around the burros, drenching them in glaring light which set them neighing as they dipped ladles into the water and drank from them. A foreman went around offering diced coca leaves from an open bag.

Then Chuck Benjamin struck his cane down against a stone, and a clipped noise rang out across the clearing, giving back one single echo and stopping all chat and movement, save the discreet chewing of mouths.

'I shall send Lee out since you insist upon it,' he said.

The child, pipe in mouth, bounded ably across the black stones until he was standing directly above Flores and Esa. He knelt down, waved at Esa, and then saw Flores's face and grimaced, sticking his tongue out in disgust.

'Well?' Benjamin called. 'What is it, boy?'

Xiaoguang Lee winked at Esa, cocked the pipe in his mouth. 'Two little monkey, Mr Benjamin,' he shouted back. 'They dying. Very sad, Mr Benjamin. Very sad.'

The purple curtain ruffled. Chuck Benjamin raised his cane and waved it. The caravan began picking itself up, lurching and struggling forward once more. Men helped one another to their feet; the lantern-carriers sloshed water in their mouths, spat balls of coca out, trotted back into place around the flanks – all slunk forward as one.

As the convulsive, flicking tails of the last burros disappeared into the forest, and the moon's reflection was the sole light left on the clearing, Flores looked towards Esa and saw her moonlit face glossed by tears. He led her by the hand, and they followed the cut and beaten path the caravan had left in its wake, Flores feeling beneath the huge trees like an insect beneath a blade of grass. They skirted around the mountain, and then Flores abandoned the trail the caravan had hacked out, not wanting to arrive at the place from where it had come, and they continued on, holding hands.

All night came unfamiliar sights half-submerged in the living forest like sunken ships, fragments hinting towards a vast civilisation now cloaked in the green monotony of proliferate destruction. Once they chanced upon an overgrown town, every stone of which was clothed in mosses and grasses, making the entire purlieu look like a huge, urban plant, soft and gentle. Trees grew through roofs and skylights; ruddy stalks cracked open cut stone; maize grew sporadically across flowery roads, all of it swallowed up in the forest's afterthought, merging wordlessly with leafy darkness. Later they climbed over a toppled lookout tower that if standing would have been taller than any structure Flores had ever seen, and near midnight, they chanced upon a statue of a fire-breathing man with insane, bulging eyes sitting on a throne amidst some marshy trees wrapped with rotting vines. Flores stared at it, and then he fell down into a faint. Esa tried to gather him up, but she was too exhausted, as well, and she sat down next to him.

When he came to, his head was in her lap once more. He felt a hot pain in the very core of his missing eye, and the night breeze murmuring deep inside his face, deeper than it had ever been, and he grew afraid again of his own body. Once the humming sound behind his frantic breath had relented, he began to hear the sparkling babbling of water close by.

They rose and followed the sound of water until they came upon a lagoon shaped like a stream, but it was not the water they had heard. The water before them was too silent to drink; a fetid steam of decay curved off the banks. He couldn't even hear any creatures moving on its surface. They went along this stagnant body until it joined up with a small, rushing tributary. Here, Esa knelt and drank while Flores looked around, feeling his way through the undergrowth by touch. There was a static light, dim and singular, hovering behind some brush, too low to be the moon, and he went towards it and found himself suddenly on the edge of a stony bay that stretched out into the distance, where it became wrapped up in a dense, grey fog that had slunk down from some faraway coastal mountains.

The light was coming from a narrow two-storeyed building, solitary and proud against the congeries of rocks. Below it, a small pier jutted into the water, off which three small fishing vessels clacked against wooden fenders, their heavy nets piled so high they peeked over the bulwarks, short masts bare and cruciform, the sails pleated in the bows.

They moved cautiously, tiptoeing now that everything had turned to jagged rock beneath their feet, and as they got closer, they saw the yellow light was a lantern hung under a colonnade around which a vector of flickering moths drifted in a suicidal tornado. As they got closer, the sole window of the building flickered into illumination, too, and a lean African woman appeared holding a candle in her hands, and the unexpected sight sent a sudden gust of gooseflesh blooming across Flores's neck. The woman's hair ran down to her waist, and she wore gold earrings and a cotton dress that left her breasts discernible behind a slight muslin veil. Suddenly, four more women were all jostling for space behind the window, flattening their noses against the glass, their mouths contorted Os of astonishment, trying to catch glimpse of the man and the girl who had stepped out of the midnight forest. A squat Latin woman, who wore a seashell necklace tight around her neck, waved a handkerchief, and then a man within shouted rudely, and the candlelight retreated.

The colonnade was held up by two whitewashed pillars on which some black paint proclaimed crookedly *Taberna y otras*. There was no door, only a hole in the wall that looked like it had been blasted open by a barrage. Batting their way through the storm of moths, Flores and Esa stood on the threshold, blinking in the light, and saw, inside, a single room laid with uneven, long flagstones. Scant illumination came from candles plunged into bottles placed on barrels, and from the bottles where the bunched candlewax hadn't entirely choked the glass, green shadows twisted across the wood. In one corner a spiral staircase ran, and in another sat a square piano missing several white keys. Above a teak cabinet of spirits there was a child's drawing of a smiling cephalopod, done with the same black paint as the clumsy sign on the pillar outside. A red-eyed man – the proprietor, Flores assumed, from the louche authority of his movements – lay on his back across an unvarnished counter; he wore a soiled cravat and a half-buttoned waistcoat over his naked chest. The five whores now pretended to be laconic, disinterested, lounging across a long divan in various poses, legs sprawled out, exposing bloomers and the soles of their sandals. The only customer seemed to be a small silver-haired monkey who sat cross-legged on a stool by the bar, looking around curiously, clutching the neck of a bottle of beer that was almost half the size of its body.

'Boi noite,' Flores said. 'Eu preciso de um doutor.'

The red-eyed man scratched the stubble on his cheeks, and then reached under the counter for a black hat whose crown was rounded with a sash and a gold buckle. He put it on his head, coughed chestily into his cravat.

'Hablen español aquí, degradado.'

'Esto es Brasil, no?'

The man glanced at the monkey and the women, and then burst into a laughter so raucous he had to grip the counter to stop himself from falling to the floor. One of the African women giggled discreetly behind a fan, the only part of her face visible being her shaved scalp and tattooed eyebrows, both ends of which terminated in upward spirals. The monkey bared its fangs at the noise and hugged the bottle closer to its chest; Flores stared at the creature for a moment. In Spanish, he said:

'I know this monkey.'

This renewed the red-eyed man's laughter.

'A friend of yours?'

Flores stepped forward into the light of one of the candles and the man, seeing his broken face, flinched and covered his eyes with the back of his hands.

'I need a doctor,' Flores said, 'and somewhere for the child to sleep.'

He reached into his pockets, took out Hieronimo's pistol, and placed it on the counter.

'I've no money; take this.'

The proprietor peeked at the gun through his fingers, then picked it up, and nodded his head. He took two wooden cups off their nails above the bar, wiped down their rims with his waistcoat, filled them with cachaça and handed one to Flores and one to Esa. Flores drank his off immediately while Esa grimaced and sipped at hers, tears still tumbling silently from her face.

'The doctor might not want to see you.'

'Una más,' Flores answered.

The proprietor, careful not to look at Flores's face again, poured him out another, more liberal measure of cachaça, drinking some directly from the bottle himself. One of the African women stood up and went over to the piano, the fabric of her skirts crinkling audibly. She played three descending keys over and over again. Flores swayed, leant against the counter; he felt very cold.

An angular European woman was kneeling down beside Esa and whispering to her, and Flores felt certain that she was the ugliest woman he had ever seen in his life. She looked like a human-sized rat, rail-thin, tubercular, with a narrow jaw that caved in on itself below the cheekbones, and centring her lengthy face was a pair of huge green eyes that gave her the aspect of one constantly surprised. Her name was Biddy Tanner; she was twenty-three, of Scottish stock, and from one look at her, Flores could tell she would soon be dead.

'Yo los cuidaré,' she said, and the proprietor gave a nod, went behind the counter, pulled open a trapdoor and sank into a cellar below.

Biddy led them up the spiralling wooden stairs into an unlit room with five dishevelled beds. In the one closest the far wall, some sleeping man was hunched up under the covers; the other four were empty. Biddy gave Esa a jar of milk, and then, with a cloth, she washed the child's face, hands and feet and helped her under the covers. Esa accepted all this passively, while in the next bed over, Flores sat, his hands startled by the softness of the sheets, watching tears slip out of the child's closed eyes.

When Biddy was finished with Esa she came over to Flores, looked down at him, and shook her head once. Then she went over to a mirrored dresser on which lay a mess of open ointments; looking glasses; hairbrushes; powders; whiteners; rouges; barrettes; curlers; wigs; eyelashes; ribbons, a candelabra; and there she prepared something for him in a small metal pipe. She lit it, told him to inhale deeply.

'Es tabaco esto?'

'No.'

'Qué es?'

'Ayudará con el dolor.'

He sucked in a profound breath of smoke and felt like he was falling down from a very great height. Biddy Tanner caught him as he fell; covered him up until he didn't exist anymore.

———•·•———

Warm breath fluttered into his open mouth; hands were loosely clasped around his neck; he was splayed out amidst crumpled sheets, dazed among a plentifulness of pillows. For a moment, he

150

remembered nothing, not even his own name. He sat up, dragging a sheet along with him, and found himself wearing a nightshirt that reached down to his knees; the sleeves longer than his arms, hiding his hands. Biddy was asleep beside him, on her side, her legs laid out on top of one another, curled up so that her shift rode up to her waist. The hips tapered down to the knees in a strawberry shape, and pressed between them lay her golden-haired sex, the upper part of the labia dark, compressed and protuberant. It swelled and fell slightly with her breathing, reminding him of something, but he couldn't remember what. Amidst all the warm comfort, a bubble of serenity expanded in his chest as he gazed at Biddy's sex. He stayed staring at it for a long time until he realised that it reminded him of the aperture of a conch.

He got up, swinging his legs over the side of the bed, and saw by his feet a bowl filled with water, tinted pink and vibrating with ripples. Next to it were a few handkerchiefs drenched in blood, scattered across the floor like cast roses, and then he ran both his hands through his hair, and they came in contact with a thick layer of bandages. Under his hands, the face seemed enormous, like it belonged to someone else. He touched the covering over his right eye socket and felt the stitching beneath. The torn eyelid had been sewn together, wefts running so thick across the thin strip of flesh that it was like someone had slipped a coin under his eyelid while he had been sleeping. Then he felt his nose; it had been splinted and wrapped, two holes pierced in the cloth for breathing. He went over to the mirrored dresser and saw that most of the damaged side of his face had been hidden, but along his cheek and chin was a soft, poisoned mark, like a ghost almost finished consuming him. He noticed, in this mirror, that the four other beds were empty.

'Esa?' he said.

There was no answer, and then a small mewling came from somewhere on the floor. He went down on his hands and knees and saw that concealed beneath Biddy's bed were several jars of milk; a faded likeness of Saint Nicholas of Myra; a wooden rosary; a button-eyed doll with hair like seaweed, and a wicker basket. He pulled out the basket and saw nestled within it a jaundiced baby, no more than four months old, its fists clenched tight around its ears. It groaned, and shifted its pose, raising one arm above its head, before relaxing down into sleep again. Gently, Flores pushed the basket back beneath the bed, and made his way down the staircase.

'Esa.'

The tavern was empty, save for the proprietor who slept face down across the counter, one hand under his cheek, the other wrapped around Hieronimo's pistol. The women and the monkey were gone, and the candles on the tables had burnt down to their stubs; dried waterfalls of wax grafted the bottles down to the table, their wicks spent. Out of the little window, Flores saw blue dawn.

'Esa.'

The proprietor stirred and grumbled, and then was still. Flores snuck behind the bar, opened the trapdoor, and looked down into the cellar. No one was hiding there; there wouldn't have even been room enough to stand up if the trapdoor had been closed over. Bottles of spirits lined damp, weed-covered walls, and the floor was heaped high with burlap sacks, one of which lay open, untied. Inside it lay a treasure of delicate black seeds whose shells were ridged with patterns like honeycomb.

'Esa.'

He went outside, and immediately the wind stirred up pleasant gooseflesh across his scalp, neck and bare legs. It blew across the water, swirling dust up around his feet, and making plaintive howling sounds beneath his bandages. Two of the fishing boats were already out in the bay, little white triangles drifting into the purple space over the horizon; the third vessel had just cast off from the pier, and a man was frantically raising the sails, and another, younger man was checking the traps. He tossed one over the side, watched it bubble away, and left a marker there. Then he looked up and waved at Flores.

'Esa.'

Flores went down to the pier, and suddenly he could see the vastness of the earth curve away from him. He called out Esa's name, cupping his hands around his mouth. The sea was darker and calmer further out, but there was, protruding from the near headland, one long stretch of water of a light cyan shade over which breakers angrily toppled. Below the pier was a protective row of big rocks shored up by sand. Water hissed and stirred seaweed as it rushed out from between these large boulders, bursts of froth like rabid mouths sparkling out of the flowing crevices.

'Esa.'

He saw a splintered seashell like a smile, glowing in a little pocket of water in a sandy hollow. The shell was perfectly ribbed, edged with a soft pink rim, and, thinking Esa might like it, he climbed down to get it. As he approached, minute crabs side-stepped under sheaves of seaweed, translucent fleas hopped ahead of him, and a seagull, catching sight of him, spread its wings and, without once beating them, floated away. Flipping over the shell, he saw that its core, where the creature had once lived, was perfectly white polished bone, and its back had the same colour and consistency as the sunrise in front of him. Then he saw another shell nearby, jammed between two open-mouthed mussels, but this shell was spiked and a strange hexagonal pattern ran unevenly across its swirls. Flores rolled up his sleeves and clambered down towards it, balancing between boulders, careful not to slip on the sopping algae that fringed everything, and by the time he had collected this second shell he had already spotted several more. It was a glimmering graveyard of molluscs. He started bowing down and picking them up, one by one, and then some saltwater splashed onto his face, soaking his bandages, and he glanced up just in time to catch sight of a shining jellyfish, the breadth of leviathan, breaching the surface with a pulse of its enormous, bulbous head, effulgent tentacles shimmering bluely after it in a slowly collapsing arc. It crashed down with a surging roar, and began throbbing its way out across the bay, and trailing after it came its innumerable children: a storming bloom of tiny, bubble-like creatures flapping hurriedly against its frothy wake, whitening the ocean with little explosions of propellant motion.

'Esa.'

It was unspeakably magnificent, but it left no trace. The creature and its progeny disappeared beneath the deeper water, the purple drained from the horizon like blood seeping out of a wound, and the listless sun shimmered cold and low in the sky.

'Esa.'

The wind blew higher, and the surface of the ocean became agitated with white scars, but the pressing of the swallowing waves undid each one, remaining forever languorous and calm in effortless immensity. There was a perfect conch by his feet; he picked it up – he wanted to show it to her.

'Esa.'

Flores leapt between the rocks, searching for the girl, glancing every now and again at the path of sunlight dappling the water, wondering why it always seemed to be following him.

'Esa.'

His arms were full of seashells.

Dear pápa,

Are you good ? Me, also, am goode. Thank you very for ask me but the true is that am no very goode. The sister Carmen say me salute Virgen Mary hundreds time for casitgate me for have the bads modals ¡ i hope alone !¿ why i am hurt Pápa ? ¿ why the life so sad ? ¿ why she is no juste ?¿ why am lone in the nigt is long ? ¿ why you no here pápa ? I want see you but alway at Bastaña in writing you estupids libarys. i hate yes . valley, i cry. The noel who come i must take 2 birds beautifuls from you so no am no so sad.

That the LORD bless and guard you, ETERNALLY,
Mlle. BT, &c.

II

Colony

S HE WAS CARRIED through a starless night by her mother. The sound of footsteps padding through sands came from far below. Slant of cheek, vast and pale. The sea that boomed forever. The thrashing darkness. Along a beach, inside the rhythm of panting. An orb of light glowed beyond the quivering spine of wave that separated the land from the ocean. She asked where they were going, and her mother told her not to be afraid.

Hyacinthe stirred, withdrew her hand, and Esa awoke, leaving her eyes closed so as to perpetuate the dream, but it had grown false. The presence was gone – the sea, her mother; none of it remained.

That evening, as she had combed Hyacinthe's hair, she had seen her shoulders rise and fall deeply and she knew her mistress was crying.

'Shall I stay here tonight?'

'Please, Esa.'

She had rolled out a pallet and held Hyacinthe's hand through the curtain of her bed.

'Were I to be Mr Benjamin's first wife rather than his second,' Hyacinthe said, 'it would make life somewhat gentler, I feel. I wonder that his son mightn't be jealous. He is older than me, you know. And I wonder if he is very different from his father.'

They had held hands, and now, awoken from her dream, she saw the hand had withdrawn. She listened. Hyacinthe's breaths behind the curtains of the bed came steady and soft.

She left quietly through the adjoining door into her own room, gathered a brass chamberstick, and carried it out into the corridor. She went down the staircase, steps hushed by carpet, into the main hall of the sleeping mansion where a grandfather clock ticked echoey against the nocturnal quiet, its shaded face reading twenty to four like a pair of whiskers. Then she passed into the kitchens between pots and pans stacked high and topsy-turvy along the counters. By the stove, a brace of doves and a calf leg hung. She put a spill to a half-buried ember and lit the candle, covering it with her palm, and stepped out the back doors.

The darkness was immense. The half-moon rolled between the gentle ridges of the valley where the coffea plants grew. She stepped across the gravel, her bare feet sinking in quick crochets that returned her with a shiver into the dream where her mother with ragged breath had splashed through shallows, and then she passed into the more profound darkness of the arbour and felt beyond the twined stems and flowers to the back of the convex latticework that held up the verdant dome.

Her outstretched fingers at once touched and displaced the message hidden above. Eight years, Lee and her had been exchanging secret correspondence in this manner. The message fell, then hung, twirling, in front of her eyes; he had tied it to an overhanging trellis by a yellow ribbon.

She sat on the teak courting chair and held the candle near the sheet. He had written closely, in their private language, telling her she must immediately stop all preparations for the uprising at Christmas: Señorita Soares had it on good knowledge that a sailor with a cross on his head known to both of them had learned about the arms shipment. It would be resolved within the week. Señor Verato Domingo and Señor Osgood Benjamin were also in agreement. He knew she would be, too.

It was written in a code incomprehensible to any but her, yet she put it to the flame. Orange light flared, wobbling shadows, suddenly large behind the drooping heads of pink flowers and she caught the strips of ash in the saucer and buried the remnants in the soil. With the yellow ribbon, she tied back her hair, then extinguished the candle and stole back inside.

The handle to her room creaked slightly when she opened it.

'Esa.'

Placing the chamberstick on the floor, she wiped her feet and her hands in a bedsheet and opened the adjoining door.

Hyacinthe was sitting up, gauzed behind the mosquito net, her shift melded with the sheets so it seemed her pale face emerged bodiless.

'Where were you?'

'Nowhere.'

'There was a light outside. I was afraid.'

Esa went over and took Hyacinthe's hand between her own.

'I am here,' she said.

'Your hands are cold.'

'I am here,' she repeated. 'Don't be afraid.'

<hr />

In Panama, a giant and drunken whoremaster called Lazar García Higgins mistakenly thought himself cheated out of some cufflinks that his recently deceased mother had given him on his third wedding day. Yi Jeongjo, not hugely taken with the cufflinks, offered them back, but the man waved him away.

'No, no, no,' he said, in Spanish. 'She's already dead.'

'Who?'

'Wait here.'

'Sí, claro.'

The man shambled off, and a little later Jeongjo saw him in the distance returning with a pistol and three muchachos all wielding machetes, so he collected his cards, his Yut sticks and his dominoes, rolled up his straw mat, stacked his wooden cups, recorked the rice wine, slung it all in a sack over his shoulder, and ran back to his lodgings above a haberdashery, where he settled his rent, wrapped up his few possessions into a knapsack, and took the first coach out of the city he could find, casting the cufflinks into the River Chagres.

He had been drifting for some eleven years; had left behind hundreds of cities and towns and had fled from dozens, but he had not wanted to leave Panama, not yet. Despite the floods and the fevers and the wind-haunted houses always collapsing on their rotting stilts, he had loved the city.

One thing, though, he could never fathom was someone who would linger anywhere long enough to get murdered. History, to Jeongjo, was nothing more than the story of people who stayed put a day too long.

———◆———

He travelled for weeks, never stopping anywhere longer than it took to earn passage aboard another southbound coach, afraid to ask his fellow passengers the date lest he find out he had already turned twenty-five somewhere back in the distance without noticing it – and then one morning he was jolted awake as the coach he was riding careened down a hill. He had been sleeping on the roof, wedged in between two lashed-down suitcases, and when he rose, he saw below him a pod of dolphins following a fishing boat, peppering the ocean with their leaps, the sun beyond them rising across the rim of the earth, and a weight that he hadn't known he had possessed lifted from his heart.

The driver bade him good morning and gestured with his whip towards a hilly outcrop of glowing buildings like broken honeycomb in the distance, telling him they were approaching Santa María.

In the markets by the teeming harbour where Jeongjo debarked hawkers cried wares of peeled Yucca; fragrant pastes; roast mice wrapped in perforated leaves; fried lizards skewered on bamboo; faded maps; hemp necklaces; dark varnishes; black tobacco; stone amulets; spiked fruits; cloudy liquors; calf legs; monkey flesh; panthers' teeth; blue-veined cheeses whose only cohesion was the berries running through their sopping flesh like amethysts; vast, sagging squids; grimacing fish; petrified flowers, hookahs, knives, and many sorts of potato.

He found a suitable space amidst all this to lay out his mat, and waited, batting away with his fan the occasional brazen seagull, insect or stray dog. His first player was an Indian who spoke very little Spanish. The man placed two reales down, and Jeongjo gave him a cup of rice wine, and together they played high-low. The Indian lost almost immediately and then asked for his money back. Feeling guilty for taking advantage of an imbecile, Jeongjo returned the coins, but then the man laid down the two reales again, and Jeongjo waved him away. There were no other players for some time.

The sun moved behind the spire of a church, its thin shadow falling across Jeongjo's face; a youth dressed somewhat eclectically as a soldier struck a slave woman several times with the back of his hands, and, later, as Jeongjo was filling his pipe, his kneecap was tapped by the side of a sheathed sword.

It was another soldier. This one accused him of corrupting the Indians with gambling, and Jeongjo, knowing himself to be on the cusp of some extortion, started to gather his cards together. The soldier kicked one of his wooden cups away, and then a man approached and dismissed the soldier with a wave of his hands.

'Señor Lee,' the soldier said. 'No sabía qué—'

'Piérdete.'

This man wore a double-breasted green jacket with gold buttons, and a green bandana. A polka dot cravat concealed the lower part of his visage, most of which seemed to be discoloured by burns. His teak eyes were unusually alive and attentive, like mice shuffling at the edge of an enclosure.

'Es vino de arroz?' he asked.

Jeongjo poured him a cup of rice wine as the man untied his knee-high leather boots and hunkered down barefoot on the mat, saying he wanted to play stud poker, but with some Caribbean variations where all the eights, nines and tens were stripped from the deck so that the seven and knave were consecutive; aces and jokers wild. They played.

The man – who introduced himself as Xiaoguang Lee, bodyguard to Mr Osgood Benjamin – asked him questions about his childhood in Busan and his travels southward through the Americas, turning over his cards casually, lace cuffs spilling over the palms of his tan gloves, and then Jeongjo saw that he was being cheated. He did not mention it, losing slowly for a while, and then, when the pot grew large with three quick parries of mindless raising, Jeongjo undid all of the cheating with a sleight of hand so that on the very final turn Lee lost thirty-two reales.

'Joder!'

The man examined his cards several times before rising from his hunkers and walking down the crowded harbour a little way, then coming back, and sitting down, this time with his legs neatly crossed. He looked at the cards once more, and asked:

'Do you speak English?'

'Yes.'

'Well?'

'Very well.'

'Why?'

'After Canada, I spent four years working aboard a British frigate that went up and down the west coast of Mexico.'

'Spying?'

'The British might have been – I was swabbing decks, picking oakum, marling yarn, peeling potatoes, and reading Henry Fielding to the blind chef whose company I kept.'

'Can you ride?'

'I am a fair rider.'

'Could you drive a coach-and-two?'

'I could.'

'Why did you cheat?'

'You cheated first.'

'You make first impressions so awful they do not allow a second. You are perfect. I must have you in my employ. Would you deliver a man for me today? It is less than half a day's ride, and I will let you keep the thirty-two reales you stole from me and will give you eight more for your labours. Then, if you please my master, I will give you something else.'

Jeongjo poured his new companion another cup of rice wine; upended the final remnants into his own cup.

'I will not stay, I think,' he said. 'The soldiers here are loutish; the slaves scarred, and the Indians insane and sad.'

'It is violent everywhere.'

'Not so.'

'The Spanish do not send out sufficient protection anymore, so the Benjamins have had to supplement with their own private militia – and they can be lively, I grant you – that is mostly what you are seeing, but they will not pester you again. I promise. Perform this one task, and then say if you will stay.'

Jeongjo was a little dazed by the rice wine and the heat; it seemed to linger on his skin like a kiss.

'Do you know any who sell rice wine?'

'Follow me. I shall fetch you a bottle.'

'Where are we going?'

'Hotel de los Benjamines.'

———•———

Blissful warmth unclasped his mind and lowered his eyelids. He was dozing off as he drove the horse-and-two up through the narrow, twisting streets where gangs of screaming orphans ran ahead, seeming to enjoy nothing more than shaking him out of his stupor by pretending to dive beneath the horses' legs at every crossing.

'Here the Spanish may govern, but the Benjamins rule,' Xiaoguang Lee was saying, in an easy manner, smoking a thin-stemmed pipe. 'Whatever is, in Santa María, works, in one way or another, for my master, Mr Osgood Benjamin, and his family. In this one fell swoop, my dear Jeongjo, you have aligned yourself with that force. Isn't that something?'

'Yes.'

'Do you have any politics?'

'No.'

'How do you feel about republicanism?'

'I feel nothing.'

'Very wise.' Lee nodded. 'And yet a republic will come, as for the greater questions – who knows? Independence is inevitable, freedom impossible, for all republics, no matter how remote, still need the support of the European banks, lest they become vassal once more to another, more exacting, empire.'

The vista of a treeless plaza opened up as they came over a rise on whose far side stood a three-storeyed hotel that, if it had not been for the hilliness of the environs, would have naturally dominated the town.

An enslaved child of eleven or twelve rushed out to meet them, introducing himself breathlessly as Noel Christmas, and holding the two horses' bridles and leading them up the avenue.

Lee fell silent and stared at the boy.

'He's new, this one,' he said.

Jeongjo fanned himself with his hat; the daylight was too bright, and then the tap of a hammer broke through the midday sleepiness, complementing the horses' steps. The avenue curled around the corner of the hotel, and Jeongjo cast back a glance at the sea, glimpsed it between two buildings, blue and curved on the horizon like a disembodied iris; atop its gentle crest, like white envelopes, the square sails of a patrolling warship, and then the sea disappeared, and in his field of vision swooped another huge building, attached by a short, thin corridor to the hotel like an artery running between two organs; along this corridor was strung a beige canopy, beneath whose shade several bearded masons argued over some designs spread across an easel. The building possessed an elliptical shape, its external façade of varnished wooden panels set between broad stone pillars. There seemed to be a great many arched entrances draped with wisteria from which blue hummingbirds occasionally burst.

'What is that?'

'An indoor theatre – the largest one for two hundred leagues in any direction, and those men are more fully integrating it with the hotel; checking the integrity of all those subterranean passages so necessary for the thespians' illusions. All this, too, sponsored by the Benjamins. They oversee all the programming. They show revolutionary plays, patriotic and republican plays, magic plays, American plays, liturgies. They believe these things important for the morality of the common man. You should go sometime. A chap comes back to life in one, right in front of your eyes. It's really something.'

'I prefer cards. You can lose more.'

They passed the kitchens, and both hopped off the trap, letting Noel Christmas bring the horses through the gardens down towards the stables. Lee led Jeongjo through a back door, and he found himself beside a scarred table stacked high with leafy tubers at which a slim Wolof scullery maid in a turban was chopping carrots. She interrupted this work to fetch them a basin of water so they could wash their faces; and then, without warning, she began rubbing Jeongjo's ears and wrist with some heady perfume, peeling off his coat and draping a new, grey one over his shoulders. Finally, she dropped to her knees and slapped at his boots with a trapo.

'Qué está pasando?'

Lee was adjusting a new cravat in the reflection of a barrel of water. 'No Spanish. Here a man who wants to get on and not just get by speaks English. You are about to meet Mr Osgood Benjamin. You must be presentable. Actually, perhaps it would be best if you didn't speak at all.'

'You promised me rice wine.'

'When you've delivered.'

'I'm hungry.'

'We are expected.'

As they were leaving Jeongjo snuck a few carrots into his pockets, the lush greens protuberant as though growing out of the fabric of his new coat. They went through the lobby and along a corridor until they reached a door guarded by a teenage captain of the local militia who was running a sword's edge along the sole of his boots.

The room they entered had a high ceiling and was flooded with light from two tall sea-facing windows. Osgood Benjamin sat at a mahogany desk, empty save for a jug and a glass of water. He wore white pantaloons and a white jacket. A damp handkerchief was plastered across his forehead. Above him on the wall was a landscape portrait of himself and someone who was obviously his brother, laurel wreaths across their heads. There were potted palm trees in each corner, a modest couch, and underneath one of the windows, another man sat at a smaller table on which lay a closed bottle of ink, a fresh quill, and a neat pile of untouched paper.

'I expected you this morning,' Benjamin said, moving the damp handkerchief down over his eyes and thus intentionally blinding himself. 'Have you settled with Cricklow yet?'

'No, sir; this evening.'

Benjamin lifted half the handkerchief so one revealed pupil darted out.

'Why are you here if it's not done?'

'I need to lure him away. The two players are still there; the woman is there; his child. They can't see me.'

'Charles is back from the Indies in two days. I am marrying Miss Dalkey in five days. The builders will be arriving in San Ángeles in nine days. What are you doing?'

'I need—'

In the high ceiling of the room a crunch echoed out, and all eyes turned on Jeongjo. He had bitten into a carrot, but now each further mastication seemed inordinately loud and prolonged. He swallowed the little bit in his mouth with difficulty.

'Buenos,' he said, bowing.

Osgood Benjamin tossed the handkerchief across the table. 'Lee, would you care to explain why there is a Chinese standing in my office eating carrots?'

'This is my man to deliver Cricklow. If he possessed a letter bearing your seal it would be done before nightfall.'

'Fritz,' Osgood said, still staring at Jeongjo, 'prepare the wax. Lee, this is Fritz Odendonk, my new amanuensis. My brother gave him to me. He has the finest position in the Americas for if he ever writes down anything I say, I'll kill him.'

'Another new face. This is a lot of new faces, sir, at this time.'

'You'll understand when you get married yourself, Lee. – You're happy here, aren't you, Fritz?'

'Yes, sir.'

The secretary had taken a red candle out of a drawer and was attempting to light it.

'Fritz, bring it here, and a blank sheet.'

The amanuensis picked up a piece of paper, and brought it and the candle to Benjamin, who folded the blank sheet on his desk, dipped some wax on it, then impressed it with the signet he wore.

'Try not to get an unreasonable amount of carrot on it,' he said to Jeongjo. 'Do you have papers?'

'No, sir.'

'The seal should suffice, but your papers will be here when you get back. What name do you want given on them?'

'Yi Jeongjo, sir.'

'No,' Lee said. 'You'll use an American name. What name would you like?'

'I would like to be called Osgood Benjamin, sir.'

Benjamin dipped the handkerchief in the glass of water and spread it once more across his face.

'Lee,' he said, 'if you ever bring this murderable son of a bitch into my presence again I will have you flayed in your favourite cravat and served up to Momma Dearest. I'll see you at a quarter to eight.'

Jeongjo was given the sealed piece of paper, and a simple map that showed a single line along a trail that led through low mountains and the forest that covered them, towards a small town by a river called San Ángeles, quite near the coast. There, he was to find an Englishman called Quentin Cricklow, and bring him back to the hotel. He was put on a trap with two fresh horses by an elderly slave named Verato Domingo who was using the opportunity to teach the new child, Noel Christmas, how to properly fit the harnesses.

A shimmering butterfly landed on one of the horse's eyelashes, and when the creature flapped away, Noel Christmas ran after it. Jeongjo watched the child twirling in pursuit of the butterfly for a moment, and then nodded at the old slave, and stirred the horses to a high-legged canter, greatly amused to find himself unexpectedly a coach driver.

Once clear of Santa María he pulled up in the shadow of an abandoned church tinted subaqueous green by the trees that towered over it, its roof and crucifix layered by years of overlapping laminae of bird droppings. Jeongjo let the horses graze in the untended, overgrown graveyard, pulled his hat over his eyes and fell asleep.

<hr />

A butterfly glancing against his lip woke him. Bells pealed faintly in the distance. He was in rocking motion, amidst a haze of swirling midges, in the soft light of early evening. Birds cawed with hysterical splendour and an undercurrent of insects swelled and fell in fizzing murmur. The horses were walking through a forest, their heads bobbing up and down, moving towards San Ángeles of their own accord, and the butterfly was now above Jeongjo, its cream wings hectic as the spasming of an injured muscle.

He decided to race it, and brought the horses to a trot, and then slowed them to a stop, and waited, and then he saw the butterfly, infinitesimally small against the foliage, blustering and twirling towards him like an autumn leaf. It alighted next to him on the seat, and he laughed, overjoyed. He rode with the butterfly beside him for another hour or so, against slight inclines and invisible declines, glancing occasionally at its gently pulsing wings, delicate and vast, the compact furriness of its body, and then, as he clattered across a load-bearing bridge that traversed a river, the cream butterfly shivered its wings and floated away. The landscape suddenly opened up. He descended into a waterlogged quarry. Some way off in the distance, shaded by its close proximity to the scar of a quarry wall, stood a two-storey wooden house with a gabled roof. It rested upon brief stilts, behind a porch that had once known paint. There, in the solitary upstairs window, a candle glowed, its glint doubled by flashing off the lens of a telescope that charted his approach. Jeongjo saluted the sparkle, and directed the trap towards the porch, where he tied the horses in front of a wetted trough, loosened their bridles and removed their bits.

He rapped on the door and then, removing his gloves and hat, entered a stale gloom wherein rested a few disarranged stools, a barrel, a counter, a meagre bar, all clad in a sticking coat of dust save for the shelves on which the spirits lay. A ferment of arching cobwebs spanned the room like latitudes and longitudes gone slack.

On a stool by the counter a slave was breastfeeding her baby.

'You can't come in here,' she said, in Spanish.

Jeongjo took the letter from his breast pocket and showed her the seal.

'Is Señor Quentin Cricklow here?'

She nodded up at the ceiling.

'There is a man dying upstairs.'

'Señor Cricklow?'

'No, otro.'

He went up and knocked. There came no answer. He entered the room to find a jaundiced man wearing a nightcap in a narrow bed, the sheets transparent with sweat and too short to conceal his booted feet. He was muttering to himself, rocking his head from side to side.

At a table by the window, a man whose stubbled face looked like a loosely adorned leather mask sat in a faded, collarless shirt and knee-length breeches, drinking whiskey and fiddling with a shrunken monkey hand that he wore around his neck, strung up on a thong alongside a pouch and a wooden cross.

Both of these men sported faded scars across their foreheads.

'Mr Cricklow?'

The eyes of the man by the window widened.

'Lee?'

'No, I am Yi, Yi Jeongjo. I am to take you back to Santa María. I have a letter from Mr Benjamin here.'

'Sit down.'

'I've been instructed to transport you presently.'

172

'La, i'n't that nice? And I presently instruct you presently to sit down presently.'

There came a rattle in the throat of the man in bed that sounded like a stick being dragged across flagstones. He blinked at Jeongjo as if waking.

'Are you my angel?'

'Now, why would your angel be a Chinese?' Cricklow said.

'Should a doctor not be summoned?' Jeongjo asked.

'Wouldn't do no use,' Cricklow said. 'He ate something very bad many years ago, and now it's caught up with him. – La, i'n't that right. But we had some wild times, didn't we, old dog?'

'No.'

'Come now, dost remember old dancing Richardson and Percival with the fish and mad Bevilacqua and old Hieronimo who drowned in the pit of hisself?'

'No.'

'Dost not remember the ghost in the tree, with Captain Graham Phillips, and his eyes at midnight crying? And merry old Amado as fell asleep on the barrow of guano and sank? And Starry Gertrude with her huge teeth and eyes like a cow? And Ilse Tasso, with her hips like a sinking ship and her ledger in which was kept all them twelve circles as to let you go on upstairs to the secret room?'

'No.'

'Marry, some people,' he snorted, and then turned his chin up at Jeongjo. 'Now show me this letter.'

Jeongjo handed over the letter and Cricklow examined the seal.

'Which brother were it?'

'Mr Osgood Benjamin.'

'Not the one I want.'

He unfolded the sheet and beheld the blank sheet of paper.

'Marry, she's blank, la. Have they smoked me? It were that dark bitch, Soares, I know it. Me and whorehouses – there should be a law. There probably is . . . Bellringing savages on Christmas day – it ain't civilised, John Joe! Guns in the hands of heathens! Mr Osgood Benjamin has been a very, very naughty boy. And if he knows I knows how naughty, la, I must out; I durst, and though you be my courier one peep at you says you i'n't my assassin; I'd chafe your neck for you. You'll get me out of here and I'll lay me aloft on you afore the hotel and you and hisself'll be none the wiser. What makes you of that?'

'I have no idea what you are talking about, Mr Cricklow.'

The man lit a cigar off the candle and rapped the table with resolution.

'Exactly. Let us go hence.'

'Don't leave,' the man in bed said. 'I am dying. Tarry with me, Quentin . . . for old times . . . not so many of us as is left to boast.'

'Do you think me quite heartless?' Cricklow asked. 'I shall give thee until the end of this smoke.'

The man in bed was whispering to himself again. Night was falling; soon Jeongjo could not see across the quarry; only his own soft reflection thrown vaguely back at him, and then there was a single, powerful knock against the far side of the wall as though a large bird had flown against it. And then there was another. The horses outside neighed.

'What was that?'

'What were what?'

'The knock, it didn't come from outside. Is there some other room here? I saw only one door upstairs.'

'Hush, John Joe, it is only the players. They are kept here for rehearsal whenever there i'n't a show on, so hush up for I am ruminating my way out of a very steep shithole.'

Jeongjo listened out for another sound, but none came. Finally, Cricklow's cigar was a stub between his teeth. He put on his hat, pocketed the telescope, and placed a new cigar behind his ear.

'Are you dead yet?' he asked.

'No.'

'Well, you had your chance. Might I borrow your overcoat?'

'My mother is here. She's crying, Quentin. Why is she crying?'

'Mayhaps you was her disappointment.'

Cricklow put his own coat on and then the other one over it. He corked the bottle of whiskey, and then sat on the edge of the bed, leaning over the dying man so their faces were very close together.

'Would you like me to kill you?'

'No.'

'Only so as to ease the pain a little.'

'No.'

'Are you sure?'

'Please, no.'

'All right, then, old dog, have it your way. Come to, John Joe; can't lag about all bloody day, la.'

———•———

The bobbing lanterns on the trap floated onwards. Slim portions of the trail rose up ahead, as though shaken into being by the glow's soft-moving orb. Long-legged flying insects batted in endless cavalry against the lanterns' glass like tiny comets sucked into stars. Jeongjo blinked them away, keeping his mouth closed against the flurry of brittle wings brushing at his cheeks.

Cricklow was nearly finished with the bottle of whiskey, seething under two coats. Hunching his face into his collars, he dozed off and then slipped downwards, his legs about to get caught in the spokes of the wheels; Jeongjo grabbed him, and hauled him back up, and he floundered, gasping as he came conscious once more.

'I see it,' he said. 'I see it.'

'Mr Cricklow, please—'

'I see it. At last, I see it.'

He tried to grab the reins, and one of the horses reared. Jeongjo wrested the reins back, and in the tussle Cricklow tumbled sideways off the trap. Jeongjo pulled up the horses, and swung out a lantern like a fishing rod, and in the brief arc of its illumination he saw a cloaked figure stalking towards the Englishman, who had gotten to his knees and was pulling a razor from the pouch around his neck. He cut his palm trying to unfold it, dropped it, and then began crawling out beyond the cone of light. The cloaked figure picked up the razor and grabbed Cricklow by the hair.

'Look at it happen.'

Cricklow stared up at his assailant.

'Tha'art still but half a blister and the second-best loved boy.'

Xiaoguang Lee cut Quentin Cricklow's throat, dragged him by the boots into the trees, tossed the razor onto the wheezing body, then came back to the trail, and mounted the trap.

'Drive on,' he said. 'We must get back.'

Jeongjo didn't move. He had been still for so long that insects had gathered on him; they were irritating the stationary horses, too.

'I know you have been shocked,' Lee said, 'but we have to go now.'

'I will bring you back to the hotel, and then you will not see me again.'

'As you wish, but now you must drive.'

They rode in silence, the only sound the forest simmering with its confluence of tiny breaths and secret glut of feasting mouths. Perhaps an hour later, Jeongjo pulled the horses to stop again so as to allow a troop of long-armed apes to lumber across the trail, their faces obscured, their eyes starlike in the lanterns' reflections.

'Let me explain,' Lee said, filling a pipe. 'Mr Benjamin, my master, will deliver this colony an independence that will, in the very act of its founding, abolish slavery and give natives the right to hold property. It is to this end I work. For years I have been establishing contacts and spies in the big houses, in the fields, even in this forest where I followed you. The woman in the kitchens who gave you that coat – her name is Loah Soares – she is with us. The old ostler in the stables – Verato Domingo – he, also is with us. There is another world inside the world you see, Jeongjo, and I can show you it, if you like.

'On Christmas Day, several hundred negros and Indians will rise up, and stifle the slack remnants of Spanish rule. Mr Benjamin's soldiers, the last authoritative force of order, will then broker a peace between the parts, and the landowners will support whatever saves their estates. The Spanish, due to the war in Europe, will have neither the time nor the means to intervene for at least three months, and in the meantime a republic will be quietly declared. A limited and bland parliamentary democracy in the British manner will suffice to let Mr Benjamin run his affairs as he would. You see, I trust Mr Benjamin because I already know in the new republic he shall plunder the earth at will – that's what he wants, and he may have it, no? It will either be a man like him, or it will be another man like him from across the ocean. The one you picked up tonight, Quentin Cricklow, thought he could manoeuvre a fortune for the information I have just given you. He would have never stopped. He would have gotten many people killed. You can only kill a man like that, nothing else will do. Do you understand?'

'Yes.'

'He was a killer himself. He hurt children.'

'Yes.'

'And now you know everything he knew.'

'I said I would leave.'

'Stay: the revolution could use a man like you,' Lee said, gesturing with his gloved hand out at the night. 'There are many submerged lives here. We will help integrate them into one society, a society of wages. Wages will bring it all to the surface, let these Africans and Indians up for air where they can breathe a bit easier, and it is the Benjamins who got the wages going here, and that is why, despite it all, I have stayed with them for all these years. The future is here. This colony is magnificent and hideous. It is everything. We are on the edge of the world, but we're really at the heart of the miracle, and you could be a part of this. I don't know why, Jeongjo, but when I'm with you I feel like I can breathe more freely. Come work with me.'

The final ape had passed, and the troop's sentry, a large, hulking male, stared at Jeongjo for a moment and then disappeared into the undergrowth. Jeongjo shook the reins, and the horses plodded on. Nothing was visible outside this little light, and yet the quickening scent of throbbing life was everywhere.

'No,' he said.

'Do you not believe in the revolution?'

'No.'

'Do you not believe in the joyful century? The happiness of all mankind? The rise of the many? The downfall of tyranny?'

'No.'

'Have it your way.'

'No.'

               —•—

In Santa María, the streets were thronged with sombre faces all moving towards the hotel.

Lee hailed a soldier who was passing by.

'Qué está pasando?' he asked.

'Señor Benjamin is dead.'

'Which Benjamin?'

'Señor Osgood Benjamin.'

Lee stared down at the pipe in his gloved hand, his posture straight and awkward. Passers-by overtook the trap, their numbers growing as they drifted uphill. They came to the plaza where the crowd thickened until it became impassable at the perron of the hotel, its steps completely blocked off by soldiers facing outwards, guns leant across the perch of their elbows.

A lieutenant of the militia saluted Lee, grabbed one of the bridles and led the trap towards the steps, waving his bayonet and calling to clear a path. As they came closer, Jeongjo could distinguish by the guttering of torchlight a man standing at the top of the steps behind the soldiers, very similar to Osgood Benjamin, but slimmer and older with startlingly blue eyes. One of his hands lay on a wheeled wicker chair that held in it an old woman cocooned by blankets so that only the wedge of her crenellated face was exposed.

'Where were you, Lee?' she called down. 'You were supposed to protect him.'

The crowd fell silent. A gust of wind rolled in off the sea, rustling gabardines and hats and bringing with it from the harbour below the faint pungency of the morning's discarded catch. Silhouettes flitted behind the candlelit windows of the hotel. Two soldiers sat on the roof, their bayonets ranging over the crowd.

'I was in San Ángeles, sending his messages.'

The old woman closed her eyes, began keening softly.

'Hush, momma,' Chuck Benjamin said. 'Now we must come together as a family, and this one, too, is my family. My boy, will we forget the past?'

He opened wide his arms. Stiffly, Lee dismounted and climbed up the steps, soldiers parting before him, and then Benjamin enfolded him in an embrace.

'You are always safe with me,' Chuck Benjamin said, 'and I will always entrust to you that which is most precious to my heart.'

Lee wiped the tears from his face with his cuffs. 'What happened?'

'An Indian of the forest killed him, a one-armed man trying to get out of a contract he'd given his mark to, but I am only a few hours back from Saint-Domingue so who am I to rule out a wider conspiracy? You will help us, of course.'

'Of course. Always.'

'Good,' Benjamin said. 'Wrangle me some information, then, and tomorrow morning I will accustom you to your new duties. There are going to be changes.'

Benjamin brushed a tear from the corner of Lee's eye with a thumb, kissed his forehead, and then dispatched eight soldiers to him. Lee mounted the trap once more, and Jeongjo drove the horses, already exhausted beyond their capabilities, at such a pace as would allow the soldiers to follow easily on foot.

'New faces,' Lee said, once they had left behind the plaza. 'He was not supposed to be back yet.'

Along narrow streets stacked with dark shanties, they proceeded, rising and falling with the hills. To their right was the immensity of the ocean, blacker than the sky. They passed a drunkard who spat at a closed door; a pariah dog with cancer around its eyes who waited patiently beside him. A woman in a rebozo fell to her knees as the trap passed, placing her forehead to the ground, hands outstretched for alms. A seagull swooped close overhead, the sound of its gliding wings causing Jeongjo to look up and see a muffled grey light traversing the shallow skyscape, and he understood then that a meteor, invisible above the clouds, was winding its way around the world.

'Here,' Lee said.

A derelict house, its sun-bleached adobe walls punctuated by three boarded-up windows like ellipses. When the soldiers had fallen into line behind the trap, Lee gestured towards it.

'Allí,' he said. 'Quiero tres mujeres nativas. Tráemelas.'

The soldiers dispersed into formation around the building, and Lee debarked and went in the opposite direction, towards a squat edifice covered in dead growth like a huge, shaggy nest. He pushed in through a bead curtain and disappeared. Jeongjo tied off the horses and followed after, finding himself inside a spare cantina whose only customers were four Chinese men hunched over in a corner playing dominoes. Lee waited by the counter, whispering to a plump barmaid in a language resembling nothing Jeongjo had ever heard.

'Qué haces?' he asked Lee.

'Only English.'

'What are you doing?'

'I must bring something to Benjamin he can use.'

The barmaid placed a cup of cachaça on the counter.

'You've been found out,' Jeongjo said. 'Why are you still here?'

'He's shaking the tree to see what falls. If I hold on tight for a few hours, who knows?'

'You can't control anything. There's going to be a riot. Can you not feel it? Leave now. Take the horses. They are good horses. Trade them for fresh ones at a post.'

Lee drank off the cachaça.

'There is a girl.'

'Take her with you.'

'She wouldn't come.'

'Then leave on your own.'

'No.'

'Stay and die, then.'

'I want to live,' Lee said. 'I'm in it pretty deep now, so I see only two ways out. I lock every door leading to her. I might manage this with three, four bodies – and these amongst the people I have loved the most.'

He held his two gloved hands flat before his own face to see if they were still shaking, and then picked up the cachaça again, and for the first time Jeongjo understood how much younger than him the other man was.

'I don't want that,' Lee went on. 'I want to continue as before. Everything is in place, save the damned guns. Money is not enough; we must also have silence and security accompanying their transit, and the only way to assure this is the seal and the contact. If I can get the seal, I think I can make it.'

A splintering sound came from across the street. The four men playing dominoes started to rise, and Lee shook his head at them. Just beyond the bead curtain there was a brief shout, and then a slump. A little later, an Indian wearing loose robes stumbled in through the bead curtain, bent over so profoundly his hands nearly dragged off the floor. His mouth was dark with the blood that had dripped into it from his nose, and on his shoulder sat a cockatoo whose majestic crest was slightly flecked with the same blood.

The Indian leant heavily against the doorframe, half-draped in rattling beads, and spoke at great length in the strange language, the cockatoo clicking its beak into his ear all the while.

Lee answered him briefly and turned back to the counter to take another drink.

'I played cards with that man today,' Jeongjo said. 'What did he say?'

'This is Atta. He used to hunt octopuses, and then he went crazy in the sun one day and became a Christian. He talks nonsense.'

'Tell me.'

'He says we're all going to die.'

'He's right about that. What else did he say?'

'He asked for alms.'

In the opposite house, women had started screaming, five or six perhaps, and though the screaming was getting louder, only one woman's scream was coming closer.

'And what did you say back to him?'

'Stay hidden tonight.'

Jeongjo went over to the dazed Indian, took him by the arms and sat him down in a chair. The cockatoo shied away, flexing its claws and shuffled across to his far shoulder. Then Jeongjo took from his pocket the cloth that held all his money, untied it and counted it, removing the thirty-two reales he had won that morning and putting them on the table in front of the man as Lee watched, saying nothing.

Jeongjo took off his grey coat and draped it across Atta's shoulders, and then peeked through the bead curtain. Outside, a soldier was dragging a native woman across the street by her hair. She was shrieking, her dress torn from where she had fallen, so that her navel, hip and one grazed breast were visible. Jeongjo pressed his body against the wall, waiting. At the last moment, he said to Lee:

'If you survive the night, I'll help you.'

The woman was tossed through the curtain. She tripped against a chair and collapsed to the floor. The soldier followed after her, shouting oaths and striking at her back with the butt of his gun.

Jeongjo slipped out behind them, unseen.

<hr />

The most annoying person Llewyn Chaffinch would ever meet in his life picked up his trunk one evening and started walking across the hotel lobby with it. Llewyn glanced over his spectacles, abandoning the poem he had been composing, and called after him:

'I say, old bean, what are you doing?'

The young man, who wore a Phrygian cap adorned with a huge tricoloured cockade, spun around, showing Llewyn the unseemly width of his perennial smile.

'Excuse me, citizen, I am so desolate that I violate per accident your affairs,' he said. 'I am in train of part to the grand terrestrial of the America Latin – for Santa María, yes. In my excitation for achieve it I have interrompt your writes, for I am bland, bland to the cooler of this . . . loon gauge, tu vois?'

'Luggage. Colour blind, eh? Quite all right, then,' Llewyn said. 'Just leave it there.'

He started writing again, but the completion of his poem was once more deferred – this time by an outstretched hand appearing between him and his sheet.

'I extend the symbol of fraternity.'

'It's quite all right, I assure you.'

'You are not liking the symbol of fraternity? Maybe you are not the republican?'

'I am, it's just I'm rather busy at the moment.'

'What are you writes, citizen? Are you journalist?'

'As a matter of fact, I am.'

'But how this is genial,' the Frenchman said, sitting down opposite him and nodding his head so vigorously that a lock of curly black hair fell across his forehead like an inverted interrogation point. 'I am journalist also, journalist very celebrate from the Aix-en-Provence. My name is Maxime de Sèves, and have twenty-seven, but, please, Max Sept for my friend and brother, and all the world is my brother, no?'

While he may indeed have been French and not Creole, he was certainly no more than nineteen years old, and his origins undoubtedly lay amongst the popular classes. Llewyn had seen him every single day in the hotel since he had arrived in Cap, though so far he had managed to avoid him. Every morning Maxime had marched down the stairs to breakfast with a hearty smile, shaking everyone's hand, and laughing raucously with the least provocation. He was always waving his hat at very slight acquaintances from great distances and running over to meet them.

'Are you not leaving for Santa María right now?' Llewyn said. 'Is that not why you picked up my trunk?'

'Not since two hours of the morning.'

Llewyn placed his unfinished composition in the hidden compartment of the leather folder he had spread across his lap.

'Might I help you with something else, Mr Sept?'

'Please, name me citizen or brother, I prefer, yes. What is your writes?'

'I am on a year-long tour of the Caribbean gathering information for what I suppose shall prove to be a rather voluminous work describing those fraternal societies that nurture liberty therein.'

'It cannot, no,' Maxime gasped, hands against cheeks. 'No. Impossible. It is too fantastic.'

'Are you feeling ill, Mr Sept?'

'This is the most strangest thing that have never pass me in my whole life. Never, never pass something so strange like this – also I am writing this same thing! My brother, you have should must to come with me to Santa María. There have the society very interesting of the liberty universal and the happiness of all the man. I insist it! Take a passage tonight aboard a silly bat, a ceiling boot . . . un bateau, tu vois . . . You must not unquiet yourself, citizen, for I have the big money for this voyage and I pay all the bat for you. I pay the hotel. I pay all, all. All, yes. My journal is a very grand journal, a very generous. We are agree, or yes?'

Llewyn's funds were running low; he had only managed to place two articles in the last six months, and Santa María was on his itinerary – but quite simply, he found it impossible to spend any more time in this ludicrously hale youth's company.

'Though the proposal be generous I could not accept.'

'But why not yes?'

'I await a letter from my father.'

'Mais non!' Maxime snorted. 'This is the silly. Make a transmit of this letter by courier with the name for Santa María at the hotel of the Benjamin. It is a very big hotel. All the world know it. There is no problem, no, or is?'

'Monsieur de Sèves, I thank you, but I assure you I cannot accept.'

'I am very sad. As you will, citizen, but if you will attend this foyer at the two of this morning we have the adventure in the grand terrestrial of the . . . the man looned, the . . .'

'The mainland.'

He shook his head, sighed. 'Yes, this I say, I think.'

The youth, shoulders low and feet dragging, moped his way out the front door. A few moments later, Llewyn looked up to see the Phrygian cap blustering frantically by the window, as Maxime, laughing with delight, waved it at a passing charwoman he had just recognised.

Llewyn found it difficult to fall asleep that night, nor could he continue his poem. What little peace he laid claim to had been ruined. Perhaps it was his unconscious mentioning of his father, dead five years now; or perhaps it was because he couldn't come up with any sensible reason not to accompany Maxime to Santa María: it would save him money he could ill afford, and even if his mother did manage to send him a bill of exchange from a house reputable enough to be recognised in the French Caribbean it might take yet another two or three months to arrive.

He arrived downstairs near two, had some words with the night clerk to dispatch a boy to fetch his trunks, paid his bill and left some money for a forwarding agent if any post did happen to arrive from his mother. Maxime was in the lobby, tapping his foot with his hands held behind his back, humming a revolutionary ditty to himself.

'But this is too fantastic,' Maxime said when he saw him, removing his Phrygian cap and laughing.

'I hesitate to put myself in your debt,' Llewyn said.

'No hesite, please. We are the republican, the brother, the mankind, no? I have no power on you, no you on me. For me only, we have the nice adventure for help the progress. Only this. We are agree, or yes?'

'And you understand,' Llewyn said, 'I will be working through-out the voyage, and so cannot entertain. I have to meet several quite pressing deadlines.'

'But of course. The write, the write, the write – all the day, all the day . . . And at the night, maybe we have the ladle dronk together, yes?'

'Yes, perhaps. Thank you, Mr Sept.'

'We are the best friends, yes?'

'Well, all right, then.'

'Fantastic. O yes, and what is it, your name?'

'Llewyn Chaffinch.'

'But this name is too fantastic. Llewyn, Llewyn Chaffinch. Sometime I hazard the English luggage is not so villain.'

'The English language.'

'Yes, I speak,' Maxime said, laughing again. 'Of course. Good morning, I am Max. Goodnight, goodbye. Yes. One beefsteak, please. For me and my friend, please. That will be one thousand franc. Here is your change. Thank you very much. – See, it is good, no? But what hour is this? We will be in retards if we do not go quack.'

'What?'

'On y va!'

A scarred Bossale loaded their trunks and drove them across Cap. They passed the courthouse with its marble façade; they passed the numerous bell towers where rang out the hours marked by raised Roman numerals; they passed a park bordered with teas-ingly curved palm trees, their trunks shaved, their bases encircled by an array of flowers in full bloom; they passed a mobile gallows with wooden wheels where a slave had been hanged that morn-ing, and from where she hanged still, her tongue protruding, her neck bent like a ragdoll, her bare feet covered in dust from the traffic; they approached the port where a jumble of naked masts skewered the night, wobbling like a mob of outraged forefingers, and in whose waters a gently listing schooner careened gracefully, decks clamouring with frantic sailors dropping fenders, calling commands, and coiling ropes, as on a nearby gangplank stevedores jostled with children who paced their little ponies up and down like sentries on guard, waiting for the various commissions they hoped to win – and then their carriage passed the port also.

'Why are we not stopping here?'

'We are the best friend, yes?' Maxime said. 'Well I revelate to you. I avow that I am not the journalist, but also something other secret. I do an espionage, make a mission very discreet. Let me explique you simply, of the debut – I am a shell of divine.'

'What?'

'A shell of divine – un paysan.'

'You are a child of the vine.'

'Exact! You are shock, no, for I assemble so much the aristocrat who is cruel and is a snobinard in my comportment, yes? You are think, "Citizen Maxime, he is so aristocrat very rich and is journalist only for amuse himself with the money violate from the luggage of the popular people." But the true is my parents they work the vine in the mountains so arids. The hands become durables with this difficult travail, for the mountain is so yellow and so hot, give nothing to the poor peoples. So sad! I think I become also a child of the vine. It is inevitable, but there is five year, when I have only fifteen year, a chapiter of the mason they come, and one, he come and he learn me read and I am very excite and I want to part . . . partager?'

'You want to share.'

'Yes, I want to share my learns with all the paysans of the world, the general liberty of the man canned . . . the man can't . . . the mankind. Excuse me. I am very excite with this history and I miss the English.'

'Where is this story going, Mr Sept?'

'Santa María, this night, citizen; I say, no? Yes, I say, I think. Any same, all the revolution is very intoxicant for me and my brother and we love the revolution so much, the equality, the liberty, the universal thing, the abolitions, the na-na-ni – all this, yes? Yes. It is so nice. It is the joy, and we must share, no? I think, for me – yes. And so am share. There have in Santa María the brother who is the slave. This is inacceptable. The slavery, for me, is always very bad, but I am too insufficient for change all, but I am mason, yes, and I say to the grand lodge at Paris, I say, "Pah, this is not so good, if have the slave who are also the mason, no?" I want do a liberty on the brother. So I petition maniacal, like a mania I am, and they say to me, "Maxime you are so . . . gênant?"'

'Annoying.'

'Yes. They say me, "Maxime you are so annoying, here, have the money. Do a contact with Santa María. There, have a mason who have the seal. He only you can know, and if he tell yes you and you also know the seal, we permit the transmit of the arm through the conduits locals who us only belong so no treachery of the clerk or the tyrant can discover the complot secret." So I go, yes, why not, to Saint-Domingue, aboard, for I am a Frenchman, no? And Santa María is a party of the colony of the Spain, no? Of course, yes, and have an brother in Saint-Domingue and he obtain me passage aboard an English sailing bat to Santa María who is called *The Jolly Jenkins*, what the captain Lovering is also my brother for who I give some correspondence from the other Saint-Domingue brother, but have not possible go direct in the port of Cap because she is the smoogler of the mongs.'

'Smoogler of the mongs?'

'Yes, the smoogler of the mongs, with the orange Jews.'

'I don't understand.'

'When the mongs are rape they are so nice.'

'I don't understand, Maxime.'

189

'Ce bateau fait de la contrebande.'

'The ship smuggles mangoes?'

'Yes, I say this, I think, no?'

He pulled a sprig of laurel from out of the trunk at his feet, and, beaming proudly, showed it to Llewyn.

'In final, I give the black mason of Santa María this for the present. It is from the house of my father, and also my mother is there, and I will give it for them and wait nothing return for me. Soon the liberty will everyone, and no more the slavery, and we have all the best friend in all the world!'

'Are we engaged in some hazardous enterprise?' Llewyn asked.

'No, my brother,' Maxime said, attempting to stifle the tears that were rising in his eyes. 'It is only a fruit.'

———— • ————

Above a secluded cove, a Taíno Indian bearing a lantern emerged spectrelike from the towering sugar cane and led them down a staircase etched into the side of a cliff whose every uneven step was clotted with the loosening detritus of abandoned nests. They reached an enclosed beach where a skiff lay out of reach of the breakers. Once the Bossale had loaded their luggage beneath the centre seat, Maxime shook his hand and, with a tap of his fore-finger against his crumpled top hat, the Bossale traipsed back through the sand. The two Europeans boarded, and the Indian pushed them out and began rowing. Maxime sat on the gunwale, directing many ignored questions towards the Indian, Llewyn holding firmly onto the thwart with both hands, scanning the jostling sugar plantations that dominated the coastline.

The Jolly Jenkins came into view, anchored behind a lopsided sea stack, its prow revealing itself slowly like the nose of a curious dog. She bore no pennant along any of her bare masts and a canvas sheet covered the name on her portside. A rope ladder was tossed down, and the luggage passed up by way of two officers.

Llewyn ascended the ladder after Maxime and landed on deck just in time to see his travelling companion pass over a thick package of letters to Captain Lovering, which the latter concealed under his coat.

'One is two,' Maxime said.

'What?' the captain said.

'On est deux.'

'Two of you? Two brothers for Santa María? Well, why not? Who am I to fix a ne plus ultra on the bravery of youth? Two lucky young chaps, that's all I'll say. There is very little better than those hot Santa María nights. I myself still remember the chorizos, the fragrant yams, honeyed air flush with wisteria and Madame Rigaud's pure-blooded whores: the soles of their feet were always white. – Welcome aboard, brothers! I return to bed.'

An officer named Brynling showed them to their shared quarters where Maxime laid himself down in a hammock and fell asleep forthwith; Llewyn remained awake, in perfect darkness for a long time, listening to the gurgling waves draining through the caves of the sea stack and growing ever more infuriated by Maxime's snoring.

Eventually, folder under arm, he stormed out on deck, and found himself encompassed by the starless blue of early morning. He gazed over the shimmering water, beyond the waves of sugar-cane that stretched towards the distant mountains that traversed the island in an unbroken chain, withdrew his poem from the hidden compartment in his folder, arranged his ink, his pen, and blotting paper against the bulwarks, and began to compose.

'What are you doing?'

Llewyn hastily concealed the poem and turned around. Captain Lovering stood there, in only a nightshift and a bicorne, holding an empty chamber pot under one arm.

'Nothing, taking some notes on the landscape.'

'What's in the folder?'

'Just some articles.'

'Articles about France?'

'Some of them, yes.'

'Indeed,' Lovering said. 'That accent, though – not quite French?'

'I am Welsh.'

'A good Britisher, though; loyal subject, and all that?'

It was the blithe manner in which the captain asked the question that gave Llewyn brief pause.

'O yes,' he said.

'Well, I'll have to think about this. Might I recommend for now that you and your Gallic copain stick to your quarters until we arrive in Santa María, lest you become a subject – or citizen, I suppose – of Nighttown.'

'Nighttown?'

'Wherein they darkly sleep.'

'Who sleeps?'

'The depths of the bays in these Americas are called Nighttown,' Lovering said, a gentle whining resounding from the wind playing around the rim of the chamber pot. 'Therein lie the millions. This is a slave colony, and since more than half of the devils die in transportation – or are too weak for the landing, the quarantining, the divvying out – they are tossed down here, down to that shadow world.'

Llewyn glanced down to the green waters beneath which centuries of eyeless skulls peered back up at him.

Nighttown.

Was it for this, the sugar that had sweetened Llewyn's childhood candies, dusting his mouth and bedaubing his lips? Was it for this, the comforting plume of smoke flowing from his father's pipe of a Sunday afternoon, his reclining booted feet steaming off the stove as he recounted wild stories of rambunctious youth? Was it for this, the gold coating on the locket around his mother's throat which bore inside it a lock of his own fair hair?

No, it must be more, he thought – some innocent hope, some lifelong sacrifice freely given, some future implacable and pure and grand enough to overcome the fraught throng of genocide all overtopped and silenced by this murderous ocean. For above and beyond this water that held down and smothered was the giving soil, the mighty forests, the waiting mines, the teeming rivers, the new stars, the empty and whistling plains, the delicious uncharted mass that would forever set man spinning out a little further, to span, to stretch, to luxuriate, to starve, to die and be born in the new, with all his bravery, all his glory, all his dreaming, all his wonder, all his madness whose displacement he called discovery.

But, yes, also the disappeared, the throttled screams, the severed lives, the abbreviated families, the unseen, the overcome, the defeated, the stacked out of sight, the once-starved faces whose eyes, blinded to all, had crossed the earth but had dwelt in the darkness beneath all the pennants and the flags, beneath all the signalling lanterns flashing messages through fog-bounded night, beneath the exiled mercenaries whose breaths blew hot with unrecognisable diseases, beneath the flourishing blades, beneath the acrid fires consuming the past, beneath the loyalties, heartbreaks and sacrifices, beneath the internecine feuds that leave no victor nor survivor, beneath the boisterous tempests, the ludicrous bicornes, the rusted cat-o'-nines, the blood treacle-thick upon the decks, the rumbling sea shanties, the audacious tally-hos, the patriotic arias of these sons of the nation with their songs of the lovers forever falling in and out of love – beneath these, Nighttown.

And Llewyn wondered in that subterraneous place, across the centuries, did an angel ever carry one down? Did some slowly spinning child descend into the arms of some mother? Did some shards of families ever fall until they constituted a singular wedding banquet? Here the father, here the mother, and there the children; here the guests and here the cousins; here the bride and here the groom?

Good God, Llewyn thought, no. No. No.

There must be more – but what? Some portion of us must be redeemed rather than merely murdered. But what could redemption – such a loose word and so damned late in the day – even mean? And who redeems? What God could be big enough to fit in his stomach all these swallowed sighs and tearful dawns, these lost hours and dashed loves, these crying mothers and lost sons? What God is vast enough to remember it all? And what God, in the wholeness of his remembering, would allow us the grace of forgetting so that one day we may innocently wake up to find the whole earth made new again?

To wake into light.

Light.

Only light.

The door slammed shut and Maxime shot up in his hammock.

'Not so bloody jolly, is she?' Llewyn yelled.

'Mais qu'est-ce qu'il y a? What is passed, my brother?'

In a great unburdening gush, Llewyn recounted all that had happened, save those details pertaining to his unfinished poem, while Maxime yawned, rubbing his eyes.

'Si je pourrais . . . for help the sentiment of the terror.'

He rooted around in his trunk, pulling out a bottle full of a startlingly luminous green liquid.

'What, by heavens, is that?'

'La fée verte. How do you say – the absent?'

'Absinthe.'

'Yes, of course, the absent! It is very good. Would you like a ladle dronk?'

'You're not such a bad chap, Maxime.'

'You not also.'

Scores of boots started smashing across the deck, and in their quarters, dust swirled, dislodged by the thunderous movements outside.

'What is going on?'

'The mango arrive, I think. I like very good the mango.'

'Indeed.'

As they were drinking, Maxime started nodding to himself, setting his roving forelock whipping back and forth continuously. The effect was so distracting that eventually Llewyn asked:

'Something the matter with your head, old bean?'

'I am in train of thinking, yes, brother Lovering demand if you are ungirlish subject, not if you are brother or citizen? So aggressive with the menace, assemble me like a shoulder to arms in his comportment, more than naturally the brother. It is strange, no? I think this is maybe the . . . hungerless shy honey.'

'What?'

'The ungirlish earning?'

'What?'

'You are from the England,' Maxime explained, 'and when you are from that you say the opposite from the true and it consider itself very droll.'

'English irony?'

'Yes, this I say!'

'No, I don't think he was being ironic. I think you might have been brought here under false pretences. Come to think of it, it might be that we are both in grave danger.'

'Hmm. I come to think of it no. The capitaine is my brother. We are very doughy together. I think, Llewyn, you also do me now the English irony because we are the best friend!'

'I am Welsh.'

'I am very Welsh, too,' Maxime laughed. 'Thank you for asking, my brother.'

There was a knock on the door, and then Mr Brynling came in, smiling faintly. He looked at them both, one after the other.

'The captain would like to see the French one.'

'See, I say, Llewyn. Me and the capitaine, we are the brother.'

'What's this all about, Mr Brynling?' Llewyn asked.

'The correspondence from the mutual friend in Saint-Domingue. The captain has read it now, and there is something he would like to discuss with the French one.'

'It's me!' Maxime laughed.

He got out of his hammock, put on his Phrygian cap, and thrust his index finger heavenward.

'I return, my friend,' he said. 'All is Welsh. Why reassemble you such the unquiet face? I see the sad, I am sad also and think me – where is the spirit? Where is the fraternity of all the mankind? Where is the beautiful woman? The wine? The happy? The popular man who sing and have the soul in his hurt and the food in his vent and the smile in his face? Where is the general will for help the brother in the world entire? I have so much a very nice time with you, brother Llewyn. You are the best friend. Yes, I think. But you need remember you – the revolutionary have always a good cheer!'

He left. Grinding his teeth, Llewyn tossed off two more glasses of absinthe. The ropes of the hammock tutted against their metal mounting rings; the water lapped beneath him. He felt a little thirsty with the liquor. The penny candles' luminescence had dimmed down to a hazy orange, their wicks dipping like insects disappointed to have emerged from their larvae. Outside, sailors called out to one another, straddled booms, clambered across the fore and high upon the mizzen, the voices diminishing higher and further, lost against the wind and the ruckus of canvas. A windlass turned; a chain slumped, and then the sawing scrape of metal running off wood came unbelievably loud. For a moment, it was so loud, Llewyn thought the anchor was being raised but the sound was too close for that, and then he realised a chain was being looped through the handle of his door. Llewyn jumped up and tried the handle, only to find himself locked in. He threw his weight upon it once, and then commenced to bash it.

'Open the door,' he shouted. 'You scoundrels, open the door. Let me out. Captain Lovering, can you hear me? Open the door. Captain? Captain?'

'Everything all right?' came Mr Brynling's voice from the other side.

'You've chained me in.'

'Yes, unfortunate business, that. Your friend was enjoying a mango with the captain and seems to have gotten a bit of a dicky tummy. He's taken a turn for the worse. We fear yellow fever – perhaps the mango?'

A sliding chill seemed to glisten through the empty space in Llewyn's lungs and his throat hollowed; he laid his palms flat against the door to balance himself.

'That's ridiculous.'

'I didn't quite catch that?' Mr Brynling said.

'It is impossible for fever to set in so quickly.'

'It is rather, isn't it? So, I'm afraid we've had to confine you in a quarantine.'

'No. No. Put me back on land. I'll go back to Cap. It would only take a few minutes.'

'The tide is going out, and you're much too infectious.'

Llewyn pressed his forehead against the doorframe, and spoke softly:

'Good God, man, I shouldn't even be here. Let me out.'

There came no more any answer.

———◆———

The sea resounded in vast, seething whispers. Every few moments, Llewyn glanced at the door. It rattled all day and all night, listing deeply towards the sea, and he slept in the corner near it so he could hear if anyone passed by, facing inward, almost lying upon the wall.

They tacked near dawn. The whole room tilted. Some of trunks were overturned, and now the door loomed above him; he gripped his fingers at the creaking battens of the wainscoting and held on.

During the second afternoon, his watch stopped; he had forgotten to wind it. The absinthe was finished. It had only agonised his thirst further, and when it was gone the headache he suffered was so profound that he could no longer tell the sound of the sea from the blood pounding in his forehead.

'Are you there?'

Llewyn opened his eyes into darkness, but it was not night. A blade of daylight crept under the door. He was falling asleep now constantly, but only ever for brief moments. The room had grown strange, the distance between the objects bizarre in some way, their sizes arbitrary and mismatched, as if they had been crafted by a huge and clumsy child. The headache now raged so powerfully that he felt a kind of detached awe towards it, like he was witnessing some grand battle from afar.

'Are you there?'

The door appeared to him like a tiny, jagged mouth, smaller than he remembered it being. He wondered if he was forgetting simple things.

'Can I have something to drink?'

'The French one, we couldn't save him.'

'Please, give me something to drink.'

No answer came. He watched the blade of daylight under the door advance forth slowly.

'I am a Briton,' Llewyn said, 'a loyal Briton. I have no designs. If he's dead, it's over. Please, give me something to drink. I am so thirsty. Have mercy on your countryman. Please, give me something to drink. Please.'

The winds calmed. He woke up to find his quarters at an upright angle once more, and the noise of the sea was almost negligible. A waft of tobacco snuck into the quarters, and so strong was the scent that it almost put him into a faint. He lay down on his belly, his cheek pressed against the floor and peeked through the crack under the door. Some leather boots waited just outside, their pointy ends facing towards him.

'God save the King,' he said. 'God save the King.'

The boots turned to the side.

'No, wait. Please, wait. I'm sorry. I'm so sorry. I didn't know. I just thought it was different, that it was different from what it was. I didn't know. I don't know. Do you understand? Do you understand that I don't understand? I'm sorry. I'm sorry.'

The boots walked away.

On what Llewyn took to be the third day of his confinement, he heard clinking and shuddering, but he didn't pay attention. He was laying down on his side, facing into the wall, trembling with the cold that had become constant in his extremities.

The door opened and, even with his eyes completely closed, he was pained by the intensity of the light that flooded the quarters. He shielded his face with his arms as Captain Lovering passed over the threshold, hands behind his back, bicorne so high it pressed almost against the ceiling.

'Slovenly quarters, brother,' he said, 'though I suppose it could be worse.'

Mr Brynling and another officer named Lamprey filed into the room.

'You are arrived off Santa María,' Lovering said.

He removed two sealed letters from inside his coats.

'These are not for you,' he said. 'Do you understand?'

'To whom shall I deliver them?'

'That is not your concern. They are not for you. Do you understand?'

'I understand.'

'Mr Lamprey,' Lovering said, 'place this one where it may be easily found and place this one where it may not – beneath everything else.'

The officer took the letters and arranged them carefully into one of the trunks, and then he and Mr Brynling started carrying Llewyn's and Maxime's trunks out the door, two at a time.

'You are to continue on to the hotel,' Lovering said. 'If someone in that hotel – whoever that might be – were to take the sealed letter near the top of your trunk, that would be fine. If someone were to take the other one, well, that would not.'

'What am I to do with the second letter?'

'That is not your concern.'

Leaning heavily off the wall, Llewyn made his way up to a standing position as Mr Lamprey was carrying out the last set of trunks.

'We're dropping you inside the tide,' Lovering said.

Llewyn came near the open door and, dizzied by the freshness of the air and the brightness of the day, immediately fell to his knees. Captain Lovering waited for him to get up, and once he had risen, Mr Lamprey guided him by the shoulder towards a little jolly boat that hung suspended over the bulwarks.

'Can I have something to drink?'

The captain nodded and Mr Brynling left towards the stern. Now aided by Mr Lamprey and the rigging, Llewyn climbed into the jolly to see that the officers had laid Maxime's body out in the prow, firmly lodging him beneath the centre thwart by nestling the trunks around his torso and legs.

The youth's brow was serene, his cheeks gently drawn back in a subtle smile, and his flesh was very white in the gloom; it was only then that Llewyn realised it was early dawn and not midday.

He sat down on the burden boards, his back pressed against the transom as Mr Lamprey operated a pulley to lower him down to the water. Mr Brynling returned with a bottle of red wine and passed it down to Llewyn, just before he was out of reach.

'Drink it slowly, man,' Lovering said, 'and when we meet again, I'll do you another good turn.'

Mr Lamprey directed Llewyn as to how to untie the knots, and Mr Brynling used a push pole to fend the jolly away from their hull – and then Llewyn was unbound. Behind him, Santa María, blue against the coast, resembled crockery shards scattered amongst carbuncular hills, and, in front of him, a thin grey cloud cloaked the horizon, under which the unseen sun empurpled the shadowy sails.

Llewyn sat on the centre thwart, planting his feet either side of Maxime's legs, and began to row, but soon his oars were out of time with each other, his prow pointing back towards the Indies. Drifting for a moment, he caught his breath, and saw that already a sheath of skin had been grazed off his palms. He took several gulps of wine, and then, feeling madly drunk, righted his direction, cutting the water in such a clumsy fashion that he kept dousing himself and Maxime with bursts of spray.

He shook his head, blinked, took a few deep breaths, and set to rowing again, but he failed to dip the left paddle into the water so that he met no resistance when next he pulled on it, causing him to jerk a muscle in his back out of place. The pain was unbelievable, fantastical almost. Torturous throbs diffused warm hurt through his entire body until even his eyes were shivering. He could not row anymore, nor even sit up. He lay down between Maxime's legs, the gentle motions of the sea seeming much greater upon the bottom boards and breathing shallowly so as not to expand his own ribcage too much.

The sky lightened until the sun crept up over the edge of the bobbing transom, and through the stupefaction of his aches and terrors, he realised that if he did not reach land before the tide changed, he would be lost at sea.

<hr />

Burt Benjamin sat indolently before his new bodyguard, Xiaoguang Lee, in the back of a gently listing coach, gazing out at the verdant curved greens of coffea now dulled by darkness, unchanging rows of the stuff falling underneath him like spokes flashing on an ever-spinning wheel, their shadows sleek against the black ground, dark shadow upon lighter shadow; somewhere above, the hidden moon.

The outlines of the open vistas were like a child's rudimentary sketch, all distilled under star-shot skies and disappearing up to a higher plane as they descended along a dirt trail into the Gaspara Valley, and in all this ageless splendour Burt found only decay, death, and a terrific boredom whose end he foresaw only in suicide or war.

'I don't want any of this,' he said, apropos of nothing.

He had recently returned from an abbreviated education that had primarily unspooled itself between two wickets on a field in southern England, summoned home after his father had been killed by a one-armed Indian protesting a peonage lately and drunkenly adopted.

Burt had known his father, Osgood, only vaguely; his mother he had known not at all, and the only love he could recall receiving from early childhood were those embraces given him by his wet nurse, Erica, and the thrilling friendship of her son, Luka; and so it was with an abiding sense of unreality and ensnarement that Burt had returned to the Americas at seventeen, after ten years abroad, travelling for more than four and a half months only to end up, flustered, at the foot of his grandmother's bed in the discreet backroom of some grand, colonial hotel, her one remaining son, Charles, standing behind the headboard.

All he remembered from that first, brief interview was the wizened woman's bloodied gaze visible under her bonnet.

'Why has he gotten so fat?' she had asked.

After this Burt was left to wander alone his father's estancía – his estancía, now, he supposed, though there seemed to be no duties or choices or responsibilities incumbent upon him. His father's chambers and most of the guest rooms had been locked against his curiosity, and his childhood bedroom now seemed impossibly small. He had gone into it only once; had sat on the bed, traced his finger across the decorations of smirking suns and laughing octopi, and in the unsettled dust motes that passed the hot beams, he experienced a torment of memories of Luka – crawling inside haystacks behind him; seeking him out in the coffea; splashing him as they bathed in water troughs; comparing the colour of their gums and penises in the pantry; setting snails alight to watch them bubble away; stealing scullery maidens' undergarments and over-seers' Gaucho knives; all those nights when Luka snuck from his pallet on the floor in under the covers beside him. With just the tips of his fingers, Burt touched the pillow, and left.

He slept almost naked on divans in the drawing room or on couches in the library, writhing in the famished rapture of his nightmares under the veil of a mosquito net like an en caul birth. Twice a day, women served him gazpacho and black tea, and if he ever appeared unexpectedly, they fell silent. All the houseslaves were unknown to him, and those fieldslaves and foremen who ran the estancía had been instructed neither to talk to him nor to look at him, and the few times Burt did try to address any of them they made brief excuses and turned away; but even if it had been other-wise he could not have communicated. He had lost most of the Spanish he had possessed as a child, and he had forgotten entirely all traces of the local patois.

On his fifth afternoon of aimless solitude, he wandered off the estancía, and it was only then that Xiaoguang Lee made his presence known. He emerged on a palomino mare from under some weeping trees that bordered a small stream, and trotted along beside him, his form reflected inverted, partial and blistered, upon the water. Burt blinked up at the strange rider whose shadow fell over him.

'Are you going to stop me?'

'No, Master Benjamin.'

'Why are you following me?'

'I am your protector.'

Burt paused, the burning air heavy in his mouth, took off his hat and used his handkerchief to daub his neck and brow. Without the sound of his own footsteps the click of cicadas sounded closely, the soft yet hectic susurrating of the stream, too. The horse passed by, and the two young men, of similar ages, shimmered in the heat; a distant bird soared in the solid cerulean above the haze.

'I wish to go to Santa María.'

'This is not the way. Let us return and I will have a carriage prepared.'

'How long do you think this waiting will last? I am the only son this family possesses, am I not?'

Lee turned the horse around, relinquished the reins, and played with the fingers of his glove for a moment.

'I'm sure Mr Benjamin will find you, soon.'

'What is the old boy playing at?'

'That I could not say, sir.'

For almost a month, Burt toured the bustling markets around the harbour; idled in wooden churches rendering poetry books unreadable with the sweat of his fingers; traipsed up and down the scorched hillsides, getting sunburnt and snacked upon by mosquitos, gazed out often at the spumes of the ever-shifting purple ocean while dreaming of England at Christmas – the hot mince pies and half-drunk bottle of sherry upon the shelf; the sprig of mistletoe above the blazing hearth; cool, dark evenings of soft grasses and primeval forests; worn roads, sunken dolmens and hooting owls, all now perhaps brilliantly silenced by snow. Often, he would bring himself to tears with his own reveries.

His life was a void, this reality a series of shallow and draining repetitions, and all that sustained him was the thought that Charles Benjamin's eventual appearance might bring forth something new. And appear he did, one afternoon, as Burt sat on the terrace of a café beneath an olive tree, sipping a glass of black tea. At the next table, soldiers were eating from an open basket of fried chicken parts – necks and legs and wings and breasts glistened oilily; white flesh fell in weighty hefts from steaming bones at the slightest touch; tossed carcases provoked scuffles between pariah dogs and wheezing seagulls. The wind changed, pushing towards Burt an odour of peppered skin, thick grease and burnt fingers, and a murderous sensation rose up in him. He looked around; phosphorescent surf dashed against a distant cliff; a drunken beggar sat on the steps of the abandoned church behind him; Xiaoguang Lee leant against the counter of the café in a tall hat, guns showing in flashes across his hips whenever the wind spread out his coats, speaking with a pregnant woman in a headdress who was gutting fish.

It was then that Charles Benjamin materialised from behind the olive tree; he reached out and drew his middle finger and thumb around Burt's wrist, so that the tips of his digits just about managed to touch one another.

'Pretty good, son.'

The blustering tree shade in which the two Benjamins sat was mottled with flurried spangles of light. Unsettled olives occasionally plopped down onto their table, the rotten ones exploding against the wood, the firmer ones bouncing to the ground.

'Una copa de vino tinto,' Chuck Benjamin called out, laying his cane across his lap and pulling his hat back to unshadow his frigid blue eyes.

He waited for the serving woman to place his wine on the table and remove herself from earshot. Then, he took a mother-of-pearl box from his jacket, opened it and placed it on the table – a signet ring lay inside.

'This was the seal of your father. It is yours now.'

The band was golden, the black signet engraved with what Burt took to be a bird. The design was an oval with two straight lines intersecting it like wings, and a small, inverted triangle a little above the midpoint suggesting a beak. It possessed no eyes.

'You are going to marry Hyacinthe Dalkey in February,' Chuck Benjamin said. 'She is the daughter of Frederick Dalkey who lives down in the Gaspara Valley, and who has recently had granted him the tender to build a portion of highway that will run through here on its way between Brazil and Panama, and then some. He is married to Concessa Dalkey, née Wymond. You know the Wymonds. Tensley was in your class; his family found much fortune in the East India Company eleven years ago, once that whole mess was resolved. The Dalkeys are the only family of any value whatsoever for a hundred miles in any direction save north, and they are English, thank the good Lord. Hyacinthe is very charming. You will meet her several times before February as your first public duty is to make collections for the relief of the orphans of Santa María whose Christmas dinner is annually provided for by yours truly. She is eager for that sort of thing, and so it is that the first collection will be held in the Dalkey residence. And there you shall meet your fiancée. Is that all understood?'

'Concessa Dalkey is Tensley Wymond's aunt?'

'Older sister.'

'Impossible.'

'By another mother. The first died in childbirth.'

Burt leant his head back, scintillas floating against his vision, and saw the stone crucifix atop the church, alone against the sky.

'Tensley Wymond,' he said. 'It is such a small world.'

The clouds had gone so low over the sea below they were like small toys bobbing on the water. An olive fell onto the table jolting concentric ripples through his uncle's glass of wine.

'Now, you would like to ask me about your father.'

'Yes, all right.'

'He was a man,' Benjamin said. 'That is to say, he did not need a story to propel him through this gaunt reality. The man who killed him was not a man, just a confusion. The savage put an X on a document where his name was to go, and then thought he could renege on the mark he had made because later he found the terms to be unfavourable. To honour what you have put your name to is the profound fundament of existence in a shared universe, and if a signature means nothing then this universe is not shared but rather overrun.

'We are in an enraged and envious era that seeks to pass itself off as a just and benevolent one. Tearful charwomen spend sleepless nights raving over past or imagined humiliations; chaste law students read eighty pages of Rousseau during Michaelmas term and learn to call their wrath natural and their laziness morality; insane mystics, suffering visions they do not understand, stalk this continent preaching Zion to slaves, Inca to Indians, and equality to peasants – and I am to accept that these are to be the powers of the coming century? The truth is, son, maybe I do accept it. Maybe, I don't really mind. They won't have power over me, though, that's for damned sure. If the era rages, then rage is our business. If the land is in turmoil, then turmoil pays us rent. If the king must die, then we are selling guillotines to the masses and parasols at the show. Do you follow?'

'Yes.'

'The times and its people will always change, but this does not. Any man who believes in something he cannot see, any man who enjoys hearing little stories told about himself, any man who fears and rages and loves under an invisible sign whose light or darkness he pretends has been cast upon him, that man, I tell you, is already controlled, and not only that, I say, but he is in love with his control. All we can do with such a man is let him act out his love.'

An arc of pigeons sat along the holy water font, fluttering water onto themselves. The beggar had passed out on the steps. A laughing girl ran through the terrace, chased by two boys. In the shadow of the church doors, she stopped, turned around. The boys stood still, and for a moment, none of the three went nearer the other, and then the girl ran in through the doors, scattering the bathing pigeons, and the two youths waited for her to emerge.

'There was a boy I once knew named Luka,' Burt said.

'Family name?'

'Benjamin. A slave boy. He would be my age. His mother's name was Erica. She was my wet nurse.'

Another olive dropped down, into the glass of wine, splattering out a brief wave across the table, and Burt then noticed that his uncle had never touched his drink.

'Dead.'

'And Luka?'

'We cleared house,' Benjamin said. 'All sold after he died.'

'I was wondering if perhaps you could help me find him.'

'Have you been listening to me, son?'

'Yes, uncle.'

'Take good care of your father's seal.'

And, thinking of this, two weeks later, trundling through the Gaspara Valley towards the Dalkeys' unfinished abode to meet his fiancée for the first time, he said, apropos of nothing:

'I don't want any of this.'

'Not looking forward to the evening, sir?' Lee responded.

'Being born was only the first of these family events to which I would have rather sent my excuses.'

'Miss Dalkey is a great beauty.'

'My life is a desert punctuated solely by the occasional

mansioned cretin on the horizon; the banality of this colony is destroying my higher capacities; my youth is being wasted amongst a gaudy periphery of imbeciles, and I am prohibited from eating pudding. I have heard universal report that Miss Hyacinthe Dalkey is fetching, but I still quite want to die, Lee.'

Without saying another word, the bodyguard hammered on the ceiling with his fist, opened the door, and leapt out. The carriage still rattled along; Burt looked out and saw Lee drawing his pistols and passing into the coffea, moving towards a body of orange light like a lake of fire out of which the heads of bushes emerged.

Gunshot sounded out, and then the orange light split into divergent parts. There was another gunshot, and the carriage came to a stop. A child appeared alongside the road. The child's belly was distended with hunger, wrinkles stamped her face, and her black hair was matted in knots. She held her left forearm with her right hand, and between the fingers heartbeats of blood pulsed out. Burt threw open the door.

'Get in. I shall bring thee physic,' he said. 'Aquí. Rápido por el médico.'

The child trotted around the back of the carriage, slipping into the coffea bushes to the other side just as Lee burst back onto the trail, sprinting.

'Ándale, Jeongjo!'

'A child has been shot,' Burt said.

'She will be fine, sir,' Jeongjo said, lashing the horses. 'It is a graze.'

Lee jumped onto the step and clambered back into the carriage as the horses broke into a canter. Two Indians were chasing on foot, falling steadily behind, and then they were out of sight.

'What was that?'

'Insurrectionists. Once we have delivered you, I must make urgent dispatch to Santa María to recruit some soldiers to help us enforce the curfew.'

'Curfew?'

'Since your father died there has been a curfew, and it is illegal for natives to assemble in numbers of more than four at any time.'

'Did you shoot a child?'

'Sir, please, you are at great risk. The colony is in uproar since the passing of Mr Benjamin.'

Burt raised the curtain and stared out at the coffea.

'Be that as it may.'

They reached a winding avenue bordered by yearlings, new weeds springing up around their recently turned bases. The Dalkey mansion came into view – two incomplete wings grew out of a central house where a portico was supported by ivy-veined columns, stained-glass wheel windows pocked buttressed walls, and the gawping mouths of gargoyles held flaming torches. A cloister ran into a small chapel that abutted a picketed-off patch of earth: the family graveyard which had yet to receive into its breast its first Dalkey.

'Sir, you must lend me your signet,' Lee said, 'so as to dispatch the soldiers. Trust I shall give it right back to you.'

Burt pulled the ring off his thumb, and passed it over, and suddenly all the shadows of the night seemed to grow independent of their sources, and his flesh was just a fraying veil against the encroaching elements of the universe. He was falling amidst the lively, dancing shadows, and then he jolted up.

A canteen of open brandy rotated under his nose, shaking him back into a more immediate bodily awareness. Lee and Jeongjo were knelt over him, the latter holding the back of his head up.

'I fear your diet has been too strict, sir,' Lee said.

In a stupor, Burt shambled through his introduction to Concessa Dalkey, not discerning anything around him, and it was only when she mentioned his father that he began to pay attention again.

'. . . come quite back to life,' she was saying, 'right there in front of your eyes. O, Osgood truly loved it so. He always took such an interest in the moral culture of the lower classes. We saw it in Spanish, of course, but there will be several English language performances, I believe. Your father's idea, of course. It's entitled *Saint Angel's Colony*. I insist that you take Hyacinthe . . . Why, Master Burt, you look like you'd seen a ghost.'

Burt had placed a hand against the wall.

'It is nothing, I assure you.'

Concessa placed her palm against his cheek.

'No, I should not have mentioned your papa. You are shaking all over, you poor thing. I am so thoughtless. Come into the salon, sit down, and, please, take a restorative drink.'

'I assure you, it's quite all right – please do not fuss.'

'Well, a drink, then.'

'Thank you.'

A liveried octoroon opened a door and Burt was led into a chandeliered room. On the mauve walls hung paintings of fantastically fat cattle in verdant agricultural landscapes. Taking up most of the far wall was a marble fireplace that had never been lit, its open grate displaying an arrangement of flowers bred from those lately harvested in the Amazon basin. Beside it was a handsome girl of perhaps sixteen years of age, sulking in a walnut chair that was formed by four angels holding above their heads a lyre.

'Have you ever tried cachaça?' Concessa asked.

'Thank you, no,' Burt said. 'I would partake of a port, if you had one.'

'Of course. Esa, go to the cellar and fetch some port,' she said to a handmaid who stood in the corner. 'O, that's not Esa. Yes, you do it. Port for Master Benjamin. – Darling, darling, darling: here, at last, is young Master Benjamin.'

The girl arose; her blonde hair tumbling down to the small of her back, swaying as she approached; her expression either ethereal or bored. She was, Burt admitted to himself, uncommonly beautiful.

'It's a great pleasure to meet you, Miss Dalkey.'

She curtsied and extended her hand; he kissed it.

'In likewise,' she said. 'I believe I was once supposed to marry your father.'

<hr />

Jeongjo left the stables and wandered in the direction of the servants' quarters, passing through a domed arbour, then along a path that bordered one of the wings where tarpaulin slapped against piles of alabaster and cages of bonelike scaffolding creaked in moonlight. He reached the kitchens; steam poured out the open windows. A back door opened onto some steps that led to a gravelled circle in which a large, dry fountain awaited the arrival of four marble tiers from Florence. He sat on its edge, feeling a soft weight descending across his forehead. It would be a long night, with another journey to Santa María, then back again, and then one more journey. Laughter sounded from within. It was pleasant to hear the fires blooming, the pots bubbling, the hectic shuffling and shouting of the cooks, the bustle of life and work. The stars over the valley were like a falling net, and, for a moment, Jeongjo felt like some fantasy coming apart at the seams.

A crunching in the gravel awoke him, and he found himself, boots some ways above his head, lying on his back in the huge bowl of the fountain.

He peeked over to see a handmaid sitting on her hunkers in front of a row of pruned bushes, looking up at the stars. She was sinewy-thin, cheekbones prominent, almond eyes dark; teeth slightly gapped, one of the canines placed higher than all the others, and there was something about her, taken all together, that made Jeongjo's body an impossible furnace, and he felt a moment of agony unlike anything he had ever known. If indeed I have been stricken by love, he thought, why am I in so much pain?

Too long had passed for him to emerge from the fountain without her suspecting, not unjustly, that he had been spying on her at his leisure. His position was ludicrous. Best would be to remain concealed until she had gone back inside, and then to introduce himself to her at a later point, but it seemed a reckless trifling with fate to not approach the woman who had transported him at the moment of transportation.

'What are you doing here?'

He glanced over the edge of the fountain and saw her standing in front of him; he yawned demonstratively, and rose up, stretching his arms.

'I was just having a siesta. My name is Yi Jeongjo.'

She turned to leave.

'Goodnight, Mr Yi.'

'If I come back next Sunday, will you walk the gardens with me?'

'No.'

'I will come back every Sunday until you say yes.'

'No.'

'I have been travelling through these Americas all my life and nothing I have ever seen compares to you.'

She looked away to not show him the beginnings of a smile.

'You are a fool.'

'What is your name?'

'Esa.'

'Esa, one day we will be married, and then will you walk the gardens with me?'

She stifled a laugh; Jeongjo felt his heart somersault.

'You truly are a fool. Of course I will not marry you, Mr Yi, but if you shave off those atrocious moustaches, and don't braid your hair but rather let it fall over your shoulders, I may walk with you one Sunday.'

'I will do this, then.'

'Mr Yi, please try not to look so proud.'

At that moment, Lee strode out the kitchen doors brandishing in front of him a letter sealed with black wax.

'There you are, Jeongjo,' he called. 'I knew I would find you somewhere near the kitchens. Have you been showing off your card tricks?'

'You are a con man, then,' Esa said.

'A magician, rather,' Jeongjo said.

'Are you going to make me disappear, Mr Yi?'

'O, such spirited patter,' Lee said. 'My heart goes with it, but tonight, Esa, I am the magician and he is my driver and he must ready fresh horses this very instant.'

He bowed to her.

'It is achieved,' he said.

Later, on their way back to Santa María, pushing against the incline of the valley, the sweating horses panting into the very bed of their lungs the jasmine scent of flowering coffea, Jeongjo said to Lee:

'Young Benjamin is not so haughty.'

'They grow up.'

'They are grown.'

'So is everything this late in the day. What difference does it make?'

'Until you send that letter, we have done nothing yet that could not be undone. Your position with the Benjamins is as secure as it will ever be.'

Lee put his hand on Jeongjo's shoulder.

'It is natural to have these doubts before such a drastic undertaking, but what is really the matter?'

'I've been thinking: I saw a docile idiot beaten, and a woman dragged across the street by the hair and it made me angry. In my anger, I said to myself if we were living in a republic this would not happen – but does that make any sense?'

214

'There would be fewer villains, and those that there were would be put equally before the law.'

'Yes, but why wouldn't a woman be dragged across the street by the hair?'

'You are an idealist. This is nonsense talk.'

'No. I am just saying my outrage has passed.'

'I know what is on your mind – it is that wondrous handmaid who appeared by the fountain, and you're saying to yourself, "Why was she outside? Why did she just happen to be there at that moment?"'

Jeongjo blinked a few times, stunned; it had never even occurred to him; he had been made into a child by his love.

'Is she your girl?'

'Far worse than that – she is the arch-conspirator behind the whole revolution. It was she who organised the soirée, frightening little Benjamin into handing over the seal.'

'I asked you if she was your girl.'

'Beware your affections,' Lee said. 'You won't settle her, so don't try.'

'Please,' Jeongjo said.

'Please, what?'

'Stop.'

'Stop what? What am I doing?'

Jeongjo shook his head. There could be no answer to this passion, to how deeply it implicated itself in him.

'I don't know.'

Lee burst into laughter.

'Will you stay true to the revolution another while yet, my friend?'

———— ••• ————

After Esa's first menses, Suya spent an afternoon by the river explaining that there would be a celebration in her honour at the next full moon. In preparation for this she must live outside of the town, bathing in the river every morning while it was still dark, and then she was to run towards the sea. She was to wade out until the sun had lifted the lowest point of its circumference above the horizon and then she was to submerge herself, still looking directly towards the sun through the flowing film of water for as long as her lungs and eyes could stand it, and then she was to sing an invocation. During these preparations, she was to speak to no one; to eat three days of every five from covered meals that would be left out for her, and she was to chant and pray seven times each day, until such a time as the forest produced a wounded creature to whom she could offer protection. Whether the creature lived or died, Suya explained, did not matter; what mattered was the protection it was offered – it was to the protection, not the creature, that her maturation would be dedicated. Once she found such a creature she could return to the town, eat every day and begin conversing with others, though she must continue her morning ritual of running into the sea until the next full moon.

Several women would spend the days approaching her next menses baking a huge cake inside the earth, and on the day of her maturation, every woman who had already come of age would spit on this cake and eat a part of it. Esa would greet them in a veil of pink flowers that her mother would sew for her, the left side of her face painted, and then she would dance, first with her mother, and then with a boy who had come of age in recent months, and finally she would dance on her own, and, at this point, Iaen would ring the bells of his staff, and she would be acknowledged by the town as having become a woman, and then all the women would dance.

By the second day of fasting Esa felt like she was dying. She found a shadow, marked where it fell by placing a small stone on its outer edge, and then prayed for what seemed to be half of the day, yet when she opened her eyes the shadow still remained on top of the stone. On the third day, she ate her meal so fast that she vomited it up again. After that she ate so slowly that consumption itself grew unpleasant. Nothing smelt the way it was supposed to. Her jaw creaked when she opened her mouth, her throat was dry, and her body, not digesting food, felt unreal, and a trembling would often come across her lips and her fingers. The hunger she felt was not constant, though; a pang tightened her torso twice a day, like a panic overcoming her, and then it would disappear, leaving her subdued and weaker, but no longer hungry.

In her prayers she found nothing, not even silence, and on the fifth day, she imagined herself dying and becoming the soil. It filled up her nostrils, eyes and ears, poured into her mouth, her skin unwove, waters unpooled, bones unclenched, and she was released into the ground. The wandering spirit inhabited an unsound structure. Death was not a violent separation from life but rather only a subtle abandonment from the body, and she now felt this coming abandonment as a terrible outrage.

She opened her eyes to find a spooked tribe of monkeys staring at her from a tree. Their faces emerged starkly from their black fur, white and ugly; their sexes flapping and mammaries protruding, and then she saw, in the middle of the caravan, all the babies wrapped up around their mothers. Some rode their mothers' backs; some clung to their necks, some hung beneath their bellies, sucking at the milk. Esa picked up a rock so as to hurl it amongst them, knowing many of them would drop their babies, and then she could take one and go back home.

She waited, examining the hooded brown eyes of the babies, and then a barrel-chested male swished his tail once, and padded along a limb until he had disappeared behind a tangled curtain of vines. The troop silently followed after.

In another moment, she would have done it, she thought.

The following morning she fainted while running towards the sun, and had to lie down for some time and then walk the rest of the way, leaning frequently against the trees she passed. Then, there was a moment underwater when the sounds of the ocean began to take on a gloomy echoing. A click sounded very close to her face, and the sun became invisible behind an illuminated orb. In terror, she flailed between the breakers until she was crawling in the space allowed her between the water's drag and push. Everything was loud in her ears, and she could not tell the difference between birds, wind, sea, and her own body. And then, still half in the water, she saw two men waiting by one of the dark mouths of the forest, laying barely above the sizzling froth that licked at them through jagged rockfaces. One was dark, sitting up with his back against a tree trunk, passed out; the other was pale, flailing on the earth as if being pulled apart by ropes, and it was to one of these, she knew, that she would offer up her protection.

Kiri protested against her bringing the outsiders into town, but Iaen allowed them to stay if they remained quarantined. Then, two days before her maturation ceremony, scouts from the Benjamins arrived. Iaen went missing, then Suya, then others, and then the Europeans enacted some abstruse ritual which ushered in the night of violence. Nothing remained, then, but the protection she must offer Flores.

The next dawn, she could not wake Flores no matter how she shook him, so she went out alone to complete her maturation, bathing in a fetid canal the ancient people had made, and when she emerged she encountered one of the Europeans with a cross knifed into his head, lounging on a rock. An almond-eyed monkey sat on his shoulder, its tail wrapped around his neck. He unbuttoned his shirt, exposing the barrel of a pistol, and said his name was Quentin Cricklow and that he had been waiting for her.

Several months later, Cricklow brought her to a building site in Santa María. Unassembled scaffolding lay in jumbles. Wagons bearing flagstones had had their wheels half-sunk into the earth; taut rows of coloured strings were pegged into the ground, marking off the overlapping dimensions of future corridors, and in the middle of all this was a wooden shed, its entrance guarded by two soldiers of the militia. Cricklow disappeared into it while Esa waited outside. The tradesmen had finished for the day, replaced by slaves who were weeding around the foundations with their bare hands, moving together in silent rows, all overseen by a young boy who looked and moved like a scarecrow.

The child wore an undyed cotton sack over his head with two holes cut in it for eyes; even his hands were covered in gauze, and all his clothes were loose. Still, she recognised him. He broke through the slaves and approached her, holding his thighs apart and his arms out.

Though it took some time for them to make themselves under-stood to one another, he introduced himself as Xiaoguang Lee, and he asked her if there was anything he could do for her. With difficulty, she managed to explain that she did not want to spend any more time in the company of Quentin Cricklow.

Shortly thereafter, she was delivered to the Dalkey household where she was made handmaid to Hyacinthe, the eldest daughter of the family. In the mornings, she would pray the rosary with her, brush and braid her hair, tie her ribbons, fasten her dresses, and lace her slippers, and in the afternoons, once Hyacinthe's lessons were finished, they would rehearse together scenes from French plays, Esa always taking the role of the hero, Hyacinthe that of the beloved.

When Hyacinthe was not there, Esa was nearly always alone. Her close relationship with the daughter of the house, the clothes she wore, the way she spoke, and even the English she spoke in – all meant that none of the slaves or scullery maids would look her in the face when they addressed her; and those that might have proven friendly, such as governesses and other handmaids, were discomfited by finding themselves face to face with a full-blooded Indian of the forest.

Her only true companion was Lee. He took long walks with her the three or four times a year that Osgood Benjamin paid a visit, and they were all she looked forward to. He was no longer the defeated ghostly figure she had seen standing amidst the foundations of the theatre; now he styled himself as an English dandy, spoke with a disconcerting bravado, but still, near the end of their every walk, he would always tip his hat up, join his hands together behind his back, and ask her if there was anything he could do for her, and she would always say:

'No – there is nothing, Lee. Thank you.'

Then, seven years after her arrival at the Dalkey household, Esa saw someone she had once known. She was waiting for Hyacinthe to finish a singing lesson and had wandered down to the port. It was the hour of the siesta. The water was flat, the vessels quiet and still. In a nearby café, soldiers, returned from patrol, were drinking coffee and smoking, watching the women go by, and there, in the shade of the canopy was Abo, a man now, topless and barefooted, unloading crates of papayas from the back of a covered wagon.

'Abo,' she said.

When he turned and looked down at her a tremor of ecstasy glided from the pit of her stomach to the very root of her tongue.

'Esa.'

He spoke to her then, a little gruffly, perhaps from the surprise of seeing her, and she misunderstood maybe every fourth or fifth word. It was like a song with missing notes, and then he finished with a question. She realised that while asking her about her present situation he had mentioned that she had originally led the Benjamin scouts to their town.

She stared at him, imagining herself through his eyes – shaded under a parasol; corseted; rouged; her hair in ringlets; the veiled sleeves of her white dress; her straw hat with the blue ribbon; and then she felt a wave of love for Abo so powerful that it was indistinguishable from nausea.

She tried to answer him, but no words came. His presence was distracting; she had lost all composure. Their shared language was there; she could understand it, but she could not produce it – not at that particular moment.

'No fue así,' she said, in Spanish. It was not like that.

Abo paused for a moment, and then bowed.

'Sí, señorita,' he said.

In confusion, she left without saying anything more.

The next month, when Lee was leaning against the fireplace of the drawing room, smoking his pipe, he said, 'Well, Esa, is there anything I can do for you?'

They were alone. She was sitting sideways upon a divan, tapping a closed fan off her knees, gazing out the window at the gardens where Osgood Benjamin and Hyacinthe Dalkey were walking together.

'It cannot remain like this,' she said.

'What cannot?'

'All of this.'

Her whole existence had been a silent negotiation with loss. She had always sought to maintain detachment from her own accidental survival, but now she felt that whatever it was that had suspended her over the unmappable immensity of her own life could no longer do so. Some submerged ocean of terror had whispered within her, and with this whisper something else had disappeared, and now she was sinking, unreachable, into the chaos of what had never been.

'It cannot be this way,' she said. 'This cannot be it.'

Lee laid his pipe on the mantelpiece, and walked over to the window, his gloved hands held together behind his back.

'You know,' he said, 'I met the most remarkable man recently, an older gentleman calling himself Verato Domingo with whom I have become fast friends. He is a very distinguished man, a local slave of some reputation with rather interesting ideas. Would you care to meet him?'

'Yes, arrange it, Lee.'

'Are you sure?'

'All of this must stop.'

The jolly clattered and rocked as she was boarded. A man let out a call, and a coil of rope was tossed to him which he tied to the iron ring affixed to the breasthook, and then another rope was tossed to him, and this one he looped around a cleat by the stern before throwing the remainder back. Llewyn could feel the shadow over him, the inside of Maxime's thigh under his head, the bootsteps vibrating the boards. The man picked up his legs, and Llewyn asked:

'Are you a corsair?'

The man let go and spoke rapidly.

'No entiendo, old bean.'

Llewyn pulled himself up by the transom and found the pinch in his back had slackened to a fitful twinge. They were abreast a yawl stacked high with empty lobster traps. A boy leant off the slender mast, holding the rope that had been looped around the cleat, his face obscured by the porous band of shade beneath his hat.

'Will you fellows pull me into Santa María?'

The lobsterman pointed at Maxime.

'Estuvo enfermo?'

'He's dead.'

'Infirm? Is malady?'

'No malady. He's dead.'

'Muerto, is died, pero is malady o no?'

'No malady.'

'Inocente?'

'Yes, innocent.'

Llewyn opened Maxime's trunk, grunting with strain. He rooted around and found some crumpled bills of exchange, which he waved up at the lobsterman.

'Bring me to Santa María, to the Benjamin hotel, and you can keep the boat, too.'

'No es posible así.'

'Please, I need help. Please.'

The lobsterman spoke at length until Llewyn was almost crying with exasperation.

'I told you – yo no entiendo.'

The lobsterman made elaborate motions with both his hands, mimicking an action, and finally Llewyn understood.

'Sí. If needs must, do it. Sí. Do it.'

The lobsterman called to his son, who finished rafting up the vessels, and then hopped aboard, as well. After a brief conversation, they heaved up Maxime so he was sitting upright on the gunwale, head drooping down like one in meditation, forelock fluttering in the breeze, the discreet smile yet on his lips. The lobsterman and his son went down on their knees and prayed. Then they crossed themselves, and tipped Maxime over the side.

They towed the jolly to the wharf. The lobsterman, refusing all monies Llewyn tried to push into his hands, debarked and arranged with a stevedore he knew for Llewyn to be concealed from the port authorities beneath a tarpaulin on a cart that was carrying red bananas to the Hotel de los Benjamines.

Inside, the lobby was teeming with soldiers, groups of whom milled in and out of adjacent corridors, laughing and shouting at each other. Silent slaves in white clothes were lining the walls with an assortment of evergreen Christmas decorations, and several more were carrying a long dining table down the stairs, angling themselves in awkward contortions to get the legs past the banisters without damaging any of the wall fittings or chipping any of the paint. A maid wearing a muslin turban passed Llewyn carrying a bowl of raw veal cutlets. He turned his neck after the slug-like jumble of blue meat, and with this twist his spine tautened like a pulled bell, and he cried out.

As if in response, a clerk came up through the maelstrom of the lobby. He wore gold-rimmed spectacles, a smart grey tailcoat, and placidly held his hands together, one on top of the other as though a butterfly had been caught between his palms.

'Buenos días, señor.'

'Do you speak English or French?'

'Whichever sir would prefer.'

'I would like to take some rooms on the ground floor.'

'We have no availability on any floor until the new year, though I would of course be happy to recommend sir some more or less reputable inns, and to arrange a carriage for him.'

Llewyn's throbbing back had caused his head to crackle; it was as though little bits of scree were tumbling down inside his skull, prologuing some cranial cave-in.

'You have something under the name Maxime Sept,' Llewyn said, 'or Sèves, or perhaps de Sèves.'

The clerk retreated behind the desk and flicked through a huge ledger the size of his torso, then nodded.

'You are here for Christmas Day, sir, almost to the new year.'

'Would you send me a physician?'

'Certainly,' the clerk said, 'and if you need anything else, please ask for Mr Fritz Odendonk.'

'Yes, there is one more thing – if any correspondence arrives for a gentleman named Llewyn Chaffinch, please do pass it on to me. I'll make sure to get it to him. Thank you.'

Llewyn spent a week convalescing in bed, eating joylessly five or six times a day, staring at the sliver of unchanging blue the window's vantage offered, reading British and French newspapers more than half a year old. The doctor had told him that the only cure for his back was rest, and had given him opium for the pain, dark tobacco for energy, and tincture of quinine to allay the risk of fever – all of which Llewyn had used up quickly, with neither pleasure nor improvement.

Then one morning the maid laid his breakfast out of his reach upon the dresser and sat next to him on the bed. Without moving his neck, Llewyn side-eyed her high forehead, sharp eyebrows, slender wrists. Her name was Loah Soares, he remembered. She placed her hands on his arms, and spoke softly, causing him to draw in a breath large enough to set his back quivering.

'Loah, stop,' he said. 'No, Loah. And you know that no lo entiendo.'

Her hands vined themselves through his, stretched them over his head, and then she placed one of her hands on his hip and twisted him over so he lay on his front.

A scream was wrenched from the very core of his being; she pressed a pillow against his face to muffle the cries, and straddled him, digging her thumbs into him until she touched something that sent concentric tremors rippling through his body, and then she pushed her thumb as deep into him as it could go, and wiggled it once. Llewyn was transported to some region inside the heart of the sun, eclipsed by a white plain of limitless heat, and then he flailed up, knocked her off and grabbed her by the throat – only realising at that moment that his back pain had disappeared.

He began covering her in fervent kisses, trying to force her teeth open with his tongue; she laughed and shook her head away, and then he dropped his hands between her thighs and she kicked at him a few times, disentangling herself with a backward tumble from the bed on which he was now crouched, the tip of his spine arched towards her.

'Bon appétit, citoyen,' she said, gesturing towards the breakfast, rearranging her headdress, and rushing out.

There was a pleasant humming in his chest, and from within this vibration emanated some imperative commanding him to bear witness to the beauty of the world. Eager to get outside, he went to take some of Maxime's monies – and saw that every trunk

225

in the room had been opened and rifled through. The first sealed letter was missing; the second one was still there, at the very bottom of his trunk. To be sure of it, he placed it in the hidden compartment of his folder, and then, thinking no more about it, left the hotel, and his feet guided him to the seafront where he stood, totally outraged at all the honeyed life slipping through his fingers.

He saw everything in Santa María, and visited everywhere, for now even the ugly to him had become full of wonder. The mornings were all abustle with fishermen and seagulls and children's laughter; the markets thronged with screeching hawkers, gossip and pickpocketing orphans, and then as the sun rose to its zenith the pullulation of commerce dwindled down, until by midday Llewyn wandered alone in the chalky shade of this port town of fourteen thousand souls, the beginnings of a fresh poem composing itself somewhere beyond the edge of his mind. By evening, life returned to the streets again, though of a different sort. Off-duty soldiers and sailors on shore leave, grown lustful with alcohol and rambunctious with camaraderie, stalked between terraced cafés, whistling up at the girls tinted palely behind the windows above. Hidden beyond their own candlelit reflections, these girls lingered, curious, tentative, warned back from the balconies by their fathers, dark hair tumbling down over their nightshifts, until doors locked, louvres hanged, shutters snapped closed.

On one such hot night, aimless with longing, Llewyn saw a dark-eyed girl staring down at him from a high, lit-up window. He watched her watching him, and then, without warning, she licked her fingers and extinguished the taper she held, and at the moment of her disappearance, it occurred to him that she might not have been looking at him – from her height, she might have been looking down at anyone. Had he been favoured with her attentions, or had her eyes only passed him by on their way to another? He waited beneath her window a long time, unable to accept that he would never know the truth.

The next day, he lazed in bed, no longer feeling the urge to walk the seafront; it seemed too far a journey, and he had already been so many times. Instead, he went to a nearby café and read over the many poems he had written in his jaunts through Santa María, and found them, universally, to be incomparably weak. Page after page flowed with platitudes, predictable rhyme schemes that defused all variety and tension – and there was so much of it. Llewyn was horrified by his own language, grown so imprecise and banal; it seemed the more he loved life, the more his style retreated into inanity. He took out the unfinished poem that he had been working on when Maxime had first interrupted him in Cap, and vowed to become once more an aficionado of café life until it was satisfactorily finished, but within a few minutes he was plagued by restlessness.

He felt trapped. Santa María was a backwater outpost in a nothing colony; there was no opera for a hundred miles, and he knew of no salons wherein he could ply his wit; the Latin women with their brown eyes and regular features were uniformly beautiful, but Catholicism had rendered them inaccessible, demure and stupid. There was nothing to do in this town but drink, so he remained lugubriously drunk within himself for a few hours, and then, halfway through his second bottle of wine, recalled there was a theatre annexed to the back of his hotel. He walked to it and was told there was a showing of a play called *Saint Angel's Colony* in an hour, but he had missed the weekly performance in English, so, exhausted by the punchy natter of incomprehensible Spanish, he went to bed and lay down, the room creeping maliciously all about him, until he fell into a dream-torn sleep.

He woke up to see a slave boy on the cusp of puberty rooting around in his trunks at the end of the room.

'What the bloody hell do you think you're playing at?'

'Ven conmigo.'

'I don't give a tuppeny sigh what your name is, Ben. What are you doing?'

The boy opened the window, tossed the trunks, and then dropped out the window himself, and walked away with the trunks, arms swinging like a spin drum. Llewyn saw him disappear out of the frame, and then pulled on some breeches and a hat, the remnants of the previous night's wine making it hard for him to open his eyes fully. He dropped barefoot out the window, and followed the boy, down the hotel gardens, and into the stables where three other people waited for him.

There was an elderly African, perhaps eighty, if not more, with a white beard and a series of slim scars running in regular vectors across his cheeks. He sat across a saddle laid on the ground, smoking a cob pipe, his feet hidden under straw. Behind him, an Indian woman stroked the mane of a palomino mare. She wore a green gown with a silken stole draped around her lower arms, her hair tied high with a bronze brooch. The third person was a younger man, whose face was mostly concealed behind a salmon-coloured scarf; two silver-plated pistols with nacreous handles hung prominently from his gun belt, their barrels obscured by the fall of a magenta cape.

It was at his feet that the boy had deposited the trunks and he was now unbuckling one and feeling through it.

'Thank you for coming, citizen,' he said as soon as Llewyn entered.

'Are you the black masons of Santa María?' Llewyn asked.

'That was only a code,' the scarved man said.

'I fear there has been some mistake,' Llewyn said.

'Yes, we know. The shipment, it has come through safely, but there were fewer pieces than we had agreed upon.'

The elderly man stood up, much more limberly than Llewyn

would have expected, and then he hunkered down and opened another of Llewyn's trunks, one eye pinched down against the smoke curling up from his pipe.

'I don't know anything about that,' Llewyn said. 'What are you doing with my luggage?'

'It is just a precaution,' the scarved man said, picking up the laurel wreath. 'What's this?'

A click sounded.

Llewyn looked towards the source of this almost imperceptible noise and saw the old man had somehow managed to locate and open the secret compartment of his folder and was reading his incomplete poem.

Before he realised what he was doing, Llewyn charged at him – and then was pinned to the side of an empty stall, one gloved hand around his neck, the other cupping his testicles.

Stray angles of unsettled hay swirled about. The horses rustled their hooves through the straw and looked over their partitions, the staring faces, one after another, diminishing down the row like a play of mirrors set against one another. There was a surprised cooing from the bulging nests that lined the rafters.

'Qué piensa?' the scarved man said.

The old African put the incomplete poem back in the folder and held it out for Llewyn.

He shook his head, and the younger man removed his hands from Llewyn, and patted both his shoulders.

'Let's have some calm and discuss this.'

Blushing so furiously that even the insides of his eyelids burnt, Llewyn snatched back the folder, picked up the trunks, and walked out of the stables without looking back.

Lee watched his form retreat down the gardens, as Noel Christmas rooted around in the hay; he found the laurel wreath and put it on.

'What a disaster.'

'It doesn't matter,' Esa said. 'Let's go.'

Verato Domingo went over and kissed her on the cheek.

'Nos vemos, mi corazón.'

'Claro.'

Verato shook Lee's hand and he and Noel Christmas left together. Esa and Lee remained, Esa setting up a small portable looking glass on the edge of one of the stalls, checking her hair with a comb, as Lee did a quick sweep to see if they had left anything behind.

'We need more guns. I still have an imprint of Benjamin's seal, but it would take more time. Maybe longer than we have. We could delay.'

'It won't matter.'

'How could it not?'

Over her shoulder, he glimpsed in the looking glass the stillness of her face made small, and realised, all at once, that he had delivered her into the very fate from which he had sought to offer her reprieve.

Her reflection bore the same expression – closed-off and haughty – that he had seen all those years ago, when they were both still children, and she was waiting in the foundations of the theatre, head in her hands, loitering around a door that would remain forever closed against her. He had a moment of understanding that day. The mystery of his life had been explained – he was for her. Whatever he was, it was all for her. But now all those years, they seemed to unravel.

Though he had never once so much as touched her, he came up behind her and lay his forehead on her shoulder.

She abided it for some time, and then said his name quietly, and he raised his head.

They walked side by side through the gardens, saying nothing. Butterflies, dragonflies and bees preceded them, like a lagging aura. The dryness in the air disallowed any scent but that of heat.

Some beggars idled around the steps of the theatre, one asleep against a column, face burning in the sun. Four slaves were on their hands and knees, squeezing green flies and unsuckling gastropods from vegetables. An overseer stood amidst them, legs planted apart, a pistol and a cosh stashed in his cummerbund. Two more slaves were pulling a petrified fawn silently down into the kitchens.

'Don't walk me any further,' she said. 'Hyacinthe will be here soon.'

Soundless as a lost kite, the little parcel of shade under Esa's parasol bobbed away across the plaza.

Lee watched her disappear and then returned to the stables, saddled the palomino mare, and rode to a clearing of black stones in the forest where he met with sixteen men. With a sack of firearms he had hidden in the hollow of a tree, he demonstrated to them how to load; how to aim, how to rest the barrel off some stay, and, if advancing, how to shoot from the hip; then he watched the men drill these motions for two hours, before going over their part in the rising again, tracing maps of Santa María in the earth, telling them where to position themselves on Christmas Day, only moving into action once they had heard a specific chime from the church bells that would thereafter then be repeated in other churches across the town. He hummed the five-note pattern to them, and then the men all disbanded, splitting up into four groups, departing in different directions.

Alone, Lee led his mare to the forest's edge, then rode back to the estancía, thinking yet of the stillness of Esa's face in the mirror.

Back home, he returned to his rooms so as to wash and change before he departed for the Dalkeys', but outside his door he was given pause by sounds of movement coming from within. He peeked through the keyhole but could see no one. He checked up and down the halls, prepared his pistols, and slowly opened the door.

Burt Benjamin, surprised face glimmering with grease, was sitting at his table, eating a chicken with both hands.

'I fear I have broken with my diet,' he said.

'Your stomach has grown too small for this, sir. You will get sick.'

'You won't tell uncle, will you?'

Lee poured out two glasses of brandy, handed one to his charge.

'No, sir.'

'Lee, do you like me?'

'Yes, sir.'

'Really?'

'Yes, sir.'

Burt let out a sudden gasp and turned away. Lee sat down rigid on the edge of his own bed and started filling his pipe.

'What's the matter?'

'Nothing. I am thin. Now I am thin, I look so much more like him.'

They remained silent for a few minutes; Lee smoking his pipe, Burt staring at the grey chicken carcase – and then there came a knock.

'Come in.'

Jeongjo stuck his head in the door, and just as quickly withdrew it.

'Come back,' Lee called, rising.

He went out and saw Jeongjo standing at the end of the corridor. His hair was shining and loose. He wore a new jacket and a cravat so plump that his face looked like a sunflower.

'What is ailing Master Benjamin?'

'I don't know.'

'I'll be back in a moment.'

Jeongjo returned, carrying two bottles of rice wine, Yut sticks, cards, and a cloth bag full of bone tiles slung over his shoulder.

'Let's play Mahjong,' he said.

As he urged Burt to drink more quickly, Jeongjo explained the rules and laid out the tiles. Soon the three of them were intent on the game, and by the time Burt's cheeks were flush with alcohol he was nearly falling out of his chair with laughter at the outrageous things Jeongjo was saying – his perfect mimicking of the houseslaves' obsequious responses, his impressions of Chuck Benjamin and Hyacinthe Dalkey. He even cried laughing whenever Lee flinched at the inappropriateness of the jokes.

'Lighten up, old boy,' Burt said. 'I won't tell.'

He smashed a tile down and claimed his first victory, his posture straightening so suddenly that his arms flew out, nearly toppling over the table.

'How fine,' he said. 'I can't remember when last I had such a splendid evening.'

Jeongjo gathered the tiles up by sweeping his forearm over the table so that they all fell in a heap into the cloth sack.

'You win, sir,' he said. 'Now let us go to the Dalkeys'.'

———•——

Llewyn couldn't sleep. It was too hot. Opening his eyes, he saw it was already light. No human flesh could withstand such a climate. All burned under the white skies of some endless noon. For this, he had abandoned his mother; his sleepy home; the mornings kneading dough in his father's bakery? No – it had been for the happiness of all mankind. But where was it? To what shore was it bound? From which sky did it fall? From whose soil did it grow? None of his dreams made any sense in this tropical scrag. Everything here was brutal, murderous, poisonous, sun-drenched, and the people so cruel, so simple, so uneducated, so ineducable – and it was too hot. It was a slave society, and in every face was that threat and that promise. Life here was simplified, without negotiation, without common custom. Beyond the lash – nothing. Nothing tied these people together, and nothing, any longer, tied him to them. No culture, no dream, no shared notion, no citizenry. The terrorised and the poor could never comprehend the worthiness of freedom, rationality, equality, self-rule. Some mob might coalesce for a blazing moment, but the hour of the siesta would soon dissolve it. Here, a republic was impossible. A blossom of tears rose in his eyes. He was so embarrassed by everything he had ever written; it had all been so naïve. He was so stupid and talentless and naïve and stupid and talentless, and it was so hot.

Sitting up, he looked out the window. There sparkled the heave of ocean, a glimmering and murmuring slab, like a writhing execution block set beneath a lantern – below it, Nighttown, that subterranean necropolis too horrifying to even momentarily contemplate. This anonymous mass grave scattered around the rims of the earth, this discarded human surplus of three centuries' production, this whispering hiding place wherein are tossed all our fruitless, unyielding sins – and Maxime gone ahead of him, showing the way. There was no romance to it anymore, not even the romance of lost illusion. He resolved to leave the Americas at once – their discovery had been a terrible mistake.

'So soon?' Fritz Odendonk asked at the front desk, as Llewyn settled his bill with one of Maxime's large notes. 'We had hoped you might stay until at least Christmas.'

'I received a letter calling me home.'

'No letter came through for you here, sir.'

'I have been receiving my correspondence elsewhere, a local club. Are there any ships leaving for the British Indies?'

'Alas, no. Several arrive from there soon, though they won't be leaving again for quite some time.'

'It must be today.'

The clerk opened the huge ledger and scanned through a few pages.

'You could make your way down to Santana, Brazil, from where the ships depart more frequently. It would take several days, but there is a stage departing in four hours, heading south. The coachman is on Calle de Belluno, near the top of the town.'

'That ought to be fine.'

'Would you like me to arrange a rickshaw?'

'No, no, no. No. No, thank you. I'll walk. Goodbye, Fritz.'

'Merry Christmas, sir.'

Within moments of leaving the hotel, Llewyn had to lay down the trunks and stretch out his fingers, waiting in the shade of a wall until his temperature had gone down a little, eyes squinting against the plaza that shone too brilliantly to look upon. He staggered for another hundred steps or so, and then put down the trunks again to catch his breath. He got up, walked, and sat down on his trunks twice more and then took a more substantial break, purchasing a coffee from a vendor, and drinking it sitting beneath the shade of an awning made of a sun-faded sail. He took up the trunks again, and walked once more, before this time being waylaid by a multitude of red steers flooding through the street, herded by Indians who blocked intersections with arms held wide. The mist of dust the creatures raised seemed to separate their bobbing heads from their flowing legs, and then one of the smaller steers arced its moist face towards him and began a charge in a tumbling confusion of hooves that was soon interrupted by a switch upon the nose; it fell back in with the herd.

He reached Calle de Belluno two and a half hours later, and yet he had still arrived too early. The back of his hands, the only part of him exposed to the light, itched horrendously with sunburn, and the profuseness of his sweat made his whole flesh a scabrous layer soggily ripped at by the friction of his clothes.

The blazing street was empty, as was the black coach that waited there, its four wheels wedged behind wooden chocks to stop it from rolling, riderless, into the sea. He tried one of the doors, and found it locked. He was about to try the other door when he was distracted by a gentle clacking.

A bead curtain swayed a little in a whitewashed building opposite. Its walls were plumped out by an airy heft of bougainvillea, the flowers gently alive with humming bees. A wooden sign showed an overflowing cup and a fat chicken leg, rendered in charcoal. Llewyn pushed in past the jangling beads, and found that, though the heat remained unbearable, the incandescence of the day had mercifully been snuffed out, and into this darkness, whose slumped and distant-seeming shaded forms he could not yet discern between, he called:

'Cerveza – una.'

He lay down the trunks, took off his hat, placed it on the counter, and loosened his cravat. Once his eyes had adjusted he could make out the low-ceilinged room, its loosely tessellated flagstones covered in moistened hay and sand. At the end of an unvarnished wooden counter, beneath a likeness of the Virgin Mary, two cockatoos tapped flinty beaks off the inside of a rust-black cage. A thin Indian, who wore loose robes, was flicking at different parts of the cage, teasing the birds into clambering sideways along the wires. Outside the counter, there was only space for two low tables. One was occupied by a pair of European men in blue jackets with ponytails tied off in red ribbons; they were hunched over and whispering to one another in Spanish. At the other table, pressed against the far wall, sat three more Indian men, their faces hidden under starched hats. They wore ponchos so long that only the tips of their boots were visible, and they, too, discussed something in a hushed tone, sipping occasionally out of a communal earthenware jug. One of them had something balanced across his lap, its impression visible through the cloth of his poncho like an obscene erection.

He saw Llewyn looking at him, and he stared back, his eyes lupine and calm. Then, the woman behind the counter, an Indian also, laid a metal cup in front of Llewyn. She was stocky, short; the skin of her bare neck and cheeks glazed with a sheen of sweat.

'Salud,' she said.

'Salud,' he answered.

He took a swig, coughed and tried to catch in the palm of his hand the dense and gagging liquid whose taste blossomed through him, jolting his nerves.

'This is not cerveza.'

Someone patted him on the back; Llewyn turned around and saw one of the European men towering over him.

'It is the cauim, of the manioc root,' he said. 'The women, they make it with, how do you say, the mouth water. They break it with their mouth bones, and then they –' he spat enthusiastically onto the flagstones – 'it back into the dark, and then in the dark it becomes the alcohol. Very good, I think. Very, very tasty.'

The man had green eyes, blonde hair, and stubble so fair that it was as though his face were the vacant colour of death.

'Are you German?' Llewyn asked.

The man laughed happily.

'No, not in the least. My name, for me, is Klaus Richter. And your name, for you?'

'My name is Llewyn Chaffinch.'

'Herr Llewyn Chaffinch – wunderbar! You are the man, I imagine, whom is awaited and should therefore discreetfully come hitherwards?'

'I am not him.'

'What shame! Is this how you say? What shame? Still, you must join us good, peaceable drinking-fellows.'

His hand exerted a gentle pressure on Llewyn's back, guiding him downwards until he was sitting at the table.

'This is my friend for me, Herr Ernesto de Díos Salgado,' Klaus went on, 'one of the only few and little natives born from this lonely and Spanish little colony.'

'How do you do?' Llewyn asked.

By the counter, one of the cockatoos bobbed its crest side to side, its protruding black tongue swinging like the tongue of a bell. Ernesto stroked his moustaches, and then cocked his head back and stared at Llewyn for a long time.

'Te dije que no vendrían,' he said.

'Esperamos un poco más,' Klaus answered, and then to Llewyn: 'The word for the waiting and the hoping is the same in the Spanish. Very, very tasty idea, I think, and very typical of the Latin fates whomso meet these colonies most every day.'

'Might I ask for whom it is you are waiting?'

'Cometh a man,' Klaus answered, 'for whom believes only nations can happen from the stories of the murdered ancestors when they are within the stories and the songs and the poems that make you cry and make you very enraged and sacrificial in such an enervated manner that you are believing the living is the dying and the vice versa. It is for this man for whom we are awaiting for.'

'Without the poem, there is the nothing,' Ernesto said, raising three fingers. 'Tres copas, Consuela.'

'Not for me,' Llewyn said. 'I'm leaving soon.'

'Why are you not drink?' Ernesto said. 'Relax in you self and have you some drink. Feel major than before. You look like an infirm, an very white infirm, like a little gusano who have hope in the sun.'

'Truth is, old bean, I do feel a bit ill at ease,' Llewyn said, leaning across the table and beginning to whisper. 'Are those native chaps at yon table concealing firearms under their ponchos?'

'Who is native? I am.'

'Ernesto, please,' Klaus said. 'Herr Chaffinch, those are the llaneros from the within land where all is the grass, inside the long mountains. How do you say – shackles of mountains? The fetters of mountains? Nevertheless, they bring forth bulls to be executed

238

in the charnelling houses of Santa María, and therefore they are firearmed against those bulls whom might escape and whom are always in a rage for their freedoms – for is not the chase for freedoms the most natural estate of even the littlest of the beasts?'

The barmaid arrived and put down three more pewter cups. Llewyn took another sip of the cauim. His teeth clenched with a shudder, his throat briefly closed over; still, he gagged less profoundly than the first time.

'Do the suffers of the poors make you to cry, Mr Chafing?' Ernesto asked.

Llewyn blinked, coughed.

'What?'

'That I say – do the suffers of the poors make you to cry?'

Llewyn nodded. 'I think so. Yes.'

'Sometime I am think of all the past and I have want to scream,' Ernesto said. 'Sometime all the poors, from all the time, they is with me, and I think of all the suffers and the loves of the poors and all the sons who come of the poors and how they always have the suffers and the loves, and I can no breathe. I can no breathe and I have want to die. Who have make suffers the poors? Who have do this?'

'I don't know.'

'Someone have do this, Mr Chafing. Who is?'

'I don't know.'

'Have you make suffers them?'

'No.'

'Are you say to me the true?'

'Never have I done it.'

'Bien. Bien,' Ernesto said, raising his cup. 'Salud.'

Klaus and Llewyn raised theirs, too. They smashed their cups together.

—◆—

239

Esa looking over her shoulder as she walked away; bare face early in the mornings, dripping wet from the river; the pursed lips refusing the smile, so close all perspective was lost, lashes brushing against cheeks, a horizon of skin swallowed up by water; the shadowless form diminishing over the hill; the parasol glimpsed through a window too hot to touch; blinking against the mirrored lanternlight and the rainbowed coronas of midday; the windswept ends of hair fallen into her mouth; staring too long at the drunkard passed out on the steps; the sweat caught in the hollow of the throat; wrists deep in the field through which she waded; the cream butterfly that landed on her ribboned wrist; the moonlight that immobilised her skin.

'Soft, listen,' she said. 'I wanted to love, and you have showed me something of this. For this, I thank you.'

'Is it Lee?'

'Don't be trivial, please – not now.'

'Are you and he lovers?'

'He is more to me than a lover; he is more to me also than a brother.'

'What is more than that? A republican?'

Esa ducked through the bower into the domed arbour draped with heavy vines from which pink flowers dangled, their bells like the forlorn heads of habited nuns, her outstretched hands glancing off them as she passed. Jeongjo hesitated at the entrance, and then followed her in. It was dark; the rich fragrance of earth rose against his breath. She sat on a teak courting chair, one hand pressed against her own cheek and forehead.

'I know you are joking, but it is Lee who is a republican, not I,' Esa said. 'I am no European, and, unlike him, do not pretend to be one.'

She leant over and plucked a flower, twirled it between her forefinger and thumb. There was a yellow ribbon tied around her wrist; he had never seen her wear it before.

'Even that it is on Christmas Day is his idea,' she said. 'All these meaningless symbols.'

Jeongjo couldn't bear to look at her any longer; he turned towards the trellis, leaves and stems and flowers flowing across his jacket, and stared out at the blurred valley of coffea plants that backdropped the vast gardens, the unfinished mansion, the fountain where they had first met. It reflected brilliantly the sunshine, white and incongruous. A lizard darted around the circumference in the slim clemency of shade granted by the lip of the bowl.

'So, all this has been for what?'

'He believes in it.'

'And you, what do you believe in?'

'I believe in him; I always have.'

'Perhaps he only does it all out of love for you?'

'No one could ask someone to do what he does, and I have never asked him, and I never will.'

'For you, then, what is it for?'

'This is my land.'

Streams of vapour shimmered upwards out of the fields, obscuring the features of the valley in the unfinished insinuation of a mirage, and somewhere inside this shimmer multitudes of golden warblers flitted and called to one another.

'It is your land, is it?'

'It is not theirs.'

'And that is enough?'

'Yes, I think so. That is enough.'

Jeongjo broke off a flower from one of the vines dangling from above and placed it in a buttonhole.

'I am going to wait out by the carriage,' he said. 'I cannot say when I will see you again.'

He could not help himself from casting one final glance at Esa, but she had already turned away, the slender bones around her throat still risen from the turning away, the featureless cheek and depression around the eye all he could see.

Putting his hands in his pockets, Jeongjo walked down through the gardens.

Later, once Burt Benjamin, Hyacinthe Dalkey and Esa had boarded the carriage, Lee went up to Jeongjo, who was moving between the horses, checking their breeching straps.

'I'll see you after the play,' he said, 'in my rooms.'

'No, you won't.'

'What?'

'You won't see me tonight. I'm leaving.'

'I don't have time for this. I'll see you tonight.'

Lee put one boot on the mounting step.

'Not sitting up with me, no?' Jeongjo asked, bent halfway under a mare's belly, his hat pushed low over his eyes.

'What do you mean?'

'Strange how they don't ever make you sit on the rumble, with the rest of them. Always by their side wherever you go. You and Esa, both – the two revolutionaries.'

Jeongjo continued moving between the horses; he was only pretending to check the straps, now. Lee waited for him to go on, but he didn't.

'Do we need to talk?'

'Not to each other.'

'Come, friend,' Lee said. 'I will see you tonight, after the play. There will be time then to discuss what we must, or whatever you think best.'

Lee held out his hand. Jeongjo didn't acknowledge it. He walked past, and then climbed up to his seat, covering his mouth with his scarf. Then he picked up the reins and waited. Lee drew in a breath, about to say something, then shook his head once, and got into the carriage.

———◆———

242

The bead curtain shimmered again, swaying lines of shade beneath the tails of steam that rose from the illuminated portion of ground. By now the table was covered in empty cups and coils of ash like broken towers, and the ceiling was concealed beyond a mist of blue smoke, little ragged wisps of which disturbed the perfect diffusion.

Squinting over someone's pipe, Llewyn looked up. The man with the cockatoos had disappeared; the three other Indian men had left, too. The barmaid was nowhere, and then he saw her, dead, sprawled face down in cruciform across the flagstones.

He flinched, almost falling off his stool, and then the fingers on her right hand twitched, some small dark bauble passing between the knuckles. She had prostrated herself below the likeness of the Virgin Mary, wooden beads snaked around her wrist, silently wording the rosary.

'Faith, you have something of mine.'

Llewyn blinked and found a squat man in a chequered waist-coat sitting next to him, smiling broadly.

Klaus hiccuped and groaned, his head stooped below his shoulders, both his fists pulling at his ponytail so as to turn his own face upwards.

'Are you the one for whom we await?' he asked. 'Or the one for whom we hope?'

'Neither.'

'Pues,' Ernesto slurred, his tongue slow to retreat from the touch of his teeth, 'nadie vino.'

The man laughed and nudged Llewyn with his elbow.

'Pues, I followed himself here.'

'Me?'

'Yes, you, yes, you.'

It was so ludicrous that Llewyn burst into laughter, and then they were all laughing, their laughter becoming wilder and more hysterical until Klaus was sobbing, and Ernesto was punching the table. The man was laughing, too, slapping his knee so fast his hand blurred.

'I have seen you before, I think,' Llewyn said, massaging the mirthful strain from his cheeks.

'We met in Nighttown.'

A thrum flickered in Llewyn's throat, and a sudden sobriety glided across his cheekbones, as if something were moving his awareness closer to the front of his face. He attempted to maintain the impression of his smile.

'What did you say?'

'When you thought you'd be trapped in with all those bodies forever. Do you not recall?'

'Who the hell are you?'

'My name is Marianne Lynch.'

A cloud from beyond the mountains thinly veiled the sun, and the slanted rhombus of patterned light thrown through the bead curtains dimmed, and then the light came back again; the cloud was floating out to sea now, disintegrating above the waves.

'I think I missed my carriage.'

Lynch winked and rapped at the table smartly three times. 'Here, Consuela, acushla,' he called, 'would you ever stop your praying and bring us four glasses of whiskey. None of that slobbered American shite you've been making these poor foreigners sup upon.'

Silently, her back still to them, Consuela arose from her prayer and retreated behind the bar.

'Would you not look at that fine heap of a woman,' Lynch said. 'Wouldn't she shine something bright? There is love in these women, I tell you, and so it is they shine. Her grandmother named her Bachue, but she calls herself Consuela. Look at her. She is from a civilisation greater than my own. It is dead in dark corners, covered in forest's mulch and secondary upon its own land, and yet it is she who kneels and prays – not me. Maybe, she will be saved in that last clamouring moment, but most likely not. Most likely it is that no one comes to save, and the sacrifice is for naught. That saving was never my concern, though. My concern was only ever how to stop the screaming.'

She arrived from behind the counter with four glasses, put them softly on the table, poured generous fingers of whiskey into each one.

'Deja la botella, mi acushla.'

She put the bottle down, and Lynch pinched the inside of her thigh, winking up at her as she left.

'What screaming?' Llewyn asked.

'Can you not hear it?' Lynch asked. 'There is a scream in their eyes. In the movements of their hands; in the breaths they skip; in their stupid ideas and choices; in their pride in what is dead and unreturnable. I hear it even in the closed way they look at their own children.'

'What on earth are you talking about?'

'The screaming.'

'You hear screaming?'

'I do,' Lynch answered, 'but it's not real. It happens once and then it is gone, but they keep repeating it.'

'I don't understand what's happening. I want to go home.'

'You are a liar.'

'I do want to.'

'Aren't we not always home?' Lynch said. 'But look at this – we have grown dour with our chat. What'll we drink to? Something pleasant. You, Mr Englishman, you decide what we drink to.'

Llewyn raised his glass; he hesitated.

'For the happiness of—'

'No, no, no,' Lynch interrupted. 'Not like this. Close your eyes, and think about it, for it might come true.'

In the cantina, no lanterns were lit, nor candles neither. Long ellipsoids of shadows interpenetrated, forming upon each other layers of irregular crosses. Ernesto and Klaus were also two black fingers of shadow at the other side of the table, their features obscure hollows. Somehow, the bottle of whiskey was already nearly empty. Llewyn could hear a long-legged insect flitting its wings against the wall in fruitless trajectories. A roiled cat in heat called, and then, beyond this sound, the waves of the ocean.

Llewyn closed his eyes.

———•———

Wombspitted into rockabye darkness. Little sister expelled, too, rode out on the second wave, size of a pip. They used to speak in the womb, through navel pipes like hollows in the tree where the macaws' screech echoes through the limbs and messages through the roots. Her soul flew up to a swallow. Little swallow went north. Swallow dropped her off into the soul of that man who now comes to meet him. Here he comes. Here comes. Here comes Noel Christmas. All these bodies. All these dying. All these flesh-less backs rotting the wood with the damp of their blood. All these gangrene. All these jumping down into Nighttown. Mother died too in the crossing in the unbreathable loathsomeness, eyes closed for eighteen nights and it was all night everywhere. The chains were short because wide eyes wind their necks up in the chains and jerked their heads down to die. Not for me, they said. Not for me, this place. Here. Here comes. Here comes every-thing. He had a wife once. Her name was Yetunda. She was older than him by eight years. The first time she touched him. A cold morning, a cold June. Saw her watching him. He had come in from the fields, hungry as the. When she was putting the yams down her arm touched his left hand and that hand tingled for so long he doubted he would ever know peace again. She had secrets he must find out. They made love in the shade of the sugarcane, and he could smell the sugar like it was inside of him. There was something separate in her. The children and their life passed through, and still she was hidden. He is waiting for her in that doorway, always seeing her go along the river. He is always. From her, with him, came Olumide, Abbey, Benin. It is coming. They are breaking the. She is dead now more than forty years and still. He made money. He bought horses. Another man called King Lekan. They called him Pirate Lucky. Used to go fishing. In a skiff he would lie on his back and look at the sky. In the beginning he wanted to have a boat as big as Cuba and sail everyone home. You will come with me, Verato, he said. No, he answered. This is my home. I come from the sea, and I arrive. Here I am. This is my home. And in the days beyond the reckoning, after all these eyes that are born, there will not be enough boats left in the world. Pirate Lucky told him about his plans to be free, to go beyond. This is good, Verato said, but I do not want to lose my family. He had three children then. He had eleven horses then, and he wanted to buy his freedom. In the hold, his eyes had never opened, scabbed and teared and pussed, and in the bright light of day when it is blue sometimes he sees a shadow falling yet. King Lekan said, What day will you lose your family? I will not lose them, he said. You will lose them, so what day? I will not lose them. Understand me. You will lose them, so what day will you lose them? In his anger was some other world and Verato wonders if he ever got there. He wonders what King Lekan touches now. They hanged him on the plaza for a year and a day. His ribcage tapped against the wall like the man who came knocking. Click clack clock. When the marrow was gone the bones whistled high notes. The wind goes in, the wind goes out. His skull was the ashtray in the Janssen-Pereira billiards room. His scrotum was an overseer's tobacco pouch. His index finger was carved into a key that sits in a box of trinkets in the Leguizamón plantation. It unlocks a doll's house. It is fine. His ghost is fishing. They killed one man from every family for six days and then the slaves had to cut the sugarcane, so it stopped. His ghost is fishing. For twenty years there was peace, but peace is the glance over the shoulder as you dive into the sea. Peace is a little creature swaying the leaves above your head. You see the rustle of its wake. Look. It is already gone. The Spanish become more inside themselves, and more of the slaves began to plant gardens and wake up late. Verato was the richest man in his community. He cultivated, lent money for men to buy themselves. He bought horses. He sold horses. Olumide went north. Abbey married a gardener who lives yet above Bastaña, and he rode a horse all day and all night and all day to see her twice a year. Benin, he worked horses like his father. Older men came to Verato to settle their disputes. Younger men asked him which woman they should marry. He celebrated the ancestors, all confused now after the crossing. He blessed the descendants. He used to take his two boys fishing. Used to take his eldest to the mart and decide together what is traded and what is not and Yetunda chose the garnish for the meal that. In the morning they hooked the lines. Used to go fishing. One morning she went to fetch water and when the sun was high the canteens were empty and across the trail the water trickling yet. Even then, he called himself an old man. He was convinced to marry again. She is young, they said. You are rich, they said. This is not yet your dotage. You have children who need. Three years later and Eva was her name and she was always laughing at him, and he was always asking why. To me, you are funny. It was like living with a bird who kept flapping her wings, but when you opened the door of the cage to let her go she would stir no more. Things go less deep the second time. It is like a dream. He learned not to ask why. Sometimes she would have to stop speaking because her mouth was full of tears. With her, there came Yaa, Erica and Verato II. So without cost, then, even in the begetting. Eva only loved him once Yaa was born, and then only a little and only for a little while. Even without affection, the moments so precious. Life happens anyway. Life lived together but not with love is still life lived together. All these years. Seeing her grow old more shocking to him than seeing his own children wrinkle. There is a white that blinds. Dark is the blood swallowing. The Benjamins arrive. Charles Benjamin came to buy a mare, rapped his cane against the porch. He has two blue eyes that go out and eat up the earth. These are the eyes that are alive. He leant over and his mother whispered in his ear. What ilk of a broken-backed bitch of a place is it, he asks, where the only breeder of horses worth any salt is a freedman who must bend over his neck to fit in door-ways? His mother whispered into his ear again. If you would like to work with real horses, you will work for me. No, Verato said. I work for me. Ten thirteen fifteen years after the Benjamins arrived, Santa María was alive as it had not been since his earliest childhood. Big ships rolled in off the high seas. Boys and dogs swam out to meet them. They brought circuses from Europe. They brought Chinamen from Panama but they forgot to bring their women. Roads went everyway, between the mountains even. They put a clock on everything. They put men with guns to protect the carriages who ride the coast. Here it comes. Here is the. There was a man called Pedro Emilio Vásquez. His holding was small, weak and in disarray. He saw Verato II leading a string of eight foals down the road one day, and said, in the cunning of his drunkenness, that one of them was his property. Verato II laughed at him. They had the papers. But Vásquez said it again. He said it again. He said the Domingos talk spells to horses at night. He said, I will have the law, but this man he only talked. But he talked. In the taverna, in the street, he talked. Verato could see how it would have to happen so he went down with a colt that was worth as much as half Vásquez's land, and this man made him wait outside for more than an hour. What he had done to the soil. Seeds scalded dead above ground. Every creaking fence falling. Broken nags not worth the knackering. Creatures thirsty in the morning. When he came out, he lay on the hammock. Already

Verato knew you could not talk with a man like this. Maybe you could beat him, but only for a time. He offered him the colt. Why a colt if your child is innocent? I want two, he said, and he held up two fingers. Two for my time. Later Vásquez said, Big Domingo gave me two spellbound horses that answer not Spanish nor the lash. Mouth will not. Like a broken door. The jaw apart. The hot breath of this summer morning. The man who comes darkening the door. Who is this that I descry? That man knocking at. Out the window was the sea. He looks abroad. Vásquez drank and drank, and whenever his slates were to be cleared he would speak of Verato II, scheming for another horse. Horsethief, they called Verato. Horsewitch, they called his son. Everywhere they said it for a year. His name was no longer a name. No one bought from him. His fortune was said to be born from witchery. What should have happened before then happened too late. Pedro Emilio Vásquez tripped on his way home and lay there undreaming and that night his spine was trampled by a herd of his own suffering creatures. By a spellbound horse Verato II incanted, they said. Murder, they said. They burnt down his house once the tavernas closed. His family hid in the forest, covered in nets to escape the snakes. The stable was in uproar and when he went out he saw two children fleeing, the soles of patting feet, moonlight on dripping blades. The horses had tears in their eyes. Their tendons cut. They were all gelded, or only half-gelded, the slip of flesh hanging like a. A drop of blood in the eye. A red drop turns the. Leaking. Plashing. Flash of. Obscures and then light once more. It was a bird. A bird just flew by the window. In the chill of a rainy twilight, under the tree, breaths visible and steam on his arms as he strode through some monsoon's dripping aftermath, Charles Benjamin's cane flashing tap tap tap, and his hat always askant and his legs almost crossing one another as he walks. You, he said, it is you, and his blue eyes. You have heard of my son, Verato said. It is lies. And what do you want me to do about it? I'll give you everything. For? For nothing, I will say. He said, A good trader. You have found what play to make, the only play to make, maybe too easily. I'm going to have to put a halter on you, ain't I? As to stop the kick that follows the yoking of a sly man. No, sir. I will give you me, my son, his family, and all his issue hereafter. And? And all my horses, all my stables, all my knowledge, all my land, it is yours. I offer myself in perpetuity to the Benjamin household, he said. Inclusive of your offspring, Benjamin said. Verato II and me only, he said. Tutting, No deal. I cannot give what is not mine, Verato said. No deal. I have nothing else. But I want something else. He bent down and his mother whispered in his ear. Tell you what, Benjamin said, we got some sprouts need watering. Get me one wet nurse from amongst your milking daughters, and I will allow you to be my slave. And I tell you what else I offer, Verato? Nothing, that's what. Nothing, but that my property is mine and not someone else's. And when it comes to it, I will not be responsible for every sparrow that falls, nos entendemos? It is Erica who offered her freedom to save. Behind the eyelids, brightness. So long torqued the gush stymies. Head heavy like a. Work in another man's stables was easy. He gave himself over to riding in the evenings. Old now. Fell asleep smoking a pipe and burnt a hole in his beard. The birds looked through it. Got yams in his beard and tears in his eyes just from waking. Cracked his fingers at dawn. Learned something new every day, but didn't care. More than seventy years in the light now. A king to his people, but didn't care. The sun went up and it went down and he didn't care. He thought about the mosquitos all the time, shaped his days so as to avoid them. Habits rode him into the ground until they broke him. Since I was a child, he told Erica, I knew why the horses run. Now I only used to know. His mother was dead a long time now, buried under more children who fell off those ships. The years a man possesses outlast the man. Lozenged in alcohol, drank for years to ease the moments.

It was effortless to be king, to solve disputes, to give others counsel, to work someone else's stables. It was easy. He drank, arms outstretched towards his dotage. Fell in love with death. Sometimes in the middle of a sentence he stopped speaking, because some decade past he had already said this sentence. Most of life is above the surface, already seen. God has gone north. His breath wants to come out his mouth. The carnivals in the forest were silent. The smile on his face was a show. The trees which shaded his childhood are long dead. Those girls he fell in love with as a youth have parted ways with the wind and the stars. Welcome to the sun. Welcome. In violence or not, it comes anyway. Eyelid forced open and a flame held to the. Eye pops like a waterdrop touching the glass off which reflects the dreamed city. All these falling circles. When Erica was giving birth they wouldn't let anyone tend to her as the big rains were coming in from the sea and it was the harvest. They were cutting the coffea then. She was bleeding only a little at first. One hour to help his daughter he believes would have been enough to stop it. They would not give it. A cloth and some hot water, they would not give it. Drunk when he heard. Benjamin, come out. Come out, Benjamin. He called in all the streets. My daughter has suckled your young. She has stifled their tears with the song of her voice and the love of her heart. You want us to give birth in the fields when all the beds are empty? Enough, I say. Enough. A soldier aimed a gun at him and he walked straight out of town. A bottle of spirits. A cobweb detached by the wind, blown high through these empty streets like a ghost carriage. All the way into the forest, he walked, taking off his boots, so the snakes could bite him if they wanted to. Drank till he was beating his head against the ground, insects big in his ears, tears burning. Bumbling bees and dead monkeys whose fur moved in the wind. Panthers who laughed in the trees. Snakes drifted down the river from the mountain. A dead town upriver that had been made dead. He went into the sea, felt the waves coming in, telling his heart to swallow the water. The waves pushed him back. In the breakers, someone pulled him out, breathed into his nostrils. He looked up, saw no one. He went back into the forest and came into a town where the dead were thronging, always moving but going nowhere, and their faces white and their eyes black and then in the middle of all these was a table under a tree around which his mother and sister were sitting. They were drinking palm wine. There were cooked yams and plantains on leaves, but these they had not touched because they were waiting for him. They were the same age as they always would be and he so much older. I have missed you both so much, he said. Every day, I have missed you. Where is Erica? I say. Not yet, sister said. Not yet. A shadow on the ground, a shadow on the leaf, a shadow close to the ground, taut to the feet beneath the ladybug's spotted back, a shadow against the hibiscus, a bee reverberating from the stamen, its arc older than the planet, the lilies on the stream, and my Erica, faded out into the sun. He sat around the fire, watching stars, and when he fell asleep it was in his mother's lap. Even if all the love was murdered it remains and it never stops. Near dawn he couldn't hear them anymore. The sound of the ocean was everywhere and he said, If I live another day, I will do something. If I live long enough, someone will come. The sun is. The sun is. It is the sun that is knocking on this skull of mine. When they came, her name was Esa. The pain ended, wore itself out and he was free again. He rode a bird out to the horizon, but when he reached the curve of the earth he said, Go up, bird, go up. Drop me in the sun's mouth. Eight years I slept in the sand. Erica. Erica. It is not a man who comes, but a woman who. He saw a white dog alone in a room, a woman smoking hemp naked in a cave. He saw a doorway in an ocean. He saw a woman washing clothes in the rivers, scree loose upon a mountain. He saw the tip of the cloud coming apart. He saw the woman in bed on the sad day of big rain. He saw the soldier whistling on the galloping horse. The laughing child bathe in the waterfall, a seagull flying into the cave, an empty crib dragged across a desert, monkeys climbing a beached shark, a lover whisper yes, a plantation of screaming women, a girl slower than the water's reflection, the flea and the ghost, a black tree grow out of the sea. He saw his love look him in the eye as one day he will look back into hers. When it finally came he said, Thank you. Thank you, God. Thank you. Kyauta, Lumusi, Erica, Verato, Yetunda, Olumide, Abbey, Benin, Yaa, Maria, Eva, Yetunda, Jon, Lekan, Édouard, Luka, Sina. Yetunda. Erica. Mother. Sister. Yetunda. Yetunda. Thank you, God. Thank you. Thank you.

———— ·•· ————

'Open your eyes.'

Llewyn did so and saw Marianne Lynch tucking a letter beneath his shirt.

'Well, what are we drinking to, lads?'

Llewyn raised his glass once more, spilling whiskey onto his lap. 'To the happiness of all mankind.'

'To the happiness of all mankind,' Klaus and Ernesto repeated, out of time.

Lynch's tallowy flesh was in wavering illumination.

'O, I'll drink to that.'

In his right hand, he held a fiery rectangle, from whose lowest edge he lit the pipe that had been at some former point in Llewyn's mouth, and between his legs lay Llewyn's opened trunk, its contents a jumble.

'Is that my folder?'

'It is,' Lynch nodded.

He parted his fingers, letting the folder fall onto the trunk, and the fire took quickly, snatching away papers and clothes and bills of exchange in grasping spires that waxed and waned like the phantom of a child's toy castle, and then Lynch hauled the burning trunk up onto the table, unsettling most of the cups thereon, and all four men around the table watched the fire augment, their faces spellbound and flickering.

Llewyn, his eyes yet transfixed on the smoke rising from the sagging cage of fire, shook the final drops of whiskey into his cup. The glass neck of the bottle was hot, and when he put it down its label remained blistered across his palm.

'Consuela,' he shouted over the roar of the fire. 'Whiskey. Más whiskey, Consuela.'

The leather of the trunk began to buckle and wheeze; glowing cinders floated across the room, and Llewyn laughed. He felt relieved far beyond the point of any satisfaction he had ever previously known.

'She's gone,' Lynch said. 'No more.'

He stood up and kicked over the table, sending the blazing trunk rolling across the straw before it collapsed in on itself, bellowing from its mouth snatches of fiery cloth, and gouts of flaming papers that floated like seeds around the room, blooming little fires wherever they landed.

Klaus had fallen off his stool and was stumbling through the smoke towards the bead curtain. Ernesto had been struck in the hip by a table leg and was crawling across the floor.

'Follow me,' Lynch said.

Llewyn staggered outside and blinked. It was still broad daylight, hot and unbreathable. He saw the visible slip of the ocean glistening beyond the shade the crooked shanties threw on one another and then looked up and down the street.

'I missed my carriage.'

Very slowly, like a dancer almost, he fell over, and then was dragged along by Ernesto and Klaus, who were speaking Spanish above him. Marianne Lynch was far ahead. He kept passing out, only to be woken whenever his shins clattered off the ground, but his waking was just some agitated awareness concentrated in

255

the blocked tunnel of his throat where some horrendous liquid simmered.

In front of the trees, amidst an ocean of fallen leaves and within a dense haze of midges, lay a long, one-storeyed wooden shack faded grey with age. Ambitious, thorned weeds, some taller than the building itself, grew along the purlieu; powerful grasses fringed the roof, the rainbow-tinted highways of spiderwebs that criss-crossed their blades clotted with blustering seeds, and all the windows were lit up, their interiors obscured by gauzed curtains behind which intent coupled shadows swarmed repetitiously.

A woman dressed in black, her silent face austere, stood in the doorway. The penny candle she held guttered for a moment as she gestured briefly for them to enter, and then, without any warning, the candle went out.

Dear papa,

¿How are you? Am fin. have no novel notices no no nice history for you Brenice remain the best friend and Fatima remains in her self the bich, also am think is very nice eat custard ¿ Are agree ? the best with the jalli is the custard, &c. en inglish the medusa is the jallifish, very silly for is not of all fabricate of jalli. jajaja . jallifish no have eye, are the most scardyest by agreement generale. Also ¿ other question of animal of me for my self is dificullt ¿ the bird that not fly have liberty ? ¿ also if bird is not liberty in eschool am so me ? is difficullt question ¿ no ? yes. valley, i believe terminate here is suficient for this times.

I remain your most OBEDIENT, AFFECTIONATE, and LOVING DAUGHTER until DEATH,
Ms. BRIDGET TANNER, &c.

Play

A NGEL IS WRITING a message on a slip of paper. He blots it, then lays it on a pile at the top of the desk. He dips his quill back into the well, sighs and gazes out the window.

'I am so sad.'

There is a knocking at the door. Patrick Edgeworth storms in, throws himself atop the bed and begins perusing the books by the nightstand. 'Still at thy studies, lad?' he asks. 'How goes the law?'

'O,' Angel says, 'well enough.'

'Life – all that!'

'This melancholy is of the wasting sort.'

A pigeon lands at the window. It bobs up and down, coos, flutters away. Patrick, meanwhile, flicks through a few books, laying them down again, one after the other.

'Let me touch upon his spirit thusly – no, that'll not . . . No, no joy. No, not Voltaire, egad, nor Rousseau. No, not temperate Montesquieu, neither, shall encroach upon the dishumoured canals of this busted frame. 'Sblood, I have it.'

He arises from the bed, takes the Bible from out of his coat, and hands it to Angel, a finger against his lips.

'Soft, I go.'

He departs, and Angel glances towards the window once more, then down at the book in his hands.

'Well, then?' he says to the book. 'You are come to save me again; come to save the whole cracked universe. Whene'er I am shrunken in despair; whene'er I have forfeited all longing, grace, hope, am without lightness and without light, then, always, I have turned to your leaves and have found the roots, wherein, I believe I have found me.'

He flicks open a page, places his finger down.

'And I beheld another beast coming up out of the earth; and he had two horns like a lamb, and he spake as a dragon. And he exerciseth all the power of the first beast before him, and causeth the earth and them which dwell therein to worship the first beast, whose deadly wound was healed.'

Angel snaps the Bible closed.

'How curious! What will I with this? Well, what is a beast but a kingdom, and what is a kingdom but a nation in utero? Ay, it is fixed, then: the beast is the nation. And if a beast is a very great animal, then it must also be a very great nation. "And I beheld another beast . . ." What of this "another"? Surely, a new one, no? Well, then it is the Americas. This is fixed, too. "And he exerciseth all the power of the first beast before him." Who is this first beast if not Europe? ". . . whose deadly wound was healed." Yes, those European empires would have claimed disintegration total had it not been for gold-hearted Americas . . . All this flow of taxes from the Americas to Europe and not in the vice versa – is this just? But, what's this? "He had two horns like a lamb, and spake like a dragon." The lamb of God, of course. But these horns – Christ and the goat are entangled again. O, it must be the Americas, ay. "And he spake like a dragon." Surely, this means he will be the first beast amongst beasts. It is the age of the American come upon us, though his Spaniards have yet to be fully cast out. There, it is also fixed . . . Already, I am half-decided to become a colonist, but shall I cast loose my lines, relinquish all family and love by the chance of having alit upon these few verses? – Yes, I shall!'

He rushes across the room, takes a pile of clothes from the wardrobe, and begins packing them into a trunk.

'I will abroad,' he says. 'These European states are too flawed and unrecoverable, yea, and they have invented and inherited an European peoples as cannot be saved no more. So, I'll to Brazil where justice may yet be found in her natural estate. I'll to Brazil, where the sun is merry and bright; where the air is flavoursome honey and the birds do twangle larkily; where each carrot and celery grows luscious and thick, and each solitary purple grape is so full she might, by herself, replenish wholly the wine cask; where gold and rubies are plucked from the lap of the earth like berries ripe from the bush; yea, I'll to Brazil where native lasses, nude as Eden, pass idle days romping through forest and floating down Amazonian rivers, beauteous cheeks smiling as I come to wash them clean with the word of the Lord.'

There is a rumbling like the whole room is about to come apart, and the door suddenly bursts open. A grinning man with a face too large for his body stands there.

'Did somebody say Brazil?'

He does a few clumsy cartwheels across the floor, overturns the desk, knocks the wardrobe on its back, and, finally, stands to attention.

'Who are you?'

'Sure, amn't I only Marianne Lynch!'

The man bows so deeply that he falls, ludicrously tumbling until he has somehow landed on the bed. Then, he pulls the blankets up around his body, and begins snoring.

'Awaken, scallywag,' Angel says. 'What is your mischief?'

Lynch yawns. 'I'm in search of a situation.'

'You've situated yourself in my bed.'

'I wish to attend upon a gentleman.'

'Attend me, now – get off my bed!'

'I would be in your employ.'

'It is my sheets you have employed.'

'I seek a place.'

'Is that place my bed?'

'It is Brazil, sir.'

'Well, then, give account of yourself.'

Lynch leaps out of the bed with a delighted whoop, falls into another cartwheel, and while spinning around the circumference of the room sings:

'Well, I'm an orgy porgy spruggling sprat, a palpeen moodling spalpering brat. I'm a boreal sporeal cosmical buachaill, a toothering-floothering murthering manookle; a skizzering flithering mithering beakle, and a befeathered, be-weeping, be-creeping eekle. I'd be a patterer and a splatterer, a flatterer and a wratherner, a crooner, a distuner, a mooner and a looner; a creeping—'

'You are my man, so,' Angel interrupts, taking a sealed envelope from his breast pocket and handing it to Lynch as he spins by, 'you must deliver this letter to Molly Sheridan, informing her that I am parting forthwith to Brazil.'

'Now, mark, what is this that does betide?' Lynch says. 'Why isn't that not only the lass that I did descry out mithering the halls as I was a-passing by yonder and heard me master within speaking of Brazil? Sure, I'll call her in.' He begins shouting: 'Molly! Molly Sheridan! Molly, would you ever get yourself in here?'

A young woman appears in the doorway.

'Is this my own true love?' she asks.

'My own true love,' Angel says. 'I am to Brazil.'

'It cannot be – across that lonesome ocean!'

She staggers against the doorway, but Angel manages to rush across the room and catch her before she faints. Lynch walks apart, near the desk he has destroyed, and wraps his thumbs waifishly around his lapels.

'Across that lonesome ocean,' he sings, 'it's true I must be a-sailing; my love and I must forever part, for it's true I must be a-sailing. Once there was a time for love, when love was never failing, but space and time have come apart, and I must be a-sailing. Well, dear Molly, I love thee well, with a heart that's always swelling, but, you and I, my love, must part, for it's true I must be a-sailing.'

Molly shudders awake in Angel's arms. 'So, you're off to Brazil?'

'I am.'

'Do you not like me?'

'It's well I like you.'

'Well,' Molly says, with exasperation. 'If it's so well you like me then why in the name of God are you leaving for Brazil today, across that lonesome ocean?'

Lynch steps forth, wraps his thumbs around his lapels once more and sings: 'Across that lonesome ocean, it's true I—'

'Quiet, Mr Lynch!' Angel says, waving his fist. 'Dearest Molly,' he goes on, 'it is in the name of God I am leaving to Brazil.'

'You are so passionate,' she says. She walks a few paces, and then glances back over her shoulder at him, coquettishly. 'Are you quite so passionate about me?'

'I am, of course.'

'Well, take me with you, so.'

'We shall be married.'

'And my handmaid shall be my companion. Georgie Finch, attend me.'

A plump, middle-aged woman in a drab dress appears in the doorway. Marianne Lynch, on seeing her, shudders his eyebrows and faints loudly, his legs flying up in the air.

'We are off to Brazil, Mrs Finch,' Molly says.

The handmaid curtsies. 'Very good, ma'am. I'll fetch me bonnet, so.'

———•••———

Whispering forms in boxes shuffled past one another, small and inconsequential in the scarlet plush of the theatre, and, in the pit, men lit cheroots and pipes, their murmuring a dark ocean between the lanterns' orbs trembling along the aisles where faceless forms filed towards the privies. Hyacinthe stared at them milling below through mother-of-pearl binoculars, not looking back when the door clicked open.

A soldier approached, his bootsteps silenced by the carpet. He bowed and handed Burt a piece of paper that bore a waxen imprint of his uncle's seal. Next the seal was scrawled:

Come to carriag out back. Urjent. CB.

He folded it and put it in his pocket. 'I have been summoned by my uncle,' he said. 'I shall return presently.'

'As you like,' Hyacinthe said.

Then her handmaid fixed him with an unsettling look so ferocious that he stumbled against a chair. He glanced back again and saw his initial impression had not been mistaken; hurriedly, he left.

'Did you see that?' he said to Lee once they were together on the spiral staircase.

'No, sir.'

'How the Indian girl looked at me?'

'No, sir, I didn't.'

'Utterly rabid. Brazen. She has gone quite mad.'

They stepped outside. It was the hour of the siesta. Oily grasses and scorched leaves shimmered as a wave of dust swept across the gardens. From the stable, two horses neighed. A matronly figure wended towards the kitchens followed by a slave whose arms were laden with a basket of vegetables still warted with specks of dirt. A second slave tramped behind, carrying four geese by their broken necks, two in each fist, their webbed feet dragging in the dirt.

The carriage was parked a little way up the avenue. A hatted figure in a black cloak and scarf occupied the driver's seat.

'Who is driving this coach?' Lee asked, and then one of its doors opened, and Chuck Benjamin's cane poked out.

'Get in, son.'

'Where are we going?' Burt said.

'Nowhere far.'

'But the play . . . Hyacinthe is waiting.'

'Get in. The play is not for you.'

Burt stepped in, and then Lee after him. Chuck Benjamin closed the door and sat watching his nephew for some time.

'Did you ever give anyone your ring?'

'No.'

'Did you ever give anyone your ring?'

'No.'

'Did you ever give anyone your ring?'

'Never.'

'Do you swear it?'

'Yes, uncle. What's going on?'

'Enough to spoil the peace of this colony for a decade, perhaps more. Take a peek down the gardens.'

Through the far window, Burt saw Jeongjo and three soldiers emerge from the broad entrance of the stables. Two of the soldiers had their guns trained on his back, and the third led him by a rope that had been looped around his wrists.

'Are you going to hurt him?' Burt asked.

'Yes, very much. When it comes to the help, Burt, you must either break it in, or give it suck. It's much better to give it suck, but that does take some time. That one there, you neither broke in nor gave suck to.'

Benjamin rapped the ceiling with his cane, and the carriage began to rumble forward.

'Now, this one,' he said, nodding at Lee, 'is a lamb. I gave him suck. I remember when he was just a little orphan, robbing old ladies by the harbour. I took him in, a dirty little boy, and I made

265

him something. See, I needed someone who spoke the language that has swollen up our fortune, and he was my boy. What I'm saying, Burt, is, I trust little Lee completely, with all my heart, but that other fellow, I don't know him. – I'll get to know him, though.'

The carriage had travelled along the avenue to the front of the hotel, and there was the straight line of the sea, like a mirage flatly folded between sky and land. A troop of soldiers were marching across the plaza, large packs across their backs. About a score of dishevelled children skipped behind the swirling dust they raised in their passage, and then the coach came to a halt.

'Here?' Burt said. 'The hotel?'

'Yes. I have something to show you.'

He undid the handle with his cane, and debarked. Burt followed, and then Lee. The three went up the steps, through the empty lobby, and then they were walking down a corridor where all the glass covers of the lanterns had been removed. At its end, darkened by the tall window behind them, were three soldiers holding bayoneted rifles. Chuck Benjamin opened the final door on the left, and they all went in.

In the centre of this large room was an elderly man tied to a chair. Two teenage soldiers crouched over him. One held a rifle, its butt pattering blood onto the stone floor, and the other was using his thumb and forefinger to pry open the restrained man's left eyelid, while ushering a candle towards his face, lapping up towards his eyeball.

'This is Verato Domingo,' Benjamin said, 'the king of the slaves.'

The door closed behind them, and then Lee unholstered one of his two pistols, cocked it fully, and shot the soldier holding the candle.

———— •◦• ————

'This is the only place,' Marianne Lynch says. 'There is no heaven, only this. Feel the wonder of it. In its wounds, we sow the seeds. It is here you are most fertile. And, after a lifetime of seeking, I have at last found my villain. From him all the children flow, and he is always hidden. Here nothing dies, nothing is lost. Here, all the messages are received. It was always this that was paradise, always here, but who is the witness?'

He passes by a glass cauldron full of water, and a leafless black tree beneath which four men are feasting on some ill-looking meat. They are naked, on their hunkers, every part of their skeletal flesh and hair coated in ashy sediment.

'Am am.'

'Am am.'

'Am am.'

One grasps at another's meat, attempts to flee with it, and immediately the other three descend on him, raining down blows upon his body. Then, without warning, they scurry away, leaving the injured one behind. He drags himself across the ground until he manages to conceal himself behind the tree, leaving a slick trail of blood in his wake.

Lynch gallivants by the tree once more, singing:

'Well, we're in Brazil; where we do what we will; and we eat our fill; and we drink till we spill, and go green at the gills, and are never ill. Whoopsy!'

He slips on the blood and collapses on his back where he sees the black branches above his head.

'Master,' he calls, 'begob, if I am not mistaken this tree is an Olea europaea.'

Angel walks over, looks up at the tree. 'An all-a-air-a what?'

'I mean it is of the genus, Olea. Now, sir, I'd be quite familiar with the various twenty-eight genera comprising the taxonomic area that'd be fairly claiming to be covering the Oleaceae itself, including trees, flowers and the lianas, and this wouldn't be a

Nyctanthes of the subtribe Myxopyrum, and it wouldn't be a Fontanesia of the subtribe Fontanesieae, and it wouldn't be a Comoranthus of the subtribe Schreberinae, and it wouldn't be a Syringa of the subtribe—'

'Do get on with it, Lynch!'

'Well, sir, 'less'n I'm wrong, and the cosmopolitan distributions of this genus has fairly escaped me, I'd say it'd be fair to be surmising that this isn't Brazil.'

'By God!'

Marianne Lynch places his hands flat on the earth and then brings his knees under his chin and slowly spins his torso upside down, extending his legs until he is doing a full handstand.

'Well,' he sings, 'we're not in Brazil; where we won't do what we will; and we won't eat our fill; and we won't drink till we spill, and we won't—'

A soft keening comes from behind the tree. Lynch, still upside down, cups one hand behind his ear. Then he spies the trail of blood and follows it behind the tree. He reappears once more, on his feet now, carrying the injured, ashen man.

'Why, it's a poor little Indian,' Angel says.

Once the ashen man is let go, he crawls to Angel, where he prostrates himself, face in his hands.

'I am Angel. What is your name, little Indian?'

He shakes his head.

'Not even a name. Would you like to be baptised?'

He nods his head vigorously.

'First you must learn,' Angel says. 'Say after me – In the name of the father . . .'

'Am am.'

'No, no, no. Not like that at all. In the . . .'

'Am am.'

'Name of . . .'

'Am am.'

'May I, sir?' Lynch says.

He goes over to the tree, takes a wooden mallet that was concealed behind it and hits the ashen man on the head with it.

'Am am,' he sobs.

'Mr Lynch, stop!' Angel says. 'I'll try again. Repeat – In the name of the Father . . .'

'Da nam fada.'

'And of the Son . . .'

'De so.'

'And of the Holy Ghost . . .'

'Deh only go.'

'Amen . . .'

'Am man.'

'Fantastic! Now, let's say it again. In the name of the Father, and the Son, and the Holy Ghost. Amen.'

'In the name of the father,' the ashen man says, 'and the son, and the holy ghost. Amen.'

'Begob, he's making a fair go of it, I'll admit,' Lynch says, rubbing the wooden mallet regretfully.

'I think he's ready to be baptised. We'll call him Jacques. Grab him, Mr Lynch.'

The ashen man is lifted again and, kicking uselessly, is brought over to the glass cauldron where Lynch dangles him upside down by the legs.

'I baptise you Jacques Kelly,' Angel says, 'in the name of the Father.'

Lynch dunks him into the water.

'And of the Son.'

Lynch dunks him again.

'And of the Holy Ghost.'

Lynch dunks him once more.

'Amen.' Lynch hauls Jacques out and turns him right side up. The ash that covered him has washed away, and now his skin gleams; his hair too has come unmatted and flows long and free over his shoulders. He stands up straight, hands on his hips, and Angel passes him a handkerchief.

'Thank you, master,' Jacques says. He dabs some moisture away from his brow with the handkerchief and then looks down at himself. 'Might I borrow some cloth with which to cover myself?'

'I have just the thing,' Lynch says.

He pulls out a seemingly endless length of green cloth from his trouser pocket and passes it to Jacques who wraps it around himself into a loincloth.

'There is a savage town just up the river,' Jacques says. 'They are ripe for the word of the Lord, but I warn you, we must hurry. At night, terrible things happen in this forest.'

'I'm concerned about Molly's wellbeing, and safe passage,' Angel says.

'But, sir,' Lynch says, 'didn't you say that under no circumstances whatsoever was Molly to leave camp and come looking for you; no matter how long you took, or no matter what happened?'

'I did say this many times.'

Jacques points at the sun. 'Look, master. Night falls.'

'To the savage town!' Angel says.

They all run away, and once they are gone, Molly wanders under the tree, circumambulating it absentmindedly, reading a letter.

'This, my Angel did write me – "My love, she is so pure and true, like Adam without's navel. Her eyes alight with great delight, 'pon those oceans we must travel. My love is like a summer garden, her breath is scented hazel, and she will be my loving wife when we have gone to Brazil." O, he loves me so! I must write him forthwith.'

She takes another piece of paper and a quill from her skirts, sits down against the tree, and begins to write. The three ashen men appear, their outstretched arms curling at the fingers and wrists like octopian appendages, and they tiptoe towards her.

Molly puts her quill down, sighs, and smiles at the letter.

'This I have written my Angel. "My heart is an ocean," she sings, "that in him shall abide; and if I do not find my Angel, then surely I will die. If I find my Angel not, then die surely I will; and I'll never marry another, in this forest called Brazil. O I miss my Angel so, that I should die for love of him, and so bonny and so sweet is he that . . ." O!'

She glances behind her to see the three ashen men.

'Good evening,' she says. 'Have you seen Angel?'

'Am am.'

'Am am.'

'Am am.'

They cover her entirely with their ashy bodies, pressing their naked fleshes against her, thrusting and shuddering. The sheet falls from her grasp, and they bear her away.

When the three ashy men return, one is nibbling at some pale meat; one is wearing Molly's bonnet and dress, and the other is entirely darkened with blood, arms held wide. They are all three smiling.

———— • ————

Lee dropped the spent pistol and unholstered his other one, cocking the hammer. The remaining soldier charged with his bayonet. Lee sidestepped, clumsily backhanded the muzzle to the floor, and brought his pistol against the soldier's neck and fired, sending a spray of blood smacking up against the wall. He tossed this smoking pistol, too, picked up the fallen soldier's bayonet, and raised it on Chuck Benjamin.

There was a snap, and Lee flinched. It came from his left; he turned the gun towards the source of the sound and saw only a stuffed white mastiff perched on an escritoire, one paw pointing forward, and then he found himself on his knees, dazed by a loud retort. Blood was seeping out from beneath his cloak; the left side of his torso felt tight. He unsheathed the dagger on his belt, at which point Chuck Benjamin struck the knife from his hand with his cane, and thrashed him until he was on his back, covering his face with his arms.

The air was acrid and dense, and Burt's throat was raw with it. Breath roared from Verato's throat, every exhalation blowing away a sheet of blood that bubbled up from the slit septum of his tongue. The skin around his burst right eye had swollen over like a purple blossom. Fritz Odendonk, the amanuensis, laid the hot pistol on top of the escritoire.

A door opened – a door closed. Three soldiers waited behind Burt, rifles trained on Lee, but Burt was following Verato's line of sight. The old man had thrown his head to the side, and was glancing out the window: the mute, persistent buildings; the stupefying light; the uneven band of ocean wavering between the roofs and crucifixes; the gutters braced with pigeons; the unblinking gleam of the sun in the upper-right panel of glass; a wagon of soldiers bobbing across the plaza, their legs dangling over the sides like fishlines.

'Somebody has been using my family name to buy guns,' Benjamin said. 'Somebody who was loved a little too much.'

He pointed his cane at Verato.

'And this one was one whose life I also saved,' he said. 'I took him into my possession and saved him when the mob would have had him swinging from the bough, and then when a bad pregnancy takes his daughter off, it is my fault? It's my fault she died of the fruit of herself? A woman like a cow, pregnant every year of her grown life, and it is my fault? Every sparrow that falls is my fault?'

He bent over and picked up Lee's dagger from the floor, gesticulated its blade at Burt.

'A woman whose own milk nurtured you – practically your mother, and if she was your mother what is he to me?'

He shook his head and walked behind Verato.

'Using my good name for purchases,' he said, 'wreaking havoc with my ledgers. They gave guns to the Indians. These Indians. These Indians that live here. In this colony. Good gracious God. These ain't Mexican Indians with big castles on mountaintops, rotating crops and holding court. These are Indians that you couldn't stop from dying even if you wanted to. And you, king Domingo, a man who lives in my stables and cleans the shit from the tails of my horses, have given them firepower, firepower with which they hope to destroy what I have created.'

He drew the old man's face up to look at him by pulling on his beard, and then Lee lunged towards the rifle laying across the floor between the corpses, but before he reached it two shots were fired behind Burt, the twin blasts immediately jolting pain through the veins across his temple.

One of the bullets went into the floor, splintering shards of wood in a thunderous hail, and the other went into the flesh of Lee's thigh, and he yelled in shock, holding his leg, the blood seeping between his gloved fingers.

'Is this who you were trying to protect, Lee?' Benjamin said. 'Or is it someone else?'

'Do you reject Satan?'

'Am am.'

'And all his works?'

'Am am.'

'And all his empty promises?'

'Am am.'

'Do you believe in God, the Father Almighty, creator of heaven and earth?'

'Am am.'

'Do you believe in Jesus Christ, his only Son, our Lord, who was born of the Virgin Mary, was crucified, died, and was buried, rose from the dead, and is now seated at the right hand of the Father?'

'Am am.'

'Do you believe in the Holy Spirit, the holy Catholic Church, the communion of saints, the forgiveness of sins, the resurrection of the body, and life everlasting?'

'Am am.'

'God, the all-powerful Father of our Lord Jesus Christ has given you a new birth by water and the Holy Spirit and forgiven all your sins. Amen.'

'Am am.'

A line of expressionless Indians, all naked, file past Angel and he submerges each one into the cauldron, one after the other. They each wander away, alone, until the last dripping convert crosses themself and stumbles out of sight.

'How many is that, Mr Lynch?' Angel asks.

'Begob, that'd be sixty-six thousand, one hundred and thirty-eight souls.'

'Yes, but there's still three missing,' Jacques says, 'and night almost upon us.'

'Still, that's a fair job of work you done on them savages. O, you've fairly nomine'd and filii'd and sancti'd them, to be sure.'

'It is the necessity that binds me to the new world – which is not Brazil,' Angel says.

'Master,' Jacques says. 'If you'll excuse me, I'd like to see if I might find those three who bilked their rightful baptism.'

Angel pats Jacques's head. 'Would you not rather be sitting at the foot of our table and eating Molly's hearty stew?'

'You are such a good master,' Jacques says, 'but I should find the other three. The stew shall furnish my purpose well enough cold.'

Jacques heads south; Angel and Lynch head north.

Night falls, moonless and starless, obscuring the tree and the cauldron, but from this darkness comes scurrying and growling. Indiscernible whispers mutter to one another. Heavy weights thwack, and then a slump. The limbs of the tree creak, and there is the strain of twanging ropes stretched to tautness.

A jaunty whistle twitters nearby, and, in response, silence envelops the tree once more. The good-humoured whistling passes by the invisible tree.

'Back this way already,' Jacques's voice says, 'back in this sweet nativity of mine. Not long now till I am supping on Molly's hearty stew and regaling my new family with marvellous tales of the south, that land that abides inside the peace of unfragmented silence, beneath flocks of wandering birdsong, unwitnessed waves, the passage of the moon.'

The whistling starts again.

'Am am.'

'Who goes there?'

'Am am.'

'O no!'

There is a snap, and then a frenzied feasting is heard. Breaths suck and splutter; tongues flutter wetly over gapped teeth; bubbles pop, gulping, satisfied moaning. At last, the footsteps plod away.

All is silence.

The sun rises, illuminating the tree from where Molly Sheridan hangs. She swings lightly by the neck, wearing only an oversized grey shift that flows down loosely over her partially limbless body. Elsewhere, near the cauldron lies Jacques's perfectly stripped skeleton, sparkling brilliantly in the dawn.

Angel walks by, and then comes to a halt, seeing the letter. He picks it up and reads it. Then he looks up and sees his fiancée. He drops the letter, covers his face with his hands, his shoulders rising and falling with silent tears.

'Alas!'

Three huge shadows, like vast fingers, seep onto the tree until they grow so big that they bleed into one huge shadow. Then the shadow diminishes as the three ashen men come out from behind the tree, slinking towards Angel in strange flowing motions, nimble arms spinning back and forth.

The naked man and the blood-soaked man lift Angel up and toss him headfirst into the glass cauldron. The third ashen man, who is now not only wearing Molly's dress and bonnet but also Jacques's green loincloth as a scarf, takes a lid, some nails and a mallet from behind the tree, places the lid atop the cauldron so Angel cannot escape, and nails it shut.

They tiptoe away again, and Angel is left sealed in water, staring widely about. He knocks against the interior of the glass prison. Distended bubbles blast from out of his mouth, and then his jaw begins working against some invisible force. The tendons in his neck rise; his fingers grasp, his chest heaves, his legs thrash. Even behind the softening blue of the water, the surging redness in his flesh is apparent.

Finally, he drowns.

Burt looked down at his hands, and saw they were twitching in the same manner as Verato Domingo's, as though there were one electrical current running between them both.

'Who?' Chuck Benjamin said.

He hunkered next to Lee and raised three fingers, which he proceeded to count off one by one.

'There is you, Lee, skulking intriguer; there is the great man over there – and then there is the third. Who is it?'

'Osgood Benjamin,' Lee said.

'Idiot. Who is the third?'

'Osgood Benjamin.'

'The girl, I think, the one who waits on Hyacinthe Dalkey. It is her, isn't it?'

'It is Osgood Benjamin,' Lee said. 'He is the third.'

Chuck Benjamin made fists which he pushed against his own eyes and grunted in frustration.

'It's a woman,' he said. 'It has to be.'

'Your brother, Osgood Benjamin, conspired with the natives and the slaves to bring about an independent republic on these shores, and I helped him.'

'Idiot. Wrong. Idiot. Idiot. Wrong. My brother used you and some other idiots to destabilise this colony and its landowners, under my close guidance, and when your little sweetheart found this out she had him murdered.'

Cold with sweat, Lee glanced up at Verato now trembling softly above him, and then he looked at Burt.

'He is lying now,' he said, 'at the end, because you are here. Whatever this is, it's all for you.'

'Great dandy of the Americas,' Benjamin said, standing up, 'cut down and stupefied by a savage handmaid. Good God almighty, what a joke you've become. By the time you'd have gotten to my age, you couldn't have picked her out of a crowd of the sullen-faced bitches. Where is my momma? Call her in.'

Fritz Odendonk rang a handbell. The door opened, and a soldier pushed in Burt's grandmother in a wicker wheelchair. Her tiny body was wrapped snugly in blankets and bonnet, only her face showing.

'Is that Cicero?' she asked.

'Yes, momma,' Benjamin said, stepping over one of the soldier's corpses, and laying a proud hand on the scruff of the dog fixed upon a wooden plinth. 'I had him stuffed for you.'

'And is that Charles?'

'That's Burt, momma. I'm Charles.'

'It's very smoky in here. I'm scared.'

'Don't be scared, momma. Do you remember Osgood?'

'Yes. I remember my Osgood.'

'Well, it's a very special day. See over there. That's Lee, and he had our Osgood killed. We're going to finish burning him up now, like we should have done way back when. We're going to take—'

'You plotted out the death of your own brother,' Lee said, his breath coming fast through his nose.

'What did he say?'

'Don't pay him any mind, momma. He ain't making too much sense because we're gonna set him on fire.'

'Don't burn him,' Burt said.

He hadn't known he was going to speak until it had already happened. He looked down at his hands, as if he had forgotten something.

'What did you say, son?'

'Please, don't burn him.'

'He said not to burn him, Charles.'

'Well, then, he must do it himself.' Benjamin said. 'If he doesn't want him burnt, he must do it himself.'

From the drawer of the escritoire, Fritz Odendonk removed a fresh pistol, poured a measure of powder into its barrel, tamped the patched ball down with the captured ramrod, half-cocked the hammer, and primed the pan.

'The filth you turned me into,' Lee said. 'The things we did. Those people. Time was I thought it better I had not been born, but of late I have lived well and truthfully.'

He pulled off his hat and his cravat, exposing his mottled pate, the rift of old scars weaving the burnt flesh to itself. A plump welt had risen across his cheek from where the cane had recently struck him.

'You were my closest family,' he said. 'For my part, I forgive you. For the others, you must be counted. I have nothing else to say, not to any of you.'

He reached out for Verato's hand.

'This is me,' he said. 'This is me. Here I am.'

———•———

'O, who will sail with Angel now,' Lynch calls, striding by the tree, 'and cut in twain the plumèd wave? And who arrives on Eden's shore – to yoke its messenger to slave? It is the tinted star that breathes; the blackened sea who, restless, craves? Is it the girl within the tree; the forgotten forest, her ancient graves? Angel? Angel? Where are you?'

Angel blinks and pulses his body forward through the clear water. He presses his whitened face against the glass. No bubbles issue from his mouth, but he is alive, after all this time under-water, incuriously staring out. He knocks against the glass of the cauldron, but the water that suspends him mutes his blows, and Marianne Lynch does not hear them.

'Angel?'

Lynch accidentally stomps Jacques's ribcage in. Lifting his boot, he sees a furrow of bones dangling there like a windchime.

'Ay de mí, poor Jacky, I hardly knew ye! Where's your pluck now, you darkly creature? O, the crosses we wove and the souls we saved; all forgot now, is it? Y'are but a bone, a mere bone, a hollow arrow signposting back towards a man that once was. Up above you lurk there in heaven, Jacky, and me down here, alone in a sorrowful dawn. Sure amn't I only undone by grief?'

Shaking his leg, he frees his boot of the jangling encumbrance, then he takes one little rib bone from the heap, kisses it, and falls to his knees, holding it above his head.

'In my heart, a very great weight is,' he sings, 'for he'd be the only man I'd e'er like to spake with; who ever thought that fate'd; take such a fine young lad for the old oblative; a Christian man as ne'er could be bated, and, Jacques, it'd been some time since I ate with – such a fine, loyal and upstanding native. Hark!'

He stops, suddenly looking up at the corpse suspended from the tree.

'Ah, would you look at that? Awful stuff altogether.'

Lynch puts the rib bone behind his ear and swipes a finger against the earth, brings it close to his face, and strokes his upturned chin.

'Ash upon my little finger . . . I feel I may have some idea as to who's been up to this particular concoction of nightmare!'

The three ashen men, as though summoned, emerge from behind the tree.

'Here comes the three ashy Indians,' Lynch tuts. 'Begob, would you look at them? Had your sup of Christian flesh, ay?'

'Am am,' the blood-soaked one says.

'What's that you say?' Lynch says. 'You are softening up our Angel in yon cauldron till he is tender? Well, I'll not let you, you infinite darkness.'

He throws himself on the blood-soaked man and they tussle until they are both rolling on the ground. Lynch is overpowering the man, throttling him with his fists and then the other two fall upon him from behind, covering his body, rendering it invisible.

'Is this the end of old Marianne Lynch?' he shouts. 'No, I must save Angel!'

His hand emerges from the pile of entangled bodies and grasps at the mallet lying beside the cauldron. He swings it into the blood-soaked one's face, sending him crashing away. Then he pushes the other two men off him and runs over to the cauldron where Angel still knocks against the glass. He attempts to pry off the lid, but the two ashen men drag him down once more.

'Will there be no end to your bemithering devilry?'

He whacks the naked one on the back of the head with the mallet, putting him down, and the one wearing Molly's dress scuttles behind the tree.

'Now, I have done for you, scallywag,' Lynch says, standing over the fresh corpse.

Angel knocks on the interior of the glass once more, and Lynch drops the mallet and rushes over and begins fiddling with the lid again. The last ashen man crawls from behind the tree, Molly's dress blustering around him as he approaches, and picks up the mallet. Lynch undoes the lid, and tosses it aside, as the ashen man rises up, brandishing the mallet high, and then Angel emerges from the water, drawing in a huge breath, and yelling:

'Behind you!'

Lynch turns and takes Jacques's rib bone from behind his ear and stabs the ashen man through the heart with it.

'Lover of death!' Lynch cries. 'Rejector of the message!'

The last ashen man staggers against the tree and dies. Lynch helps Angel out of the cauldron.

'You were resurrected, sir,' he says. 'You were good and drownded and came back to life.'

'All who follow me shall never die,' Angel says, 'and I shall build a town here by this very tree – a fair and just town where all who love God and fair, honest work are welcomed. San Ángeles shall be its name.'

'And no more Spanish tyranny!' Lynch says. 'Begob, their tariffs, duties and taxes are extortionate, their administrators slow and unwieldy, their laws contradictory and completely unrepresentative of the needs of this colony!'

'Yes, no more Spanish tyranny,' Angel says. 'Many will come with false messages, claiming they have been writ in my name; many will deceive, for these are the days of vengeance.'

'O, ne'er a truer word.'

Lynch spins a quick cartwheel, then wraps his thumbs around his lapels, and places one foot on one of the ashen men he has slain.

'Well,' he sings, 'our master, Angel, staged a strangely fable; he came to Brazil, least as much as he was able; and somewhere along the way became a baneful saintly saviour; manfully averring savage behaviour; baptising bloodthirsty cannibals who ne'er deserved it – with me, his sprugglin' sprat of a servant; spreading God's word and defeating his death; drowned for eternity yet still drawing breath; bringing back life where it could be brought back at all – and now setting up a town that shall be the new capital! Well, we emerged from the sea, and we mastered the day. We came to this place—'

'San Ángeles,' Angel sings.

'—and I believe that we'll stay.'

———•———

The curtain rippled from ceiling to floor. The pit was emptying out, men funnelling towards the doors. At the foot of the stage, Esa glanced over her shoulder and saw inside a broken wheel of purple smoke three soldiers speaking with Hyacinthe in the box. She slipped off her heels, pulled herself up onto the stage, and crawled beneath the hem of the curtain.

A horizonless landscape of shadows confronted her. It was all a lie, she remembered, staring at the stage until the tree achieved in her pupils' bloom a discernible silhouette. Its veined branches slanted, cumbered by the hanging body. A brief bubbling sounded from the cauldron, seizing her into stillness. Angel had been there so long, impossibly long. Between the acts, the curtain left up, he had just floated there, dead in front of all of them. It was impossible. It couldn't be. She moved past the tree and the cauldron, feeling her way by touch of floor, and then her hands reached out into nothing. Laying down flat, she grasped about. Her fingers pressed against a wooden step, and she began to climb down backwards.

The stair led to a subterranean corridor that curved away, out of her sight. A faint band of light flitted high along each dripping wall, and her own steps echoed out whispers that seemed to come from far ahead. The light grew brighter, and now propped low against the walls and scattered along the floor were old-fashioned blunderbusses and cutlasses; hats, leather aprons, jerkins, riding cloaks, frockcoats, steel breastplates, epaulettes, carnival masks; a telescope with a cracked lens; a fanged monkey skull; a green key; a half-scrolled likeness of a blonde girl in a blue dress; a violin's bow whose few loose horsehairs floated upwards, disappearing into darkness; a pierced concertina lay across the ground, its wounded bellows stretched wide.

Then, the corridor was intersected by another. The way ahead continued on into darkness, but to the right, turned into the wall, sat Marianne Lynch, removing with a cloth the paint that had given his face a terrible and corrupted femininity.

He was perched before a candle-studded dresser in front of a tall mirror, its edges de-silvered and spotted with age. An open trunk lay at his feet. His form, in the obscurity of the reflection, was of a greenish pallor.

He was staring at her in the top corner of the mirror, and she saw herself there, too, faintly behind him.

'It wasn't like that,' she said.

He remained facing the mirror.

'You have seen the play before?' he said. 'It changes night to night. I improvise so much, but none of it matters so long as the miracle at its heart remains the same – the raising of Angel from a death you all have witnessed. That is why you keep coming back. And no, acushla, I will not tell you how I do it.'

'No. What you show, it isn't true.'

'You audiences can be so unforgiving,' he said, 'but look to your own lives, I say. Look how they are botched together out of lacunae, an embarrassment of incongruities, pain, the false dreams of idiot hearts. I give you back the dream so you can say that it is courage and not fear, but the truth is that it is fear and it is weakness. In the end, you are just cruel. You don't dislike the brutality, you love it. All the weak and fearful do. You just want it to be the good who brutalise, and you are always the good.'

'It is not the truth.'

'I gave it to you how you wanted it, and for this you haunt me. I gave you the dream made new.'

'You don't remember me.'

He laid down the cloth, its edges starkly whitened from the paint, and placed his left hand beneath his jacket. Then, his face loomed larger in the mirror, and he cocked his head to the side, birdlike.

In the theatre above, she heard the curtain winched open, its drawing blowing a draught down through the passageway that raised the hair on her nape. Footsteps trod the stage, and then something heavy was dragged across it. Gobbets of silt-like dust splattered from the ceiling of the corridor, and she looked up – a cord of wet sediment dropped and joined her right eye, and she was doubled over with the pain of it, blinking desperately, hands touching off the damp wall.

'Angel,' Lynch called, 'do you remember this one?'

A soft padding sounded from the darkness, and then Angel arrived, barefoot and dripping wet, into the corona thrown by the candles. For a moment, the only sound was the water falling from his body.

He stared at her and shook his head.

'I am Esa,' she said. 'Remember, you were sick, and I cared for you. You were sick for weeks. We thought you would die.'

Angel didn't answer; a pool of water was forming steadily around his feet like a liquid shadow.

'Why are you here, Angel?' she asked. 'Were you always with them? Were you with them when I brought you to my home?'

His mouth opened slightly. He blinked.

284

'Why won't you speak with me? In the granary, we stayed together, when I was a child. Angel, you have to tell me – were you always with them? Were you with them when I brought you and Flores to my home?'

Lynch turned around, facing her eye to eye for the first time. His left hand was still beneath his jacket.

'You know Flores?' he said. 'What are you to him?'

She took a step back.

'Answer me, girl. What are you to him?'

'I don't know.'

'Pay attention. It is important you tell me.'

'A friend.'

Waving the finger of his right hand, Lynch smiled.

'I am going to save your life, Esa.'

He twisted around, unsettling the dresser so the mirror shivered both their reflections, and then, using his feet, he drew the open portmanteau towards himself, and pulled it up onto his lap. Inside were many leathern compartments stacked with reams of papers of all different dimensions and thicknesses; some handwritten, some printed, others scrawled with verse, cross-written or blank, and then he pulled out a little gathering of veined leaves folded into a quire, tied off with a black ribbon, and stamped with a seal.

'Nearly four years ago I intercepted an exchange of letters between Flores and his daughter. Not only did I read their correspondence, but I confess I kept several of the letters in my possession. I couldn't bear to part with them, but it is time they were returned. Would you please give them back to him?'

He held out the papers to her.

'He lives hard by in a little fishing village, about two days' ride south from here. It's called Bastaña. If you leave now you will arrive there just in time for Christmas. I'd give much to see him again, but I must stay here, with the play. Even tonight, I have another performance. Here, Esa, take them.'

285

She reached out, and at the same moment Lynch took from inside his jacket a short, golden knife. He tossed it so it spun thrice in the air, caught it by the tip of the blade, between thumb and forefinger, and held it out to her like a flower, hilt first.

'It is a letter opener,' he said. 'Would you not like to read them?'

The splotch of black wax next the ribbon was impressed with a sort of bird. She took the letter opener, and then, in the corner of her eye, saw Angel move. She glanced up, and saw his lips drawn back into a sort of grimace, his face slightly turned away from her. He had shaken his head at her; she was sure of it.

'They are not mine to read.'

'Well done, my darling,' Lynch said. 'Well done. Now, if you go back the way you came the soldiers will find you, and I want those messages delivered, so continue on this way. You'll come to a window. Go through it and you'll find yourself free, nothing between you and that blazing world, but make sure you don't stop and certainly don't think about coming back. Keep going no matter what you see. O, and, Esa one more thing . . .'

He arose, arms held wide, and sang:

'Could I steal a kiss?'

He lunged. Esa screamed, waved the letter opener wildly at him. Lynch shimmied easily out of her reach. She stabbed at him again, and he spun out of the way once more, overcome by laughter, his hands on his knees.

'Only messing,' he said. 'It's not real. None of it is real so why are you still pretending?' He winked at her, tongue pressed against the inside of his cheek. 'Now, get you gone, acushla, and I'll be sure to remember you next time.'

The golden edge of the letter opener trembled in her grasp. Angel blinked slowly twice, and then, on the third blink, his eyes remained closed. She ran down the dark corridor ahead, and soon came across a wall in which a small black square was set, high up. She touched it and felt the glass hot, though no daylight penetrated. She pulled it in, spilling down on herself a few rectilinear strips of moss that had overgrown the frame, and hauled herself up through it.

Willowy branches quivered across her face; brittle, fallen leaves and the half-buried bark of emergent roots scratched at the palms of her hands. She crawled, breathless, through arid undergrowth, into greater light, and emerged from a row of bushes that lined the front of the hotel.

She stood up and saw, there, in the heart of the empty plaza, some new tree.

<hr />

In a room on the first floor of Hotel de los Benjamines, hands still tied together in front of him, Jeongjo dropped his last card on the table, taking the final trick and the game with the queen of clubs.

'Otra vez.'

Rául, the captain, leant back. He was thickset, perpetually sweating; his dense moustache twitched each time he got a passable hand.

'Well played, Jeongjo,' Santiago said, gathering cards and dealing them out again in pairs and triplets.

Santiago was the youngest, an affable and gangly Mestizo with a bony Roman nose. Whenever he wasn't concentrating on a task, he would begin smiling to himself.

The third soldier hadn't given his name, and it hadn't yet been called. He sat at the foot of the bed, gun across his lap, holding the end of the rope that bound Jeongjo's wrists, and he didn't approve of his captain playing cards with the prisoner.

'Ábrelo, Tiago,' Rául said, fanning himself.

The youth stood up, opened the window, sat down again. Jeongjo picked up the cards and scanned them. He had gotten the queen of clubs again.

A wasp whizzed in through the window, hovered in its new surroundings, its yellow stripes shining brightly. Santiago robbed the three of hearts, and the captain led with the five. The wasp bounced against the windowpane twice, then looped around and flew out again, a disappearing speck against the bright blue of the sky.

They played another game, and then there was a knock at the door. The captain drew his chair back, gripping the rifle that leant against the table.

'Ángeles,' a woman's voice said, on the other side.

'A woman?' Santiago said. 'It's a trick, no?'

'She knows the password,' the captain said.

He took the key from his breast pocket, but before he could pass it to Santiago the lock inside the door clicked. The third soldier pulled at the rope, and Jeongjo found himself yanked down onto his knees. The door opened, and the captain overturned the table. Loah Soares, wearing a wooden mask, flickered across the doorframe. There was a loud retort, and a panel of glass in the opened window shattered. The third soldier aimed his gun, and Jeongjo raised his arms so the rope's end and the gun both flew out of his grasp. Santiago jumped on top of the loose rope, but by then Jeongjo had managed to climb up onto the windowsill. He tipped over the side, his weight dragging Santiago across the room so the drop was slowed as if by pulley, and then the rope was unsuspended above Jeongjo, coiling around itself as he fell. He landed heavily on the balls of his feet, overbalanced and tottered into some bushes. He looked up. Through the vectors of branches, he saw, out of the window from which he had just leapt, a gun barrel pointing down at him, and he stared into its hollow eye, frozen, until it blurred behind smoke.

The captain shoved the third soldier out of the way and rested his own gun atop the windowsill. Jeongjo pushed himself up and ran around the corner of the hotel. Suddenly, he found himself thrown onto his back, and he wondered if he had been shot, but it was only the trailing rope tangled amidst the roots of some shrubbery. He scrambled back on his hands and knees, gathered up the reams of loose rope in his arms, and kept running, past the theatre and down the gardens, towards the stables.

'Señor Domingo,' he shouted. 'Necesito un caballo.'

The stables were empty save for four horses who turned surprised faces towards him. A fork lay tilted upon a barrow of hay. He placed it on the ground, sat on his hunkers steadying it between his boots, and worked a tine through the knot around his wrists, pulling at it until it was loosened enough that he could undo it with his fingers. Unbound, he became aware of a warm tickle moistening his scalp – a palomino mare was puttering her black lips against him, gnawing at his hair. He crawled below her snorting bites, unbolted the stall, and climbed onto her.

They trotted down through the gardens, and then Santiago and Rául rushed out of the kitchens. The captain commanded the youth to kneel and aim his rifle. Jeongjo leant flat against the mare's back, urging her forward with his thighs, his face hidden in her mane, and though Santiago had closed his eyes long before he took the shot, the ball still struck so close to the mare's front hooves that Jeongjo felt dirt ricochet up across his cheek. The palomino reared, shimmied to the side, and then broke into a gallop, and they spilled together up the avenue, her shoed hooves tattooing a perfect glissando, Jeongjo delirious with the certitude of his escape.

Then, around the corner, he saw, in the middle of the plaza, stark, alone and absurd, a leafless tree weighted down by two bodies, and Esa stood before it, and the sight of it was so strange that Jeongjo imagined he might already have become, unawares, the habitant of some sparse afterlife.

The sun shone its light down in unceasing, contiguous waves. Low buildings on the periphery of the plaza shimmered, their edges trembling like beating hearts. The tree was shadowless, austere, the vertices of its naked limbs possessing a symmetry remote from the bursting sprawl of life. It was fake, Jeongjo realised, a prop tree from the theatre. The palomino would go no closer, spooked by a crescendo of droning flies that gauzed thickly the wounds, making the two corpses appear like stirring oceans.

Hanging upside down from one of the boughs, was Xiaoguang Lee, shaded by the funnel of his own fallen cloak. On another branch had been strung up the body of Verato Domingo, wizened and crumpled. One gelid eye, half-closed, turned downwards, as if looking to the wooden sign that hung around his neck which read:

¡Muerte al rey!
¡Libertad al pueblo!

A third noose dangled from the tree – Esa gazed up through this vacant loop, directly into the white circle of the sun.

'Esa.'

She turned around, and a spangle of light flashed in Jeongjo's eyes from the letter opener she held in her hand.

'Jeongjo,' she said. 'He's gone.'

They rode away, beyond the plaza, up narrow, empty streets. Twice, Jeongjo came across long convoys of soldiers moving inland towards the forest, so he changed directions, riding to the top of a town where a large and solitary river of smoke coursed upwards, marring the blue perfection of the day.

On the mesa of a hill, they rode past a small church; and then past the terrace of a café closed for the siesta where two pregnant women yet sat in the shade speaking amongst themselves quietly – and then Jeongjo no longer felt Esa's arms around him.

He wheeled the mare around and saw her on her hands and knees on the earth.

'Esa.'

She pushed herself to her feet and began walking back in the direction from which they had come.

'Esa, what are you doing?'

Beyond her was the blur of the sea, mute from this distance, its intricacies invisible. White spumes flashed against a cliff where large breakers crept up; a seagull caught a gust of wind, floated behind the bell tower.

'Esa.'

She walked across the terrace, beneath the gaze of the two women who had fallen silent. Then she climbed up the steps of the church and tried the door, but it was locked. She knocked and waited in the slim vantage of shade the portico offered.

The clop of hooves sounded hollowly, close by.

'Esa.'

With the sun behind him, she couldn't see his face. He was featureless, an anonymous rider wrought of shadow. It was not Lee. He would never call for her again. She closed her eyes, felt the narrowness of her senses, the subtle life that animated, the constancy of the heat and silence within.

One of the doors of the church creaked opened. In its aperture stood an Indian maid holding a bucket of water with a cloth draped over her shoulder.

'Buenos días, hermana.'

Esa pushed her aside, and walked by, but the woman grabbed her passing hand.

'No se—'

She shook the maid off, and took another step forward, and then the maid reached out to her again and grabbed her once more, this time by the wrist.

'No se puede—'

Esa slammed the woman against the door, and pushed the letter opener into her neck, forcing it in all the way to the hilt. Blood sprayed up, setting her blinking. The maid slid down into a sitting position, the bucket of water she held sloshing unbalanced waves of water across her front, and Esa went down the aisle, past the rows of teak pews, disappearing into the sacristy.

Jeongjo dismounted, climbed up the steps, and stood over the maid. Tears had risen in her eyes. Blood gouted steadily around the hilt. The bells started to sound out a pattern, and they rang for a long time, and where Jeongjo waited, far below in the portico, he could sense the sound coming up through the flagstones, could feel the reverberations in his throat and the palms of his hands.

Later, Esa, her face a bloody mask, walked out the church door, and looked down at the dying woman.

'It's too early,' Jeongjo said. 'No one is ready.'

She touched her ear with her forefinger.

'The bells,' she said. 'I can't hear anything.'

The terrace was empty now. She looked around.

'They'll be coming soon.'

The maid wheezed and crumpled more profoundly against the door. Training her eyes up towards Jeongjo, her lips trembled in the failed beginning of some word, and then a bubble of blood spread across her left nostril and she started choking. He had thought it wrong to stand, so was on his hunkers next to her. There was a flower in his buttonhole he couldn't remember putting there; he placed it in her open hand. The woman opened her bloodied mouth, the pink folds in the back of her mouth fluttering, gritted her darkened teeth and drew her head back. She was trying to smile, he realised.

Jeongjo left her and went down the steps. He found the palomino at the side of the church, nuzzling at the weeds which flourished in the cracks along the walls.

Through the clamour resounding inside her, Esa saw him pass silently by above her. He said a word, but she could not hear it. Then he reached out his arm. She took it and climbed up behind him again, wrapping her arms around his waist, pressing her forehead against his back.

Together, they fled south.

———•◦•———

Three knocks against the glass and then again, the same soft pattern. If there were a fourth, Llewyn decided, he would rise, but there was no fourth. He twisted on his side, winding the sheets about him, and implicated immediately the knocks into the lunar landscape of the dream whose sense he could no longer maintain without them.

'Who is knocking?' he asked, in the dream.

A hunter scratching on the other side of the door answered:

'O, Llewyn. It is your father.'

'He is dead, and I am not him.'

The hunter stopped assailing the door.

'You can only love,' he whispered, not unkindly, 'the one you love.'

Glass broke – a woman screamed. Llewyn opened his eyes and saw fingers picking away at shards of window. A woman was yelling at him in what seemed to be some sort of Chinese, her hand on the door bolt. She wore a frilled corset that didn't cover her breasts and a straw hat adorned with four pink flowers whose stems had been woven through the embroidered tulle. Llewyn felt very dull and wanted nothing to do with any of this.

'Calm down, woman,' he said.

There was a face in the cracked glass, and Llewyn watched this face watching him, and wondered if he should get up.

A rifle butt swept along the pane, shattering and clearing the rest of the glass in a single tracing motion, and then an Indian stepped in through the window, but his poncho got snagged behind him so that he was left hunkering like a huge bat within the frame. Someone else behind him tried to unhook the hem without tearing it.

293

The woman had already gone. Llewyn rolled off the bed and crawled out in time to see Ernesto de Díos Salgado emerging from another door across the hall, naked save for his boots and a pair of long, linen drawers.

'Mr Salgado,' Llewyn whispered. 'Mr Salgado.'

Ernesto looked both ways, but in his fluster didn't see Llewyn. A woman dressed as a sailor brushed past him, and disappeared into yet another room, and Ernesto, crouching low and keeping close to the walls, crept along the unlit hall, and then left through the front door. Llewyn followed him to the door, which Ernesto had left ajar behind him. He peeked out and was surprised to learn that what he had taken earlier in the day to have been some dense and limitless forest had been in fact four saplings, a tree, and a line of diminutive shrubs planted decoratively around three sides of a water trough. He was still in Santa María.

Across the street, Ernesto was discussing something with two Indians who were carrying guns. More Indians were running up the street and joining them, and still Ernesto talked. He raised his hands and turned away. Someone said something to him, and he turned back around, gesticulating. Then he pointed his finger at a man whose face was hidden by the slant of his hat brim, and this man placed his hand on Ernesto's shoulder. Ernesto slapped the hand away, and the man's hat fell off. The man reached for his shoulder again, and Ernesto caught his wrist and pulled it so that the man doubled over and fell. Another Indian in the crowd stepped forward and seemed to only lightly touch Ernesto on the back of the head, but with this touch Ernesto collapsed face down. Immediately, five or six people surrounded his body, and began kicking him. There were about thirty Indians in the crowd now.

One of the first two men Ernesto had been speaking with walked over to the man sitting on the ground whose hat lay next to him. He offered the man his rifle, but the latter only put his hat back on, and remained sitting there. The man with the gun then went back to Ernesto and shot him in the head, and the people who had been kicking him scattered.

Llewyn closed the front door.

Inside, to his right, the three Indians who had come in through the window were going in and out of all the rooms, moving in his direction. Two of them were armed. Llewyn opened the front door again, and walked along the thronging street, keeping his head down. There were about fifty people gathered there now, and still more arriving.

An Indian child came up to Llewyn and started speaking to him in a rapid patois occasionally punctuated by Spanish. He nodded at her, keeping up his pace, and she put her hand in his trouser pocket, and when he didn't stop walking she started screaming. He pushed her away, broke into a sprint, and then heard behind him several men shouting, and, though he didn't look back, he was certain they were giving chase.

Up the street, he passed a boarded storefront where a bearded man in a leather apron knelt in a doorway, a rifle propped against his shoulder.

'Pasa.'

Llewyn stopped, raised his hands.

'Pasa.'

'Where should I pass?'

The bearded man shuffled sideways so he was pressing his kneeling body against the doorjamb, and nodded for Llewyn to enter, but then the men chasing Llewyn arrived, halting suddenly on seeing him with his hands raised.

A shot went off. Llewyn turned around to see if anyone had been hit, and saw eight youths, all without weapons, looking at each other. The door slammed shut, and then they all rushed towards the store. One kicked at the door handle; two started prying at the boards, and one climbed onto the shoulders of another, shimmying his way up onto the roof.

Llewyn realised they had forgotten about him. He ran again.

After a few minutes, he paused to get sick, but nothing came up. There was a sound like sand blowing across a beach, but it was coming from inside his head. Holding his sides, he staggered along a street, passing by three slaves who were carrying a divan with a Venetian mirror, a rug, a clock, a pistol and a steaming apple crumble all balanced on top of it.

Llewyn slowed down to a limp, gasping hot air, and then he heard the plaintive lowing of cattle in the distance. He went towards the sound and saw a huge, uninhabited structure set off at some distance from all the others, surrounded by a dense crown of floppy weeds adorned with spiky violet flowers, many of which commenced their growth far up in the walls.

He looked inside the entrance. A dismal metal maze was fixed atop a beige slatted floor. Grids of fences and gates faced onto one another, the myriad quadrants of poles dulled and rusted, their undersides bumped with the gathered residue formed by the oceans of blood and faeces that had sprayed across them over the decades. Blackened chutes hung off the walls, and at regular intervals were set huge vices on raised platforms below scaffolds of harnesses and swings.

It was a deserted slaughterhouse. He felt it all: imbibed the terrorised secretions, the tumbling viscera sluicing down into the runoff, the last animal gasps, those dimming eyes. There was another opening across the killing floor, the same size and dimensions as the one on whose threshold Llewyn stood – but he could not cross. The aroma of murder was too powerful.

He went around the outside of the building, to the back, where he found a pen full of red steer. There were perhaps twenty of the creatures, so closely packed that when one drooled or shit it was always upon the flank or face of another.

The enclosure was in the middle of a lot where clumps of grass grew high in peaceful desuetude. The violet flowers were there, as well. An aureole of flies rose and fell. A lonely cricket clicked and whirred. Tiny birds glided in pairs from out of concealed scrape nests, flying around the steers' heads as though taunting them, their beaks sporting bright fragments of leaf and petal.

Llewyn walked up to the gate of the pen, so close that he could see the insects crawling upon their black eyelids. He felt the breath groan from their nostrils across his fingers, and then moistly across his thigh and crotch, and he looked down and saw that his trousers and drawers had been torn open, and his right pocket was missing.

For the first time since he had been woken up by the three knocks, there came some slight unclenching of his fear, and all his enormous drunkenness came spinning up inside him once more.

<hr />

A high sea; an immobile sky; white sun's unblinking eye; a light no ghost could withstand; the darkening of the reverie; since he was a little child, this man who had followed him; a frozen fragment, mutilated and fractal; the déjà vu; the vast inheritance coming down; the slaves who fell silent when they heard him unbolting the front gate; the naked woman who smiled in the shade; splayed innards of chickens unreadable in the courtyard; the scream that made no sound; the never knowing; the child who was lost; the child who became the nightmare.

'Wake up.'

'I am tired, uncle. Let me rest, please.'

In the heart of a convoy of marching soldiers, the Benjamins trundled through the forest in a black carriage, its curtains closed over.

'Open your eyes. We are almost there.'

'Please.'

'I know you gave your ring away, Burt, but it's all right. You don't need to pretend anymore. We are family.'

Burt opened his eyes, their lids swollen from a slew of baleful dreams, to see the pacific gaze of Chuck Benjamin trained upon him, and this gaze he held.

Beside his uncle, his grandmother slept with her mouth hanging ajar, wrapped tight in swaddling and strapped back into a raised seat by a leather harness.

'I have invited the British in,' Chuck Benjamin said. 'I have withdrawn my bodyguard, leaving those loyal to the Spanish exposed upon the coast – exposure was always the problem with Santa María. It will fall soon, but after today the Spanish will not offer so much resistance.'

He paused, lifted the curtain slightly, and Burt saw in the slender gap between glass and rippling cambric, the side-profile of six soldiers who flanked the carriage, their visages greened and murky, their shoulders and hats scored with fresh streaks of guano.

Benjamin let fall the curtain again.

'What is a republic? What is a colony?' he said. 'It is nothing, nothing. The only question of any import is whether it is French or whether it is British. For now, I favour the British, and so do the banks. There are more French, but British ships are superior, and, in connecting this world to itself, we must live yet upon its rims until such a time as we can burrow between the continents or leap over them. I choose the British – that is all. And these so-called Spanish, these arrogant provincial landowners who have sat on contracts as though they were their personal chamber pots for the last hundred and fifty years – after today, they will be begging the British to come in and lay down order, because, tonight, the slaves and natives, in their grief, will burn Santa María to the ground.'

Burt felt tears fall upon his cheeks; he swiped at them with the back of his wrist.

'Good,' he said.

'O, you like these little tantrums, do you? This righteous rage, vaguely addressed? You believe in the terminally unsaved who scream shrilly about freedom, but who only want to be kindlier enslaved? Would you like to throw your own tantrum, Burt? And to what end?

'Listen – I said no more pretending, and I meant it. Now, because I trust you, I will tell you the miracle. There is only one but it is everywhere, and this is it. Pinch the mother's dugs, the more she milks. Pilfer the honey, the longer the bee labours in the glade. Snip the bud, many flowers grow. Strip the ewe, her next wool weaves thicker. Kill the son in war, the mother begets more boys. Offer up one body to the masses, they give back a thousand. Sow a nightmare into a man, he returns it to you in the light of day. Tell a man he is just, and he will sentence everything he sees to death. Have him deliver one single message without a fixed address, and he will spend his only life spreading it to the whole world.'

'Stop!'

Benjamin tapped his signet off his cane thrice, never averting his eyes from his nephew's face.

'Is this your tantrum?'

'I can't do this,' Burt said. 'I have nothing. I can't. It's too much. I don't want this, any of this. I can't have been the one who . . . I can't have done that, not that. I don't want to live here. It's too hot. I don't want to be his son. This family . . . This . . . I can't. This is my life. I think about staying here and I can't breathe. This is my . . . I can't breathe, uncle. I can't breathe. I can't be the one who did that. It was . . . Help me, please. Help me. O my God, I'm so scared. What have I done? It hurts too much. I hate it here. I hate this life. I hate it all so much. Uncle, please, I have nothing. O, my God. Please, uncle. Please let me go. Please. I have nothing. No one. Please, uncle. All this, I don't want it. I can't do it. Please, there has to be another way. There has to be a way out. O, my God. I can't. Please.'

In his effort to stop himself from crying, Burt started gagging, and then, with a painful flutter, his throat constricted. He muffled his mouth by pressing it against the upholstered interior, and then knocked his forehead against the lacquered wainscoting.

'What have I done?' he said. 'What did I do to him?'

Burt squeezed his own thighs, and rocked back and forth, his eyes clenched shut, his breath coming fast and shallow.

'You feel very alone, yes?'

'Yes, uncle.'

'Even with all your family, still you feel alone?'

'Yes, uncle.'

'What do you want?'

'A way out.'

'No.'

A sudden yell escaped from Burt, so brief that it seemed already unreal the moment it was finished. He began to sob openly while his uncle waited.

'I can't. I can't have done that to him. I can't.'

'Hush now and tell me what it is you want.'

When Burt's eyes eventually cleared, he saw his grandmother was awake, watching him silently from within her harness.

'This can't be,' he said. 'I can't do it.'

'Tell me what you want.'

'Luka. I want Luka.'

'Domingo's grandson? Not possible.'

'Get me Luka. He's my friend. I need a friend. I need someone, a friend, someone to love, someone outside all of this.'

'He's not outside of all this.'

'I don't care. I want him. Find him and buy him for me. I've given up everything, and I want him. I want my friend.'

The carriage rattled briefly across the timber planks of a bridge, and then they were planing smoothly, the scroll of the wheels only syncopated by the intermittent click where the long wooden boards met.

'All right,' he said. 'We'll see.'

They rolled to a stop. There were calls of formation, the shuffle of horseshoes clipping by, and Chuck Benjamin leant forward and opened the door onto a guard of soldiers standing to attention. He gestured with his cane for his nephew to go first, and Burt ducked his head down and put one boot onto the mounting step and found himself amidst a ramshackle village of flapping tents pitched crookedly atop a mucky terrain where hundreds of soldiers waited.

He looked to the west, away from the impromptu garrison and the forest that overshadowed it. The falling sun and the rising full moon were concomitant in the sky. Below them a mist of clouds darkly gathered in the ventral gaps of mountains furred by a simmering foliage that stretched towards him, terminating in the hewn hollow of this murdered town once more in embryo, where seven webs of scaffolding rose up out of the earth like the backs of a surfacing gam of whales. The nearest scaffolding enshelled the skeletal beginnings of a stage wrought around a black tree. It plunged upwards out of a black circular plaza where a road was to bisect, flowing from north to south, its future dimensions and coordinates already marked between rows of pegs staked into the pale earth. The markings stretched all the way through the forest, between the mountains, and then out of sight.

Burt Benjamin took a step down, alighting into San Ángeles.

<hr />

A prospect of smoke turrets weaved brightly across the sky. At first, they blossomed, separate and proud, like chained tornadoes, and then those that weren't blown out to sea blended into each other, forming myriads of vaporous castles, as if the burning town had projected out of its own death throes a shimmering mirror of itself.

There was the clank of metal, and then its shriek as it was dragged across stone. A solitary pair of feet pattered through the desolate slaughterhouse, each step slapping out two conjoined echoes that arced down to where Llewyn lay on his back, his eyes turned upwards seeing the featureless underside of the cattle's heads fanned out above him like the petals of a flower, framing from his supine position the swirling skyscape. He flipped onto his stomach and tried to spy through the forest of legs into the back entrance, but could make out nothing, and then the trapped herd all shuffled together, as if bound atop a tilting axis, lowing furiously. He saw the bare feet only when they were almost on top of him, and he pulled himself under a fence post, and crawled through legs until he was concealed in the steers' midst. His intrusion threw the animals into a stumbling panic, the whites of their eyes showing as they attempted to shove their heft away from him, but having no space to give, eventually they fell back into place, a perfect firmament of hanging bellies above him, hooves hesitant and flinching whenever they came near him.

A woman was whispering to the creatures, reaching out and touching bobbing noses and slavering lips. Llewyn turned slowly to watch her; and then a hoof tapped against his side, tearing his shirt and grazing the skin. He swallowed back a gasp, as two steers away, like a leak in the ceiling, the propulsive force of a stream of hot urine dug a little hole into the loose dirt whose boundaries it immediately overflowed. A tail flicked up, exposing outside the slick rim of the anus a cluster of ticks, and a tube of green dung splattered down on him. The encrusted tail dropped down, the bony rear swayed, and finally, another steer rummaged its curious head down through the tight press of neighbouring bodies and lowed in his face.

'O, for God's sake,' he shouted.

The bolt unlatched; the gate of the pen was opened, and the steer began to flow out, slowly at first, bifurcating around Llewyn's crouched form, but then, once they had more space, they began leaping and kicking. A stray hoof clipped his backside, sending him into a tumble. He twisted around. Another passing shank knocked him flat on his back. He could feel the vibrations of the trampled earth around him in apocalyptic hailstorm, and then a dehorned steer tripped up sideways across its own legs, and Llewyn witnessed his own inglorious death bearing down upon him. The steer's right hindleg stamped down in the V between his thighs, its flesh stretched over him, the wriggled veins thereon uncoiling like striking serpents, and then it planted two front hooves either side of his head, blocking the sky out by its belly. The rear curled messily into itself; the left hindleg swept diagonally above his face, and the hoof came down on Llewyn's outstretched right hand, breaking fingers, one after the other – one, two, three.

The three snaps rushed from his fingers to his palm, up through the tunnel of his wrist and arm, climbed up the ladder of his spine, and from there jolted into the sealed chamber of his skull where they terminated their cracking with three sharp raps against his brain. He heard the clicks again, then, though it was all already finished – a vivid triplet of sundering bones, not entirely synchronous, but consecutive so he could hear each break separate in the quick arpeggio. He stared across at his flattened hand. Neither his wrist nor his palm had been broken, only compressed into the merciful give of the soil. Along his back he could feel the beat of stampeding hooves diminishing into the distance. He sat up and cradled the twisted fingers in his lap. They were already darkening to purple; little calluses and wrinkles disappearing before his sight, filled out with the swelling.

'Cómo te llamas?'

A woman in a white dress stood above him. Only her chin and mouth were visible beneath the wooden mask she wore, just a circle with two holes in it, uncanny in its simplicity. She blinked down at him a few times, and with her eyes deep-set behind the mask, it was like the creaturely blinking of a third set of eyelids.

'Respóndeme,' she said, 'eres Maxime?'

'Yes.'

She bent over, grabbed his right forearm and brought it behind his back.

'You am not Maxime,' she said.

He went to swing at her with his free arm, but she squeezed his broken fingers together and he lost all strength. Manipulating his hand, she brought him up to a standing position.

'Listen to me,' he said, the right side of his face spasming, 'Maxime was my friend. I had to use his papers because I had nothing of my own. We are the same. Los mismos. Maxime and me – los bloody mismos. I am a republican, a periodista republicano. I hold no slaves. I am a friend of the poor. I am a friend.'

'Vamos.'

She exerted a slight pressure on his ring finger that propelled him forward. Pain seared through the right side of his body in waves that numbed the root of his tongue so that he could not contain his drool as he screeched, yet within fewer than five steps he had learned to intuit her movements so well that it was almost as though he were leading her by the hand.

When they passed in front of the slaughterhouse, the woman brought him to a halt. They stood shoulder to shoulder, waiting, his fingers pulsing occasionally inside her loose grip as though each of the three digits possessed its own heartbeat.

'I don't belong here,' Llewyn said. 'I was waylaid. This is a mistake. I was going home. My name is Llewyn Chaffinch. I am from Llanfairfechan. It is a coastal town in Wales. My mother lives there. She has red hair and she likes to garden. She likes to sing too. She is clumsy and shy. She doesn't understand why I left. I never write to her. Sometimes when visitors come by, she hides in the pantry so they will think that no one is home. My father, he was the sociable one. His voice was very loud, loud and deep, like it was coming out of the bottom of a bowl. He died in bed.

We don't know why. He was just dead one morning. I am a baker's son. My mother is alone. She is alone. Do you understand me? When I speak do you understand?'

The woman made no response, nor looked towards him. Soon, a child appeared around the bend, scanned the street, and then ran back. Four dancers in motley robes came into view, spinning with palms raised to the sky, raising dust as they tripped lightly forward. Next was the young boy who had brought Llewyn out to the stables that day. He wore low over his ears Maxime's laurel crown, brandishing a ringing staff with some bluster and swagger. He passed in front of a creaking two-wheeled bier scattered with so much greenery it was as if a mobile garden were being drawn through the dimming streets of Santa María – and atop this thick strew of flowers lay spread-eagled an ancient African man whose ravaged body had been cowled under a tarpaulin so that only the face remained visible under its garland of pink flowers. Following the dead man came the glimmering cortège in their closely packed hundreds; their many rows of faces intermittently apparent behind the waving of the white torches, and then Llewyn understood that the greatest part of the light that emanated from this mournful parade issued not from the torches they bore, but from their flames' reflections made manifold against the scythes and the guns and the panga machetes and the cutlasses, and in their many rows of eyes that passed the penumbra into the light, Llewyn could feel himself touching up against the agitated limit of a void whose trespass, no matter how accidental or fleeting, required death, and he was overcome then by the profound sense of having arrived at the end of all things.

'Vive la république!' he shouted. 'Vive la révolution!'

The masked woman struck the broken parts of his ring finger against one another as though she were striking sparks from a flint, and, in breathless horror, his skin opened all at once, exuding through a thousand yawning pores a cold ocean of sweat, and the stench of slaughter that had until now covered his surface, imbued him utterly. Three cracks tore through him like eviscerating peals of thunder and, when he could open his eyes again, he was on his knees, gasping.

She had her hand on his shoulder and was shouting at two men in a language he had never before heard. The parade had already passed by. Whistling whooshed through the twilight, and the choral screaming of the multitude rose to meet it. Then the screams and the gasps fell apart. A blast ran like a shiver through the land, disunifying their pain, tremoring the landscape and scattering its people. Across the street, inside the doorway of a burning house, shimmered the silhouette of a young man.

'Maxime,' Llewyn said. 'Is that you, Maxime?'

The shade turned away. The masked woman was gone; the two men, too; Llewyn rose to his feet, and stumbled towards the burning house, but then a child collided with him, and he tripped backwards just in time to hear the click of the transom that preceded the splitting of a beam. The burning building screeched, sagged, then tumbled down into a roaring pile of rubble that immediately extinguished the fire within it.

When the storm of dust dispersed, Llewyn could see, through the gap the collapsed house had left behind, down to the harbour below. Outside its curved walls floated three British men-o'-war, naval pennants drooping along the spars, sides popping and winking sparks. Llewyn, bathed in ash and choking, crawled over the threshold into the debris, and squinted; from where he knelt the bombardment seemed merely like the lighting of a strip of matches against the hulls of a few toy ships.

A muzzle flashed near a portside prow, bringing a brief clarity to the gold lettering above it that read: *The Jolly Jenkins*. A cannonball whistled by, tearing through something as it passed. Llewyn looked about himself, feeling it had flown very close. There was a creaking, a snap, and then the neighbouring building fell down on top of him.

———◆———

As night was falling, Esa and Jeongjo came to a river too wide to cross. They followed it towards the sea, hearing invisible fish surfacing and swallowing the insects that had gathered around the rotting branches caught in nestlike piles along the banks. Drooping, bearded trees leant down, the branches overhead fragmenting the moon and separating the starry sky from itself, and then they came to an outpost, its open door a portrait of light against the gloom of the avenue. Opposite it, a flat ferry that could support two carriages clacked against a pontoon.

Jeongjo went to turn the horse around, but the ferryman had already emerged, and was hailing them. Two soldiers followed him out. They wore white leggings, plumed hats, and red coats.

'British soldiers,' Jeongjo said. 'I can still outstrip them.'

Esa let go his waist and dismounted.

'Don't worry.'

'Your face is covered in blood.'

'My face is fine.'

She took the piece of yellow ribbon from her wrist and used it to tie her hair back, and then she walked towards the outpost, holding up her dresses, and when her bloody countenance became apparent, the soldiers trained their bayonets on her. She raised her arms.

'Me llamo Esa Benjamin,' she said. 'Queremos cruzar el río.'

'Muestremé sus documentos,' the ferryman said.

She reached into her dress and took out the bundle of letters Marianne Lynch had given her, and held them out, but the ferryman wouldn't come any closer to her. The soldiers waved her inside to a room where three mattresses were laid out upon the ground in a triangle. Several cloaks hung from the wall beside a shelf stacked with dried meats and jars of leaves. There were two chairs and a desk on which lay four bottles of wine, one half-drunk, a ledger, and a pipe that was still smoking.

The two soldiers spoke to one another, standing in the doorway.

'That's blood and she's not bleeding.'

'An Indian. The other one, too. Will I bring in the one on the horse?'

'Do it.'

'Barquero – el otro, el hombre, lo quiero ahí.'

The ferryman went to approach Jeongjo, and then Esa said:

'Look at my papers.'

The three men stared at her, and she glanced away from their eyes towards a lantern lapping a soft halo against the wall. A moth careened by, disappearing in a single flicker. She thought it had gone into the flame, but then she heard the flapping of its wings yet audible in the darkness.

'No one crosses tonight,' the ranking soldier said.

'Please look at the seal on the papers which I am holding.'

He took them, and passed them to the other soldier, who went over to the ledger on the desk and opened it on the very first page. She saw, stuck within, a printed bill spotted with a series of designs – twelve of them in two vertical rows.

'I work for Mr Charles Benjamin,' she said, 'and I am transporting for him this missive. It is of great importance to the colony. I must cross the river tonight.'

'You have nothing else – no other papers?'

The soldier by the desk tapped his forefinger against one of the designs. Esa stretched out her right hand to receive back the letters.

'This is all I need.'

———— •—•• ————

Wang Sin-Hua – María in front of patrons – blew gently into Klaus Richter's nostrils. He groaned and turned on his side, so she leant over him and traced the tip of her tongue around the concha of his ear.

'Qué quieres?' he said, into the pillow.

'Hay una campana.'

He listened, and indeed, a small bell was ringing somewhere outside. He opened his eyes. Everything in the room was milky, hazed, as though cloaked in a soft aura. From the placid quality of the light, he knew it was late morning. He felt delicate, sleepy, wonderful, like a child almost.

Yesterday afternoon Sin-Hua had led him out the window, and they had waited behind a tree – him sitting on a root, her sitting on his lap – and they had kissed each other in the shade until the mob had gone away. Then they had climbed back in the window, and spent the rest of the evening making love, drinking wine and smoking opium.

Presently, he sat up and kicked at the tangled pile of sheets and clothes on the floor, then turned around to ask Sin-Hua where his leggings were and saw that she was wearing them. He tried to peel them off her; she wriggled away; they wrestled. When the leggings were down about her knees, she covered her sex with both hands. He stuck his tongue into her navel so with laughter she would lose her strength, and then he pinned her wrists and buried his face deep into her pubic hair, inhaling her scent and the scent of last night's lovemaking. He dragged his nose up and down between her labia. She pressed her thighs against his ears, making them pop, and twisted so he had to fall out of bed to save his neck from being broken, but the leggings were still in his hands, save for one cuff that remained snug around her ankle. He yanked them free, kissed her big toe, and, hopping on one foot, put them on.

When he was sufficiently dressed, he leant over and kissed her.

'I do not know when I'll be back again,' he said, in Spanish.

She spat a little into his open mouth.

'It's all the same to me.'

Tying off his ponytail and grinning, he went down the corridor. He passed a room where the window had been broken in so violently that several shards of glass had become lodged in the opposite wall. The mirror was in pieces, and the bed was foul-smelling and wilted with the remnants of a fire that hadn't taken, though it had blackly streaked the space above the headboard like a chimney flue. He pushed open the front door – it fell off its hinges, slid down the steps, and glided into the little garden.

Across the way, a collapsed building was still smoking, its orange embers rendered invisible by daylight. Three slaves were attempting to drag away a crushed steer by its lassoed hindlegs. Several brown discolorations marked the earth where its blood had evaporated. A single stocking was skewered flatly across the pins of a cactus, and a dead woman was laying back in a shallow water trough, her blonde hair floating like sea anemone, dress ballooned up about her.

A tiny boy, perhaps no more than seven years old, walked by, ringing a handbell. He wore a red coat whose sleeves hid his hands and whose tails dragged through the dirt. The crown of his tricorne fell over his eyes, so he had to keep his head tilted very far back to see where he was going.

'Hark me, hark me,' he called. 'You is now a British protectorate. The Spaniard's tyranny is done. Long live the King of Great Britain, defender of the faith. Long live him. Long live faith, et cetera, et cetera. Hark me, hark me.'

The child took a long breath and began yelling and ringing again.

'Hark me, hark me. Any males who is without property and possessing of the King's English capable of either labouring or clerking, what is also betwixt twelve years of age and twenty-nine years of age, get you hence to the hotel of the Benjamin. Otherwise you is liable to death by hanging, and also confiscation of personal effects for costs incurred, et cetera, et cetera. Hark me, hark me. You is now a British protectorate—'

'You are a very little boy,' Klaus said.

The child leant back his hatted head even further to see his interlocutor.

'Not that it's none of your affair, but I happens to be twenty-one years of age.'

'Your pretensions are redoubtable.'

The child waved his bell up at him defiantly. 'Why, you native lout – is that English you speaks?'

'Most definitely I am speaking it.'

'Well, go on down the hotel, then, you and all, or you'll be made to do the census, and that won't like you one bit. Be on your way now and leave decent folks to their work.'

The child wandered away, ringing the bell and crying out the same message, looking from behind like a coat and hat become sentient. Klaus went in the other direction, and soon found the way ahead blocked by a restless crowd. He pushed through and saw five British soldiers standing guard over nine Indians, all of whom sat in a row on their hunkers, manacled together by their necks. The soldiers had formed a barrier with their bodies to keep the crowd and the prisoners apart, and a gouty man went to spit at one of the Indians, but his saliva landed on the boot of a soldier. A kerfuffle broke out.

Sticking close to the wall, Klaus slid past. Up ahead, a fire-blackened beam whose span was comfortably longer than the width of the street had been laid across the flat roofs of two houses opposite one another. From this overhead beam dangled eight empty nooses, and beneath one of these nooses, a soldier was arguing with a portly man in a cloth jerkin and a straw hat who was trying to sell him a footstool. Klaus continued, ducking between the nooses and passing the slanted guillotine of shade the beam cast, and next he came across an admiral admonishing a distraught Indian who was being restrained by two soldiers.

The admiral turned his imposing bicorne in the direction of Klaus.

'You, varlet – do you speak Spanish?'

Klaus saluted. 'Yes, sir,' he said. 'I am very nicely acquainted with it.'

'English?'

'The tongue of the Englishmen is, with the big luck, the companion of my mouth and also of my heart.'

'Very good, then you shall translate for me,' the admiral said, joining his hands behind his back. 'Tell this Indian that it may as well be today. All he loses from it being today is some few meals – some corn on the cob, in his case, I presume – a few uxorious embraces; a few sunrises he wouldn't have noticed anyway; a ritual or two. What else? Some chanting, some drum circles, eh? Perhaps, there is someone he wants to apologise to? Well, you tell this creature that if His Majesty's Royal Navy hadn't come along and introduced some urgency into his life he wouldn't have apologised to them, anyhow, so what difference does it make? A man's life is not just his final moments, but his display of character on the path leading hitherto.'

Klaus approximated the spiel into Spanish as the Indian grimaced, his lips high over his teeth, twisting his agitated face back and forth between the admiral and the soldiers and Klaus.

When Klaus fell silent, the admiral cleared his throat and went on.

'Tell him not to plead,' he said. 'Mercy can have no occasion here. Mercy is the avowal that life is a gift, freely given, but this gift could only ever be comprehensible in a universe of scarcity and punishment – else from what is it that we are delivered into clemency? Mercy is the universe's admission that not every little sparrow is held to account – but what if you are not the little sparrow? You are not. Tell him he is not the little sparrow. Tell him he must hang and tell him it's war. It's war forever, tell him.'

As Klaus was translating, there was a smash in the near distance. Stunned cries rose in a chorus, followed by yelling, and then the echoing report of a gun. A moment later, an Indian with a noose around his neck and hands tied behind his back jogged past, the standing end of the rope bouncing off his heels as he fled.

'Will I shoot him, sir?' one of the soldiers asked.

The admiral shook his head.

'Let him go, Johnny,' he said. 'He seems like a rather carpe diem sort of fellow – not like this snivelling reprobate.'

Another man in uniform ran up to them, bowed, and then also saluted.

'Admiral Lovering,' he said, smartly.

'Mr Lamprey, what trifle compels my attention?'

'The beam broke, sir. We shall have to delay the hangings.'

'That's fine.'

'The local populace is becoming somewhat overwrought, sir.'

'Well, shoot them, Mr Lamprey.'

'Sir.'

'By God, we shouldn't even be hanging without trials and logbooks, but, alas, my poor clerk is drowned! I'll have to speak with Charles. His buffoons should be helping with all this ruddy brouhaha. We shall head down presently.'

'Sir.'

'All right, Mr Lamprey, all right. You have always been the incorrigible angel of my better nature. Requisition a boat from the harbour and hang them from those spars whose integrity you deem sufficient for a dangling of the rascals.'

'Thank you, sir.'

Mr Lamprey bowed, saluted, and trotted stiffly back in the direction from whence he had come.

Admiral Lovering pointed his bicorne back up at Klaus. 'You there – why have you stopped interpreting?'

'This Indio, sir,' Klaus answered, 'he has no ability of Spanish properly. He is not understanding so many words. He is addressing and pleaing with me, yes, intimating that he was not here in the revolutionary time that passes yesterday, but I am not understanding so much, in return. He is speaking of something of his family that I am not understanding. It is so strange, yes, and antagonisticatory, and purposeless.'

'Well, then, varlet, don't faff about here or you'll be shot. You're dismissed.'

Klaus saluted and left, passing down a ruined street where almost no buildings remained, only huge, smouldering heaps through which the occasional hand or foot poked like a gristly fungus dipped in prehistoric smut. Then, he stopped, seeing the way was blocked by debris. A gang of slaves was tossing rubble into wheelbarrows and dumping it off to the side so as to clear a path. Two foremen watched with arms crossed, pistols on their hips, whips twisted snakelike around their forearms; one of them was eating a banana. Klaus leant up against a sliver of wall that remained intact and gazed out at the sparkling sea. Beyond the harbour walls, a man in a white shirt was singing an aria while rowing a yawl between two ships, each stroke of his oars throwing up spouts of water that briefly glinted the sunlight before joining once more into the great mass of sea; a dog swam happily beside him.

A string of burros wrenched free a wooden platform atop a wheelless axis and dragged it away. This set off a collapse that seemed to loosen a terrible odour into the air, reminiscent of sewage but stranger and less human, and when the dust settled a crevice had appeared through which it seemed possible to pass. Klaus climbed through, covering his mouth and nose with his handkerchief and looking up at the sky as the tumble of detritus had exposed the corpse of a dusty child lodged upright, eyes closed and waiting, like the bust of a statue carved in a niche.

On the other side of the rubble, a few slaves were hauling someone from the wreckage of a house. It was a man, dressed scantily in rags and entirely whitened by dust, and one of his hands was almost twice the size of the other, the fingers all twisted over one another. When the slaves let him go, he remained standing, staring down stupidly at the obliteration from which he had just emerged.

'Good morning, Llewyn.'

Klaus went to shake his hand, thought better of it, and patted him on the shoulder instead; Llewyn blinked a few times up at him.

'Mr Richter.'

'Yes, I am he. Are you as much hangedover as I have occasion to so be? The cauim, I find, does not forgive so much its gustative participants. Let us go now then to the Benjamin place where we shall avail you of some clothes and some baths and unguents and wooded splinters for your fingers, and so on and so forth.'

Taking his left arm, he gently propelled Llewyn forward in dazed silence until they came to an open plaza unscarred by the riots or fusillades of the cannons, where the hotel shone pristinely in the sun. Out of its front doors snaked a huge queue of perhaps two hundred young men, and Llewyn and Klaus joined this queue.

'Have you seen my good and gracious friend Ernesto de Díos Salgado?' Klaus asked. 'I misplaced him in my orgy.'

'He's dead.'

'Alas,' Klaus said. 'Send to know, the poet hath quoth, for whomst the bell is tolled.'

Llewyn swayed a little, Klaus steadied him with a touch; Ernesto joined them in the queue.

'Who is tell the bell?' he asked.

315

His face was blackened with soot, and his hair seemed to have been singed and lopped off in uneven chunks. He was still naked save his drawers and one boot.

'Thee,' Klaus said. 'We bethought you dead.'

'No. Is other.'

The line moved forward slightly; Llewyn limped along with it.

'I saw you shot in the back of the head.'

'No,' he said, 'can be the hairs, yes, but no the head.'

He pulled at a burnt scruff around his temple, and it came apart between his fingers like oil. He crinkled his nose at it and wiped his fingers off his solitary boot.

'The native mans is very scaring and annoy,' he explained. 'Also have say want make a castration for me, but I tell no and I go –' he clapped his hands together – 'like this.'

'I saw you die.'

'No, Mr Chaffing, is other is die. His head is depart. You is drink a very lots the day is past. Too much, I am think.'

The line moved forward again. Admiral Lovering clopped by on a grand chestnut stallion, surveying them all; Mr Lamprey and Mr Brynling walked either side of him. When he passed them, Klaus saluted him.

'Do I know you, rapscallion?' the admiral shouted. 'I do not think I know you.'

He pulled up the horse, squinted down, and then his gaze fell upon Llewyn.

'Egad! It's the Frenchman! Mr Brynling, you recall the Frenchman?'

'Yes, sir.'

Admiral Lovering held the pommel and swung himself down as Mr Brynling took the reins and Mr Lamprey caught the admiral's boot on his shoulder, kneeling down so as to soften his dismount.

'My lad, come with me,' Lovering said. 'I told you I'd do you another good turn, did I not? You, take the reins, and do not let

Aelfweard see you come up on his left side. He will not abide rogues on his left.'

Klaus was left holding the horse, and Mr Brynling and Mr Lamprey stood either side of Llewyn and ushered him forward. They skipped the queue, turning all heads they passed as they went into the lobby where two lieutenants were passing out folded British flags from a crate to an ill-dressed group of attentive children, and then they went down a hall to the left. The queue terminated outside a corner room where four soldiers stood guard. They were not British, but when they saw the admiral they all saluted.

'Announce him, Mr Brynling,' Lovering said.

Mr Brynling rapped smartly on the door three times, then entered. As they waited, a little boy wordlessly made his way up the line, beating the dust from everyone's boots with a straw switch. He came to Llewyn, looked him up and down a few times, and then beat at his feet twice, and left.

The door opened and Mr Brynling came out of the room with Fritz Odendonk, who pushed a befuddled man in a crownless straw hat out ahead of him.

'In you go, my lad,' Lovering said to Llewyn. 'I'd join you myself, but there's a chap I just met needs shooting.'

Llewyn limped into a large room illuminated by two tall windows. The walls were bare, marked by the recent removal of all paintings and ceiling fixtures, and there was hardly any furniture save for a broad ochre kilim spread out across the middle of the floor. A pair of similar-looking gentlemen sat legs crossed on two wooden chairs. They were both dressed in a debonair fashion, but the younger was gaunter and more tanned; his pale blue eyes like icy shocks above the ruddy brown of his high cheekbones. In his lap, he fondled a sleeping puppy, a stark white creature so young its eyes had not yet opened.

317

'My name is Charles Benjamin,' the elder said, his voice echoing slightly in the high, emptied room. 'This is my nephew, Burt Benjamin. We hear you are a man of the press.'

Llewyn noticed there was a small stain on a lower part of the wall that had dripped down onto the wainscoting; it had been scrubbed away, but still left a very slight discoloration.

'Yes.'

The door opened again, and Fritz Odendonk came in carrying one of Maxime's trunks. He placed it at Llewyn's feet.

'This belongs to you,' Benjamin said.

'It's not mine.'

'Whose is it, then?'

'Maxime's.'

'You are not him?'

'No.'

'Where is he?'

'Nighttown.'

'He's dead?'

'Yes.'

'Keep the trunk,' Benjamin said. 'Listen – our local newspaper recently ceased production under quite tragic circumstances, but, luckily, there are two new printing presses ready and waiting in a little town called San Ángeles, not far from here.'

Suddenly, Llewyn's head jerked back three times. When it stopped his right eye was twitching.

'Did you hear that?' he asked.

'No.'

'The knocks – maybe at the window. It clicked when it opened.'

Benjamin glanced over his shoulder. There was nothing out the windows, save a pigeon asleep in a narrow parcel of shade, its beak buried in itself.

'You like to write, don't you?'

'Yes.'

'Would you like to run your own newspaper?'

'I don't speak Spanish.'

'Good. Would you like to run your own newspaper?'

Llewyn was staring at the trunk by his feet, holding his swollen right hand by the wrist; it throbbed slightly whenever he breathed too deeply, and it was throbbing now.

'Mr Benjamin,' he said, 'I am a republican and an abolitionist, and any paper I oversaw would necessarily bear the stamp of truth and liberty.'

'That's just dandy.'

'It is?'

'I'm a republican and abolitionist, too.'

'You are?'

'Of course! That's why I think you're just the man for the job, but remember, you can't just declare a republic, you have to have a people first. And we don't have a people – what we have here is a mess. You see that, don't you? Look at what's left of this town. Look out that window. Are you looking?'

There was nothing out the window, save the sun and the sleeping pigeon.

'Yes,' Llewyn said.

'You have to tell them the little stories about how some mean, old tyrant hurt their mommas or something of the like, and nowadays the pageantry and the plays and the ballads just aren't enough. You need a newspaper, too, and you are the one who will give them, every damned day, a sense of themselves – as a people, as a republic. I'm just like you, brother: I'm an idealist, a universalist, an egalitarian, a lover of liberty, and a firm believer in the happiness of all mankind, but recollect that the universal must travel along the same road as the particular, and one of these must be ferried about on the other's back. You sell me enough papers, and I reckon it'll take only about eleven years until we can declare ourselves a nice, little republic. That ain't such a long time. Right

319

now, you're thinking: "Well, Chuck, why not sooner?" I'll tell you why. If we were to declare a republic right now every shopkeeper with a stick up his ass could hold the nation to ransom over some storefront licence. He'd get him and his fifteen sons to vote us all into Armageddon by sundown. Imagine paying court to a shopkeeper for the rest of your life. Think about it, a man with your capacities forced to consort in such a manner. You're like me, ain't you?'

'I am?'

'You'd happily die for the rights of the common man, but you wouldn't spend an evening listening to him. Now, think for a moment about what would happen if we abolished slavery this afternoon: packs of wild you-know-whats in their thousands roaming through the countryside, with neither food nor shelter nor work, raping, razing and murdering every blessed thing in sight until some raggedy lunatic of a preacher hellbent on final things inspires them to become an army. It'd be worse than the Indians of the forest, who at least . . . You know what? I can't even talk about them I'm so sore . . . When I think of our beautiful town . . . But let me ask you, let me ask you – that mob last night, did that look to you like a jury of your peers? Did that look to you like a reasonable expression of popular sovereignty amongst a gathering of rational citizens? No, don't answer. I can tell just by looking at you that of late you have encountered some faction of the general will . . . No, not yet, not yet. This is not just the happenstance of our passing through. It'll take eleven years for a republic, and another twenty for abolition, give or take. Maybe less if we have a good newspaper, and not at all if we don't. Well, are you in?'

'Yes. Yes, I'm in.'

'Welcome aboard – what's your name?'

'Llewyn Chaffinch.'

'Welcome aboard, Llewyn. Pick up your luggage, there, and Fritz here will take you to a nice room upstairs where we'll get you cleaned up and get those fingers seen to. You'll be in San Ángeles by nightfall, and – you mind me now – I want that first issue circulating before the new year is in.'

Llewyn, his head jerking back and forth violently, picked up the trunk and limped out, and Fritz Odendonk followed, leaving the two relatives alone together. Burt touched gently the shivering ears of the yawning puppy, and Chuck Benjamin rose and stretched his limbs so his cane wavered high above his head. He went over to the windows, causing the pigeon there to wake up and fly away.

'See, with a bitch like that, you can do anything,' he said, 'so long as they think it was their idea.'

He stared up at the sun and smiled.

'Damn!' he exclaimed. 'It's a heck of a nice day.'

———— • ————

They rode into Bastaña on Christmas morning. There was laughter everywhere. Children in robes were performing the Nativity outside the open doors of a church. A little magus with a cotton beard, charcoal eyebrows and a paper crown pointed up at the North Star – a glum girl clad in a sparkling dress suspended from a tree, her face painted golden. The little magus attempted to give a speech, but kept forgetting the words, and then the donkey turned around and knocked over the crib and crushed with its hoof the baby Jesus made of wood. The child playing Joseph ran into the crowd to bury his face in the belly of his mother, and the Virgin Mary scrambled, screeching, to pick up the pieces of the broken doll. The magus continued with his speech as though nothing had happened, and then a sheep started to munch at one of the angel's straw wings, and the angel started screaming and trying to shrug her wings off. A shepherd sat down and cried, and the archangel Gabriel was picking his nose and eating the snot from beneath his fingernails. The magus said they had followed the North Star all the way from the east, when the breeze picked up, catching his paper crown. It fluttered away, and then he chased it across the seafront plaza, the white crests of the waves tumbling behind him. The two remaining magi started to pull each other's hair, and the Virgin Mary ran, alone, into the church.

The priest was red in the face from laughter.

'Basta!' he said. 'Basta!'

A farmer wearing his Sunday best tried to lead the donkey away by the bridle, but, breathless with laughter, he kept having to stop and lean on the animal. The laughter was general over the crowd. Flores was there amongst them, and he was laughing, too. His one eye shone with tears he was laughing so much. He had a paunch now; a perfect streak of white ran through his hair, interrupted only by the strap of his eyepatch. He was laughing and waving up at the sad-faced North Star.

'Papa,' the North Star called down to him, in Spanish. 'Papa, I want to come down.'

'Sí, claro,' Flores said. 'Where is Arturo? Arturo?'

'Arturo?'

'Arturo?'

'Arturo, Arturo, Arturo?'

Soon the whole town was shouting for Arturo to come, and then, at last, a fisherman emerged from a shed, and all mouths erupted in whistles and cheers.

Arturo waved at them, his head poking out between the rungs of a ladder, its sides balanced on each shoulder, and he swaggered forth, but within a few steps it became apparent he was drunk. He bumped the ladder against the church wall twice, the second time only narrowly missing the stained-glass window, drawing gasps from the crowd. It took him so long to get to the tree that the children had started calling out his name again, making a song of it.

Flores tried to take the ladder away from him, but he spun away, causing several people to duck and yell as the back end swung out.

'No gracias,' he said.

He planted the ladder down in the ground and then tried to climb up on it without having propped it up against anything. He reached the first rung, wobbled and then fell forward, and the ladder cracked apart underneath him, and the whole town was laughing again as Arturo sat up amidst his own wreckage, beaming happily.

Esa made her way through the parents, past the singing and quarrelling children of the abandoned nativity and climbed the tree. She reached the limb where the North Star hung and gazed down at them all. She could see Jeongjo walking towards her through the village's only street, having watered and fed the mare. She saw the little magus chasing his paper crown across the beach. The sand seemed to be coming apart in layers. She could see the paper crown blustering away, whirling out to sea; and Flores was looking up at her, and he was laughing.

She raised her arms and tiptoed out across the limb. The crowd were calling encouragement up to her as she bent down and undid the knot.

When Flores and the farmer were standing directly below, Esa let go of the rope, and they caught the North Star. The whole town started cheering as one, giving their applause, and Esa stood up, walked backwards towards the trunk and climbed down again. The moment her feet touched the ground, Flores wrapped her in an embrace.

He held her for a long time.

'Esa.'

'Here I am.'

He kissed her forehead, looked at her face, and smiled. The North Star came up and held Flores's thumb, leant her head against his side.

'This is Biddy,' Flores said. 'This is Esa, my friend. Kiss her cheek. Kiss her and say thank you. Un beso por Esa. No? Por qué?'

For a moment, Esa stared at the child, and then took the bundle of letters from her dress and held them out for Flores. He received them, and examined them, his one eye squinting.

'Thank you. This is a kind gift.'

'I am only returning them to you.'

'It is a gift,' he said. 'I have something for you, too. Biddy, wait here.'

He tried to pry the child's fingers from his thumb, but still she clung to him.

'Quédate, Biddy.'

Up through the crowd came Jeongjo, and introduced himself, and then he went down on his hunkers before the child, fanning out a deck of cards. At first, she looked away, and then, at Flores's urging, she took one. Jeongjo blew on his palms, rubbed them together, clicked his fingers, and then her card appeared in his hands.

'Cómo?'

She snatched the card back and picked out another one.

Flores and Esa went down to the beach together. The wind was higher there, deafening, whipping long sheets of galloping spray across the water in which myriad rainbows briefly shone. White crests like knife edges emerged and sank before they reached shore. She could feel the sharp grains of sand dancing off her legs. The little bareheaded magus stood in the shallows, holding up his trouser ends so they wouldn't get wet, shouting something into the sea. In the distance, between the endless curved thread of breakers, a black dog bounded back and forth. Seagulls hovered above the jetty, and then Esa and Flores passed onto the darker sand where thousands of little heaps lay in a great complexity of twists, cast off by the worms who strove and ate beneath the wandering tide, and then they passed carefully across the slippery rim of popping yellow seaweed that flapped madly like the wings of trapped birds.

She turned towards the grey horizon, feeling the spray flicker against her cheeks. Flores knelt down and picked up something, and then she saw his mouth moving, but she couldn't hear him over the wind.

He held out a conch; she took it in her hands.

'It's a gift,' he shouted. 'I knew you would come.'

His voice came to her faintly though there was only a little space between them. She stared down at the conch.

'I waited for you,' she said.

He grimaced and looked out at the sea; his hair was shaking in the wind, his shirts fluttering.

'For years, I looked for you,' he shouted. 'And then Biddy needed to go to school; I had to remain in one place. I couldn't keep searching, but I knew we'd meet again. I swear I knew it, Esa. I knew you would find me.'

'I needed you, and you weren't there.'

'You found me.'

She shook her head.

'I met you the day my mother died, and you carried me back into life,' he said. 'Without you, I would be nothing. You are there in my dreams. You saved me, Esa. Every day you saved me.'

She shook her head again; a tear seeped from the corner of her eye, flew upwards into the heavens.

'No.'

'When she died,' Flores said, 'I couldn't understand. I hurt so much, for so long, and then one day I forgot to suffer, and then I kept forgetting, and the more I forgot, the more I loved. She was perfect, my mother, but she's gone. I forget, and I love. Nothing needs my pain. To love, there is no past. It is without history. I am free, Esa. I am home. This is my home, and I am free.'

More tears were flying off Esa's face, the wind carrying each drop, scattering it far out to sea. Her hands were shaking so much that the shell vibrated. She closed her eyes, feeling like she was choking.

'No.'

'I swear to you that it's all resolved,' he said. 'I swear to you that this is paradise. You are wonderful. You are a miracle, Esa.'

'No,' she said. 'Stop.'

The tide was coming in; bubbling froth whooshed over their feet, sucking the sand away from beneath them. She opened her eyes and stared through her tears out at the sea. The breakers were growing taller, coming in faster. A spangle of sunlight flashed coldly upon her face, and, seeing this, Flores started to laugh again.

Dear papa,

*¿ how are you ? blablabla. alway the same history to write.
always comence how are you. wake me this morning and say me
« ¡ no mor the sister Carmen ! » « ¡ no mor the inglish ! » « ¡ am
tire of write that it what happen me the history ! » but i no say
with her for i have the nowledges of the castigate she make me so
i rebel secret. ¡ jajaja ! valley, i invent you the very nice history
for you that why because am genias. have a gentl boy, he is
always love me, used to was a good boy nambe roberto, but at
this hour is very annoy, say « Biddy am so love and you am so
beautifule and so intelelligente » &c. send me mensages, but am
not read them, he send to me the litlle light in the evenings that
is senal for me but close the eye, « marry with me » have said
much times, i have respond « ¡ no ! ¡ is no possible ! » in final, in
one day in futur am say « ¡ yes ! ¡ i marry with you ! » and so do
the happy history. valley, estop at this hour, is very boring the
writes. ¡ is too much ! Alway am miss you.*

*Your obedient and humble daughter, evermore,
Ms. BIDDY TANNER, &c.*

III

World

I N   TWILIGHTS, ESA lies flat over quiet rockpools holding the
torch as Atta perches with a spear held high. He waits for the
tentacles to unfurl. He waits for the boneless flab of head to
emerge into the light with that flow and that silence known only
to water and dreams. The black eyes reflect the guttering of the
torch. Atta entices them into cages with the fresh hearts of birds
tied to a piece of string. As he carries them home, they blast tubes
in their heads until they suffocate in the air, collapsing in on
themselves. Sometimes they crawl between the pools and he
spears them, their tentacles mad and flapping. Sometimes they
seethe in the cage, their heads bulging through the bars, trying to
wrap themselves around her. They are all poisonous. They have
many hearts. Their legs are full of brains. Atta hangs them from
the ceilings.

The tide is going out, Atta says. The moon is leaving.

Then, she cannot find him. She wanders across town and forest
and beach. There is much life scrambling between the tides. She
cannot find him there. There is no trace of the man that once was.
She searches all night. Her head hurts, and she thinks she will die
she is so tired.

Sometimes he goes away, her sister Suya says.

The tide continues retreating. Crabs make vast sideways
pilgrimages to their eggs. Hatchlings wander inland by accident.
Vast meadows of seaweed burn in the sun. Every dawn, the

fishermen bear their boats across their backs further out. By the time the river runs into the sea, it is a trickle. The birds are all gone. The moon is as small as a star in the sky. No one makes love anymore. Then, beyond the plains of sand, a bridge of stone appears. It arches up from the seafloor, and every day more of it is exposed by the retreat of the ocean.

Someone is coming, Esa's mother says.

A rider crosses the sea, hooves dashing water, and then he crosses the bridge, and then the plains, and then he rides into town. A pale squid sits upon a chestnut mare and he is dressed as a European corsair. He wears high leather boots. He wears a long black coat. He wears a black tricorne with a gold-threaded rim. He wears his tentacles tucked into his shirt so that they look like a row of cravats. He dismounts and tries to speak, but his mouth only pops and suckles and hisses. Iaen offers him a roasted chicken. He devours it with the puttering tube in his face. He pulses his face into darkness, and then he pulses his colour into paleness again. Grease drips from the swelling sacs beneath his eyes. He hands Iaen a sealed message. He rides away.

Mr Squid grew a spine, the message says.

The next day, while all the others sleep, Suya wakes Esa up.

It is you, she says. You are the one who must go on.

I want to stay.

No.

I love you. I want to stay here. I want to stay with you.

You are the one who must go on.

Esa walks towards the sea. It takes her a day to get across the seaweed. It buzzes with insects. It steams with pestilence. It suffocates. She cannot breathe with it. She gets sick. Then she is crossing sand, passing between great lakes where trapped shoals of fish are eating themselves, and then she is on the bridge. The drained sea falls away, and by nightfall, she is walking above huge canyons, guided by moonless starlight. In the day she can see far below. Dead octopi hang from seaweed trees in great, purple forests. Schools of sharks lie mouldering atop mountains, their rows of teeth reflecting the sunlight. An ancient ship is lodged on its side, its mast broken. Either side of the bridge falls away so sharply that she cannot see all the way to the ground beneath. The crevices are so deep. She throws a stone down and does not hear it land. She is so high above the seabed that she thinks she is among the clouds, but she is not. The clouds still flow above. She comes upon Nighttown. The many silent faces turn up towards her and she walks by, not looking down. The bridge narrows and it starts to rain. It rains for days. The cords fall beneath her, disappearing into the abyss. Then, there is the echoing sea sloshing at the bottom of the canyons. As she goes on, the sea starts to rise once more. Soon the bridge will be submerged and she will have to turn back or swim out further. The water comes up to her ankles. The water comes up to her knees. The water comes up to her waist. She can still see the bridge beneath the water. She goes further. Ahead, a dead cephalopod lies across the bridge. It is vast. Atop its collapsed head grows a tree, and beneath this tree is a desk where Angel sits writing messages.

I am so sad, he says.

Have you seen Atta?

He passed this way three days ago, walking an octopus on a leash. They were both dying.

Esa crawls across the slippery flesh of the cephalopod, trying to get to the other side.

Why don't you rest for a while? Angel says.

I cannot stay here.

Why not?

Mr Squid grew a spine.

I know, but you can hide in the tree. Stay for a while to keep me company. I get so lonely.

She climbs the tree and falls asleep. When she wakes up the sea has risen, and they are floating atop the dead cephalopod. There is only water all around.

Why didn't you warn me? she asks.

I was asleep, too.

Angel hangs from a crucifix, now. They float for many days and then a ship comes into sight on the horizon. It disappears many times, and then eventually it sails abreast, its keel tilting away from them even as it passes. She sees the faces above the bulwarks, watching her. She sees Angel, younger, amidst their number. He is there, but he is here, too. Someone throws her a rope. It lands upon the dead cephalopod, and she watches it slip away.

Take it, Angel says. It might be different this time.

No.

The ship sails away.

I cannot stay with you, she says.

Goodbye.

Would you like me to take you down before I go?

No, thank you. Goodbye, Esa.

Goodbye, Angel.

Esa dives into the water, then floats on her back, and then she lets herself sink. Her feet touch the ground, but her mouth is still above water. She turns around. Angel is far away now, too far to ever follow. She wades southward, hoping that one day the waves will carry her home.

It is night and then it is day.

The sun rises behind her, and she walks away from it, but the sun never crosses her head, no matter how far she walks. It seems to be following her, growing larger in the sky.

Go away, she says. Give me night.

I want to stay with you, the sun says. I get so lonely.

Did you see Atta?

Yes, he is here with me. Will you look at me, Esa?

Where is the moon?

She is with me, too. Look at me.

And where are my family? Where are my sister and my mother?

They are all here. They are all with me. Will you look at me?

You are too bright.

You have looked upon death. Now you must look upon me.

I cannot. You are too bright.

Then, Esa, the sun said, swelling out to embrace her, then you must feel the heat of my love.

Only light.

Discover *Nobber*, Oisín Fagan's debut novel

'Amid a strange, dark tale come glimpses of a striking new talent'
THE TIMES

'Oisín is a true original. *Nobber* is brilliant, innovative, relevant, zany, and highly readable'
IRISH EXAMINER

'A skilled storyteller with a rich command of language and rare comedic flair'
IRISH TIMES